A Perilous Perspective

ANNA LEE HUBER

BERKLEY PRIME CRIME
New York

BERKLEY PRIME CRIME
Published by Berkley
An imprint of Penguin Random House LLC
penguinrandomhouse.com

Library of Congress Cataloging-in-Publication Data

Names: Huber, Anna Lee, author.
Title: A perilous perspective / Anna Lee Huber.
Description: New York: Berkley Prime Crime, [2022] |
Series: Lady Darby mysteries
Identifiers: LCCN 2021059049 (print) | LCCN 2021059050 (ebook) |
ISBN 9780593198469 (trade paperback) | ISBN 9780593198476 (ebook)
Classification: LCC PS3608.U238 P47 2022 (print) |
LCC PS3608.U238 (ebook) | DDC 813/.6—dc23
LC record available at https://lccn.loc.gov/2021059049
LC ebook record available at https://lccn.loc.gov/2021059050

First Edition: April 2022

Printed in the United States of America
1st Printing

PRAISE FOR THE LADY DARBY MYSTERIES

"[A] history mystery in fine Victorian style! Anna Lee Huber's spirited debut mixes classic country house mystery with a liberal dash of historical romance."
—*New York Times* bestselling author Julia Spencer-Fleming

"Riveting. . . . Huber deftly weaves together an original premise, an enigmatic heroine, and a compelling Highland setting."
—*New York Times* bestselling author Deanna Raybourn

"[A] fascinating heroine. . . . A thoroughly enjoyable read!"
—National bestselling author Victoria Thompson

"Reads like a cross between a gothic novel and a mystery with a decidedly unusual heroine."
—*Kirkus Reviews*

"Includes all the ingredients of a romantic suspense novel, starting with a proud and independent heroine. . . . Strong and lively characters as well as believable family dynamics, however, elevate this above stock genre fare."
—*Publishers Weekly*

"[A] clever heroine with a shocking past and a talent for detection."
—National bestselling author Carol K. Carr

"[Huber] designs her heroine as a woman who straddles the line between eighteenth-century behavior and twenty-first-century independence."
—New York Journal of Books

"[A] must read. . . . One of those rare books that will both shock and please readers."
—Fresh Fiction

"One of the best historical mysteries that I have read this year."
—Cozy Mystery Book Reviews

Titles by Anna Lee Huber

For my Grandma Emma,
who at least partially inspired
Kiera's daughter's name.

A Perilous
Perspective

CHAPTER 1

We know what we are, but know not what we may be.

—WILLIAM SHAKESPEARE

JULY 1832
ARGYLL, SCOTLAND

There was nothing quite like the sight of proper, normally reserved ladies and gentlemen flailing and dashing about a moor. Their natural habitats of stately homes and the theaters and clubs of Edinburgh and London offered little opportunity for them to behave in such a carefree manner, and even less for me to enjoy observing it.

We had all gathered at Barbreck Manor along the northern tip of Loch Craignish to celebrate the wedding of my dear friend Charlotte, Lady Stratford, to my cousin Rye Mallery. Charlotte had endured a tumultuous and difficult first marriage to the late Earl of Stratford. One that ended with him trying to frame her for murder and then attempting to kill her—an effort I had helped foil. And I was pleased to see her find happiness again with my strong and steady cousin.

Though matters with her soon-to-be stepchildren seemed to be progressing less smoothly.

Charlotte darted to the side and flung out her racket in a vain attempt to bat the shuttlecock back toward her fellow players, only to watch it fall to the ground, nearly tripping on her skirts in the process. The look on Rye's daughter's face clearly communicated her disappointment in Charlotte's prowess. The fact that her cousin and Aunt Morven demonstrated such skill didn't help matters.

I empathized with Charlotte, knowing I wouldn't have shone in comparison with my cousin Morven in this regard either. She had always been lithe and quick, and accomplished at games like battledore and shuttlecock. Though how she managed to move about so effortlessly in her fashionable gowns with their voluminous gigot sleeves, I could not fathom.

I squinted across the windswept field toward where Rye stood with his son, his dark head gleaming in the sunlight as he bent over to help repair something on the kite they clutched, oblivious to his fiancée's struggle. Not that there was anything he could do about it. In truth, his interference would have made the matter a larger problem than it was.

The crack of a ball hitting a cricket bat drew my gaze toward the far side of the moor, where most of the men were playing with Morven's two older sons. The day being warm and fine, they had all discarded their coats and hats, and rolled up the sleeves of their shirts. I spied the golden head of my husband, Sebastian Gage, bent over to speak with one of the boys as he demonstrated something with the bat. The sight brought a smile to my lips as I imagined him doing something similar with our own daughter in some years' time.

For now, Emma, being only three and a half months old, was content to loll about on the blanket beside me, grappling with a ragdoll she drooled and gnawed on. That is, when she was able to successfully get it in her mouth. I retrieved the soggy twist of cloths as it tumbled to her side out of reach and lifted it to her chest, tickling her with it. She squealed and giggled in delight, the sight of her happy grin filling me with joy.

My Aunt Cait gave a warning cry, alerting me to the wildly kicked ball headed toward us. With a deftly placed foot, I stopped it before it reached the blanket, then tossed it back toward Morven's youngest child, who, at barely two years old, was doing his best to kick it toward the octogenarian Lord Barbreck.

The entire party had joined in the games and antics with the other children. Everyone, that is, except Lady Bearsden, Charlotte's great-aunt. She was supposed to be keeping me company but instead sat behind me softly snoring. She had nodded off in one of the chairs the footmen had lugged up the hillock so that the two oldest members of our excursion would not have to try to lower themselves to the blankets laid out in the shade of the ruins of an old castle.

Not that I blamed her. I stifled a yawn. Given half a chance, I would have nodded off myself—the warmth of the afternoon and the clean, fresh air lulling me into slumber. When I was lucky, Emma woke me only twice in the middle of the night and went straight back to sleep, but the past week she had demanded more feedings than usual. It was normal, our nanny Mrs. Mackay, had informed me. Merely an indication that Emma was about to outgrow her little gowns.

I attempted to smother another yawn, but not fast enough to hide it from Morven as she sank down on the blanket beside me, settling her goldenrod-patterned skirts.

"Still up at all hours?" Her lips curled upward in commiseration as I nodded. "It won't be much longer. Before you know it, she'll be sleeping through the night, and *you'll* be the one waking with a start, wondering if she's taken ill."

The idea of Emma sleeping through the night sounded heavenly at the moment, but I could also well imagine what Morven was saying. I probably would rush over to Emma's cradle to make sure she was breathing if she slept longer than four hours at a spell.

Though some members of the nobility hired wet-nurses for their infants, it had become increasingly more popular and acceptable for ladies to nurse their own children. In any case, it was something the women in the Rutherford branch of our family had insisted upon for generations, and frankly I found the prospect of sending my child off with someone else to be fed and cared for horrifying. We had a nurse to help care for Emma, as did all noble families, but she slept in her cradle in my bedchamber or the adjoining nursery every night.

Charlotte knelt on the blanket a short distance away, her gaze directed over her shoulder toward where the two young cousins now batted the shuttlecock back and forth. Her brow was marked with worry lines.

"Don't take it to heart," Morven murmured, reaching a hand toward her along the blanket to draw her attention. "Children can be brutal at Jane's age. They don't yet understand how to politely mask their reactions, or fully grasp the concept of empathy." She chuckled. "Especially for the fallibility of adults." Her gaze dropped to Emma, who offered her a drooly grin. "The important thing is to keep trying," she cooed as if she was speaking to the baby, even though she was still addressing Charlotte. She tapped Emma on the nose before straightening and continuing in a normal voice. "It might not seem like it, but children value most the time you spend with them, regardless of the activity you might be pursuing. It's how they know that you care."

I tipped my head, contemplating this advice, which seemed remarkably sound.

Charlotte reached up to smooth back the loose wisps of pale blond hair that had escaped their pins and offered her a smile of gratitude. "I fear I'm rather green at all of this and hopelessly out of my depth."

That she had admitted such a thing told me how vulnerable she must feel. The forlorn look in her soft gray eyes tugged at my heart.

"I think you're doing splendidly," I told her.

"You are. You truly are," Morven echoed in encouragement.

"After all, children don't exactly come with instructions." I glanced down at Emma. "A mother isn't instantly blessed with the knowledge and insight about how to best care for her child the moment he or she is born. There are bound to be a few stumbles, a few mistakes." I realized my tone had turned pensive, revealing a bit of my own insecurities in being a new mother, and shrugged a shoulder in commiseration with Charlotte.

"Well, I think you're both doing marvelous," Morven declared, squeezing my upper arm. "Now . . ." She flicked her dark curled tresses off her shoulder and turned to survey the remnants of our picnic scattered across the blanket. "Where is the lemonade? I'm positively parched, and it's only a matter of time before we're descended upon by sweaty boys and men, who will undoubtedly finish it off."

"I believe it's in the basket beside Lady Bearsden," I said as Morven began rising to her feet, having already spied her quarry.

Charlotte fondly shook her head at her great-aunt. "When did Auntie doze off?"

"Not long after everyone abandoned the blankets."

"And abandoned you."

I smiled softly. "I don't mind." I gestured toward the panorama before us. "Not with a view like this one."

I had never traveled to Argyll, which perched along the western edge of the Scottish mainland, but it was beautiful. A multitude of rivers, lochs, and inlets divided the coast into peninsulas, and at the farthest edge were the Inner Hebridean isles. Much of the landscape reminded me of my brother-in-law's castle on the shores of Loch Ewe in the northern Highlands—its colors in undulating greens, browns, amber, and even red ochre; its terrain of deep forests, boggy moors, and windswept rocky crags. Loch Craignish also happened to be a sea loch, opening into the Atlantic Ocean at its southern end. Situated at the northern tip as we were and raised on a hillock overlooking the steel blue water, we could gaze down the length of the loch for some distance.

I tipped my head back and breathed deeply of the Highland air thick with the scent of pine trees and the salty brine of the loch, as well as the faint aroma of old stone. The castle ruins providing us shade were little more than two stubby walls of a former tower while a number of larger stones straggled across the hillock. Lord Barbreck had explained that the rest of the rocks had long been carted away, most of them being utilized to help build the new castle in the early seventeenth century near the spot where the manor now stood. That building had been burned to the ground by Hanoverian troops following the Jacobite rising of 1745, but if I looked to the northeast over the treetops, I could just spy the decorative chimneys and crenellations of the Georgian manor which had been built to replace it some fifty years ago.

At the sound of the loud snuffle behind me, I looked over my shoulder to find Lady Bearsden blinking up at Morven.

"Rise and shine, sleepy-head," my cousin teased as she poured herself some lemonade from the pitcher she'd located.

"I wasn't sleeping," she countered, pushing herself upright, then patting her snow-white hair to be certain it was in place. "Merely resting my eyes."

Morven nodded toward her chin. "Then I suppose you'll blame that bit of drool on little Emma?"

Lady Bearsden swiped at her face but, upon seeing the

smirk Morven had failed to hide behind her glass, narrowed her eyes. Morven bent forward to return the pitcher to the basket, but the older lady halted her with a thump of her gold figure-headed cane, narrowly missing my cousin's foot. "Aren't you going to offer to pour some for me? My, but isn't it warm today." She fanned her face with her hand. "And you ladies dashing about in this heat."

"I suppose you and Kiera had the right idea," Morven replied good-naturedly, handing her the glass of lemonade she'd demanded in retaliation for Morven's impertinence.

Lady Bearsden accepted it with a nod of thanks. "I told Kiera I was surprised she'd not brought her sketchbook with her, as I've scarcely seen her without it the past three days."

She had, indeed, already remarked such just before dozing off and apparently missing my answer.

"There are many interesting sights to capture at Barbreck," I replied. "But I suspected it would be much too blustery on this hill to fumble with paper and charcoals, and I was correct."

"All the same, that view must be beckoning to you," Charlotte interjected, admiring the aspect before us.

"Yes and no."

This admission was met by a quizzical glance.

"Kiera is only curious about people." A twinkle lit Morven's eyes as she sat beside me again. "Landscapes are much too dull and less prone to foibles."

I laughed. "I suppose that's partly true. But portraits are definitely where my talents lie. I wish I could paint a landscape half so well as Gainsborough or Constable," I added wistfully.

My cousin made a derisive sound at the back of her throat. "Well, I wish I could paint more than a blob with arms and legs. You happen to be one of the most gifted portrait artists in all of Britain, so don't expect me to feel sorry for you."

I smiled at her taunting tone, hearing the pride behind it.

Though she *had* been exaggerating, at least a little. It was true that, second only to my family, my art was my greatest passion. But while my portrait paintings had recently become all the rage, that was more due to my scandalous reputation than my talent. And my decision some months past to stop accepting portrait commissions had only seen the demand for them rise. In the past three weeks alone, I had turned down two outrageous offers from one of the highest-ranking peers of the realm and a wealthy industrialist. Had money been my chief consideration, I might have been sorely tempted, but Gage's fortune was more than adequate, and I was much more interested in pursuing my own portrait projects.

"I've two Gainsboroughs up at the hall," the Marquess of Barbreck declared, shuffling over to rejoin us with the aid of his walking stick. "A few Van Dycks, Titian, Reynolds, Zoffany . . ." he continued rattling off artists' names, some of whom made my ears perk up with interest. I had already spied a pair of portraits by Thomas Lawrence and a delightful watercolor by Thomas Girtin, but I'd not yet had time to explore the rest of the manor, what with the demands of motherhood and preparations for the wedding to be completed.

"Yes, Barbreck is quite proud of his art collection," my Aunt Cait said, breaking into this litany as she herded Morven's youngest child toward his mother. As always, dressed in the first stare of fashion, my late mother's younger sister appeared elegant and unruffled even after chasing a toddler and his ball about.

"Rightfully so," Barbreck trumpeted in his deep brogue as he settled in the other chair. "'Tis one o' the finest private collections in all o' Scotland. Nay, all o' Britain!" He gestured upward with his walking stick before lowering it to point at me, his scraggly white eyebrows arching. "I'll take you for a tour myself one o' these days." He thumped the stick down between his legs, leaning against the silver filigreed head. Between his and Lady

Bearsden's canes, I expected someone's head or knuckles to be rapped at any moment. "At least I ken *you'll* appreciate it."

"We appreciate it," Aunt Cait assured him. "But I gather you're eager for a more captivated audience."

Given the fact that I could spend hours studying the paint strokes in a masterfully rendered painting, that would most certainly describe me.

"Yes, I'm sure Kiera would love to hear all about Great-Uncle Alisdair's expeditions and savvy bartering skills," Morven added cheerily, before leaning toward me to mutter under her breath. "For the rest of us have already heard his tales no less than two dozen times."

Emma began to fuss, and I reached down to set her on my lap, using the movement to conceal my amusement. I knew full well how much Morven adored Barbreck despite his cantankerous nature. Her grandfather and grandmother had died before she was born, and for all intents and purposes, Barbreck had assumed the role. It was a natural fit given the fact he'd remained a crusty old bachelor, and Morven's father—my Uncle Dunstan— was now his heir.

"Aye, Alisdair had quite the eye for artistic treasures," he proclaimed with relish, leaning toward me as if he were imparting a secret even though the entire party could hear him. "'Twas quite the artist himself, as weel." He straightened, shaking his head. "Though, sadly, no' o' your caliber, try as he might."

I was trying to decide how to politely respond to this comment when Aunt Cait interceded. "There'll be time enough to show her your collection and share all these tales later." She glanced toward the west. "Right now, I think we need to begin making our way back toward the manor, lest we get caught in that rainstorm."

I followed her gaze, noting for the first time the dark gray clouds forming on the horizon. They were still some distance off, but the manor was not a short stroll away, and while Lady

Bearsden, Lord Barbreck, and the younger children could ride in the cart used to transport the items for our picnic, we couldn't all fit.

She called her granddaughters over and sent them across the field to interrupt the cricket match, before nodding for the pair of footmen hovering at the edges of our gathering to begin packing up. Five or ten minutes later we set off across the glen, following the cart as it rocked side to side down the grassy track. Though I could have claimed a seat in the conveyance, I elected to stretch my legs since I'd been sitting most of the afternoon. Emma snuggled into my shoulder, rolling her head back and forth in a manner that told me she was sleepy. Eventually she settled, clutching my tartan shawl in one of her little fists.

Morven's second son came running past, and then Gage soon fell into step with me, having finished escorting the boy into the bushes at the edge of the clearing. The boy tugged on his sister's hair and was met with predictable results. His sister squealed and began to berate him for his unclean hands, forcing Morven to take her aside to try to calm her while her husband, Jack, gave his son a stern lesson in manners. I couldn't help but smile at the mundane family dramatics. Twenty years ago, the same scene might have played out between Morven and one of her older brothers.

"Is this what I missed, then, not having a sister or female cousin to rile?" Gage queried.

"This, and so much more," I jested as I turned to look up into his handsome face. His golden curls were in more disarray than usual, and his skin had bronzed from all the time he'd spent in the sun over the past week. It made the pale winter blue shade of his eyes all the more arresting. My husband was a well-favored gentleman in any circumstance, but confronted with his relaxed smile, tousled hair, and the evidence of his recent physical exertion, he was exceedingly difficult to look away from.

As if reading my thoughts, one corner of his lips curled naughtily as he bent his head nearer. His deep voice thrummed in my ear. "Perhaps Emma will nap long enough for us to enjoy one of our own." And when he suggested we nap, I knew he was implying something altogether different.

I thought it more likely Emma would wake the moment we returned to Barbreck Manor and demand to be fed, but one could always live in hope.

"Would you like me to take her?" he asked as the roguish glint faded from his eyes to be replaced by something more tender.

We carefully transferred her to his shoulder. She grunted in protest, before turning her face into his neck and settling comfortably. As always, the sight of our child cradled in his strong arms made my heart do tiny flips. Though my muscles were also glad to be relieved of the duty. Emma might weigh less than a stone, but after a time, she still made my arms ache.

I took Gage's coat of deep blue superfine, folding it over my arm as Lord Henry Kerr fell back a few paces to stroll along my other side. Though the wedding party was to be a small one made up predominantly of family, I had asked Charlotte to invite him for my husband's sake. Just four months past, Gage had learned that Henry was his half brother. Though at first he'd reacted with anger and disillusionment at the discovery that his father had betrayed his marriage vows to his mother, whom he'd adored, Gage had soon after embraced his half brother.

Since that revelation and reconciliation, however, they'd not been able to spend as much time together as they'd both hoped.

Henry was the sixth and final child of the Duchess of Bowmont and had grown up in the bosom of that rather notorious family. The duke had claimed him and raised him as his own, just as he had all of the duchess's children, no matter the truth of their conceptions. As such, Henry was still close to all the members of Bowmont's family, and he was often called upon to assist with various matters at the duke's numerous estates and holdings, keeping him away from Edinburgh, where Gage and I had been residing.

I looked back and forth between them. Though their coloring was different—Henry's hair being an auburn shade that glinted in the sun and eyes the silvery gray of their father's—the two men flanking me shared striking similarities in facial structure and physique. As such, I was somewhat surprised that no one had remarked upon it yet. Or perhaps they were too polite to do so.

"Lord Jack told me there are a number of hillforts and standing stones in the area," Henry said. "I gather he holds a keen interest in ancient sites."

"That he does," I replied with a light laugh, recalling the story Morven had once told me about her *then* newlywed husband, and how he'd made her stand in the rain for hours while he tried to examine the grooves in the stones around a Neolithic cairn.

"Well, he and Rye have offered to take us out to see them tomorrow." He glanced over his shoulder toward the gray clouds that were drifting ever closer. "If the weather clears. While I can't say I am altogether enthused by such monuments, I would welcome the chance for a good gallop."

Much like Gage, Henry enjoyed the exertions of physical activity—riding, shooting, hiking, climbing, as well as the requisite gentlemanly sports—boxing and fencing. Activities they could fully indulge themselves in here at Barbreck's estate in the Scottish countryside.

"As would I," Gage replied in a soft voice, so as not to wake our daughter. His gaze shifted to me. "That is, if Kiera doesn't mind."

"Of course not," I said. "Go and enjoy yourself. I will likely be busy helping Charlotte with wedding plans." It being only a fortnight until the wedding was to take place, there was still much to do. "And if not, I'm sure I can happily entertain myself examining Barbreck's art collection."

Gage grinned, knowing this to be an understatement. I would be ecstatic to have some time to myself to quietly study and contemplate the paintings gracing the manor's walls.

In any case, I could only be separated from Emma for three to four hours at a time, making a long ramble on horseback already difficult and, with Jack leading the excursion, all but impossible. Such long ventures would have to wait until my child was older.

"Then, tell Jack I would be pleased to join you," Gage told Henry before reaching out to wrap the arm not cradling Emma around my waist to pull me closer to his side. "And I hope *you* will be able to indulge to your heart's content. May an enjoyable day be had by all," he declared lightheartedly.

If only that had proven to be the case.

CHAPTER 2

The following morning Gage and Henry set off on horse-back with Jack and Rye while I joined Charlotte and the other ladies in the rose parlor, which had largely been given over to wedding preparations. Even for such a small, private ceremony, there were details to be attended to. However, not so many that the tasks became tedious, or so laborious that we couldn't gossip while completing them.

Unsurprisingly, Charlotte's great-aunt, Lady Bearsden, possessed the most titillating information, as she was an incorrigible rattle. Though I knew from experience she also understood when to hold her tongue. As such, she and Aunt Cait had more to say than all the rest of us combined, though Morven's comical facial expressions were perhaps the most amusing.

Our gowns had been designed and sewn by a modiste in Edinburgh, but there were still a few minor alterations to be made by the manor's resident seamstress, and a large portion of the morning was taken up by this task. All the ladies had chosen to have new gowns made, not simply Charlotte and myself, as her attendant. Rye's six-year-old daughter, Jane, seemed charmed by the confection she was to wear, and I could tell how much this pleased Charlotte.

However, I couldn't help but feel a pulse of concern seeing how much my friend's gown needed to be taken in. Her last fitting in Edinburgh had been barely three weeks prior, yet she'd lost enough weight in that time that the seamstress would need to cinch the bodice in further. Charlotte had already possessed a slender figure, and she didn't have the excuse I did that I was slowly shedding the extra weight I'd gained while with child. So there was no reason that she should be dropping inches. No reason except nerves.

As such, I made it a point to thread my arm through Charlotte's as we all scattered to our various pursuits following luncheon, sticking to her side like a burr. Once we'd slipped away beyond the hearing of the others, I diverted our steps toward a bench situated in an alcove beneath the grand staircase fashioned of gleaming oak and finely carved spiraling balusters.

"Now, tell me what has your stomach so tied in knots," I ordered lightly. "And don't try to insist it isn't," I hastened to add when she opened her mouth to do just that. "If the amount of fabric your gown is being taken in wasn't indication enough, the fact that you barely ate a bite of luncheon confirmed it."

A vee formed between her pale brows, as if she were cross with me for broaching the subject. But then she gave a deep sigh, either weariness or distress pulling down the corners of her mouth.

I urged her to sit beside me on the bench upholstered in cream silk. "You aren't having second thoughts, are you?" I asked, trying to mask the disquiet I felt at such a possibility. After all, Rye was my cousin and a gentle soul. Should Charlotte decide now not to go through with the wedding, I knew he would be tremendously hurt.

But she reassured me immediately on that score. "Oh, no! No, that's not it at all. I *love* Rye."

"Then, is it the children? I know you're anxious for them to like you."

"I am," she conceded. "But I know that will take time. Such matters can't be rushed."

I watched as she smoothed her pale pink muslin skirts over her lap, diverting her gaze from mine. "Then what is it?"

She seemed to struggle with herself, though it wasn't clear why she was so hesitant to speak. Did she fear my reaction? Or maybe she was worried that putting her misgivings into words would only make them more concrete?

"Is it the governess?" I guessed.

Charlotte seemed startled by the suggestion, and then uneasy. It was an expression I had not seen on her face since the early days of our acquaintance, when her rotten blackguard of a husband, Lord Stratford, was still alive. Then, she'd tried to mask her pain and insecurity with icy disdain, but now she merely gazed back at me in apprehension.

"I noticed that the manner in which she addresses you isn't entirely . . . respectful," I clarified.

No one could have taken fault with Miss Ferguson's words, but the few times I'd observed the young governess, her brittle tone of voice and the look in her eyes were a different matter. She might not have displayed outright contempt, but she came very close to it.

"Then, I'm not just imagining it?" she murmured uncertainly.

"Definitely not."

She seemed to exhale in relief. "I worried I might be misreading her intentions or expecting too much."

"So you haven't spoken to Rye about it?"

"No, I . . . I didn't want to raise the issue. Not when I wasn't sure." She flushed. "The children are so fond of her. I suppose she's the closest thing they've had to a mother since theirs died four years ago, God rest her soul. And I . . ." Her gaze dropped to her lap, where she worried her fingers. "I didn't want to upset them."

I could appreciate the compassion she was showing her new stepchildren, and the delicacy of the situation, but that didn't mean she should discount her own feelings on the matter. I also knew from experience that if the staff were allowed to treat you with even a whiff of disrespect, things would merely get worse. My late husband, Sir Anthony Darby, had permitted and even encouraged his staff to disregard me, so I'd possessed few allies in a household where I had desperately needed them.

I reached out to clasp her hand to still her fidgeting. "That's all well and good, Charlotte, but you know as well as I do that it's best for all if you begin as you mean to carry on. If you allow Miss Ferguson to eye you with contempt now, she will take greater liberties later. And her tendency to countermand you in small ways with the children will only grow bolder. There's no need to be unkind, but you must make it crystal clear what conduct and comportment you expect from her. From *all* of your staff."

She nodded. "You're right. To be honest, given the way she dismisses me, I've wondered what things she says about me when I'm not around."

I'd wondered the same thing. I'd also wondered whether Miss Ferguson held some sort of hopes that Rye would fall in love with *her*, for she was no more than a score and ten years of age and attractive in her own right. But there was no need to heap more worries on Charlotte's head. Not when my suspicions were unsubstantiated, and Rye was so clearly smitten with the bride he *had* chosen.

"Then you'll speak to Rye?" I prodded.

"I will."

"Good." I squeezed her hand once more before releasing it.

Sitting back, I scrutinized her pale complexion. Its normally porcelain tone had lost some of its vitality. "But I know that's not
the only thing troubling you."

A pucker formed between her brows.

"Will you tell me, or must I guess?"

She heaved a mock sigh. "I suppose I only have myself to
blame for befriending such an annoyingly observant woman."
She turned to stare at the wide panel of windows glinting in the
sunlight across from where we sat. "My father . . ." she began.
"You know he's been abroad."

"Yes."

"That he's due to arrive in a few days' time."

I nodded. His absence from the country had been one of the
reasons Charlotte and Rye had postponed their wedding until
nearly August. The other being concern over Rye's older brother,
Brady, and his family traveling such a distance while the cholera
morbus still ran rampant through parts of Britain.

Whereas before she'd carefully smoothed the fabric of her
skirts, now she began pleating it into neat rows between her fingers. Rather than stop her, this time I let her continue, hoping
the soothing motion would help her find her words. "Father has
met Rye just once. Briefly."

I waited for her to continue, but her tongue appeared to have
become stuck to the roof of her mouth, forcing me to prompt
her again. "And what happened? I can't imagine Rye made an
unfavorable impression."

For all that Rye was shy and retiring, he also possessed impeccable manners and knew how to present himself among society so that his quiet demeanor was not seen as odd but rather
becoming. It was a talent I had never acquired, though my stilted
awkwardness had eased somewhat now that I was more settled.
Marriage to Gage and the accomplishment I felt in solving our
inquiries had given me a confidence I'd lacked. Even if occasion-

ally I said the wrong thing or missed a cue, my worth wasn't tied
to either.

"No, no. I could tell that Father liked him well enough. But . . .
we weren't engaged to be married then, and Father . . . well, he's
rather a stickler to propriety, to . . . to rank." She looked up at
me after this last statement, and I could see the desperation in
her eyes, the desire to make me understand without having to
say the words outright.

"You're afraid your father won't approve of the marriage," I
stated succinctly for her.

Tears glistened at the corners of her eyes, and I touched her
shoulder.

"Oh, Charlotte."

She sniffed and reached up to swipe away the wetness. "It's
not that it really matters. I don't require Father's permission to
marry, and I'm certainly not going to let him stop me. But . . ."
Her voice choked on a strangle of emotion.

"But he's your father."

She nodded.

I rubbed my hand up and down her arm, waiting to speak
until she had gotten herself in hand. I knew very little about the
Earl of Ledbury, only the few things Charlotte had told me and
my own impressions drawn from the facts I knew. When her
mother had died, the earl had become somewhat of an absent father, passing her off to his favorite aunt, Lady Bearsden, to manage. Although this wasn't entirely surprising. Many gentlemen
had little to do with the rearing of their children. But because
he'd never remarried, even though his wife had given birth to
but two daughters, meaning he lacked a direct male heir, I'd perhaps erroneously assumed he was a romantic. That he'd not taken
a new wife because he could not bear to replace his first one. Unless Charlotte was the one who was not seeing clearly.

"Maybe you're putting the cart before the horse," I told her.

"Rye is, after all, a gentleman, and one from a good family. He may not bear a title, or be likely ever to do so, but his father will one day be a marquess. Even the most priggish of individuals can't wrinkle their noses at that."

"You're right." She dabbed at her eyes with her handkerchief. "I'm probably being ridiculous."

"Now, I didn't say that," I countered. "But I *am* curious what gave you the impression your father might object, for I know you didn't make it up whole cloth."

"It was my sister."

I didn't bother to hide my adverse reaction to her mention of Alice. I knew my older sister and I had our differences and our fair share of disagreements, but I still considered her my dearest friend, and I knew that she would always be there for me even in my darkest hour. Charlotte could not say the same for her older sister.

"In her last letter, Alice said that Father had confided in her that he'd held hopes I would endeavor to capture the interest of a lordly widower. Perhaps even Lord Melbourne."

Melbourne currently served as the home secretary and was expected to one day reach as high as prime minister.

Her lips twisted sourly. "She even recorded his remark that, though nine-and-twenty, my beauty still rivaled that of any debutante, and so he'd expected me to reach higher."

"She must have choked on her spleen writing that," I replied, knowing well the jealousy Alice felt toward her younger sister for not only being more beautiful but also having wed a man of higher rank. I was glad her sister had been unable to travel to Scotland, and thus Charlotte had been saved from her malicious company.

"Which means it must be true. She would never have been able to stomach sharing such a thing otherwise, not without knowing it would hurt me." She flushed angrily. "She even suggested Melbourne would be glad to have me as a wife to give him another son. One without complications."

Such a comment was unspeakably cruel on many levels.

"I take it you haven't told her of your difficulties," I said, knowing Charlotte was unable to conceive children.

"Heavens, no! And have her throw it back in my face at every opportunity?" She laughed scornfully. "No, she can never know. And neither can my father."

"I'm sorry, Charlotte," I murmured.

She flicked her hand as if to say what was done was done.

"But just because your father thought and said those things doesn't mean he won't approve of your marriage to Rye." I took hold of her hands before she hopelessly wrinkled her gown and squeezed them between my own. "You said yourself that they'd barely met. With more time, I'm sure he'll come to love Rye. You'll see."

Though, truth be told, I wasn't certain I cared much for his good opinion—for Rye or myself. Not while knowing he'd heartily approved of Charlotte's first husband, Lord Stratford. Stratford might have been an earl, and a wealthy one at that, but he had also been a score of years older than Charlotte, and a notorious rake and scoundrel. I supposed I couldn't hold it against Lord Ledbury that Stratford had also proven capable of murder, as that had happened years after they'd wed. But the very fact that Ledbury should have been so eager to see his naïve and innocent daughter married to such a depraved man like Stratford, and yet was possibly unwilling to embrace a good and kindly man like Rye, told me all I needed to know about his character.

However, I said none of this to Charlotte, hoping it would be unnecessary for me to point it out. In any case, whether it was my reasoning or my determined optimism that persuaded her, I was relieved to see a glimmer of assurance in her eyes. "You're right. I'm borrowing trouble, aren't I?" She exhaled a long breath and then nodded determinedly. "I'll stop anticipating the worst."

"Good." I smiled in encouragement. "It's going to be a lovely wedding, Charlotte. And I couldn't be happier for you both."

Her cheeks reddened again, though this time for a much more pleasant reason, and then she pushed to her feet. "I'm on my way to the nursery. Are you coming?"

"No, Emma should still be napping," I replied, knowing she was under Mrs. Mackay's careful watch. "I thought I'd take the opportunity to view some of the paintings Lord Barbreck has been bragging about."

An impish twinkle lit her eyes. "I could fetch him for you, if you'd like the full tour."

I clasped my hands together to plead. "Please, be merciful."

She laughed, turning toward the stairs. "I'm going to tell him you said that."

"No, you won't," I replied as she pattered up the steps.

She glanced over her shoulder to make a face at me before hurrying on.

I grinned at her retreating figure until it disappeared and then turned to the large painting hung on the wall next to the bench. It was a winter landscape composed of skeletal trees, snow-covered houses, and ice skaters on a frozen river, either painted by Pieter Bruegel the Elder—as its gilded frame proclaimed—or his son. It was hung in an awkward setting, half in light and half in shadow, which made it difficult to appreciate the painting in the manner in which it should have been.

As such, I turned from it rather quickly and then slowly made my way up the stairs, scrutinizing the portraits which hung above the stairs, sometimes as many as three high. The paintings hung at such a great height were too far away to be satisfactorily studied, but those closest to my eye level provided enough meat to my senses that I could not be too disappointed. Paintings by some of the greatest portraitists were hung next to lesser artists. Reynolds, Gainsborough, Hogarth, Holbein. I was dizzy with delight. Whether or not the subjects of the paintings were related to Barbreck Manor and the family in some way, I would have to ask Lord Barbreck, but I suspected many of them were not. Their features were too varied, too dissimilar. It seemed clear that most of the portraits had been collected purely in appreciation of the artists and not the person portrayed.

I stood for a long time in front of a Rembrandt on the flight of stairs leading to the second floor, examining the brushstrokes and the way he portrayed character and emotion. One of my various art tutors had pointed out the manner in which he reflected light from the nose and the cheekbone into the eye socket, channeling it there in a brilliant illusion that the untrained eye would not detect, and so every time I saw a new Rembrandt, I looked for that effect.

I turned to continue up the stairs and around the corner into the long gallery. I knew that Barbreck's most treasured works of art would hang here, and I was not disappointed. Paintings spanned the length of the gallery, some no larger than my two hands placed side by side, and some large enough to cover the wall from floor to ceiling. Light spilled into the gallery from several high windows, illuminating the white walls and corniced ceiling, and highlighting the paintings and a number of small sculptures and busts. In this space, silence reigned, broken only by the soft click of my own footfalls against the marble floor.

I inched my way down the wall, savoring this feast for my eyes, examining the brushstrokes and colors, the composition and technique, the light and depth and emotion. It was like wading into a pool of euphoric delight. My fingers twitched at my side, eager to grip my specially weighted paintbrushes, impatient to discover whether I could replicate the method. I leaned close to see even the most minute detail and then retreated to marvel at its broader effect.

That is, until something jarred me from my revery.

It wasn't immediate. Rather it began with merely a whisper of uncertainty, a stirring somewhere inside me that something wasn't quite right.

I felt it first when I stood in front of the Titian—an artist I was greatly familiar with due to his popularity among Englishmen. I had seen numerous works by Titian, but this painting did not fill me with the same reverence and awe. It portrayed an equestrian astride his steed, bedecked in armor, and yet it was very dark, and the reflective qualities of the metal seemed dull. Most of the works I had seen by Titian boasted lush and luminous colors and masterful light and shadow, even 250 years after his death. Although there *were* darker, more subtle portraits attributed to him, I reasoned. Or perhaps the varnish was severely discolored with age. But still, my disquiet would not be eased, particularly when I turned my attention to the cloth and draping. I had once stood transfixed by the manner in which Titian had rendered the texture of a quilted sleeve, but this equestrian's clothing appeared flat and unrealized.

Determined to brush these worries aside as flaws in my own expectations, I moved on to the next portrait of three ladies, only to be nearly overwhelmed by a swirling sensation in my stomach akin to nauseousness. This painting was even worse. The frame stated it to be a Van Dyck, but I was certain it could not be.

As the court portraitist during Charles I's reign, Sir Anthony Van Dyck had painted during a tumultuous reign filled with uncertainty. But despite—or perhaps because of—that, his portraits were filled with life and drama and movement. He did not simply paint a person, he captured a moment in time. And there was always a sense that there was a story behind the composition of the people, a secret in their eyes, words trembling on their lips.

But this. This held none of that allure. None of that dynamic force that typified Van Dyck. This was stiff and lifeless. Even the pigments were dull, the saturated colors he'd applied—likely learned from studying Titian's works—nonexistent.

I was stunned. Utterly stunned.

This room held Barbreck's most prized paintings. He clearly believed this to be a genuine Van Dyck, and yet I could not deny the evidence before me, nor my years of visual and practical study and the instincts they'd honed.

I stood with both hands clasped over my mouth, wondering what on earth I should do, when suddenly a strong pair of arms wrapped around me from behind. I gasped and startled, only to sag back against Gage's chest at the sound of his deep chuckle.

"I'm sorry, darling," he murmured into my ear. "I did stomp my way across the room and say your name a few times, but apparently you were lost in your study. As I knew I would find you."

I exhaled a long breath. "Did you have a good ride?" I asked, smelling the musk of wind and sun and horse clinging to his clothes and skin.

"We did." He turned me in his arms, arching a single eyebrow. "Though, you were right. Jack enjoys talking about ancient monuments." His lips quirked. "An interest that my half brother does not share."

I nodded distractedly, my thoughts still on the alleged Van Dyck hanging behind me.

"At one point I thought I might have to intercede when he started weighing the heft of a rock between his two hands after Jack had waxed on for too long about burial cairns."

I smiled reflexively at his jest, but evidently it wasn't convincing, for he lifted his hands to clasp my upper arms.

"Kiera," he said, waiting for me to look up at him. "You look troubled." His brow furrowed as his gaze searched mine. "What is it?"

I hesitated, wondering if I should keep my suspicions to myself. But then I realized this was Gage. There was no need to keep such a thing from him. Not when he could help me decide what to do.

"I think . . . I'm fairly sure . . ." I huffed, aggravated with myself for my vacillating, and then looked him squarely in the eye to declare with confidence. "I'm nearly certain this painting is a forgery."

CHAPTER 3

I gazed down into Emma's sweet face, her blue eyes sparkling and alert. "Happier now?" I crooned, dabbing at the milk still lingering in one corner of her mouth. As if in answer, she waved one little fist and kicked. Smiling, I sat her upright in my lap, supporting her chest with one hand while I patted her back with the other.

It had taken longer than usual to nurse her due to my anxiety over the paintings. As a new mother, I had swiftly learned that if I was worried or distressed, then that would not only translate to the baby, but my milk also would not let down. At the best of times, I took several deep breaths before ever settling down with Emma. But when she was already fussy because I was late in feeding her, that only compounded the problem.

It was moments like these when my insecurities would rear their ugly head. For months before her birth, I'd fretted over whether I would make a good mother, whether my temperament and occupations would make me a suitable one. Fortunately, those fears had since all but faded. Especially when I cradled Emma in my arms and gazed down into her little face, my love for her filling me to the brim until I felt it would surely run over. But there were still times when doubts crept in, when Emma could not be soothed, and I worried my abilities weren't equal to the task. Which made me all the more grateful for Mrs. Mackay, Emma's nurse.

This evening, she had done her best to soothe Emma before my arrival, but it had already become apparent that my daughter had a mind of her own, and that meant when she wanted to eat, she wanted to eat then and there. The nurse had made clear to us how important schedules were for children, as well as their parents, and recognizing the wisdom of this, we had done our best to comply with the suggestion. But to paraphrase the sage Robert Burns, our best laid plans often went awry, and Emma seemed to revel in breaking them.

The door to the dressing room opened quietly, and Gage peered through, knowing well how any sight or sound could distract our daughter even while she was eating, her curious mind at least temporarily overruling her hunger. Upon finding Emma seated upright, he mouthed the word *Done?*

"Yes," I replied, and he advanced into the room, having changed from his riding attire into a coat of deep green superfine and brown trousers. His hair was still damp at his temples, and I could smell the starch from his fresh cravat mixed with the spicy scent of the cologne he must have reapplied.

Catching sight of him, Emma offered him a toothless grin just as a loud belch erupted from her tiny stomach. Considering all the air she'd swallowed while she was crying, I wasn't surprised.

"Ate your fill, I see?" Gage said, reaching down to lift her from my lap. He swung her around in his arms, and she laughed—one of her most recent developments, and one I was still charmed upon hearing every time.

So I smiled, even as I was scolding her father. "She won't remain full for long if you keep swinging her about like that, and you'll be changing your coat yet again." I moved closer to tickle Emma's chin. "I can just hear Anderley's reaction to baby vomit," I crooned, as if it were the cutest thing in the world.

A chuckle rumbled from Gage's chest. "Point taken."

Although Anderley, his valet, was tremendously loyal to Gage, it was obvious he still didn't know what to think of baby Emma. I suspected that, like most men of his station, he had little experience with infants, so that wasn't unexpected. In any case, he had little cause for interaction with her, especially here at Barbreck Manor. We had been assigned a large suite of rooms at the northwest corner of the house, and while Gage and I shared the bed in my chamber every night—contrary to the practice of many members of the upper classes—Gage utilized the bedchamber on the opposite side of the dressing room to shave and change clothes, and all the other tasks his valet assisted him with. Meanwhile, Emma largely remained in my bedchamber and the small nursery conveniently placed next door.

Upon our arrival, Aunt Cait had explained how the smaller nursery had been set up when her first grandchild was on the way, and how it had been used for each successive grandchild since. Then, once the child was weaned, they went to join the other children in the nursery proper. However it had come to be, I was grateful for the arrangement, particularly in a manor as large as Barbreck.

Wide windows flanked by long drapes of smoke blue damask spanned the length of the rounded exterior wall, looking out over the boulder-strewn ridges and golden-green glens to the north and the shimmering blue waters of the sea loch to the west. The walls had been papered in a delicate ivory hand-painted silk, and the fireplace was tiled with fine Italian marble. But the heavy oak furniture had clearly been transferred here from somewhere else, for it was older than the Georgian mansion by at least a century.

Gage sank down on the edge of the bed supported by four massive posts nearly as large around as tree trunks and sat Emma on his knees, mindful of her head as she'd only recently mastered the ability to hold it upright. "Now, tell me what you meant in the long gallery?" he prompted.

I sighed, leaning against one of the posts as I continued to wrestle with myself.

"Though I understand your haste to return to our chambers once you realized what time it was, you can't simply make a statement like that and then expect me *not* to ask you to explain," he added, misinterpreting my bewilderment for reluctance. "Do you honestly believe it's a forgery?"

"Unfortunately, yes."

"I see." He seemed startled by my frank answer. "Well . . . that's not good."

I cast him a look of mild annoyance, for "not good" was quite the understatement.

From the manner in which he avoided my gaze—watching Emma as she lowered her head to gnaw on one of his knuckles with her toothless gums—I could tell he had more to say, but he was searching for the right words. Likely because he didn't know how to express his skepticism of my judgment without insulting me.

"You're wondering how I can be so sure?"

His expression turned sheepish.

I sank down on the opposite end of the mattress. "Because I'm an artist." I shook my head. "No, it's more than that." I tried again. "Because I've studied Van Dyck. I *know* his work. I know his style, his techniques. Were it a good forgery, I would not dare to voice my misgivings even if I had them, for there are any number of reasons why a painting might not appear to be entirely up to snuff. The varnish could be discolored with age, or it could have been damaged or improperly cleaned, and then someone of lesser skill tried to cover it up or fix it."

I tilted my head to the side, considering the possibility that the flaws and inconsistencies I'd detected had been caused by such overpaint, that a real Van Dyck was hidden beneath, but then I discarded the possibility. If there was an actual Van Dyck underneath—and I highly doubted it—it had been so damaged and obscured as to no longer truly be his work.

"But this is not a good forgery. Not by Van Dyck's standards in any case, or his pupils." A man of Sir Anthony Van Dyck's caliber would have had a studio of artists working under him, preparing the canvases and pigments, echoing his technique, copying his work, and even painting the elements of some of his portraits that were less in need of the master's hand.

I pressed a hand to my forehead, wondering how I was going to tell Lord Barbreck that one of his most prized works of art was a forgery, or whether I even should.

But of course I had to. I couldn't let him go on believing it was a genuine Van Dyck. Not when he might find out from another visitor to Barbreck in a far more embarrassing manner. In any case, if he didn't know it was a fraud, how could he attempt to recoup his losses, either by investigating the theft of the original or suing the fraudsman who'd sold it to him in the first place?

Unless that had been his brother Alisdair.

I cringed. This was not going to be a pleasant conversation.

"You're worried about telling Barbreck," Gage deduced.

"How can I not be?" I retorted, distress tightening my voice.

He laid Emma in the middle of the counterpane decorated with delicate twining silver embroidery and gave her the ragdoll sitting on the table beside the bed. She cooed to her little friend before stuffing part of it into her mouth. Seeing this, I couldn't help but smile, especially when she began to kick happily.

Gage slid closer, reaching out to clasp my hand where it rested against the coverlet. "He might be upset upon hearing the news, but he'll recognize it's not your fault."

I nodded, hoping he was right. Barbreck might profess a fondness for me, but he was also quite the curmudgeon and, like many Highlanders, capable of keeping ferocious grudges for even the tiniest infractions.

"Shall I come with you?" he offered.

I supposed it was better to have it over and done with, but still I hesitated, wondering if perhaps I'd made too hasty an assessment. Except I knew that I hadn't. Actually, the more I questioned myself, the more certain I became. After all, when it came to art, I'd come to realize that the first instinctual impression was almost always the right one. Certain artists and paintings made you feel certain things. They resonated inside you like the pure sweet ring of a bell or the deep peal of a gong, like the precision of a major chord or the aching tension of a minor seventh, like the lyrical cascade of a mountain spring or the grumble of thunder. Whatever tone that painting had been attempting to strike, it had succeeded in stirring only discord, and not even an intentional dissonance at that.

"Would you?" I finally replied.

"Of course. Shall we go now?"

"Yes, I suppose there's no use dragging my feet."

He smiled in commiseration and then strode across the room to rap once on the adjoining nursery door while I lifted Emma and her ragdoll. A moment later, Mrs. Mackay came bustling through the door, her silver hair tucked neatly inside a lace cap. I didn't know precisely how many generations of children she had raised in her lifetime, but Emma was certainly not her first—or even second or third—and somehow I doubted she would be her last. Despite the wrinkles which had settled into the grooves of her face and the gentle sagging of the skin around her neck and beneath her eyes, she still brimmed with energy.

We had struggled to find just the right nurse to fit the needs of our little family. One who wouldn't mind the somewhat nomadic lifestyle we led at times, for I had absolutely no intention of leaving my child behind as we traveled about. Not that I could at the moment, nursing her as I was, but I had wanted to be sure they understood that that wouldn't change even when she was older. Because most children of the upper classes remained at a country house in the charge of their nurse and her staff while their parents traveled, I knew this would not appeal to all potential nannies, particularly experienced ones.

There was also the matter of my scandalous past and Gage's efforts as a gentleman inquiry agent, which I assisted him with. We had solved a number of intricate investigations over the past two years and unmasked several murderers, and while we had recently taken a respite from such activities since Emma's birth, that didn't mean we had given them up entirely. If someone needed our help and it was in our power to give, I knew we would never say no, even if Gage had made it clear to his father—who was also a gentleman inquiry agent of great renown—that he was no longer at his beck and call. The fact that we dabbled in such matters was unattractive to some would-be applicants and downright disagreeable to others.

Not only did Lettuce Mackay possess the experience and impeccable references we desired, but she also seemed to possess a desire for adventure that she'd heretofore been unable to indulge. She'd confessed that one of the reasons she'd applied was specifically because she *wanted* to travel. Before now, she'd been trapped at a pair of manors located in the countryside of Midlothian for decades at a time. After so many years in one place, she wished to see more of Britain or even Europe, and the only way she was likely to ever do that was to find a place with a family like ours.

Given the intrepid natures of many of the members of our staff, the nurse had seemed to settle in easily. I knew my maid Bree, a fellow Scotswoman, liked her, as did our butler, Jeffers, who was still back in Edinburgh. Gage's valet, Anderley, didn't spend much time conversing with me unless we were in the midst of an investigation he was assisting us with, but I had heard him laughing at one of her jests one evening, which I viewed as an encouraging sign.

And as for her care of Emma, I was more than pleased. She was warm and kind, often singing and talking to her. When I approached the nursery, I could tell whether my daughter was asleep or awake simply by listening for the sound of her nurse's voice, for she seemed to chatter almost constantly about everything and nothing when Emma wasn't resting. Had I been the one forced to listen to her nonstop, I might have run screaming from the room, but Emma didn't seem to mind.

Mrs. Mackay was also steady and confident, and having raised so many children, nothing seemed to rattle her. Emma being my first child, I appreciated this tremendously. For Mrs. Mackay's calm often soothed my own worries, and yet I detected no condescension in her when I asked her a question or solicited her advice. I had been warned by my sister, Alana, that some nannies could be very set in their ways and determined to have things done how they'd always done them, but thus far I'd had no such clashes with Mrs. Mackay. Of course, with Emma being less than four months old, that might change, but for now it was not a concern, and I wasn't about to go borrowing more trouble when I already had a forgery to denounce.

"Did we fill our belly?" Mrs. Mackay asked Emma as she approached, offering her a gentle smile.

Emma pulled the ragdoll from her mouth, offering her a slobbery grin in return.

"She did," I confirmed somewhat unnecessarily given the fact she'd been wailing like a banshee when I'd taken her from Mrs. Mackay three quarters of an hour earlier.

I pressed a kiss to both of Emma's cheeks before passing her to her nurse. "I'll be back in time to feed her before I change for dinner like usual. And I won't lose track of the hour this time," I added somewhat fretfully.

"Och, there's no need to worry," she assured me. "The bairn just had to exercise her lungs for a wee bit, and she needs to do tha' from time to time anyways. 'Tis good for her."

I laughed lightly, feeling I shouldn't need this reassurance, but grateful for it nonetheless.

Gage dropped a kiss on Emma's downy blond head while I checked my appearance in the mirror, adjusting the epaulettes on my sleeves and the high neckline of my morning gown of small floral bouquets over a white background. Then we set off arm in arm in search of Lord Barbreck.

We found him seated with Lady Bearsden in front of the tall Georgian windows of the library which looked out over an ornate portico at the side of the house. The pair of them were perched in tall wingback chairs upholstered in regal purple silk with their heads bent together. A naughty timbre shaded Barbreck's voice as he made some sort of jest, to which Lady Bearsden tittered almost girlishly. I could only wonder what sort of mischief they were up to.

We paused for a moment in the doorway, waiting for them to notice us across the expanse of the chamber. White-trimmed bookcases spanned the length of three walls from floor to ceiling, save for two doorways—one which led into the corridor and the other to Barbreck's private study. Two sliding ladders were affixed to the tracks at opposite sides of the rooms, allowing for access to the higher shelves. Groups of furniture were spaced evenly about the medallion carpet to allow one to cozy up with a book, indulge in a tête-à-tête, or tip one's head back to admire the magnificent coffered ceiling.

"Ah, my dear Mrs. Gage," Lady Bearsden exclaimed, being the first to catch sight of us. "And your darling husband," she simpered as we crossed the chamber toward them. "If you're looking for Charlotte, she's gone for a stroll in the garden with Mr. Mallery. I believe they wished for a moment alone."

From the twinkle in her eye, it was clear she believed this was for romantic reasons, but I had to wonder whether instead Charlotte intended to discuss her concerns about Miss Ferguson, the governess. However, if she hadn't confided as much in her great-aunt, I was not going to do so.

"Actually, we were looking for his lordship," I replied, glancing at the man in question.

His chin arched, and had I not been fighting the nerves fluttering in my stomach, I might have been amused by the sight of him preening. "Aye, lass. What can I do for my favorite niece?"

I wasn't truly his niece, nor did I believe I was his favorite. Barbreck simply liked to bandy the title about from time to time when one of us pleased him, as if to pit us against each other. Or layer on the guilt.

His gaze flicked toward my husband. "Do I need to take this gentleman to task for abandonin' ye last night for a game o' billiards?" he queried with mock severity, lifting his walking stick to point it at Gage's chest before lowering it back to the floor. A corner of his mouth twitched upward. "Heard there was quite a ruckus when he and Lord Henry thrashed Rye and Jack."

"All in good-natured fun," Gage answered calmly, knowing better than to let himself be riled by the wily old marquess.

Barbreck's eyes narrowed craftily. "Aye? Naught but a brotherly tussle, then."

My eyes darted to Gage's face, perhaps giving too much away. I'd known it would only be a matter of time before someone noted the similarities between Gage and Henry. Not that it was imperative to keep the matter private, but I felt the half brothers should have the ultimate say in who was told and who wasn't. Particularly as such a revelation was not without risks and repercussions to certain people's reputations if the knowledge became too widespread.

Gage's lips curled softly in amusement. "You could call it that."

Which was neither a confirmation nor a denial, but delighted Barbreck nonetheless.

Lady Bearsden, on the other hand, was scrutinizing Gage's features with too much intensity, and I knew a far more pointed comment would pass her lips if I did not divert her interest.

"No, I . . . well, I have something a bit awkward to tell you," I replied somewhat gracelessly, not knowing how on earth to broach such a subject. My gaze shifted to Lady Bearsden before returning to the marquess. "One that might be best discussed in private."

I could tell from their rapt expressions that I had their attention now. Unfortunately, Lady Bearsden leapt to the wrong conclusion.

"Has something happened?" She slid forward to the edge of her chair. "Emma hasn't fallen ill, has she?"

"No, it's nothing like that," I assured her. "We are all well."

"Then, another guest?" She glanced at Gage. "Lord Henry, perhaps?"

"No, it has nothing to do with the family or any of the guests," I replied with perhaps more force than was necessary. I exhaled an exasperated breath, realizing I would have to be clearer if I wanted her to stop pressing the matter. "It's to do with Lord Barbreck's art collection."

The marquess thumped his cane against the floor between his legs, leaning on the silver filigreed head. "Aye, weel, then ye can speak frankly in front o' her ladyship. There's no need for secrecy there."

I opened my mouth to offer one more objection but then stopped. If he didn't mind her hearing, then who was I to oppose. Besides, it might go more easily if Lady Bearsden was here to witness the conversation. Her dark eyes shimmered not only with curiosity but also kindness.

I dipped my head once in acceptance and sank down on the upholstered bench across from them, waiting until Gage had joined me before I gathered my words. "I spent some time this afternoon admiring your paintings on the walls of the grand staircase and then into the long gallery. It's quite impressive," I confessed with sincerity, hoping to soften the blow.

"Aye, I've been told by some that it is the finest collection in Scotland. Perhaps all o' Britain," he remarked with pride, having said something similar the day before.

This assessment was definitely taking it too far. His collection was certainly fine, but not the most superb in all of Britain, nor even, in all likelihood, Scotland. However, pointing this out would only make what I had to say next more difficult.

"Yes, well, I . . . I have something troubling to tell you." I faltered, struggling to continue. Particularly in the face of the forbidding expression which had fallen over Barbreck's countenance. I searched his features, trying to understand precisely what was stamped there. Did he already have some inkling of what I was going to say, or was he merely reacting to my evident uneasiness?

Gage pressed a reassuring hand to the small of my back, and I forced a deep breath past the tightness in my lungs. "Your Van Dyck portrait. The one of the three ladies." I hesitated a second longer before spitting out the truth. "It's a forgery."

I gazed at Barbreck, pressing my tongue to the roof of my mouth to stifle the urge to rattle off all of the evidence, instead making myself wait for him to speak first. But rather than asking me why I believed such a thing to be true, he simply grew redder and redder, until the veins in his forehead became a mottled purple, and I feared he might be in physical distress. Just as I leaned forward in alarm, his voice cracked like a whip. "Lies!"

CHAPTER 4

I shrank back, feeling as if I'd been struck, memories of my first husband making me want to shrivel up into a ball.

"Lies!" Barbreck repeated, his voice growing in volume. "I welcome ye to my house, allow ye to view my collection . . ." His eyes glittered with fury. "And yet, I'd no' kenned I was claspin' a viper to my breast."

"Now, see here . . ." Gage protested.

"Did *she* put ye up to it?" he snapped, rearing forward nearly onto his feet, which was no mean feat. I had seen how much effort it took him to stand, using his cane for leverage. "Did she?" he demanded again when I didn't answer.

"No one put me up to anything," I finally managed to reply, but he shook his head in disgust and shakily stood.

Lady Bearsden, who had been staring at the marquess in mute shock, appeared to have regained some of her composure. "Barbreck, please," she pleaded. "You can't . . ."

"I can," he shouted as he strode away, thumping his cane angrily against the floor. "And I *do*."

"What in heavens?" Aunt Cait gasped from behind us. "Uncle Donald, what is all this yelling about?"

But Barbreck ignored her, retreating to his study and slamming the door behind him.

My stomach still quavering, I shifted even closer to Gage and the protective arm he'd wrapped around me, before daring to look behind me toward the trio gathered just inside the doorway. Aunt Cait's eyes were round with astonishment, while deep furrows cut through Uncle Dunstan's brow. Only Morven appeared entirely composed.

"I didn't mean to upset him," I murmured. "I simply thought it was wrong for him not to know the truth."

"Oh, we know, dear," Lady Bearsden reassured me as the others advanced into the room, though they could know no such thing.

"What happened?" Aunt Cait asked evenly, sinking down on the bench with her knees on the other side so that she had to turn sideways to face me.

Gage's warm hand moved up and down my back, continuing to offer me support.

"I noticed there was something that wasn't quite right with one of the paintings in the long gallery this afternoon." I swallowed before stating the matter outright yet again, albeit in a small voice. "The Van Dyck is a forgery."

A pleat formed between Aunt Cait's deep blue eyes—the shade slightly darker than my lapis-lazuli ones—as she exchanged a look with her husband. "You're certain?"

"I would never have said anything if I wasn't."

She pressed a hand to my arm. "Yes, yes, of course. I know you wouldn't have." She sighed. "And Barbreck should have realized that as well. I know he takes great pride in his collection, but I still can't fathom why he reacted so heatedly."

"I suppose that takes you out of the running for his favorite," my cousin replied flippantly, spreading out her dusky blue skirts as she sank down into a mahogany armchair.

"Morven," her mother scolded.

But I appreciated her effort to break the tension. In any case, she wasn't wrong.

"I'll talk to him, lass," Uncle Dunstan told me. "Dinna fash yerself." He turned to look over his shoulder toward his uncle's study, reaching up to stroke the sides of his chin covered in a curly gray beard. "There'll be an explanation." But he didn't sound very certain of that.

Regardless, my thoughts had strayed back to Barbreck's words. In particular, the comment I hadn't understood. "Who is 'she'?"

My uncle and aunt looked to me in confusion.

"He asked me if '*she*' put me up to it?" I reiterated, using the same emphasis the marquess had. "But I don't understand who 'she' is."

By the speaking look Aunt Cait and Uncle Dunstan shared, I could tell they had at least some inkling.

"When Barbreck refers to '*she*,' he usually means Miss Campbell," Aunt Cait explained with chagrin. "I'm afraid there's no love lost between those two."

Uncle Dunstan nodded. "For as long as I can recall, there's been animosity between Barbreck and the Campbells o' Poltalloch. Though I dinna ken exactly why. 'Tis likely no more than the continuation o' some feud between clans. After all, Barbreck's mother was a MacLachlan, and she despised the Campbells 'til the day she died, even though the Duke o' Argyll"—the chief of the Campbells—"helped save her cousin's lands when the government intended they be forfeit after her uncle, the clan chief, was killed at Culloden fightin' for the Jacobites."

I made a quick calculation in my head, startled to realize Barbreck's mother would, indeed, have been alive to see the Battle of Culloden. At eighty and some odd years of age, Lord Barbreck would have been born sometime around 1750, not long after the last stand of the Jacobites in 1746, and the end of much of the Highland way of life.

But for all that his mother had been a MacLachlan, his father had been an upstart Lowlander, granted these lands and a title for services to the Crown. Part of me wondered if those services had anything to do with the events surrounding the final Jacobite uprising. If so, it made sense that he would have requested his lands be at the edge of those controlled by clan Campbell, for Argyll and the Campbells had been staunch Hanoverians, helping to crush the rebels, and as such, not likely to be as acrimonious to their new neighbor.

It was possible Barbreck had adopted his mother's opinion of the matter and the Campbells, but that did not fit with what I already knew about the marquess. He was nothing if not a savvy investor and negotiator, and his politics leaned far more toward the Tories and a staunch support of a robust government and ruling upper class than the reformist Whigs.

"It wouldn't be the first time, or the dumbest reason, our countrymen held a grudge," Morven stated bluntly, perhaps entertaining the same doubts I had as to the origin of his enmity.

"Yes, but he referred simply to '*her*.' Miss Campbell. Not the entire family," I pointed out.

"Poltalloch," Lady Bearsden ruminated aloud, drawing our attention. Her gaze remained trained on the ornate ceiling; her eyes narrowed in thought. "Hmmm, I wonder."

"Have you thought of something?" I prompted, having learned

never to doubt her prodigious memory. Sometimes it took her a bit of time to sort through the reams of gossip she'd collected over the past seventy years, but eventually she found the connection she was searching for.

"Yes, I seem to recall . . . But, no . . ." She lapsed back into silence, and just when I was about to press her on it again, she shifted forward in her seat, beckoning Gage closer. "I must check something."

Whether this was to do with Barbreck and his hostility toward Miss Campbell or another matter she'd only just remembered, I couldn't tell, but I stifled the urge to badger her as Gage helped her to her feet and then escorted her from the room. Should she have something to tell us, she would, in her own time.

Meanwhile, I would have to be satisfied by the fact that at least the others seemed to believe my assessment of the Van Dyck as a forgery. Though I couldn't shake the uneasiness that had gripped me since Lord Barbreck's outburst.

"Don't fret, dear," Aunt Cait consoled me, correctly reading my expression. "He must simply be shocked. He'll come around."

"Yes, but . . ." I bit my lip, wondering if now was the time to be asking further questions. But now that I'd begun, I couldn't take it back. "How did a forgery—and one allegedly by such a renowned artist—end up in his lordship's collection?"

Everyone fell silent as they exchanged glances with each other. Not even Morven had a quip.

Aunt Cait was the first to reply. "I don't know, but let's wait until Barbreck is more accepting before we try to answer that."

"Of course," I murmured. But I knew it wouldn't be so simple. At least, not for me.

I excused myself soon after and wandered back to my bedchamber even as my thoughts were still fixated on the painting. Finding myself standing in the middle of the room, I turned in a circle, searching for some occupation. By now, Emma would be taking her last nap of the day, and I was in no mood for other company. Then my gaze landed on my sketchbook and charcoals on a table next to the pale sea green damask couch before the windows.

Sliding my kid leather slippers from my feet, I reclined on the couch, pulling my knees up toward my chest to form a prop for my book, and then flipped the pages until I came to a clean sheet. I breathed deeper as I swept the charcoal across the page in broad strokes, the smoky musk as familiar and comforting as an old shawl. Sketching had always helped to settle me when I was tired, strained, or anxious. While painting fully absorbed all of my attention, sketching merely distracted me from the present while still allowing my brain to ruminate on what it wished in the background.

Inevitably my thoughts returned to the forgery. Or forgeries—plural—for I had an unsettling feeling that the Titian hanging next to the Van Dyck might also be a fake. And what of the other paintings I hadn't even seen yet?

Brushing aside that possibility for the moment, I focused on the question I'd posed to my relatives in the library, but my thoughts didn't travel very far before the door to the chamber opened.

My maid, Bree, paused on the threshold, evidently surprised to see me. "My apologies. Should I return later?"

"No, no," I replied, gesturing for her to come inside. I knew she would be readying my attire for dinner—checking to see if any of my garments needed pressing or last-minute mending—and I didn't wish to put her behind schedule.

She closed the door softly and then advanced into the room, her hands clasped before her primrose skirts—as lady's maids and valets were not required to wear a uniform, but rather more simple garments or castoffs from their employers. I could tell from the expression on her softly freckled face that she'd heard something of what had happened in the library. Given the swiftness with which gossip traveled among the staff of a large household, I should have expected as much.

"Is there anything I can do for ye, m'lady?" Bree asked in her gentle brogue.

"No, Bree, thank you." I hesitated to say more but then decided it would be best to know. "What are they saying belowstairs?"

She moved several steps closer, sympathy shimmering in her whisky brown eyes. "That his lordship lost his temper and started ragin' like he were fit to make a Highland charge."

"Yes, that about sums it up." I turned to look at my drawing; the background and shape of a man had only just begun to take shape. "Did they say . . . does Lord Barbreck often lose his temper?"

"In general, the staff seems to think o' him as a rather cranky if fair employer. I didna get the impression he regularly yells at them."

This matched my history with the marquess. I had only ever seen his cantankerous side, not encountered the man in an actual fury.

"But Callum, the second footman, said he's heard him arguin' wi' some o' the neighborin' landowners." She arched her fair eyebrows high. "And that once he caught him yellin' at his correspondence as if he thought it would answer him."

Then my altercation wasn't an isolated incident. Though at least it appeared he was better mannered than to take out his frustration on his staff.

"Here you are," Gage declared, opening the door to the corridor. Evidently, he'd been looking for me after escorting Lady Bearsden to wherever she'd wished to go.

"I think I'll wear the orchid pink watered silk gown this evening," I told Bree as I turned to lower my legs from the couch and leaned forward to set my sketchbook and charcoal on the table.

"Aye." She turned toward the clothespress. "Wi' the pearl-drop necklace?"

"Yes."

While she busied herself on the other side of the room, Gage sank down beside me, his face creased in concern. He knew how angry men unsettled me. How my body still reacted instinctively even when my rational mind knew I had nothing to fear. I wondered how long I would face the repercussions of my marriage to Sir Anthony.

"I'm fine," I told him as he took hold of my hand, not realizing until it was too late that my right one was smeared with charcoal.

"Yes, well, I'm afraid I may have given you bad advice," he replied sheepishly, reaching into his pocket for his handkerchief.

"No, you were right. He needed to be told. And besides, you couldn't have known how he would react."

"Well, *clearly*, there's more to his reaction than simple outrage if he's accusing this Miss Campbell of being involved."

I nodded, accepting the handkerchief from him to wipe off my own fingers.

"Speaking of which." His pale blue eyes sharpened. "Lady Bearsden said she'd remembered something about her."

"Did she?" I replied, perking up in interest.

"But she said she wanted to give the matter a bit more thought." His mouth quirked wryly. "Or rather she didn't want to be disturbed from her predinner nap. She said she'll speak to us after dinner."

I smiled in half-hearted amusement. If she was prepared to wait until after dinner to share it, then it must not be that intriguing, for I had never known Lady Bearsden to be able to keep a juicy morsel of gossip to herself if it was something that should be known.

Then another thought occurred to me. "Perhaps she wants to

confront Lord Barbreck and give him the opportunity to tell us himself first."

"If so, I'm afraid she's going to find that difficult. Lord Barbreck climbed into one of his carriages and set off at a spanking pace not a quarter of an hour ago."

At this pronouncement, Bree straightened from where she'd been searching through one of the drawers and turned toward us. I nodded for her to speak.

"I forgot to say, m'lady, but Callum also told me his lordship had ordered the carriage be brought around."

I felt less irritated that she'd forgotten to share this detail than I was curious about this Callum she kept referring to. His being a second footman, it wasn't unusual that she should be speaking with him, but I also couldn't help but question whether I detected a subtle undercurrent to her tone when she spoke about him. If so, I wondered what Gage's valet, Anderley, thought about it. After all, not four months ago he and Bree had been romantically linked, even though they had since decided to revert to merely being friends. Though their relationship had been rocky and awkward for a time, things had since smoothed over, returning to the teasing comradery they had exhibited before. However, I wasn't convinced their feelings toward each other were entirely platonic, and if one of them were to become romantically involved with someone else, I was afraid there might be a great schism.

"Where was he going?" I asked.

Gage shook his head. "No one seems to know."

Bree simply shrugged.

I contemplated this for a moment. It was a little over an hour until dinner, so wherever Lord Barbreck had set off to so precipitously, it must be urgent for him to abandon his guests. As such, there was only one possibility I could think of.

"Where do these Campbells of Poltalloch reside?"

Gage's eyebrows arched as if he was surprised he hadn't

thought of that, and then lowered almost in disapproval as he considered the question. Or perhaps it was irritation with Jack. "I would wager at Poltalloch Castle. Rye pointed it out to us in the distance from the top of one of the summits we climbed looking for some ancient hillfort Jack was determined to find. The castle stands along the shore of Loch Craignish about four or five miles away, as the crow flies."

But as rocky as the terrain was, that didn't mean the roads from here to there led directly to it. More than likely, the distance by carriage was double that. Which meant Barbreck would never return before dinner. Unless he regained control of his temper, came to his senses, and turned back before he reached Poltalloch.

"Well, I suppose we shall find out one way or another at dinner," I replied with as much sangfroid as I could manage. Then we would confront whatever Barbreck had to say whenever he arrived to say it. If he chose to disregard my concerns about the Van Dyck, then there was really nothing I could do about it. It was his painting. He was free to believe whatever he wished about it.

Unless he tried to sell it. Then we might have a problem. But I didn't foresee him doing such a thing anytime in the near future. No, he was much too attached to it. Much too attached to its provenance. As such, I didn't hold out hope of his giving any credence to my concerns. Whatever the case, I had a sneaking suspicion it depended on whatever happened at Poltalloch Castle.

CHAPTER 5

Aunt Cait asked the staff to hold dinner for half an hour while the rest of us waited in the drawing room, but when there was no word from Lord Barbreck, she decided the meal could not be delayed any longer. As such, our party's procession across the Great Hall into the long formal dining room was more somber and subdued than on previous nights. And while everyone tried to ignore the empty seat at the head of the table, it was impossible not to be conscious of it. Or at least, impossible for me, my eyes being drawn to it of their own volition.

It appeared everyone was aware of my altercation with Lord Barbreck that afternoon, but much to my relief, it seemed no one blamed me for it. Although, in general, we skirted the subject rather than addressing it directly. The closest we came to discussing it outright was an artless remark made by Jack about how obsessed Barbreck was with his art.

Lady Bearsden, for her part, looked slightly dyspeptic. There had been no opportunity to speak privately before dinner, and now she sat with her lips tightly sealed, as if she was struggling to keep whatever she knew—and she knew something—from spilling from her mouth between bites of food. Charlotte kept casting worried looks her way, unaware of the real reason for her great-aunt's uncharacteristic silence.

By the time the final course was brought forth, and still there had been no sign of Barbreck, the men started discussing whether they should ride out to ensure nothing dreadful had befallen him.

"After all, the roads in this part of Scotland are not exactly the most hospitable," Rye remarked.

"And it isn't unheard of for a band of ruffians to stop an unprotected carriage traveling at night," Jack added, causing somewhat of a stir among the ladies. Even I felt a pulse of alarm.

"That's true," Uncle Dunstan conceded, sinking back in his chair as he directed a chiding look at his son-in-law. "But the same could also be said aboot most o' the roads in Scotland and northern England. Highwaymen are a problem everywhere."

"Yes, but you can't deny they're more desperate here," Jack countered, lifting his glass of Madeira. "What with the clearances having taken away any chance of their scrabbling together much of an honest living."

This was a familiar topic of discussion between the two men, one on which they normally saw eye to eye. For Uncle Dunstan was as concerned as Jack about the lack of land available to small farmers. A century earlier, the wealthy landowners had begun driving off the people who had lived and worked on the land of their estates for generations in order to enclose it for more sheep. Many of those people had ended up immigrating to North America and beyond, but not all.

However, in this case, it wasn't Jack's politics my uncle disagreed with.

"Maybe so, but there's no need to be frightenin' the ladies wi' such talk. Especially when we've no cause to jump to such a rash conclusion."

"All the same," Aunt Cait declared, ever the peacemaker, as she leaned forward to rest a restraining hand against Jack's arm. "Perhaps it would be a good idea if several of you gentlemen ventured out to meet him if he hasn't returned by sunset."

I glanced at the clock, seeing that it was almost nine o'clock, which meant the sun would be setting soon. During the height of summer, sunset did not occur until late in the evening and was followed by the gloaming—the time between sunset and actual nightfall when the soft smudge of twilight reigned the sky. Here in the Highlands, the gloaming could last for hours after sunset.

Uncle Dunstan nodded in agreement. "Aye."

Everyone's appetites being sated, if not spoiled, by that point, Aunt Cait rose from her chair but a few minutes later to lead the ladies from the room. This left the men to plan their approach over their port. I trailed my fingers over Gage's shoulders as I passed his chair, letting him know that I was content with him joining the search should he choose to do so. His hand lifted to briefly clasp mine before releasing me.

Morven was waiting for me just outside the door and looped her arm through mine to walk in step with me. "Is it just me, or does Lady Bearsden look as if she's going to burst if she doesn't tell someone what she knows?" she leaned toward me to murmur as our heels clicked against the flagstone floor of the Great Hall.

These tiles appeared to be original to the previous castle, as did the stones in the enormous fireplace and some of the weaponry mounted on the walls. However, the white stucco work, tall-corniced windows, and wide Corinthian columns were much newer.

I eyed the lady in question, who strode arm in arm with her great-niece a few feet in front of us. Charlotte appeared to be whispering solicitously to her, but Lady Bearsden merely shook her head, which made the already taut line of Charlotte's back even more rigid.

"That, or cause her great-niece to collapse in worry," I retorted.

"Then perhaps we'd best wheedle it out of her." Morven's dark eyes were lit with mischief, but in this instance, I had to admit, her mischief was warranted.

"Yes, I think you're right." For if Barbreck didn't return soon, we needed some understanding of what had sent him running off to Poltalloch Castle, or wherever he'd gone, without a moment's notice.

Aunt Cait must have harbored similar intentions, for when we reached the drawing room, she was already dismissing the footman, informing him we would serve ourselves. I scrutinized the fellow as he was leaving, wondering if the ash-blond-haired chap was the Callum that Bree had referred to twice during our conversation earlier. It was either him or the darker-haired footman who had also assisted in serving dinner.

"Morven, dear. Do, please, shut the door," Aunt Cait urged as she began pouring tea. "I feel a draft."

Morven's eyebrows arched in wry disbelief, but she released my arm to comply with her wishes.

I passed Lady Bearsden and Charlotte their tea, declining a cup for myself before I sank down on the sofa upholstered in mulberry brocade across from the pair of fauteuil chairs the two women inhabited. The drawing room being as spacious as the library across the hall, we had naturally gravitated toward the seating arrangement closest to the hearth and the metal screen depicting stags and Scottish thistles. The ceiling in this chamber was likewise ornately decorated, and the windows tall and numerous, flooding the room with sunlight during the day. But at this hour we had to be contented with the warm glow of the fire and the candles spaced throughout the room.

"Now then, Lady Bearsden," Aunt Cait declared, arranging her full juniper green skirts as she settled beside me, the width of her gauze oversleeves dwarfing my own. "Out with it. What have you remembered?"

It was moments like these when I could see so clearly the resemblance between mother and daughter, for Morven was perched in the adjoining chair with the same expectant look as my aunt. Even Alana exhibited some of the same mannerisms, and I couldn't help but wonder whether she'd picked them up from our mother before she died or Aunt Cait—Mother's younger sister—when she resided with her in London for two years as she and Morven made their rounds as debutantes in search of husbands.

Unfortunately, Lady Bearsden did not appear as ready to admit what she knew. "What makes you think I've remembered anything?" she demurred, feigning interest in the exquisitely painted porcelain Sèvres potpourri vase set in the middle of the low table between us.

Aunt Cait's mouth screwed into a tiny moue of irritation before she replied. "Because you were as quiet as a mouse at dinner, and I have *never* known you to be so."

She lifted her chin almost in challenge. "Perhaps I'm not feeling myself this evening."

Charlotte leaned toward her as if fearful she might collapse.

"Is that the line you mean to take?" Aunt Cait countered, nodding toward her soon-to-be daughter-in-law, who was visibly distressed.

Lady Bearsden's expression softened as she turned to her great-niece, and she reached out to touch her cheek. "Don't fret, my dear. It will give you wrinkles on your lovely face, much like my Lumpy. He was always working himself into a dither, and all the dear fellow got for it was more wrinkles."

I suspected that, like me, Charlotte found her great-aunt's reference to her late husband to be reassuring. I had never discovered why Lord Bearsden had been given such a mildly insulting nickname, but the affection with which his wife used it told me that he must have been a good man.

"Lady Bearsden, please," Aunt Cait pleaded, sitting forward in impatience. "The men are about to set off in search of Lord Barbreck. Would it not be better to send them off with some idea where his lordship has gone and what they might find when they get there?"

When still the older lady hesitated, bowing her head full of snowy white hair, I decided enough was enough.

"He's gone to Poltalloch Castle, hasn't he?"

Aunt Cait and Morven turned to me in surprise and then chagrin as if they felt they should have realized this sooner themselves.

When she lifted her head, Lady Bearsden's expression was far more resigned. "It only seemed right that I should allow him the opportunity to explain himself."

"Well, it seems to me he forfeited that right when he unfairly lashed out at Kiera and then ran off, leaving us to worry about him," Morven admonished, revealing for the first time the genuine concern beneath her glib façade.

"True enough." She sighed. "Then, to answer your question: yes, I believe he's gone to Poltalloch. Though I'm not entirely certain why." Her gaze shifted to each of us in turn. "The only thing I've recalled that may be pertinent is that when Lord Barbreck was a young man, he was engaged to marry a Miss Campbell of Poltalloch."

Aunt Cait straightened in evident shock.

"But the engagement was broken. I don't believe I was ever privy to the reason why." She shook her head. "In truth, I doubt they ever made that knowledge public. It was simply ended."

"And yet he never married," Aunt Cait said. "And neither did Miss Campbell."

A look passed between the two women, and Lady Bearsden nodded. "Just so."

It was clear now why she had wanted to give Lord Barbreck the opportunity to explain. Whatever had happened to end his engagement to Miss Campbell had obviously been no small matter. Not if neither of them had ever married. Not if all these years later he couldn't even say her name but still referred to her venomously as a pronoun.

I frowned. But why had he immediately thought of her when I mentioned the forgery? Why had he been so certain she was somehow involved that he set off for her home without saying a word to the rest of us about where he was going?

"Is this Miss Campbell an artist?" I asked.

Aunt Cait turned to look at me, almost as if she'd forgotten I was there. "Not that I'm aware. Why do you ask?"

"Because someone forged that Van Dyck. And given Lord Barbreck's reaction, I thought perhaps he believed it was her."

"Nay, but she undoubtedly hired whoever did," Barbreck declared gruffly, astonishing us all as he strode through the door.

Aunt Cait exclaimed in relief, rising to her feet along with Morven and Charlotte to go to him. For my part, I remained where I was, still wary of the marquess and his fury. I looked up to find Lady Bearsden watching me, her gaze kind. My stiff demeanor made it plain how I felt.

Something Gage was attuned to as he and the other gentlemen joined us. He perched on the arm of the sofa beside me, rubbing a hand up and down my back as Aunt Cait attempted to convince Barbreck to let her call for a tray of food for him.

"I'll eat when I'm good and ready, Caitriona," he retorted, having had enough of all their fussing. "Noo, sit doon, the lot o' ye." He plopped down into the bergère chair nearest the crackling fire. "I've somethin' to say, and I'd rather have it oot noo, and no' have to repeat myself." He exhaled heavily, reaching into the pocket of his coat for a handkerchief to swipe his brow with. "Is everyone here?"

I glanced around me, seeing that everyone had drawn close, either sitting, leaning, or standing.

"Good. Noo, then, Idonia," he said turning to Lady Bearsden. "You and your cursed memory recalled my long-ago engagement to Miss Campbell, didna ye?"

She sniffed. "I cannot help it if I happen to be sharper than *some* people I could name."

His lips curled into a small grin at this insult, but they flattened soon enough as he continued. "Aye, well, 'tis true. I *was* engaged to Anne Campbell some fifty-four years ago." He glared at his relatives almost belligerently, as if he expected them to argue. "'Twas a suitable match, wi' advantages to both our families."

Though no one spoke, I had to wonder if I was the only one who found it interesting that he felt the need to justify their engagement. I was not familiar with the Campbells of Poltalloch, but it seemed obvious that they must be minor Scottish nobles or at least gentry. As such, Barbreck's marriage to the daughter of such a family, particularly one whose lands abutted his own, would have been sensible. And yet his emphasis on the prudent nature of their match made me think that had not been their true motivation. That, and the strong feelings he still exhibited toward her even fifty-four years later.

No, to quote Shakespeare, he definitely *doth protest too much.*

"Then why did ye no' marry her?" Uncle Dunstan asked.

The flickering firelight made the hollows of Lord Barbreck's eyes more pronounced as he leaned forward. "Because the Campbells questioned our family's honor," he snarled. "Sir James had the audacity to accuse my brother, Alisdair, o' sellin' him a forged painting. And then *dared* suggest *I* colluded wi' him."

This was the reason he had reacted so fiercely to my assertion that his Van Dyck portrait was a forgery. It turned out this wasn't the first time the word had been bandied about in connection with his art collection. And the last time, it had not only smarted his pride but cost him the woman he may have loved.

He pounded the arm of his chair. "Alisdair secured and transported the painting at Sir James's bidding, at no small effort, and yet the old churl and his termagant daughter still dared to challenge its authenticity." He turned to stare broodingly into the shadows at the edge of the room. "I was simply glad I'd uncovered what a deceitful harridan the woman was before I married her."

"The painting Alisdair sold them," Aunt Cait queried, her gaze sliding sideways toward me. "Was it the Van Dyck?"

"No," Barbreck stated firmly. "A Titian."

I stiffened, drawing his attention for the first time since he'd entered the room.

"Then why did you go charging off to Poltalloch?" Lady Bearsden demanded to know, perhaps distracting him intentionally. "That is where you hared off to, isn't it?"

"Because she ken how much I esteemed Van Dyck. She ken any portrait by him would be one o' the most treasured in my collection." His eyes narrowed. "And so she *must* o' stole it and replaced it wi' a *fake*." He bit off each of his words with vehemence.

"Dinna tell me ye rode off to Poltalloch an' accused Miss Campbell o' that to her face?" Uncle Dunstan's aghast disbelief was palpable.

"Aye!" His gaze flicked up and down over his nephew's form as if he found him lacking. "Well, I wasna aboot to let her get away wi' it."

"Did she admit to it?" Morven asked almost eagerly.

"Nay." His jaw tightened. "Laughed in my face is what she did. But she willna be laughin' long. No' when I prove her to be the thief and the fraud she is."

I had a sinking feeling I knew where this conversation was

headed, and if the manner in which Gage's hand flexed where it rested against my back was any indication, so did he.

"Dinna ye think you're takin' this too far," Uncle Dunstan protested, his bushy eyebrows bristling like a hedgehog. "You've no proof o' any such plot."

"Nay. But I will."

Upon making this statement, almost as if on cue, his gaze swung to pin me to my seat. But this time I was prepared for it, and I did not allow even a single muscle to quiver.

"And Kiera is goin' to help me."

Feeling my temper stir, I arched a single eyebrow. "Oh, I am, am I?"

"I believe you said she was a liar," Gage remarked drolly, though I could sense the anger he fought to restrain tightening the edges. "A viper," he bit off.

"Uncle Donald, you didn't?" Aunt Cait gasped, apparently not having heard the precise words he'd spoken to me earlier but more the tone.

"Aye, weel," he grumbled. "Can ye no' understand my shock and fury?" He lifted his cane to point vaguely in the direction of Poltalloch. "That woman is tryin' to make me look a fool."

"You seem to be doing that well enough on your own," Lady Bearsden quipped with a sniff.

He turned his glare on her, but if he expected her to quail, he was going to be sadly disappointed.

"I believe the words you're looking for are 'I apologize,'" Gage informed him. "At least, for a start."

He stewed for a moment, his haggard, wrinkled face taut with displeasure before softening. "Aye, I do. I should ne'er have doubted Kiera's integrity."

As apologies went, it wasn't exactly sincere. *If* it could even be considered an apology, given the fact he'd avoided saying the actual words. But I suspected Barbreck had rarely, if ever, been made to apologize for anything in his entire life. And at four score and two years of age, he was unlikely to develop an aptitude for it. In any case, his remorse was short-lived.

"But surely ye must understand why I need your help." His eyes hardened. "She canna be allowed to get away wi' this."

I turned to look up at Gage, seeing in his face the same irritation and reluctance I felt, but I knew he would leave the decision to me. I had been the one who had been insulted, and I was the one who possessed the knowledge and skills Barbreck wished to utilize. My stomach swirled with a mixture of pity and revulsion, for I had no desire to become entangled with this vendetta between Barbreck and the Campbells. Though, truth be known, we had only heard one side of it. Perhaps this Miss Campbell had done her best to move on, harboring no ill will toward her former fiancé. Or perhaps she had not. There was no way to know unless we spoke with her about it.

I also had to admit that my curiosity had been awakened. I felt certain the Van Dyck was a forgery, but how old was it? Could an authentic Van Dyck actually lay somewhere underneath numerous layers of overpaint, perhaps originally applied to hide damage? Had I discarded such a possibility too swiftly? Could that explain the discrepancy? And then there were the questions about the painting's provenance. How did it come to be in Barbreck's possession in the first place? Was the painting hanging in the long gallery the original portrait he had purchased, or as he alleged, had it been switched out with a forgery? If so, when?

Finding satisfactory answers to these questions could be very difficult, if not impossible, but the challenge of doing so appealed to me. The artist in me was affronted by the idea of someone else trying to pass their artwork off as another artist's, be it for monetary gain or pure ego. It wasn't right. Of course, there was always the possibility that the painting had been misidentified, either by accident or on purpose. If so, the real artist deserved to have their name restored to their creation.

If I agreed to do this, it would be for the integrity of that artist, *not* for Barbreck and whatever revenge he wished to take on Miss Campbell.

But first there was another issue that needed to be addressed.

I turned to study Barbreck's features, ignoring the murmurs of the others in the room. "The Titian you mentioned. The one you said the Campbells claimed was a forgery. Where is it now?"

"Hangin' in the long gallery," he replied after a slight hesitation.

"Next to the Van Dyck?"

"Yes." This time his voice was definitely tinged with suspicion and perhaps a warning.

"Then I'm afraid the Van Dyck isn't your only problem. Because I'm fairly certain that Titian is also a forgery. Though, in this instance, it may simply be a misattribution rather than outright fraud."

CHAPTER 6

Barbreck's face flushed with fury, but whether it was the presence of the others or his own realization that lashing out at me would get him nowhere, he stifled his anger before speaking. "Fairly certain?"

"Yes, I would need to study it closer. And . . . there are a few assessments I could attempt to verify its age." I mentioned the last with some trepidation, for these could potentially damage the painting. I was no expert when it came to such things, but as an artist, I did understand how my chosen mediums worked, and the changes and processes they went through.

Barbreck scrutinized my features, clearly recognizing the other implication of my analyzing the paintings. If I uncovered evidence that they were, in fact, forgeries, there would be no turning back, no denying it. Just because he seemed to have accepted the possibility that the Van Dyck was a fake did not mean he was willing to face the prospect that there were other forgeries in his collection.

Then suddenly his shoulders slumped, and the proud angle of his gray head seemed to droop as he nodded somewhat listlessly. It was such a rapid change from his prior bristling demeanor that it seemed all of us in the room leaned forward in alarm. "Do what ye must to uncover the truth," he directed, the weariness he must have felt making his face pale. "'Tis better to ken than no'." He clamped his hands on the arms of his chair, his own arms shaking as he attempted to rise. "And noo, I'd like to rest."

Rye and Henry, being closest, hurried over to help him to his feet. Then Rye escorted him from the room while Aunt Cait bustled after them, promising to send up his valet and a tray of dinner. Meanwhile the rest of us sat looking at each other, uncertain what to do.

It was Lady Bearsden who broke the spell, planting her cane firmly between her legs. "I think I shall also retire," she declared, hoisting herself to her feet. Charlotte came forward to grasp her arm as Lady Bearsden hobbled toward the door. She paused beside my chair, reaching up one gnarled finger to pat my cheek. "The truth will always out. So do not fret, my dear." Her eyes were kind, as if realizing that was exactly what I'd begun to do. "Simply give it to us unvarnished. The rest will take care of itself."

Then with one last pat, she moved on, though not before briefly clutching my husband's strong arm. "Oh, to be young again," she lamented on a sigh, and I couldn't halt a bubble of amusement from bringing a smile to my lips. Lady Bearsden was rather fond of good-looking young men, and unafraid to comment on that fact as well as their attributes.

"I think we shall retire, too," Morven stated, crossing the room toward her husband.

Uncle Dunstan scraped a hand back through his thick, grizzled hair. "Aye, perhaps we all should."

This was probably a sound idea. After all, my analysis of the paintings in question could wait until morning when the sunlight would make it much easier. In any case, there were supplies to be gathered and prepared, and Emma would need to be fed in less than an hour's time before settling down for her longest slumber of the night. I was not about to sacrifice my lengthiest stretch of uninterrupted sleep for anything less than an emergency.

However, the look that passed between Gage and Henry told me we wouldn't be retiring to our bedchambers quite yet. So when Gage pulled me through the doorway on the floor above, just to the right of the grand stairs, rather than continue down the corridor to our rooms, I was not entirely surprised.

When Aunt Cait had given us a tour of the manor upon our arrival, she had called this room the solar, a title which was somewhat misleading considering that the house had been built less than sixty years ago, so this room could never have functioned as a true medieval solar. It was really just another parlor—one whose walls were draped with an exquisite set of tapestries. One depicted a scene from the Greek myth of Eurydice and Orpheus, while another portrayed nine dancing women who I suspected were supposed to be the Muses. Though the room was now dark, and the drapes drawn, I could make out shapes in the darkness, including the tables and pedestals spaced throughout, where a number of ancient vases, bowls, and amphorae—or the fragments of such—were displayed.

"I assume you intend to further analyze these paintings?" Gage turned to ask me just as Henry joined us carrying a brace of candles. The small halo of light in which we stood created a sense of intimacy.

"Yes, in the morning," I replied, curious to hear what he was thinking.

"Then when you confirm your suspicions, as I have every confidence you will, whether you wish to speak in such concrete terms or not . . ." His lips quirked in the soft glow of the candle-light. "Then I presume you'll want to pay a visit to Miss Campbell."

"That would be the logical next step." I crossed my arms in front of my chest. "Although, I don't know how welcome we will be after Lord Barbreck went charging over there tonight to accuse her of fraud and theft."

"Your aunt and uncle and cousins all seemed shocked by Barbreck's revelation of his broken engagement, but I do wonder at their never having guessed at it. After all, his animosity toward *her* . . ." Gage emphasized the pronoun just like the marquess did whenever referring to Miss Campbell ". . . was well known. How is it that none of them tried to find out why?"

It was a legitimate question, no matter how little I liked it. Morven, in particular, was not only inquisitive but also astute. As was my aunt. How had they never pursued the matter?

"What do you know of the Campbells of Poltalloch?" Gage asked Henry. "Has your family had any dealings with them?"

The Duke of Bowmont had vast holdings all over Scotland, as well as deep connections to many of the nobility.

Henry reached out to set the candles he held on the sideboard nearby, their light burnishing his auburn locks. "Lord Jack asked me the same thing earlier today."

"He did?" Gage replied in evident surprise.

Henry nodded, the watchful look in his eyes telling us he found it an odd coincidence as well. "After Rye pointed out Poltalloch Castle in the distance. I thought he was just making conversation, and perhaps he was. But now . . . I wonder."

"Yes." A slight furrow formed between Gage's brows as he leaned against the back of the settee behind him, considering the matter.

"But to answer your question, I'm not aware of any dealings

Bowmont or my brothers have had with the Poltalloch Campbells. They're a minor branch of the larger Campbell clan's tree, nowhere near the status of the Duke of Argyll."

"An old family no longer of great importance," I surmised, and Henry dipped his head in agreement.

Gage straightened. "Then, while you're examining the paintings, I think I'll speak with your uncle and see what he can tell me about these Campbells," he told me. "I'd like to know what sort of situation we'll be riding into."

It was a sound suggestion. For all we knew, the Campbells might be an antagonistic bunch, greeting any encroachment onto their land with hostility, especially after Lord Barbreck's accusations this evening. I doubted they would react to our arrival with violence, but that didn't mean we wouldn't be met with enmity. We needed to know how willing they would be to receive us on short notice, or whether doing the dance of social niceties and sending a request to pay them a call would achieve better results. I preferred not to give them time to formulate a coordinated response, but any element of surprise had already been ruined by Barbreck's temper.

"Is there anything I can do?" Henry asked, his silvery gray eyes intent. Though he spoke evenly, I could sense his desire to help. The same way I'd sensed it in Edinburgh during our last murder investigation.

"Not just yet," Gage replied, and I could almost see his half brother's shoulders metaphorically slump, though he was holding himself too still to visibly do so. "But I was hoping you would ride with us tomorrow afternoon."

His face lit with eagerness. "Of course. I'm at your service."

"I can't help but think it would be best to take as few of Barbreck's relatives with us as possible."

"Good luck with that," I remarked wryly as I moved toward the door. "If I know my family, and I do," I glanced over my shoulder to add, "Then half of them will be mounted and waiting for us the moment they discover where we're going. They'll use concern and politeness to mask their insatiable curiosity."

"It seems you come by it honestly, then."

His teasing grin stretched wider as I glowered at him from the doorway.

The following morning after breakfast and snuggles with Emma, I gathered up a small kit of my art supplies and asked Bree to join me in the long gallery. I half suspected to find Barbreck there waiting for me. In fact, I initially thought the wooden bench placed in the middle of the room was for him to sit on. But when he failed to join us, I began to wonder if he trusted me more than I'd believed. That, or now that he'd already confronted Miss Campbell, he hoped I would uncover definitive evidence of forgery and believed by staying away he was more likely to get it.

In any case, audience or no audience, it made no difference to me or my results. But it *would* be easier to work if he wasn't hovering over my shoulder.

Warm sunlight filtered through the high windows, indirectly illuminating the paintings. I set my bag down on the bench and removed the magnifying glass I'd borrowed from the library. Then with a deep bracing breath, I turned to my task.

I began with the Van Dyck. Once again as I stood before it, I felt a sort of uneasy queasiness swirling in my gut. There was simply a sense of wrongness about it.

"This *can't* be a Van Dyck," I murmured more to myself than to Bree, who stood quietly beside me, but then I continued, explaining why I was so insistent. "Look at the folds of this gown." I pointed. "The shapes and shadows are too . . . certain. There's no flow or movement. No sense of life. Just like their faces. There is no light or thought behind them. No allure. And Van Dyck is known for such things." I tilted my head, studying the painting from a slightly different angle. "And this blue." I swept my hand in the air over the train of the gown on the second woman. "I would swear this is Prussian blue, and yet that pigment was not used in Van Dyck's time. He would have painted with something like azurite."

The last, I knew, was a highly subjective observation, for there was no real way to tell one pigment from the other with the naked eye. But I had seen Hans Holbein the Younger's painting *A Lady with a Squirrel and a Starling*, in which he had used azurite as the background. This looked nothing like that shade.

I sighed, shaking my head. Further visual analysis was not going to change my mind. It was time to employ another method.

Bending over, I retrieved a small bottle of turpentine, a fine brush, and a linen rag from my bag. I would have preferred to examine the back of the painting first for any markings, for the rear often held more information than one would think, but there were no men nearby to assist us. I could have rung for a footman, but I felt so certain the portrait was a forgery that I decided to move forward with this swab test to try to determine its age.

A sharp pine scent filled the room as I dipped the brush in the turpentine and carefully selected a small spot in the lower left corner of the canvas and began applying it in gentle strokes over the foliage. Almost immediately I could see it beginning to have an effect, stripping away the paint. When I dabbed at the affected area with the rag, it came away smudged with pigment.

Watching over my shoulder, Bree gasped. "M'lady, isna that ruinin' the painting?" she asked as I applied more turpentine to the same spot, in short order revealing the canvas beneath.

"Perhaps," I conceded. "But considering the fact this proves it's most definitely not a Van Dyck, I should think the damage is warranted."

"Because the paint dissolved?"

Hearing her confusion, I replaced the top on the turpentine before I explained. "Van Dyck painted with oils. As I do." I knew she would grasp the mechanics of that, for I had taught her how to assist me in mixing my pigments with linseed oil, as well as other elements of the process, when I was expecting Emma because the fumes were too harsh for me and the pigments potentially dangerous while I was in that state. "And while oil paintings are often dry to the touch within a few days to a week, it can take nearly a century for the oil to evaporate so that they dry completely."

Her eyes widened, as she turned back to the forged Van Dyck. "And so if ye apply turpentine, a dry painting willna dissolve?"

"If you apply enough solvent, it will eventually dissolve anything, but not this swiftly with just a small amount. No, the painting before us is unquestionably of recent origin, likely painted sometime within the last fifty years. I'd hoped to discover an older layer of paint underneath—something that could possibly have even been an original Van Dyck—but there is nothing beneath it but canvas."

That was somewhat of a precipitous statement, for I should test other places near the middle of the canvas before making such a definitive assertion. However, I felt comfortable saying so nonetheless. There was no evidence of the canvas being joined to others or expanded upon, so this was likely its original size, and so would have been painted to its edge.

Stepping back, I gazed up at the portrait of the three ladies again, feeling outrage building inside me. That someone should have forged Van Dyck's work and succeeded in doing so—at least in fooling some people into believing it was such—was maddening and insulting. I was offended on the artist's behalf. If the forger had been able to replicate Van Dyck's style and technique more exactly, I think I would have been less upset, for then they would have at least exhibited skill equal to that of Van Dyck, or nearly so. I was no prig. I appreciated talent wherever it appeared. But to pass off this mediocre effort as the work of a master was frankly infuriating.

I turned my back on it, my lips undoubtedly curled in a sneer, and exchanged the turpentine for the magnifying glass to analyze the second troubling painting. Once again I was struck by the overwhelming sensation of wrongness. The light, the shadows, the colors, the textures—nothing felt right. Yes, there were pieces that were quite good if I separated them from the impact of the whole, but as soon as I widened my gaze, the composition once again fell flat. It was not as poorly executed as the Van Dyck, but it was certainly not equal to the genius of Titian.

"This one, too?" Bree whispered aghast.

"I'm afraid so." Moving closer, I lifted the magnifying glass to scrutinize the texture of the paint. What I saw made me grimace in disgust. "If this portrait was by Titian, then it would be over 250 years old. There should be fine cracking in the mineral-rich pigments on the surface, not this . . . soupy, coagulated mess. This has to be overpaint." I retreated a step to let my gaze sweep over its whole. "Which means something is painted underneath, possibly something very old." I debated how to proceed. Whether I should gingerly test a small section of one of the lower corners or wait until the canvas could be removed from the wall.

Then I noted a discrepancy in the coat of one of the horse's forelegs where it met the tasseled caparison covering. "Look here." I pointed at the spot where a jagged strip of paint had flaked off revealing a sandy shade underneath quite unlike the steed's deep umber coat. I knew that Titian had often layered his pigments to achieve a desired effect, but they would have dried at the same speed, and would not have flaked off or congealed as the top layer of paint had done. Clearly the portrait we now saw had been painted over an older composition.

"You were right, m'lady."

"Yes. Though it's somewhat of a sour triumph."

Bree glanced at me and then back to the painting. "So . . . what does this mean? Did someone paint *over* a Titian?"

"There's no way to really tell. Not unless the overpaint is painstakingly removed, and I'm not even certain that could be done without damaging the painting underneath." I scowled in frustration. "And even if such an undertaking were successful, there's no telling what we would find. The painting underneath might have been damaged, explaining why the overpaint was applied in the first place."

"Do ye think that's why they did it?"

I shrugged. "I suppose that would be the kindest reason. But there are also artists who believe their talent is equal to or greater than a painter like Titian and think they can improve upon his works. Not everyone is as reverent of art as I am. Or as clear-sighted about their abilities," I added dryly.

I bent to replace my supplies in my kit. "Regardless, as it now appears, this painting is not a Titian. And I doubt it's by any of the other notable artists from Venice who are sometimes mistaken for Titian—Tintoretto and Veronese and others—either." The Venetian artists were known for their distinctive use of light and color, and neither of those characteristics, nor their level of skill, were present. I straightened, gazing sadly up at the equestrian. "The Campbells were right to question its authenticity." They had been right to demand answers.

Which meant that Barbreck had been wrong.

"His lordship isna goin' to like hearin' that, is he?" Bree asked, correctly guessing the reason for my unhappy silence.

"No, I'm afraid he isn't."

Even if he was trying to coax himself into believing, now that he'd confronted Miss Campbell, he wanted the paintings to be forgeries. I knew the bald truth was that the discovery they were indeed fakes would be a hard blow. He would undoubtedly continue to insist she had somehow swapped and stolen the originals, but the logistics of such an enterprise would be staggering. Who had painted the forgeries? And how had the switch been made without anyone noticing?

There were dozens of questions to be answered. But the one foremost in my mind was whether the Van Dyck and Titian were the only fakes in Barbreck's collection, or were there more yet to be uncovered?

CHAPTER 7

It had been almost a year since I'd enjoyed the pleasure of
riding across the countryside on horseback, and nearly two
years since I'd done so in the Scottish Highlands. As such, I
began our ride feeling rather awkward atop the sturdy bay pony
Gage had chosen for me from Barbreck's stables, but soon enough
I found myself settling into her gait, becoming re-accustomed to
the saddle. Which was fortunate, for the trail my uncle had directed us to take soon after we crossed the bridge spanning the
River Barbreck veered south over rocky terrain.

The carriage road was forced to divert east, avoiding the large
stone crag standing in its way south of Dùn na Ban-òige and its
hillfort, and then turn south again to parallel the burn trick-
ling through Kilmartin Glen between the larger ridges. But on
horseback we could take this more direct route, skirting the rugged terrain where the base of the crag met the loch, and complete the journey to Poltalloch in half the time.

Gage, Henry, and I didn't talk much as we made our way

single file over the most precarious part of the trail, concentrating on the horses and trying not to be distracted by the glorious views across the loch toward the west. Sunlight glinted off the water, where seals bobbed in the waves, and the verdant rolling hills surrounding the village of Ardfern and its harbor on the opposite shore.

Gripping the reins with my kid leather gloves, I breathed deep of the salty breeze that played with the hairs at the base of my neck and ruffled the gigot sleeves of my plum riding habit. Gold epaulette trim marched down the bodice and around the cuffs, and a matching belt cinched the fabric around my waist.

On the far side of the crag, the terrain evened out and the trail led us into a forest, where the trees soon enveloped us, hiding the loch from our view. Beneath the thick canopy of downy birch, oaks, and pines, the air was cooler and redolent with the smell of moss and old growth. At first the path was nearly as narrow as it had been over the rocky terrain, with the trees crowding close and branches brushing the tops of our heads. But as we passed along the shore of a lochan buried deep within the heart of the wood, the trail widened enough for at least two to ride abreast.

Gage slowed his chestnut gelding so that I could ride alongside him. "Your uncle said when the trail passed a small rocky outcropping to the west, we would be halfway there. He even suggested that if we have time, we might wish to stop and view the cup and ring carvings in the rock."

"Perhaps on our return journey," I replied, knowing I needn't explain why I was so mindful of the time. I had, at most, three hours before I needed to return to Emma, and a glimpse at the watch pinned to my bodice told me a quarter of an hour had already passed. "But what did Uncle Dunstan say when you asked him about the Campbells?"

Gage had been present when I informed Barbreck of my

findings about the forgeries in the long gallery, so he knew the marquess had reacted better than I'd expected. At least, this time he hadn't shouted at me, instead falling into a brooding stupor. One he'd emerged from long enough to grant me permission to analyze the other paintings in his collection, and to order me to prove Miss Campbell's involvement. The latter was a difficult charge, and one I had no intention of actually pursuing, though I did plan to pry into the paintings' provenance. Whether Miss Campbell had been involved with them in any way other than her father's denouncement of the Titian remained to be seen, but unless she intersected with them in another meaningful way, I was not going to badger the woman.

After delivering this information, I'd hurried off to feed Emma and change garments while Gage and Henry arranged our transportation and somehow contrived—undoubtedly with my uncle's assistance— to discourage the rest of the family from joining us.

"What sort of situation will we be riding into?" I prompted, echoing his words from the previous evening. I knew he wasn't expecting to be met by angry men brandishing weapons, otherwise he never would have allowed me to accompany them, but I was curious what Uncle Dunstan had told him about the Campbells.

Henry urged his steed closer, as if also eager to hear Gage's response.

"Apparently, much of the time Miss Campbell resides at Poltalloch with only her younger sister, Margaret, for company. The estate belongs to their nephew, Sir James Campbell, but he and his family live elsewhere for the greater part of the year."

"Kindness or neglect?" I queried, wondering whether Sir James's elderly aunts wished to live at Poltalloch or were forced to do so.

"From what your uncle tells me, I deduced that Miss Campbell is rather a force unto herself. She may be over seventy, but she's still healthy and vigorous, and often seen riding about the countryside." He cast an amused glance at us. "He thinks it's likely *she* wields the real power at Poltalloch, and her nephew is happy to leave the management of it to her. I gained the impression he and his son, the next James in a rather long line of them, are not the most frugal of gentlemen. So the estate isn't prosperous, as they've drained many of the assets to pay for their expensive lifestyles. But it's obvious Mr. Mallery has great respect for this Miss Campbell. Says she takes care of her own."

"Then the animosity between her and Lord Barbreck must not extend to Uncle Dunstan or the rest of the family," I surmised.

"I gather not. Though I don't believe there's much interaction between them."

I frowned at the trail before us. We seemed to be traveling uphill, perhaps nearing that rocky outcropping Gage mentioned. "It still puzzles me that none of them suspected Barbreck's broken engagement to Miss Campbell." The degree of his hostility seemed too extreme to be ignored.

"I wouldn't be so sure about that."

I turned to look at my husband in question.

"Your uncle said something that made me think he's suspected the truth for some time, though it's unclear whether he ever asked Barbreck about it. Perhaps he was rebuffed, or perhaps he believed it was none of his business."

I thought back to Aunt Cait's reaction to Barbreck's confession. "I'll grant you that he may have suspected it, but it was evident he'd said nothing to my aunt about it. Did none of them question Barbreck's resentment of their neighbor?" I knew these were questions for my relatives, but I couldn't help but ruminate aloud. "I know they suggested it was naught but a clan feud. And I would never underestimate the power of such a grudge." One need only delve shallowly into the history of Scotland to uncover tales of the savage vengeance one clan sometimes enacted on another. "But I could tell they found that theory as doubtful as I do."

"Maybe they thought it was because he'd taken umbrage at her being granted so much control over Poltalloch, at least ostensibly, but were reluctant to say so," Henry remarked.

I turned in my saddle to look at him, much struck by this. "That actually makes a great deal of sense." After all, women rarely owned property and so were rarely allowed to manage it as they saw fit. In this case, Miss Campbell didn't own the property, but her nephew's carelessness or disinterest had left her in charge. Even without the added strain of their personal history, a nobleman like Lord Barbreck might have resented this, particularly if her methods ran counter to his own.

Such a resentment would not have been one Aunt Cait took kindly either. Nor Uncle Dunstan, I imagined, as their marriage had always seemed to be a true partnership. That Barbreck would disdain Miss Campbell for such a reason would not have sat well with them, and so maybe they had avoided thinking it. The notion of a clan feud was easier to stomach.

Regardless, we knew the truth now; that his antipathy stemmed from the forgery accusation and their broken engagement. Though I was certain Miss Campbell's control of her estate probably also played a role in his festering resentment. The question was, how much did Miss Campbell resent him in return?

The fact that she appeared to be friendly enough with Uncle Dunstan seemed to indicate that she didn't harbor a grudge against all the Mallerys. Though Barbreck's accusations the previous evening might have stirred any lingering bitterness back up again.

Whatever the case, we would find out soon enough, for the trees began to thin and I spied the rock formation just ahead. As we passed, I allowed my gaze to drift upward over the craggy surface, but from such an angle it was difficult to see any of these cup and ring carvings my uncle mentioned. At the far end, the trail rounded the rocky outcropping to swing to the west nearer to the loch before turning south again along a ridge at the edge of the forest. From this vantage we could see across the waters of the loch to the long narrow island near its middle. The undulating green isle appeared deserted, but perhaps there were buildings hidden from our sight by the scrubby trees clinging to the upland slopes.

We fell quiet again as the path entered another forest, narrowing so that I was forced to drop back to ride behind Gage. This wood was less dense than the last, and we soon neared the edge where the trees opened up to offer us our first glimpse of Poltalloch Castle. The tower house was old. That much was apparent even from a distance. I wagered it had been built in the fourteenth or fifteenth century, and its moss-speckled north-facing edifice testified to that age. Judging from the large divots in the stone and the sizable chunk which had collapsed from the northwest corner, it had also survived multiple attacks over the ages. That or its masonry was in such disrepair that it was falling apart.

Uncle Dunstan had told Gage that the estate was in decline and being stripped of its assets, and the castle exterior's poor condition attested to that. As did the ruins of a newer manor built in a glen some five hundred yards to the east. There was no roof, only the remains of the outline of its walls. The vegetation growing on, around, and inside those walls made clear it had sat in that condition for several decades.

The trail converged with a wider one from the east, leading us toward the castle, which loomed over us, having been built on top of a rocky mount. The builders had taken advantage of this natural formation and constructed the low walls of a courtyard around its perimeter. The gates were thrown open, and so we urged our mounts through them and up the sloped path into the enclosure.

Inside to our left we spied a row of low buildings which undoubtedly acted as stables. I suspected the far side of the castle boasted a set of stairs built into the face of the crag, leading down toward the loch. But around the corner of the tower to our right stood the unassuming wooden door which acted as its main entrance.

Someone had evidently noticed our approach, for a tall woman in a rather plain but impeccably tailored gown of the finest merino dyed in a shade of spruce green stood before the doorway. A man, whom I presumed was her butler, stood just beyond her shoulder, his back straight and his thinning hair rustling against the top of his head in the breeze. In stark contrast, the woman's iron gray tresses were tightly restrained atop her head, as if they wouldn't dare disobey the orders of their mistress. Her gaze scrutinized each of us in turn, but I could feel it linger longest on me.

"You'll be Lady Darby and Mr. Gage, then, I presume," she remarked in a lilting Scottish brogue, and leaving me in no doubt that Lord Barbreck had invoked our names, likely as a threat, when he confronted her the previous evening.

Polite society persisted in calling me by my first husband's title out of courtesy, since Sir Anthony Darby had been of a higher rank, though I infinitely preferred to be linked to my second husband by his name instead. But Lady Darby was the title I was most famously, and infamously, known by.

Miss Campbell's eyes swung back to Henry. "And who might this be?"

"Lord Henry Kerr, ma'am," he replied.

"A Kerr. And one o' Bowmont's sons, no less," she mused, proving she knew her *Debrett's Peerage*, or at least the lineage of Scotland's noble families. "Aye, well, you're welcome to Poltalloch as well. Best come inside." With this remark, she turned to retreat inside the house, trusting us to follow.

A pair of stable hands appeared to take control of our steeds as we dismounted. I hobbled slightly as I moved toward the entrance, unaccustomed to being in a saddle. Gage moved forward to take my arm, but after a few steps I found my gait again. The door was not tall. It appeared that the original opening had never been enlarged, as was done in many old tower houses. For a moment I wondered if Gage and Henry would be forced to stoop to enter, but they remained upright with mere inches to spare.

Fortunately, the interior did not maintain its fifteenth-century design. At some point, likely in the early eighteenth century, it had been refurbished and remodeled. Warm wood-paneled walls greeted us in the entry hall, and the patina of the oak floor spoke of its age. The butler gestured us through a doorway across from the main entrance, and we stepped through to find ourselves in a worn but tidy drawing room. The faded upholstery and threadbare rug had seen better days, but not a pillow was out of place, nor did a speck of dust touch the surfaces of the room's contents.

Miss Campbell stood just inside the room, waiting to greet us properly. From a distance, I had not been able to appreciate the lovely sea green shade of her eyes or the regal structure of her features. With her height—several inches above my own—and commanding appearance and presence, I could easily imagine her being a queen, let alone a marchioness, as she would have been if she'd wed Barbreck.

The niceties being observed, I expected her to directly address the reason for our being there, as her practical demeanor seemed to suggest. But she astonished me instead by remarking, "I certainly see the resemblance. You have your mother's eyes."

I blinked in surprise. "You knew my mother?"

"Oh, aye, my dear," a voice from behind our hostess said with a titter. "Quite well."

Miss Campbell stepped to the side, giving me a glimpse of the woman seated in one of the armchairs upholstered in burgundy-figured silk near the rough stone hearth where a fire crackled in its grate, the better to ward off the chill of the castle even on such a warm summer day. A tartan shawl was draped around her shoulders, which seemed to bow forward with frailty.

"Come closer so I can get a look at you," she beckoned.

"My sister, Miss Margaret Campbell," the elder Miss Campbell explained.

Miss Margaret's soft brown eyes twinkled at me as I approached, as if we might be sharing a private joke. I could see the resemblance in their facial structures and the widow's peaks at their hairline, but whereas Miss Campbell appeared tall and robust, her younger sister seemed to be small and delicate. From the manner in which she sat hunched in front of the fireplace, I would have suspected her to be an invalid if not for the healthy flush of her cheeks and that liveliness in her eyes. But perhaps her fragility only seemed so pronounced when compared with her sister. After all, both women were over seventy years of age, and life in the Highlands was hard on the body, even the most pampered of aristocratic ones.

"You are someone I never thought to have the chance to meet," she declared with relish. "But Barbreck does have interestin' friends."

"Dunstan Mallery is her uncle," Miss Campbell reminded her, as if to say the odds of us meeting had not been as remote as her sister implied.

"Aye," she replied in acknowledgment, but she didn't seem to give the comment much credence. "Forgive me for no' risin', my dear. My knees are no' what they once were."

"Of course." My head swam with a dozen questions I wished to ask of them pertaining to my mother and how they had known her, but before I could begin, Miss Margaret lifted the tambour embroidery hoop in her lap that my gaze had dipped to.

"Do you like it?"

Focusing on the intricate stitches, I was immediately struck by her skill and the artistry of the design. "I do. The depth and subtlety of variation in your shades of color, and the complexity of the motif. It's remarkable." I tilted my head to study it from yet another angle. "Is it your handiwork?"

"Why, yes." Her eyes sparkled with pleasure. "You must embroider yourself."

"Not very well," I admitted with a light laugh. "I'm afraid I never acquired the aptitude. But I am a portrait artist."

My good humor abruptly faded as I recalled the reason we were there in the first place. Lifting my gaze to Miss Campbell, I saw that her lips had tightened.

"Let's be seated, shall we?" she instructed us, gesturing toward the chairs and sofa arranged before the hearth.

I sat on the end of the floral settee nearest Miss Margaret, and Gage joined me, leaving the remaining chairs to Henry and Miss Campbell.

"Noo," Miss Campbell proclaimed once she was settled. "It's no surprise why you are here, so I shall speak plainly." Her stern gaze met each of ours in turn, ending with me. "I dinna ken where Barbreck's Van Dyck portrait is. I am neither a thief nor a liar. So, if you've come to accuse me o' either one, you've wasted yer time and mine."

CHAPTER 8

I understand why you would think that's why we're here," I replied, unsurprised by her anger but grateful for her restraint. "I'm not certain precisely what Barbreck said to you when he paid you an unexpected visit yesterday evening, but I gather it was unpleasant, to say the least."

"Called her a thief, a liar, a termagant, *and* a harridan," Miss Margaret declared almost gleefully.

My eyebrows arched. "I apologize. It appears 'unpleasant' was too kind a word. 'Vile' perhaps would be a better adjective. My point is that I'm not here to accuse anyone of anything. I'm simply trying to gather information, and as I understand it, you have a unique and, in some ways, possibly more objective perspective." I studied Miss Campbell's taut expression, trying to gauge how receptive she was to my explanation. "Will you answer my questions?"

She clasped her hands more tightly together in her lap, scrutinizing me in return. For a moment, I worried she might decline.

But then she lowered her chin, and the tiny furrow between her brows cleared. "What do ye want to ken?"

I looked at Gage, wishing I had thought to confer with him on the best way to proceed. But as there was no time for that now, I decided it would be prudent to start at the beginning. Or at least the earliest known incident to do with the art forgery.

"We understand that some years ago your father arranged to purchase a painting by Titian that Lord Barbreck's brother, Alisdair, procured for you. But then you discovered it was a forgery. Is that correct?" I'd deliberately chosen not to mention their broken engagement, wondering if it might be too sensitive a topic, but Miss Campbell seemed to have no qualms about speaking of it.

"Aye, and if ye ken that much, then you also ken it led directly to the ending o' our betrothal. Or did Barbreck omit that part?" she added dryly.

I exchanged another glance with Gage and then Henry. "He told us something of it."

She huffed. "Made a big fuss, more like. Called it an affront to his honor and that o' the Mallery name."

"Though he had no trouble questionin' Father's. Nor yours," Miss Margaret remarked almost blithely as she picked up her needlework to begin stitching again.

Miss Campbell turned to look at her, her eyes narrowing in displeasure, before she returned her attention to me. "But if ye identified the Van Dyck as a forgery, then I'd wager you've taken a look at the Titian as well."

"I have."

Her eyes glittered like hard emeralds. *"And?"*

I hesitated, perhaps out of some misbegotten loyalty to Barbreck, but then I decided she deserved the truth. "The Titian is either a blatant attempt at a forgery, or some later artist painted over the original for some unknown reason, effectively destroying it."

I'd expected her reaction to be one of immense satisfaction over this vindication that she and her father had been right to question the painting's authenticity. But my response seemed to subdue rather than delight her. In the jumble of all the emotions reflected in her eyes, pleasure was not one of them.

Miss Margaret noticed this as well, lowering her embroidery as she watched her sister closely. "Ye were right, then," she said evenly. "And noo Barbreck kens it, too."

Miss Campbell smoothed her hands over her lap, her gaze still lowered to the rug at our feet. "Aye."

But that fact didn't change the past. It didn't change the fifty-some odd years that had passed since then. She couldn't help but be thinking of this, for I was, and I was merely an observer, and a latecomer at that. I had suspected there was more to Barbreck's emphasis on the monetary and dynastic advantage to both families as the primary reason for their engagement, and now seeing how Miss Campbell struggled with her own emotions, I was even more convinced of it. It made my heart go out to her. For although it was impossible to know precisely how deep each of their emotions had run, it was obvious there had been some sort of tender feeling between them. Enough that this vindication was as painful as it was gratifying.

"How did you and your father know the Titian was a fake?" I voiced as she continued to struggle. Had our situations been reversed, I knew I would have been glad of someone prodding the topic along.

"There was a chip." Taking a deep breath, she lifted her gaze and spoke more firmly. "Near the middle o' the canvas. It had flaked away to reveal a different shade o' paint underneath."

"Near the horse's legs?"

"Yes, I believe so. It's been some time since I last saw it . . . since I last thought o' it." Her shoulders straightened. "Father invited an art expert to visit, a man a friend o' his had recommended. And when he showed him the painting, the man studied it for less than a minute before declarin' it to be a fraud. Somethin' by a lesser artist that had either been mislabeled by a fool or deliberately misattributed in order to exploit the gullible." Her eyes had narrowed as if in remembered outrage.

"So you confronted Barbreck?" Gage queried.

"Aye. And his brother, Alisdair."

"He'd acquired the painting?" Gage asked in confirmation, and she nodded. "Do you know from where?"

"He brought it home from one o' his trips to the continent. He was always dashin' off to Italy and Greece, and sometimes Spain and France. That's where he obtained most o' Barbreck's art collection. Here and there, wherever he found an eager seller."

Truth be told, that was how most gentlemen acquired their art and antiquities collections. These treasures were procured either on voyages they'd personally undertaken, beginning as young men with their Grand Tours of the continent—a journey which had been almost a rite of passage among aristocratic young men after coming of age and completing university—or through the services of one of the many dealers established throughout the continent who had made a name for themselves, and a fortune to go with it, by catering to the whims and avarice of British collectors. Unfortunately, these dealers' scruples were not always all that one would hope them to be.

I'd once had an interesting and informative conversation with Gage's friend Mr. Knightley about this acquisition of antiquities from the classical civilizations, and the corrupt means by which such items were sometimes obtained. It turned out that Mr. Knightley was rather an expert on the subject of antiquities, and one whom Gage had consulted on two previous inquiries, which was how they had met. He was also more well-versed than most in the tricks of these dealers' trade as well as the methods of the Italian restorers they worked with. The jugglery they used joining together different fragments of statuary—some ancient, some more modern—to create a pleasing piece, the methods they used to age them, and the tales the dealers wove to distract the purchaser from making a closer inspection of the item, appealing to the collectors' desires and self-conceit. Had Lord Alisdair fallen for such ploys?

I turned toward the sunshine streaming through the narrow window, contemplating Barbreck's deceased brother. Much of this mystery seemed to center on him, and yet I knew little about him. Was it possible he'd been duped by an unscrupulous dealer? Had he even used one, or had he obtained the artwork and antiquities he'd brought back to England by another method? A dozen questions sprang to mind about Lord Alisdair Mallery, most of which would have to be directed to Barbreck, but there was one or two I could put to Miss Campbell.

"Did Lord Alisdair acquire the painting in question specifically for your father?"

"Father had expressed his interest in procurin' a Titian," she said. "Told him that if he found one that could be had for a good price, he would pay him a handsome finder's fee."

That certainly made it sound like the painting had come directly to them, leaving no time for it to have been swapped or forged after its arrival in Argyll, and yet that fleck of paint bothered me.

I tilted my head, frowning at the ceiling. "Do you know how that chip of paint came off the portrait?"

Miss Campbell stiffened. "We didna damage it on purpose, if that's what yer implying."

"No, no. That's not what I meant. It's only . . ." I heaved a sigh, trying to find the right words to explain myself. "Paint shouldn't flake off like that. Not unless the canvas has been improperly treated, but we can see from the underlayers of paint that's not the case. Is it possible someone's hand slipped, and it was jarred or dropped while it was being carried? I'm simply trying to ascertain the viscosity of the paint, which could tell me when that overlayer might have been painted."

The angry glint in her eyes faded, but her demeanor did not relax. "I dinna recall the painting bein' mishandled, even accidentally," she answered crisply before glancing at her sister, who shook her head.

"I didna even see it until it was already hung." There was an odd note in Miss Margaret's voice I couldn't quite identify. Wistfulness, perhaps. Given her skill with embroidery, perhaps the artist in her wished the Titian had been real.

Regardless, I was far from satisfied with their answers, and uncertain whether I believed them. If the painting had been unintentionally damaged while it was being examined, that would tell me one thing, but if the overpaint had flaked off without human assistance, that could indicate something else. Without a definitive answer, that line of inquiry was impossible to follow.

"What of Lord Alisdair himself?" Gage asked, relaxing a bit deeper into the settee cushions. "He must still have been a rather young man at that point. Yet Barbreck and your father trusted him to acquire expensive pieces of art. Was he so trustworthy?"

Miss Campbell's gaze dipped to the arm of her chair, and from the pinched look about her mouth, I knew she was struggling with her temper. "I've no wish to speak ill o' the dead." She exhaled a fierce breath through her nostrils before continuing, biting off each word almost savagely. "But Lord Alisdair shouldna been given such a responsibility. He didna deserve it."

"Noo, is that really fair?" Miss Margaret pronounced softly, her gaze on her sister's profile. "Isna that blamin' Alisdair for his brother's failin's?"

"Alisdair isna blameless?" Miss Campbell turned to snap.

"Nay, o' course not," she agreed. "But he also didna force Barbreck to make the choice he did. You ken as well as I do that no one forces Barbreck to do anythin'."

Miss Campbell's head bowed for a moment, as if the weight of it all was too much, but then she straightened, seeming to summon her composure with an iron grip. "My apologies. I'm afraid this has all been rather . . ." She seemed to search for the right word, settling on one that was more impersonal than I anticipated. ". . . *unpleasant* to have the incident brought up again, and then have these new accusations flung at us." Her brow furrowed. "At me," she corrected, brushing down her skirts as she pushed to her feet. "Noo, if you'll excuse me. I've an estate to see to. The drainage in the south field needs to be examined, and one o' our ewes fell ill overnight." She glanced at her sister where she still sat with her embroidery. "And my sister shouldn't be overexcited. She has a weak heart."

If Miss Margaret was embarrassed by this pronouncement, she didn't show it. But then I supposed she'd been hearing it all her life. It also helped to explain the fragile nature of her appearance, though the mind behind her eyes seemed as sharp as her sister's even if she had less cause to use it.

"Of course," Gage replied as the three of us rose to our feet. There was really nothing else we could do.

"Calder will show you out," she declared, gesturing to the butler, who had appeared in the open doorway as if he'd been standing just on the other side waiting for her summons.

"Thank you for your time," I told her before nodding to Miss Margaret.

"Oh, but you must come back," the younger sister protested, shifting forward in her chair. "To see my embroidery. To talk. I have ever so many questions."

Seeing the anxious look in her eyes, I wondered how lonely her existence must be. How much did her weak heart limit her?

Did she ever travel beyond the borders of the estate, beyond the walls of the castle? Somehow I doubted the Campbell sisters received many visitors.

Miss Campbell's face softened, as if moved by the same thoughts. "We shall invite Lady Darby one day for tea," she said with an anxious look toward me, perhaps uncertain whether I would accept. "I shall send her an invitation."

"Yes, I should like that," I replied sincerely.

With that decided, Gage linked his arm with mine as we were led from the room into the entry, just as a dark-haired maid came bustling up the stairs, her arms laden with a heavy tray. She stopped abruptly at the sight of us leaving, her cheeks flushing bright red. "Kady dropped the first tray," she blurted in defense. "Made a right awful mess."

"'Tis all right, Mairi," Calder replied long-sufferingly. "Take it on in."

Though I would have preferred a sip of tea, I decided it would be best to settle for a drink of water from the flasks tucked in our horses' saddle bags.

Our steeds were waiting for us where we'd left them, and we were soon mounted and riding through the gates and back down the trail we had taken such a short time earlier. Gage opened his mouth to speak, but I shook my head. "Not here."

He studied me for a moment before glancing behind me at Henry and then nodded.

It wasn't that I was worried about being overheard, but rather that it was difficult to hold a conversation on horseback when the path was not wide enough to accommodate all of us abreast. That, and I wanted time to think over what we had seen and heard before I voiced my opinions to the others. As the only female among our trio, and a woman whom the world also viewed as unconventional, I perhaps possessed a unique insight into the Campbell sisters and what they were thinking or feeling. I didn't want my impressions to be muddied by Gage's and Henry's thoughts until I'd given them due consideration.

We rode in silence until we reached the rocky outcropping my uncle had suggested we might enjoy seeing. The one etched with cup and ring markings. I was admittedly less enthused with traipsing up and down the rock face to see the etchings as I was to rehash our interview with the Campbells, but that didn't mean we couldn't stretch our legs while we allowed the ponies to graze at the side of the trail.

The midafternoon sun beat down on the windswept rocks between snatches of clouds. I turned my face up to it as I neared the top and breathed deeply of the sea-scented air before turning to the men. Henry had squatted to examine what did indeed appear to be intricate carvings swirling over the stone only to disappear under a patch of moss or sod. I suspected if anyone ever took enough of an interest in them and decided to remove the vegetation grown over the rock surface, they would find more of the ancient etchings. Perhaps they would even be able to discover what they were for. But I brushed the thought aside in favor of the more immediate issue at hand.

"What did you think of Miss Campbell and what she had to say?" I asked Gage, who stood with his feet braced apart to steady himself at the steepest slope of the rock face, studying something his half brother had pointed out.

He looked up at me and then climbed the remaining feet between us while Henry straightened up to stand. "I think . . ." Gage broke off, removing his hat from his head to let the wind riffle through his golden tresses while he gazed off over the loch toward the Craignish peninsula. A furrow formed between his brows. "I think that forgery caused more heartache than it had a right to."

I had to agree. Despite Barbreck's and Miss Campbell's attempts to pretend that their broken engagement some fifty-four years earlier had not mattered, it was more than obvious that it had. That it still did. I wanted to shake my head at the foolishness of their allowing the painting and their outrage over their family's honor to come between them, but that was not the matter at hand, nor our charge to fix.

"As for Miss Campbell herself," Gage continued. "She seemed to me to be an intelligent, capable, forthright person, if not a bit mistrusting. But given her circumstances, one can hardly blame her."

"She certainly seems to take pride in Poltalloch," I replied. "Doing her best for it even as her nephew continues to direct the funds toward his own pleasures, if my uncle has the right of it. And I have no reason to doubt he does. Uncle Dunstan wouldn't cast aspersions unless they were well-proven."

Henry nodded. "I've met the current Campbell of Poltalloch, and nothing your uncle has reported about Sir James surprises me. He's rather a careless ne'er-do-well. And his heir, who is nearing his majority, appears to be following in his footsteps."

"Then it's no wonder Miss Campbell feels so protective of Poltalloch, or that those living on the estate feel protective of her," I murmured. "They must know what's coming when Miss Campbell passes." As such, I suspected it would be difficult, if nigh *impossible*, to get any information out of her staff. If we even needed to.

I clamped my hands onto my hips, turning my head to stare over the green treetops in the direction of Poltalloch. "Truth be told, the involvement of the Campbells seems straightforward. Miss Campbell's father asked Lord Alisdair to acquire a Titian. The painting he sold him proved to be a fraud, so he confronted Lord Alisdair and Barbreck. Lord Alisdair denied fault, Barbreck backed him, and the painting was returned to Barbreck, the money presumably returned to Sir James, and the engagement broken. That timeline of events does not appear to be in dispute, even if my confirmation of the Titian being a forgery has dredged it all up from the past.

"However, there doesn't appear to be any evidence that the Campbells had anything to do with the Van Dyck. Nothing, that is, except the fact that Barbreck believes they did."

Gage kicked at a tuft of moss with the toe of his riding boot. "Barbreck claims that the Van Dyck must have been switched, but when exactly in the last fifty-odd years does he allege that happened? And *why* did no one notice?"

I frowned. "They should have. *He* should have. If he had ever truly owned a Van Dyck, he would have seen the difference." I tilted my head. "Though I do wonder when he actually acquired the Van Dyck. We know Lord Alisdair brought the Titian back from a trip to the continent sometime shortly before Barbreck and Miss Campbell's broken engagement, but we don't know when Lord Alisdair returned with the Van Dyck."

"True. It might be a more recent acquisition."

"I find myself curious about Lord Alisdair," Henry admitted, echoing my thoughts. "How long ago did he die?"

"I don't know," I admitted. "But that's one of many things we need to find out. And the best source for that information, while admittedly biased, is Barbreck."

"Then I suppose it's time we return to Barbreck Manor. You also need to see to Emma soon, don't you?" Gage asked, tracking my movements as I checked the watch pinned to my bodice.

"Yes. Though there's no need to rush." I moved forward to take hold of the strong arm he held out to me to help me down from the outcropping. I steeled my resolve. "*Then* we'll speak with Barbreck."

CHAPTER 9

After feeding and settling Emma, I found the men waiting for me in Barbreck's study. Contrary to the dark wood-paneled affair most gentlemen seemed to prefer for their inner enclaves, the room was light and airy, just like the rest of the house. High ceilings gave over to white walls covered in landscape paintings of Highland scenes. I arrived to find Lord Barbreck, Gage, and Henry ensconced in the leather chairs and sofas at the center of the room, cradling glasses of amber liquid in their hands.

I'd opened my mouth to apologize for my delay when the portrait hanging between the two tall windows above the sideboard arrested my steps. It was one of mine. One of the paintings I'd created at Gairloch Castle following my first husband's death and the ensuing scandal. While most of my past works were painted from subjects who posed for me, this one was from a series of portraits I'd created largely from my imagination. Sometimes the people portrayed were drawn from my memories of interesting faces I'd seen in a park or a village street, but other times they were pure whim, as was this one.

I had named each painting after the emotion depicted by the subject—a title that only I, the broker, and the owner would know unless the owner chose to reveal it. In this instance, it was *Portrait of a Woman Scorned*. Her body swathed in a deep forest green gown was painted in three-quarter profile, as if she were moving away from the viewer, but her head had turned back to look directly out of the canvas. Snapping eyes, their depths stormy with emotion, captured your attention, as well as the defiant, up-turned chin perched above the woman's long, regal neck. It was not a comfortable painting, for it fairly throbbed with tension and repressed fury. It made my skin flush hot and hollowed the pit of my stomach just looking at it and recalling the memories I'd poured into creating it.

My first thought after my initial surprise was to wonder why Barbreck had it, and whether he even realized it was mine. Most of my paintings from that period of my life had been sold under the name K. A. Elwick. While that alternate identity was not so secretive now, as portraits under my own name had in-creased in popularity, that didn't mean everyone was aware of the connection.

One look at his almost defiant expression as he stared back at me told me the answer. Yes, he knew I had painted it, and no, he didn't want me to comment on it. Or perhaps he didn't want me to draw the connection I was beginning to make. My gaze flicked back up to the woman, who I now realized reminded me of Miss Campbell, or rather how she must have looked when she was younger. Barbreck's eyes promised retribution if I remarked on it, and that more than anything told me I was right.

"My apologies for the delay," I said instead, sinking down onto the sofa next to Gage and settling my skirts. "What have I missed?"

"Nothing but Barbreck's grunts of impatience," Gage replied, the twinkle in his pale blue eyes telling me he had enjoyed provoking the marquess.

"Aye, weel, I've waited all day for your report, so let's get on wi' it," he growled.

I arched my eyebrows in mild chastisement at this curt demand, but the vee between Barbreck's winged eyebrows only grew deeper. "We spoke to Miss Campbell and her sister, Miss Margaret," I confirmed. "But before we can determine anything, we need some more information." Barbreck appeared as if he was about to argue, so I charged ahead before he could do so. "We understand the alleged Titian was acquired by your brother, Lord Alisdair, in continental Europe sometime in 1777 or 1778. And he acquired it specifically for Sir James Campbell. Is that correct?"

"Aye." He frowned. "At least . . ." He broke off, considering something. But whatever it was he quickly discarded it. "Aye, that's correct."

I eyed him askance, wondering if I should press him about whatever had caused him to pause, but then Gage pressed on.

"Do you recall any of the details? The date of his trip? Where in his travels he acquired the alleged Titian?"

"Nay. Alisdair made many trips to the continent over the years. And on most o' them he acquired artwork for me." Barbreck huffed. "I canna recall the exact dates. No' for a voyage so long ago. Nor the details o' where he acquired what."

"But surely he recorded the details somewhere. Made a record of the purchase."

"Aye. But if ye wish to go pokin' through those files, you'll have to speak to my steward."

I'd expected such an answer, and Gage's resigned expression told me he'd anticipated much the same. It would be tedious work finding the information we sought, especially if Barbreck couldn't narrow the search any further.

"He must have had a dealer acting on his behalf," I interjected, thinking that would at least give us a name to look for listed at the top of the bill of sale. "Someone with the knowledge and connections to seek out interesting art for sale. Did he share his contacts?"

"I'm sure he did, but I dinna recall them noo. No' this many years removed."

My hands fisted in my lap as I began to grow frustrated with the marquess's lack of information. I couldn't tell whether he was being deliberately obstructive—determined to have the finger of blame point at Miss Campbell—or he truly didn't know. "But surely you must have at least *asked* your brother where he acquired that purported Titian? After Sir James's allegations, you *must* have discussed it."

"O' course, we did," he snapped. "But Alisdair assured me the man he purchased it from would *never* have sold him a forgery. That he was too august, too well-respected to even countenance such a thing. And to even ask him aboot it would have been the height o' insult and sever his chances o' ever doin' business wi' the man again."

"Which is exactly how you *would* react were you a dealer who sometimes traded in forgeries," Henry remarked with a cynical curl to his lips.

"Aye, weel, Alisdair was my brother and I trusted him. And *he* trusted the man. So *I* trusted him." He sank back in his chair, a troubled expression creasing his brow.

"And it was as simple as that," Gage said, laying out the logic he must have used in making that long-ago decision. "You trusted your brother, so he must be telling the truth. Which meant the Campbells and their expert had to be lying."

"Except your brother was wrong," I added in a gentler voice than I wished to use. "Whether he knew the truth or not, that Titian was . . . *is* a fraud."

His eyes rekindled with fury. "No' if they switched—"

"They didn't," I stated firmly, halting his denial. "The damage that proved it was a fraud fifty-four years ago is still evident today."

His lips were pressed together so tightly they quivered, but then he heaved a deep breath. "Near the horse's legs?"

He was familiar with it, too, then. Which most definitely confirmed it.

"But couldna that damage be replicated?"

I shook my head. It would be almost impossible to make it look natural, and I felt I could detect the difference.

Barbreck turned away, as if he still couldn't face the truth head-on.

"What about the Van Dyck?" I asked after giving him a moment to reflect. "Did your brother acquire it at the same time as the forged Titian?" There was no point in continuing to use the word *alleged* even if it made Barbreck flinch.

"Nay." He pulled a handkerchief from the inside pocket of his coat, wiping his brow with it. "Nay, he purchased that for me some years later. From somewhere in England."

"So it wasn't obtained through the same dealer?"

"Nay."

Perhaps Lord Alisdair had been more suspicious of the dealer who sold him the forged Titian than we realized. Or maybe I was trying to give him more credit than he deserved. After all, Van Dyck had painted *in* England, so one did not have to go far to find his work. While the dealer from whom Lord Alisdair had acquired the Titian had likely been based in Rome or even Venice, where Titian had done most of his painting, they were unlikely to be the same man.

Yet, they were both forgeries. And there still might be *more* forgeries in Barbreck's collection. This did not speak to Lord Alisdair's abundance of caution.

I searched Barbreck's weary face, curious if he'd done what I asked. "Have you gone to look at the Van Dyck since I told you my suspicions?"

"Aye." With the aid of the walking stick propped between his legs, he hefted his bulk so that he could sit taller.

"And?" I prodded.

"It's no' the same painting," he stated flatly. "I see what you're sayin' noo. The one hangin' there *is* dull and lifeless. There's no way it's the same portrait that arrived here years ago. It doesna even make me feel the same."

But was that because it truly wasn't the same painting, or because I had pointed out the flaws and proven it to be a fraud?

So I pressed him. "You're certain?"

"Aye, I'm certain." He was back to growling. "Ye dinna think you're the only one wi' an eye for art, do ye?"

No, but I *was* the only one in the room with a trained eye. And, furthermore, I had nothing to gain or lose from the truth.

Gage leaned forward, propping his elbows on his knees. Perhaps trying to stifle his own irritation. "But you didn't notice the painting had been switched until now?"

"Nay. And I'm no' too proud to admit it might have happened some time ago. When I'm here, I doona always visit the long gallery, and when I do, I doona always give the art my full attention." He scowled. "And . . . my eyesight's no' as clear as it once was. If Kiera hadn't pointed out the discrepancies, I canna say wi' certainty whether I would've noticed."

This seemed to contradict what he'd just claimed about his eye for art, but I did not challenge him on it.

"Then if the original painting was a Van Dyck, it might have been switched out for the forgery years ago? Maybe even decades?" I queried, wanting to clarify the matter.

"There is no *if* about it," he groused. "But aye."

"Then the original could be anywhere," Henry surmised. "If

it vanished decades ago, it could be anywhere in the world by now."

I pressed a hand to my head, trying to grapple with the facts before me and the impossibility of discovering what had happened. We didn't know when or even if, in fact, the paintings had been swapped, so we couldn't begin to examine who had been in the vicinity as potential suspects. The original Van Dyck could be thousands of miles away, and tracing it would be almost impossible. The only element that might be able to provide us any further lines of inquiry was the forgery itself.

After all, while it was no Van Dyck, the forged portrait had still been painted by a gifted artist. It was not the work of an amateur. What's more, it was painted by someone who had studied the original. Someone who must have had access to it. Repeatedly.

But Barbreck was determined to persist with his accusations against Miss Campbell. "It'll be at Poltalloch, or the Campbells sold it," he insisted.

"We're aware of your theory," I replied, not bothering to hide my annoyance this time. "But can either of the Miss Campbells paint?"

Barbreck's brow lowered thunderously.

"Are you aware of *anyone* at Poltalloch, past or present, who could paint? With great skill?"

"Nay," he bit out. "Weel, there was one woman . . ." he began, but then he abruptly broke off, giving me a strange look. "But nay, it couldna be her."

I found his expression to be suspicious, but given his vendetta against the Campbells, I trusted that if *he* didn't believe the woman could have done it, then she probably hadn't.

"What of Lord Alisdair?"

He shook his head. "My brother dabbled in painting, but he didna have the talent for it. No' enough to paint a convincin' forgery, that's for sure."

"How about any of the staff or regular visitors to the estate?" Gage persisted. "Anyone who might have been able to come and go with few questions?"

Once again Barbreck shook his head. "I canna think of anyone." But it was clear from the look in his eyes that he had. Why he wasn't naming them I couldn't begin to speculate, but I was close to losing my temper with the man. He quite obviously was not telling us everything, and how we were supposed to solve the mystery without him being forthright, I didn't know. Or was he simply determined to keep the suspicion of fault directed at the Campbells?

"Unless we can figure out who painted the forgeries, I'm afraid our investigation is rather thwarted," I stated plainly, struggling to restrain my frustration. "And *do not* suggest again it was someone the Campbells hired," I cautioned, able to tell he was about to do just that. "The artist would have needed access to the actual portrait in order to copy it. And without any idea of when the paintings were swapped, the chances of us identifying one visitor to Poltalloch over the past five decades is highly unlikely."

I'd hoped this warning might loosen his tongue, but before the threat had a chance to work on him, there was a knock on the door. The butler opened the door in response to Barbreck's summons.

"I beg your pardon, sir, but you wished to be informed the moment Master Braeden arrived."

"Verra good," Barbreck proclaimed, shifting forward in his chair in order to use his walking stick to push himself to his feet. The rest of us followed suit, standing before our seats. As he gained his balance, his gaze lifted to meet mine, sharp with displeasure. "We'll continue this discussion later."

I waited until he'd hobbled through the doorway before muttering my response. "No, we won't, because there's nothing more *to* discuss."

Gage offered me a smile of commiseration and reached out to wrap his arm around my waist, drawing me momentarily closer.

Pressing a hand to my forehead again, I heaved a sigh. "I apologize. But the man is beyond exasperating."

"He's certainly not making matters any easier," Gage agreed. His gaze remained trained on the door through which he'd passed. "He's keeping something from us."

"Several somethings."

"I noticed that, too," Henry agreed.

I noted his slightly stiff posture, evidence that he still wasn't entirely comfortable in our presence. Truth be told, he appeared more anxious now than when he'd arrived at Barbreck Manor. But I suspected that was due to the investigation. It was obvious how keen he was to win his half-brother's approval. I wanted to tell him Gage was not the type of man to base a man's worth on what he could do for him, but I wondered if my saying something would only make it worse. If perhaps this was something he needed to figure out on his own.

The sound of loud voices could be heard echoing down the corridor from the entry hall.

I led the men from the study to join the others gathering to greet Rye's older brother, Brady; his wife, Poppy; and their children. As usual, Brady's voice was the loudest, followed closely by Morven's. Sandwiched between these two bombastic personalities, I'd often thought it no surprise that Rye had turned out to be quiet and reserved. He'd probably never been able to get a word in edgewise. But it was clear they held each other in esteem all the same.

I watched as Brady clapped Rye heartily on the back, making him grin at his enthusiastic salutation. When he turned to greet Charlotte, rather than politely taking her hand, he swung her off the floor. For a moment, my dear friend appeared aghast, but then she began to giggle. A sight that brought a smile to my own face.

Poppy turned from Aunt Cait, shaking her head good-naturedly at her husband's antics, and stepped forward to take my proffered hands. "He can't help himself," she declared in her gentle voice. "But you already know that." Her dark eyes twinkled with mischief. "You're probably next."

For all of Poppy's serene appearance and soft-spoken manners, I knew she possessed an impish streak to rival her husband's. She was simply slyer in how she wielded it. Between the pair of them and Morven, I was doubtful that the remaining days until the wedding would pass quietly.

As if to illustrate this, Brady suddenly hefted a bottle of dark spirits. "Tomorrow night, gentlemen. I've uncovered the most delightful recipe in the pages of *Blackwood's*." He clapped Rye on the back once again. "We shall toast to my brother's happiness with the flowing bowl."

All the men cheered in approval, and I turned to meet Gage's eye, rolling my eyes in resigned amusement. All of Edinburgh society—perhaps all of Britain—was well-acquainted with the recipes for Punch touted in the pages of *Blackwood's Magazine*, often in the column *Noctes Ambrosianae*—Ambrosian Nights. Rum Punch, Brandy Punch, Hot Whisky Punch. And while the ones I'd tasted were often delicious, they were not without risk, for depending on the formula, it became all too easy to imbibe too much. Punch often being the preferred beverage at clubs and other gatherings of gentlemen, Gage had more experience with the flowing bowl, as Brady and other wits called it. Usually he kept his head about him, but once or twice he had returned home giddy and rather amorous after a night of Punch-swilling, and woke the next morning with a pounding skull. Not that I'd minded his impassioned overtures. Not in the least. But with an infant already interrupting my sleep, it did complicate matters somewhat.

Heat sparked in Gage's eyes, and I turned away even as he sidled closer, leaning down to murmur in my ear. "Perhaps I should ask Mallery to make up a bowl for the ladies as well. I seem to recall how much you enjoyed the Punch that Dalmay served the night before his wedding to Lady Caroline."

I flushed, my skin prickling as much from the gust of his breath over the sensitive skin behind my ear as the titillating memory. We had been married for less than a month when Michael and Caroline's wedding took place, and the Punch in question had made me rather uninhibited. Certainly more so than usual. Though my recollections were somewhat hazy, I did recall saying several things aloud that I couldn't believe I'd actually uttered unbidden and even now made me blush to think of. Fortunately, Gage hadn't minded in the least, though he seemed to delight in teasing me about them. From time to time, he even used his considerable powers of persuasion to convince me to say them again.

I lowered my head and coughed, trying to shield my red face from the others, lest they notice.

However, Brady chose that moment to literally sweep me off my feet in one of his crushing embraces, expelling all the air from my lungs. "Kiera, it's been an age. And I hear you're a mother, noo. Imagine that."

I gasped more than laughed, though I had to appreciate my cousin's enthusiasm and the steady transformation his accent underwent. The longer he talked, the more rolling his brogue became. Now that he was back in the Highlands with his father and great-uncle, who never bothered to mask their accent, he'd softened the crisp British accent all gentlemen learned to emulate in the English public schools and universities. It was the accent used by the Quality in Parliament and to conduct business. Sadly, to be taken seriously among the nobility and London society, it was all but required.

"Best put her doon, lad," Uncle Dunstan said with a chuckle. "Looks like you've driven the wind from her."

"Oh! Apologies, cousin." He grinned unrepentantly as I stumbled back a step. "I dinna ken my own strength."

I thought it was less his strength—for he was shorter and sparer than many of the men in attendance—and more the energy that bristled through him like a voltaic pile conducting an electric current. Even his chestnut brown hair seemed incapable of being restrained, sticking up in tufts around his head, much like mine constantly escaped from its pins.

"It's good to see you, too, Brady," I replied, and meant it. With him around, the festivities would undoubtedly be livelier, and maybe that's exactly what we needed. The art forgeries had distracted us from the real reason we were there—Charlotte and Rye's wedding. While serious, the only clear victim of the frauds and possible theft was Barbreck, and since those crimes had been committed some time ago, there was no real need for urgency. Not when there were other more important matters to attend to.

I moved to stand next to Charlotte, who glowed with happiness. I'd not had time to even think about, let alone ask her about, her concerns over the governess and her father, and I was relieved to see they didn't seem to be troubling her then. Of course, that didn't mean they were resolved, but at least she wasn't letting them steal her joy over the upcoming celebration.

She turned her radiant smile on me before reaching out to thread her arm through mine. I squeezed it in affection as she tilted her head to the side, resting it on my shoulder.

CHAPTER 10

Since I'd spent much of the past two days distracted by the art forgeries, I deliberately banished them from my thoughts that evening and the next day, and focused my attention alternately on Charlotte and baby Emma. I would be lying if I said that part of me wasn't also doing it in retaliation for Lord Barbreck not sharing everything he knew about the frauds with us. If he wished to know the truth, then he needed to stop keeping things from us.

Dinner that second evening was spent segregated, with the men inhabiting the library, study, and drawing room in the southern wing of the castle and the ladies cloistered in the rose parlor and morning room to the north. Though none of the ladies anticipated actual harm from the gentlemen toasting Rye with copious amounts of Rum Punch, we knew our men well enough to realize that mischief was not out of the question. So as an unspoken rule, we kept well clear of their impromptu party.

However, that did not stop us from making merry ourselves. Morven and Poppy confiscated multiple bottles of wine and porter from Barbreck's extensive cellars, and we gathered before the hearth in the rose parlor to toast Charlotte with much laughter and delight. At the edges of the room were scattered the fruits of our labor in preparing for the wedding, but in the warm glow of the fire, we amused ourselves with songs and stories and discussions that would likely have shocked the men—the spirits and company loosening our tongues and hearts in more than one way.

A companionable lull fell over the gathering at one point— one that I was more attuned to, as I'd chosen to limit the amount I imbibed. After all, I had a wriggling infant to nurse in a few hours. As such, I found it impossible to ignore the sight of Poppy and Morven with their heads bent together giggling nearly uncontrollably.

"What on earth is so funny?" I asked them with a smile.

"We're just expressing our appreciation for Great-Uncle's art," Poppy managed to reply before she began tittering again, nearly spilling her wine down her pale blue gown.

"Especially the painting of Mars," Morven concurred. "Or is it Ares?" She waved her hand through the air as if to brush the question aside. "One can't help but admire his *attributes*." A wicked grin split her face as she shared a look with Poppy. "Or is that arse-tributes."

This set both women off into peals of laughter, and their hilarity spread to Lady Bearsden and then Charlotte, who snickered into her glass. Even Aunt Cait chuckled after rather half-heartedly chiding her daughter for such a joke. I had no trouble deducing what they were referring to, but I wasn't certain I'd yet seen this particular piece of art.

"Where is that painting hung?"

"Very well," Poppy quipped before dissolving into another fit of mirth.

I shook my head at her ribald humor before persisting. "Who's the artist?"

"It's in the long gallery," Morven replied with a gasp. "Surely you've seen it."

"Oh, I do hope it's not a forgery," Aunt Cait said, her voice taut with concern. "Not that it matters. It's still an exquisitely rendered painting."

At this pronouncement, Lady Bearsden began guffawing so hard she nearly fell out of her chair. Charlotte tripped on her skirts, struggling to control her own hilarity as she tried to help her great-aunt.

I laughed. "You're chirping merry, the whole lot of you."

"Aye, well, only you, cousin dear, wouldn't notice such an . . . an *exquisitely rendered* piece," Morven managed to retort with a titter, consciously repeating her mother's words. "Too lost in the brushstrokes and glazing and high impasto."

I couldn't help but smile, for I *had* been waxing on rather poetically about such things to her the other day. The painting of Mars must have hung among the artworks on the side of the long gallery I'd yet to examine. However, I wasn't about to let Morven's remark go unchallenged. "Well, *I* hardly need to look at a painting to see a spectacular male form."

This set everyone off again into gales of laughter, and for once my cousin did not insist upon having the final say. Instead she tipped her glass to me. "Touché."

We fell quiet again, long enough to hear the faint echo of male voices on the other side of the manor. Aunt Cait sat forward as if she meant to rise. "I do hope they're not damaging anything." Then she lapsed back in her chair with a sigh.

The fire crackled in the hearth, silk rustled, and a servant could be heard passing quietly along the corridor outside, but no more was heard from the men. However, a vague sense of unease suddenly stole over me—just a momentary ruffling of my nerves—but unsettling, nonetheless. I reclined deeper into my corner of the sofa, listening to the others with half an ear as I tried to identify the source of my sudden twinge of worry.

As always, my thoughts first went to Emma and then Gage, but I knew if either of them was distressed in any way, I would soon hear of it. I sent up a brief prayer for them anyway, as well as for my family farther afield, considering all the recent political troubles. My gaze dipped to Charlotte, who had yet to rise from where she'd stumbled to her knees beside Lady Bearsden's chair. She sat with her head resting lightly against the chair cushion, her spine for once less than perfectly straight as she leaned to the side. I searched her face for signs of apprehension, but she seemed entirely at ease—her worries about the wedding, Rye's children, and her father forgotten.

When the conversation shifted to Lord Henry, I perked up, but they were merely attempting to play matchmaker. It was an irresistible urge for ladies who were currently or formerly happily wed to see those they liked similarly paired off.

Which left only the conundrum those forgeries presented. They were, of course, still nagging me at the back of my mind, urging me to solve their riddle. I decided that was the likeliest explanation for my disquiet, and then did my best to dismiss it from my mind. But it would not dislodge. Not completely.

So when Charlotte confessed her desire to retire a short time later, I told her I would join her. Even if Emma was asleep, I could still look in on her to ensure all was well. We bid everyone a good night and turned toward the doorway only to be brought up short by the appearance of Miss Ferguson, the governess to Rye's children. Her simple dress was neat, and her honey blond hair was plaited in a coronet on her head, telling us she hadn't yet retired. For her to be on this floor at this hour of the evening could only mean something was wrong.

"Miss Ferguson, has something happened?" Charlotte said with a gasp, hastening toward her.

The governess retreated several steps into the corridor, forcing us to follow her, and I was instantly irritated by such a maneuver. Rather than dip a curtsy as was customary, her chin arched upward, and her dark eyes flashed. "I was instructed no' to disturb Mr. Mallery, but rather that I should inform your ladyship." She glanced toward the doorway as her mouth grimaced ever so briefly in disapproval. "Though I do hope I wasna interruptin' anything important."

My eyes narrowed, letting her know that I was aware of her disrespectful demeanor despite the correctness of her words and the polite manner in which she'd uttered them. If she noted my displeasure, she gave no indication of it. Her attention remained fixed upon Charlotte, whose brow had furrowed uncertainly.

"Go on," she murmured.

"Jane has an earache."

Charlotte's eyes widened in alarm. "Oh, no! The poor dear. Should we send for a physician?"

"I took the liberty o' consultin' with Mrs. Mackay." The governess nodded toward me. "She told me that pourin' a few drops o' oil in her ear should help." She rolled her shoulders, clasping her hands before her as if congratulating herself. "Jane appears to be restin' comfortably noo."

A soft "Oh" was all Charlotte seemed to be able to manage, but I was not similarly distraught.

"I see. Then, you've done your job and managed the situation." I arched a single eyebrow, echoing the same barely concealed scorn she had shown Charlotte. "Well done. I'm glad Mrs. Mackay was able to assist you. Now you shall know better in the future."

Miss Ferguson's gaze lowered to the floor. "Aye, weel, I simply thought ye should ken." She sniffed. "Since you're to be her stepmother shortly."

I couldn't help but feel this was meant to be yet another jab at Charlotte, and perhaps she realized it as well, for she regained some of her self-possession.

"Please let me know if it returns," she replied crisply.

This time Miss Ferguson remembered her curtsy before spinning on her heel and hurrying away. Charlotte waited for her to disappear around the corner and then turned back to me as if she knew what I was going to say. I told her anyway.

"Charlotte, you cannot let her treat you this way."

She sighed. "I know."

"It is possible to live amicably with your staff. In fact, such a situation is ideal." I was fond of all the servants in our employ, from our stable lads and kitchen maids to the butler, lady's maid, valet, and nurse. I shook my head, threading my arm through hers as we began to stroll down the corridor. "But not if they don't respect you."

She nodded.

I directed our steps toward the grand staircase. "You must exert more control over your interactions than you might wish, at least for a time, or she will continue to try to exploit the anxiety you feel about becoming a stepmother." I frowned at the stair riser before me, lifting the hem of my gown with my free hand as we began to climb. "I have experience with these sorts of manipulations," I added more softly. My chest tightened in remembrance. "Sir Anthony employed them often." I lifted my head to stare blindly at the paintings hanging on the wall of the landing before us as I struggled not to become lost in the dark memories. "He liked to remind me who held the power, and that it was his choice alone whether or not to wield it."

"Stratford did, too," she murmured hollowly in reply.

I turned to look at her face. Moonlight from the tall windows glinted off the soft curls of her pale blond hair and cast a silvery, ethereal glow over her creamy porcelain skin. But her eyes were flat and her mouth tight with remembered fear.

I was fully aware of what a monster her late husband, the Earl of Stratford, had been. After all, he had murdered his mistress and their unborn child and attempted to frame his wife for the crimes, and then proceeded to try to kill her, and me when I got in the way. But we had never discussed what their marriage had been like before those terrifying events at Gairloch Castle. I knew that he had forced her to try strange and unpleasant remedies and methods that were supposed to aid her in the conception of a child when Charlotte failed to become pregnant, but we had never talked about his treatment of her otherwise. Though, it had not taken a great deal of deduction on my part to know it was at best cold and unfeeling.

I squeezed her arm where it was linked with mine, offering what comfort and understanding I could.

Her lips curled into a sad smile.

"Then you know of what I speak. If you allow Miss Ferguson to continue to control your interactions, if you let her continue to make you feel guilty for things that, as a new stepmother, it is unreasonable to expect you to know, or that are out of your control, then she will never respect you, and you will never have an amicable relationship or a contented household."

And she would never know whether the governess would allow Charlotte to direct her or if the woman needed to be replaced.

Charlotte nodded. "You're right. I just . . . dislike confrontation."

"I can understand that." I turned to face her as we reached the corridor outside her bedchamber. "But think of this as less a confrontation and more that you're standing your ground. You're not skirmishing with her but merely exerting your authority." I reached up to untangle a strand of hair that had become snarled in her pearl and gold earrings. "Frankly, if your interactions turn into an actual confrontation, then I think that tells you it's time to look for a new governess."

My gaze lifted to her soft gray eyes still clouded with worry and then back to the earring. "What did Rye say when you spoke to him about this?"

"Well, I haven't *actually* spoken to him yet."

I'd suspected as much, but I still turned to her with a chiding look as her hair came free from the earring. "Charlotte, why are you so hesitant to speak to Rye about this? Don't you trust that he'll listen?"

"No, it's not that." She fiddled with the clasp of her matching bracelet. "It's just . . . I wanted to be sure I wasn't wrong . . . about Miss Ferguson."

"You're not," I stated flatly and then softened my tone. "You're not."

I understood what my friend was doing. Her first marriage had been horrible, and now on the cusp of her second, she was afraid perhaps she didn't know best. While she had already battled that particular demon in regard to Rye and his character and love for her, she had yet to face her insecurities about motherhood and the rest of the life that would soon be hers—permanently. So if she needed reassurance, if she needed a bolster of confidence that her thoughts were not wrong, then I was happy to give it to her.

One corner of her mouth lifted in acknowledgment of her dithering. "I'll speak with him tomorrow."

I bussed her cheek and then waited until she'd closed her bedchamber door before retreating to the stairs. But then realizing where I was, I paused. My gaze strayed toward the entrance to the long gallery.

My curiosity had been aroused. There was something about the muscular structure of the figure Morven and Poppy had described that made me wonder if the painting of the god of war was the work of Caravaggio. While I knew the lighting at such a late hour would not be ideal, that I should wait until morning to examine it, the artist in me was too inquisitive not to take a peek. And yes, admittedly, part of me was also interested to see what had made all the other ladies titter and flush. In any case, I was already here. I might as well look.

I entered the long gallery to find it dark save the pale wash of moonlight filtering through the high windows. The hush of night had fallen over this part of the manor, broken only by the faint swish of my silk skirts and the soft tread of my leather-soled slippers. It felt cooler here, but that was to be expected with there being no source of heat except for what rose from the floors below and what sunshine filled the room during the day. Clouds covered the moon, shrouding its glow, and I stood still, debating whether to return to the corridor in search of a candle, when an arm suddenly snaked around me from behind.

I gasped, nearly leaping out of my skin. Only the familiar sound of the perpetrator's chuckles and the scent of his spicy cologne restrained me from lashing out with an elbow to his solar plexus.

"Good heavens, Sebastian," I scolded even as my husband's mouth pressed to the skin at the junction of my neck and my shoulders.

"Did I surprise you?" he drawled, before his lips trailed up my neck, leaving a string of tingling nips and kisses in their wake.

Warmth pooled low inside me, and I angled my head to give him better access. "You know you did. But what are you doing here? Did you follow me?"

"Hmmm," he hummed, doing something to the skin behind my ear that made my breath hitch in pleasure. "Saw you going up the stairs," he replied distractedly, his words slurring slightly.

Meanwhile, his hands had begun to wander, leaving licks of heat wherever they touched.

I swiveled in his arms, gazing up into his heavy-lidded eyes in the pale moonlight. "Enjoyed the Punch?" I asked, unable to repress my amusement.

"Not as much as I enjoy you." His mouth lowered to my neck again, and he began slowly but inexorably to back me toward the nearest wall.

I was torn between laughter at his determinedly amorous state and the heated pull of desire. Gage was astonishingly good at making me forget myself, pulling me into a haze that encompassed only the planes where our bodies met. But he was normally rather punctilious about making certain it was in places where we had privacy. The long gallery at a country house party where anyone might happen upon us, even if the space was dark and the hour was late, was hardly that.

"If that's so, then maybe we should retire to our own chamber," I suggested between quickened breaths.

His hands found my bottom even as my back met the wall between two paintings, and I found myself being lifted. The feel of his body pressed against my length, and the evidence of his desire for me, sent a sudden thrill through me. And when his voice murmured huskily in my ear, "Oh, Kiera, my love," it drove me out of my senses. So much so that I ceased resisting and simply wrapped my arms around his broad shoulders and gave myself over to his kiss as his mouth opened against mine.

It could only have been a matter of a minute or two, for Gage had just begun hitching up my skirts when I heard a strangled gasp and then a shriek.

I pushed against Gage, thinking at first that someone had stumbled across us in our embrace. But he was slow to come to his senses and lower me to the floor, allowing me time to process the sounds we'd heard even as my heart still pounded in my ears.

Something about the shriek seemed amiss. It had been less an exclamation of shock and more one of horror or fear.

As soon as I felt steady on my feet, I strode toward the opposite side of the gallery, while Gage followed more slowly. It was several steps before I could distinguish the shape of another person in the cloud-shrouded moonlight. Which meant it was unlikely they'd known that Gage and I had been engrossed in a passionate encounter on the far end of the room. A suspicion which was confirmed when their shadow jolted in fright and began to scramble backward.

"Please, don't be alarmed," I called out to them. "We heard your shriek and came to see what had distressed you."

As I drew nearer, I was able to distinguish more details of the figure and recognized it was Miss Ferguson, the governess. She stood stiffly, her hand pressed to her mouth as she gazed back at me with wide eyes.

"Are you well?" I queried in concern. "What made you shriek?" When she didn't immediately respond but instead dropped her gaze, I began to wonder whether she had merely let the darkness play tricks with her. "Did you think you saw . . . ?" I broke off as my eyes better adjusted to the gloom, and I was able to discern a small mound on the floor near the wall. I realized then that Miss Ferguson had not been lowering her gaze in embarrassment but rather looking at the object lying there.

And as I strode closer, I discovered the reason for her fright. For the mound wasn't an object at all. It was a woman. And unless I was very much mistaken, she was dead.

CHAPTER 11

I hurried forward the last few feet, kneeling beside the woman. Her wide eyes stared unseeing toward the shadowed ceiling.

"What happened?" I gasped.

"I . . . I dinna ken?" Miss Ferguson stammered. "I just found her."

Alarmingly, blood trailed from the woman's nose and the corners of her eyes and mouth, leaving gory streaks and blotches across her face. Though it was obvious she was dead, I still reached for her wrist, checking for a pulse. Finding none, I lowered her hand back to her side. My heart hitched in sadness for the poor woman.

"Who is she?" Gage asked, coming to a halt behind me.

From her clothing, it was obvious she was a maid of some sort. And a relatively young one.

"I . . . I dinna ken that either," Miss Ferguson said. "But she's no' one o' the maids here. Least, no' one *I've* ever seen."

Then what was she doing here?

The question flittered across my mind before I redirected my thoughts to more pressing matters. "Are you recovered?" I turned to ask the governess. "Can you go and fetch Wheaton for us?" The butler would be the first among many people who would need to be told. "Have him inform Lord Barbreck." He would know whether the marquess was in a state to hear such news or too inebriated from the Punch to understand clearly. "And tell him we'll need candles, blankets, and a footman or two."

She nodded and hastened back the way she must have come. I spared a moment to ponder why she'd been crossing the long gallery at such a late hour and then filed it away to be addressed later.

"What would cause her to bleed from her orifices like that?" Gage asked, lowering himself to one knee beside me. I noted that his speech was still less precise than usual, but he seemed to be mostly in control of his faculties even if he was a trifle disguised. So perhaps two sheets to the wind rather than three.

"Well . . ." I sighed. "Several things, actually. But I'll need to examine her in better light to be able to tell you more."

He nodded and then stumbled to his feet. "I'll find you a brace of candles." I turned to watch him cross the gallery, walking in more or less a straight line. So perhaps he *was* three sheets to the wind, but thank heavens he wasn't spoony drunk and useless at four. Regardless, had he been in full possession of his senses, I knew that he would never have left me alone. Not without knowing whether the maid had met with foul play, and if she had that the killer was not still lurking nearby. It didn't matter that I suspected they were long gone.

I shook my head at this turn of events. What a night for all the gentlemen to be cup-shot.

But perhaps that had been intentional.

I frowned at the possibility. *If* the maid had been murdered, and it had been intentionally done here, then I supposed the killer might have taken advantage of the gentlemen's plans. That would also indicate premeditation. But I was getting ahead of myself.

Turning my head, I surveyed my surroundings, trying to understand what had brought the maid here. It had almost certainly been dark, as it was now. Her body was still quite warm, suggesting she'd died but a short time ago.

My gaze lifted to the wall above us, and I realized with a jolt that she was lying underneath the forged Van Dyck. A sickening swirl began in my stomach, for I knew that could not be a coincidence. Had she come to view the painting, or perhaps she'd been lured here and then killed? I knew from Bree and Anderley's reports that the servants were aware of the forgeries—and aghast at the news. It seemed a natural curiosity that they should wish to see the objects that had caused such a stir among the guests. Or had she been moved here?

Either way, I couldn't help but wonder if the maid's death was somehow connected to the forgeries. Whether it was a warning to those of us who might attempt to probe deeper.

I shivered at the thought, wishing Gage would return soon. How far would he have to venture to find a brace of candles?

I studied the woman's face again, her unseeing eyes. Though it would stain my fingers with her blood, I decided to reach out and close them. Perhaps the gallery would seem less unnerving without her flat stare. Perhaps it would banish the sensation that I was being watched, though from where, I couldn't have said. There was no way to sneak up on someone here, nowhere to hide except in the shadows at the ends of the room, and if I couldn't see them, then they couldn't see me.

Tugging my handkerchief from my tufted sleeve, I wiped my fingers and then tilted my head. Something about the maid seemed familiar, though I couldn't say why. Maybe it was nothing but a family resemblance. After all, in rural and remote areas, many times parents and children, brothers and sisters, and even cousins served in the same grand household, generation after generation. Half the staff of my brother-in-law's estate at Gairloch Castle were kin, related to each other in one way or another.

The gallery was quiet—too quiet—with naught but the sound of my breathing and the rustle of my garments. Even the wind appeared to be calm that night. I found my ears straining at the hint of any noise. Was that a door closing farther along the corridor? A child crying? A dog barking? Were those footsteps?

I stilled, my muscles tense until I was certain that I was, indeed, hearing footsteps. Multiple pairs of them. A faint light appeared at the end of the gallery, growing ever brighter, and then Gage and Wheaton, Barbreck's butler, appeared, followed by at least one other servant. They each held a brace of candles, making me blink at the sudden brightness as they approached.

Something of my unease must have communicated itself to the men, for Gage's eyes anxiously scoured my face. "Is something amiss?"

I shook my head, not wishing to dwell on my own fevered imaginings. "Bring those candles closer."

The bleeding from the maid's orifices was even more ghastly in the light. The red blood mottled her features and stained her dark hairline. However, I was still able to recall now where I had seen her.

"This is one of the Campbells' maids," I exclaimed. "From Poltalloch."

I looked up at the men for confirmation, and Wheaton and the darker-haired footman both leaned closer.

"You're correct, m'lady," Wheaton declared, sorrow settling over his features. "That's Mairi MacCowan. Her father is an old retainer o' Lord Barbreck. Lives in a cottage no' far from here," he added in his gentle burr. "Just up the river."

"Is?" I repeated. "Then he's still alive?"

"Aye. He'll take the news hard, I imagine."

I frowned at the maid, puzzled by another of the butler's comments. "Her father served Lord Barbreck, but she chose to work for the Campbells?"

"Aye, my lady. The people here need the work. And they'll take a position wherever they're offered one."

I studied his sturdy features. At no more than two score years of age, he was one of the youngest butlers I'd met and couldn't have been in his position long. However, he spoke confidently about the locals, making me suspect he was one of them, perhaps having worked his way up the ranks here to his current position.

I recalled what Jack had said at dinner—about the lack of land and employment. Those who hadn't been driven off by the clearances—moving to Glasgow or Edinburgh to find work or immigrating to America—must take employment where they could. After all, what good was clan loyalty when your stomach went empty?

All the same, the dubious nature of a Campbell maid being found dead here, under the forged Van Dyck painting of all places, by pure chance could not be ignored. And the fact that her father had been a loyal retainer of Lord Barbreck set off even more alarm bells.

"Do you know how she came to be here?" Gage asked, swaying slightly. "Did she have friends among the staff?"

"I would have to ask," Wheaton replied. "But I imagine so."

"Mairi went aroond wi' Liam," the dark-haired footman interjected, drawing his superior's gaze. "Ye ken, regular-like."

What the butler thought of this comment, I wasn't entirely sure, but he seemed doubtful.

"You mean, he was her beau?" I tried to clarify.

The footman nodded. "Aye."

Wheaton continued to eye the younger man askance even as

he explained. "Liam Gillies is our first footman. And if what Callum says is true . . ." He hesitated briefly, as if to indicate he would be verifying that assertion with the remainder of the staff—a task easily done—so he'd better not be lying. "Then the fact that Liam disappeared from his duties earlier this evenin' is troublin'."

Callum's brow tightened, clearly disliking having his honesty questioned.

So this was the footman Bree had spoken of so often during the past few days. I couldn't say I blamed her. He was a good-looking lad, possessing a youthful vigor and a rugged Highlander's physique that was certain to turn heads. However, I found myself wondering what it said about him that Wheaton didn't entirely trust his word. Was this merely an indicator of the inherent rivalry that must exist between a first and second footman, or something specific to Callum?

Whatever the case, Liam's absence was, indeed, noteworthy if not outright suspicious.

"Please let me know when he turns up," Gage told the butler.

"O' course."

I lowered my gaze to scrutinize the maid's face while he instructed the two men to leave their candles and collect blankets and something sturdy to carry her on. As they hastened away, I offered my husband a tight smile of gratitude. He knew I preferred to conduct my examinations without others looking on in shock and disgust. That my reputation preceded me—having been forced to sketch my first husband's dissections for the anatomy textbook he was writing—lessened their astonishment somewhat, but not the revulsion many still felt at the idea of a gentlewoman assessing a corpse, no matter my and Gage's renown as inquiry agents.

Gage made a slow semicircle around me and the corpse, scrutinizing the floor carefully before he stepped, and set a brace of candles near her head and feet. "What do you think? Was Miss MacCowan curious about the portrait Lord Barbreck accused her employer of forging and stealing? Maybe she overheard him blaming her. So she asked her beau to sneak her up here to see it."

"Maybe," I replied obliquely, leaning closer to examine the maid's nostrils.

"But then what?" Gage continued in bafflement. "He attacked her? With what? How did he make her bleed from her mouth, nose, and eyes?"

I pulled down on the maid's jaw, peering into her mouth. "Bring that light closer," I instructed him as I tilted her head to get a better look inside her mouth.

"What is it? What do you see?"

"Ulcers," I replied absently, sinking back on my heels as I racked my brain for something that would cause these symptoms. Furrowing my brow in consternation, I felt her lymph nodes and down her neck. I examined her head for any indication of a blow, but there was no fracturing, and the only blood appeared to be from her facial orifices. A brief scrutiny of her torso and limbs showed there were no punctures, abrasions, or scrapes, and no defensive wounds either. There were no injuries of any kind save a small burn on the inside of her arm, and she could have easily suffered that from mishandling a clothing iron or dropping a pair of curling tongs.

"So strange," I murmured to myself, scrubbing the blood from my hands as best as I could with merely a handkerchief to hand.

"What is?" Gage asked, gripping my elbow to help me rise to my feet.

"It seems she was poisoned." I gestured toward the body, the flickering light of the candles casting it in a yellow glow. "For I can find no evidence of physical violence. But I've never heard of a poison that causes bleeding from the eyes, nose, and mouth." I tilted my head. "Not that I'm all that versed in poisons to begin with. But I did familiarize myself with the symptoms of the most common ones after the events in Edinburgh last spring."

"A poison?" Gage repeated.

I nodded. "Yes. One she probably ingested. At least the ulcers inside her mouth seem to indicate so."

"Then the footman—Liam—might not be responsible? That is, if he's the person who helped her gain access to the long gallery."

"Not necessarily. Some poisons act quickly, but others do not. She might have ingested it hours ago, long before she arrived at Barbreck Manor." My mouth flattened. "But you raise an interesting point. Clearly an outsider *could* gain access to the long gallery. An outsider from the Campbells' household. Though as far as we can tell, she wasn't carrying anything." I lifted my gaze to the Van Dyck, verifying it was the same one I'd examined two days prior.

"You think someone was trying to make a point?" He widened his stance, planting his hands on his hips. "But to what end? And why poison the maid?"

"To prove that an outsider could have switched the paintings. Though the person trying to make that point and the poisoner need not be the same person." I scowled, scrutinizing the body and the floor nearby again. "And yet, it doesn't make sense to even try to make that point unless she was intended to be caught. Or unless she left something behind."

"Perhaps Liam took it with him."

"Perhaps."

Gage turned his head sideways to look at me, but I kept my eyes trained on the deceased maid before me—Mairi—searching for the explanation, the anomaly. But I feared it wasn't to be found here.

"What's bothering you about this?" he asked.

I finally looked up at him.

He offered me a gentle smile. "I know that brilliant brain of yours. Your artist's eye. Your instinct. And I can tell when something has you flustered. So, what is it?"

I sighed. "You mean, other than the obvious?"

"Of course. Murder—whether suspected or proven—is never pleasant."

I'd noted that the longer we talked, the more sober he'd become. Had that not been true, I might have brushed his question aside. But while I still wouldn't trust him to carry me steadily down the stairs, I could tell his intellect had not deserted him, and there was no risk he wouldn't recall this conversation tomorrow.

"It simply doesn't make sense," I blurted. "What was Mairi doing here? And why? If it was simple curiosity, then *how* did she end up poisoned? And if it *wasn't*, if she was sent here to make a point, then how did she make it to this room without raising Liam's alarm?" I shook my head in frustration. "She must have experienced *some* symptoms before reaching the gallery. Cramping or nausea, an elevated heartbeat, sweating, *something*! It's highly improbable she just dropped dead without any idea of what was happening."

"Are we certain she died here?"

It was a logical question, and I gave it due consideration. "I'm sure you already spotted the drops of blood on the floor and wall, there and there." I pointed. "And there may be more underneath the body. Her hands are covered with it, as would be expected if she lifted them to her face to try to find out what was happening. The pattern of the blood pooling on the floor and onto her bodice seems consistent with the way it would have flowed from the position she was found lying in." I glanced in both directions down the gallery. "You didn't spy any blood droplets leading away from the body?"

"No, but whoever moved her here might have cleaned them up."

"True." I clamped my lips together, reviewing everything I had said for flaws. "But I still think this is where she died."

Gage nodded, trusting my judgment. "Then we have a whole slew of questions that need to be answered. Starting with how she gained access to the manor."

Hearing the sound of footsteps approaching, indicating the return of the butler and the second footman, I knew we hadn't much time for further private consult. "Has Barbreck been informed?"

"I told Wheaton not to bother. He was already as drunk as an emperor when I left the library. I daresay he's insensible by now. We'll inform him in the morning." He grimaced. "And what a pleasant conversation *that* will be."

Considering the ferocious headaches and hangovers I'd expected all of the gentlemen—and even some of the ladies—to have, I'd already been anticipating a fraught morning best spent in the garden or the long gallery, far away from the grumbling and growling. But it looked like that was no longer going to be possible.

"I'll make certain Wheaton secures Miss MacCowan's body someplace cool, and then take Anderley with me to uncover the likeliest path of her entry and speak to what servants we can. Perhaps one of them saw something or knows where we can find her alleged beau, Liam. The rest will have to wait until the morning."

"Good. And I have Emma to attend to," I replied, wondering how I was going to settle myself before then. She could sense even the smallest hint of anxiety and would then begin to fuss rather than feed.

I took a deep, calming breath, stepping back from the body as Wheaton and Callum drew nearer. "Mairi's father will have to be notified. As well as the Campbells."

"Tomorrow," Gage asserted and pulled me in close, draping a protective arm around me. I turned my head into his broad chest and shoulders, drawing strength from his warmth and solidity. After one final inhalation of his scent, which always seemed to steady me, I stepped away. Then with a nod of farewell to the men, I slipped away in the direction Miss Ferguson had come and gone.

Exiting into the corridor, I discovered an opening to a second set of stairs directly to my right. I realized that these must lead down to the staircase across the hall from Gage's assigned bedchamber. Then *this* corridor led to the nursery and the governess's room, as well as several other bedchambers. If so, then perhaps Miss Ferguson utilized the long gallery as some sort of shortcut. But to where?

I continued to puzzle over this question as I descended the stairs, confirming their position inside the manor. However, the faint sound of a baby's cry soon drove everything from my mind. Emma had awakened early, and it sounded like settling her to feed was going to be difficult enough without me adding my worries to the matter.

CHAPTER 12

One blessed consequence of motherhood, and being awakened at odd hours to nurse, was that when I *did* get to actually sleep, I fell into it faster and more deeply than I'd ever done so my entire life. There was something incredibly soothing about cradling my child skin to skin and knowing that I was meeting her needs. Some nights I sat holding her long after she'd fallen back into a milk-induced slumber simply to study her tiny little face. But once I'd settled her in her cradle, I would stumble back to bed and collapse, barely making it under the covers before I drifted back to sleep.

So I did not stir when Gage climbed into bed sometime later, my hearing only being attuned to wake me at the sound of Emma's crying. But when I woke to collect our daughter for her three o'clock feeding, I discovered he was there. He rolled over and grumbled, so when I was roused by her again around seven o'clock, I decided to leave her in Mrs. Mackay's care rather than bring her into our bed with me as I did on some mornings. Her giggles and chatter and drooling baby grins were the perfect start to the day.

However, I returned to our bedchamber to find Gage propped up by his pillows with one arm flung over his head. His torso was bare, and the sheet had slipped down to his abdomen, revealing his muscular physique. His gaze shifted to me from where he had been staring, unseeing, at something across the room. I could already see the thoughts churning in his head, analyzing the previous evening's fatal discovery, but he made an effort to alter them, smiling softly at me as I strode across the room.

"No Emma?"

"I thought you might be suffering some ill effects from last night's indulgence," I replied, lifting aside the covers to slide under them. The tightness of his brow and the slight pallor of his features told me he hadn't escaped entirely, but he was in far better condition than I'd anticipated.

He slid his arm underneath me and turned toward me as I snuggled in close. His voice was still husky from sleep. "It's just as well, for I *do* believe we were interrupted in the middle of something last night."

"Hmm, yes. In the *middle* of the long gallery." I teasingly arched my eyebrows. "Where anyone could have stumbled upon us."

Rather than turn sheepish, as I expected, Gage slid his other hand up my leg under my nightdress, pulling the limb over his hip. "Not the most sensible place for a seduction, I admit, but the configuration that developed proved interesting."

"Did it?" I replied rather breathlessly as he rolled me beneath him.

His lips found the sensitive skin behind my ear, the bristles on his jaw lightly abrading my skin and making me arch my back in pleasure. "Don't tell me you didn't find the idea of my making love to you against that wall exciting. I know you did," he drawled, reminding me that my husband had never been meek when it came to bedroom matters. Even if he had been tamer in recent months because of my being heavy with child and then recently delivered.

"Yes," I admitted. "Until . . ." I broke off, some of my ardor fading at the memory of what had come next. "Maybe we shouldn't . . ."

Gage lifted his head to gaze down at me, his pupils wide with desire, but tenderness was there as well. "Kiera, if we stopped coming together for every murder or crime we encountered, we would practically be celibate."

"True," I conceded. An alarming number of murders did seem to occur within our vicinity, though more often they happened *before* we were summoned to the scene.

"It's a hazard of the profession. But in all earnestness, if facing death and murder doesn't make us embrace life and cherish what we have . . ." His voice dipped, throbbing with intensity. "If it doesn't make us hold tight to those we love, then what will?"

My heart swelled at the truth of that statement and my love for this man. I responded by pressing my mouth to his and giving myself over to the passion I felt for him.

Sometime later, I still lay wrapped in his strong arms, cocooned with contentment. But that serenity and satisfaction began to slip away as the reality of what we faced intruded. Somehow Mairi MacCowan had been poisoned by an as-yet-unknown substance, either intentionally or by accident. Somehow she had died beneath the recently revealed forgery of a Van Dyck, one her employer had just days before been accused of swapping for the real portrait. These were factors which could not simply be written off as coincidence and ignored.

I lifted my head from where it had lapsed on Gage's chest, expecting to find he'd fallen back to sleep after his thorough efforts, but I should have known better. He had never been the type of person content to rest on his laurels when there was an investigation afoot, and the alertness of his pale blue eyes told me that even now he was contemplating the matter.

"What did you and Anderley uncover last night?" I asked, lowering my head again to his warm skin.

He inhaled deeply, causing his chest to rise and the muscles along his torso to do interesting things. It seemed he was as reluctant to return to the matter at hand as I had been, even if his thoughts had already wandered there. "Several of the scullery maids recalled seeing Miss MacCowan arrive through the servants' entrance. Apparently, her presence wasn't entirely noteworthy, as she and the footman Liam had been courting for some time, and she would often walk to Barbreck on her days and half days off to see her father and to visit Liam."

"Then she was familiar to the staff?" I ruminated, idly swirling my fingers through the chest hair several shades darker than the golden locks on his head.

"Yes, and with Liam being her confirmed beau, he is the most likely person to have shown her up to the long gallery. No one Anderley and I spoke to recalled seeing him after dinner was finished being served and cleared. But, of course, some of the members of the staff had already retired. We'll have to speak with them today."

I tried to piece together her movements in my mind, but they were mired by several thorny problems. "She must have spoken to some of them. Did she tell them why she was here?"

"Of course, but they all claimed to exchange no more than small talk and local gossip with her. And they assumed she was merely here to see Liam, as usual."

I lifted my head, propping myself up on my elbows. "But surely that was an odd hour for her to be here? So late in the evening."

He lifted his hand, scraping it through his hair and further rumpling his already tousled tresses. "I asked the same thing, but I gathered Miss MacCowan often visited with her father first and arrived here late in the afternoon into the evening. Especially during the summer when the sun sets so late, and the gloaming lasts long after that. Liam would escort her part of the way back to Poltalloch before returning." His hand rasped through the bristles along his jaw before hooking the pillow behind his head.

"You look thoroughly tumbled," I remarked in amusement. Rarely was he ever anything but immaculately groomed, and seeing him thus always melted something inside me.

"Speak for yourself," he replied with a wolfish grin, reaching out to flick the end of my braid that trailed over my shoulder. It had come partially undone, and I could feel waves of my hair caressing the sides of my face and tickling my back. But given the fact that Gage was prone to removing the braid entirely, burying his hands in my chestnut brown tresses, I considered partially undone to be rather tidy.

I grasped his shoulders and pulled myself higher up his chest to press a kiss to his lips. "What are our next steps?" I queried, as much to myself as him. "I suppose the remaining servants will have to be interviewed, and Mairi's father must be informed, as well as Lord Barbreck and the Campbells."

"That will be a good start. And I suspect you also want to consult what books are available on the topic in Barbreck's library to find out what poison the maid ingested."

I doubted his collection on such a subject was very extensive, but I had to begin somewhere, and that was the obvious place.

He brushed several loose tendrils of hair back from my face. "But first, I think we should meet with Bree and Anderley. Anderley intimated your maid has become quite friendly with the staff here and might know some things the rest of us don't. Perhaps that will save us some time and allow us to better divide and conquer."

I tried not to read anything more into Anderley's comments to Gage, but I couldn't help it. Especially when I could tell my husband was couching his words in the best terms possible. I'd wondered what the valet thought of Bree's renewed self-confidence and her friendship with the second footman, Callum. Bree fit in well here, she was comfortable, and the attentions of an attractive man had brought a welcome flush back to her cheeks. It appeared Anderley didn't look upon all of this quite so favorably, but was that just jealousy talking, or was there really cause for concern?

"I'll ring for her and order our breakfast brought up on trays." It was doubtful any of the other guests would be up and about at this hour anyway, if they were awake at all. "We can talk after we're dressed."

I shifted to pull away, but he clasped the back of my head, pulling me back to him for one more devastating kiss.

"Any more of that, and we'll never make it out of this bed," I quipped.

He heaved an aggrieved sigh. "The things I sacrifice for the good of the rule of law."

I smiled before turning away to search for my nightdress. I found it tossed carelessly toward the end of the bed. "Such nobility. Don't worry. I shall reward you for it later," I told him, pulling the garment over my head.

"Will you?" His eyes heated with promises. "Then, I shall hold you to it."

I slid from bed and, with a provocative wiggle, tugged my garment the rest of the way down. "I'm counting on it," I replied, tossing a saucy look over my shoulder to find his eyes fastened on my lower extremities.

He made a lunge for me, but I dashed away, laughing, and yanked the bell-pull.

Perhaps half an hour later we found ourselves seated near the rounded bay of windows in our bedchamber. Gage and I perched side by side on the couch, finishing our breakfasts, while at our urging Bree and Anderley settled into the chairs flanking either side. I brushed the crumbs from the royal blue skirts of my riding habit and picked up my cup of warm chocolate, savoring it slowly as I observed them both while Gage explained the situation.

Bree looked fresh and lovely this morning in a gown of dusty lavender, her strawberry blond curls becomingly restrained. She reacted with appropriate concern and empathy to the topic of Mairi MacCowan's death, but it did not dim her natural cheer and good humor. Meanwhile, Anderley was quieter and more reserved than I'd grown accustomed to his being when we were all speaking in private. He appeared almost brooding, which I noted was no detriment to his dark good looks, but perhaps he was merely fatigued from lack of sleep.

Having finished reviewing what we had already discovered, Gage took a drink of his coffee before sitting back against the sofa cushions. "We will need to finish interviewing the rest of the staff today. A task I would like to leave in your hands," he told them both. "But first, Miss McEvoy, I would like to hear your impressions of the staff and everything we've learned so far."

"O' course," she replied, folding her hands in her lap. "What would ye like to ken?"

"First of all, did *you* have any interactions with Miss Mac-Cowan?"

"Aye, I spoke wi' her for aboot . . ." She tilted her head in thought. "Five minutes, I would say." She glanced toward me. "I was mendin' a rip in one o' m'lady's hems."

"And how did she seem?"

She shrugged. "She seemed nice. We didna have time to ex-change more 'an the usual pleasantries and lighthearted grum-bles o' a maid's life." Her eyes narrowed, lifting to the ceiling. "Though, noo that I think aboot it, she did seem a trifle pale and nervous. And she had a bit o' a cough. I thought she was merely anxious to see Liam, and a bit embarrassed, feelin' in the way wi' all the comings and goings from both the gentlemen's and ladies' dinners, but maybe I was wrong."

Gage's gaze shifted to meet mine. "What about the footman Liam? What do you make of him?"

"As far as I can tell, everyone seems to like him. Kens his business and doesna make trouble for others. But he's quiet and mostly keeps to himself. I dinna think he's said more 'an a dozen words to me since our arrival, but he's always verra pleasant." She nodded toward the valet. "He's said more to Anderley than me, so he's probably able to tell ye more than I can."

Gage neither confirmed nor denied this, instead pressing her on the point he clearly wanted to know most. "Do you think he might have been capable of violence or discreetly poisoning someone?"

Bree straightened in surprise. "Weel, I dinna ken. A brief acquaintance doesna really tell ye much aboot a person, noo does it? But if I had to give ye my best impression, then nay. At least, not o' the violence." She shook her head. "And I canna say aboot the poisonin'. That's trickier to tell."

Gage nodded, turning to his valet. "Has he turned up yet?"

"No. The last thing I heard of the matter before answering your summons was Callum grumbling about having to manage Liam's duties as well as his own."

A tiny pleat formed in Bree's brow and then smoothed away.

"Are the other staff members concerned about him?" Gage queried.

"Aye," Bree replied. "The housekeeper told me it's no' like Liam to disappear or to be slack in his work. That he's always been as reliable as the sunrise."

I lowered my cup to the table. "Then I suppose the question is, do we think Liam had anything to do with Mairi's death, or has he made himself scarce because he's afraid of being accused?"

Gage's eyes searched my features. "What do you think?"

"I think it's the latter for several reasons. She was killed by a poison she ingested. One that I strongly suspect was slow-acting. Otherwise, we should have found evidence in the gallery or on her clothes that she ate or drank something." I began ticking off the possibilities. "Crumbs, a spilled cup, remnants in her mouth." I gestured toward my maid. "Bree says she was pale, nervous, and coughing, which could all be indicators she already wasn't feeling well when she arrived at Barbreck. Yet upon first glance, the bleeding from Mairi's facial orifices made her death look violent. She looked as if she'd been beaten." I turned to Gage, knowing he would agree with this statement. "Imagine Liam standing next to Mairi, his sweetheart, and suddenly she begins dripping blood down her face. Perhaps he tried to help her, getting blood on himself in the process, and then she drops dead. He must have been shocked and bereft, but also terrified. He wouldn't know how to even begin to explain it. Given all that, it's understandable that he might have panicked and fled."

Anderley nodded. "As the only person present at the time of her death, he must have known blame and suspicion would fall on him." The taut expression on his face told me he empathized with the footman. As a fellow male servant, he was the likeliest person among us to understand precisely what Liam had been thinking and feeling, and what he'd faced with such an accusation made against him.

"Then we all agree he probably ran out of fear rather than

guilt," Gage concluded. "But he still may know or have seen something that could tell us what happened. We need to find him."

"Speak to the butler and housekeeper," I directed Anderley and Bree. "Find out if Liam has any family living nearby."

"I'll speak to Callum as well," Bree said. "He and Liam were friends, so he might o' told him things he wouldna told the others."

"They're also rivals," Anderley pointed out with a dark look. "With Liam gone, he'll be promoted to first footman. Or I imagine that's what he's counting on, at any rate."

Bree frowned. "That's a rather unworthy sentiment. He's expressed nothin' but concern for Liam."

"Between grumbling about the extra work he has to do in his absence," he reminded her.

She arched her chin. "Weel, I imagine you'd be grumblin', too, if you were in his place."

"Maybe. But perhaps it's best if *I* be the one to speak with him. I suspect he's all too aware of your sympathy for his plight and likely to take advantage of it."

"I'm no' so easily gammoned as that," she retorted, bristling with anger. "Besides, he's no' likely to talk to *you*. Thinks you're stuffy and self-important. A regular English nob."

"Does he, now?" Anderley drawled warningly, leaning forward in his chair.

"Enough." Gage cast a quelling look at both of them. "Miss McEvoy, because you are already on friendly terms with Callum, you will speak with him."

Out of the corner of my eye, I noticed Anderley's hands tighten on the arms of his chair before releasing. This may have been done chiefly in frustration at not getting his way, but I suspected the rather smug tilt to Bree's lips provoked some of it. However, Gage wasn't finished speaking.

"But you should know, Miss McEvoy," he added soberly, repeating her name in order to reclaim her full attention. "That Callum was the first to point out Liam's connection to Miss MacCowan *and* his absence. And I couldn't help but notice that Wheaton was not impressed with the young man."

The smirk faded from her lips, and her gaze slid toward me, perhaps seeking confirmation of these assessments.

"Bear that in mind as you weigh what he has to tell you," Gage warned.

She nodded, and the conversation moved on to my and Gage's intentions for the day. Some of which should have been abundantly clear, as we had both dressed in riding attire. Mr. Mac-Cowan lived just a short distance from the manor, and we would need to leave soon if we were to return in time for Emma's mid-morning feeding. Then we could depart on the lengthier trip to see the Campbells.

"Bree, I would like you to be ready to ride with us to Poltalloch," I told her. "We need someone belowstairs to assess the reactions of the staff members to the news of Mairi MacCowan's death, and as a fellow Scotswoman, I'm hopeful they'll be inclined to speak with you."

"I suppose that means I'm to remain here," Anderley remarked in a voice that was carefully indifferent. Too carefully, to my mind.

Before Gage or I could reply, reminding him of the mistrust many Highlanders held of outsiders, Bree spoke up. "Oh, I dinna ken. I suspect ye could still prove useful." A glint of devilry lit her eyes. "Puttin' that legendary charm o' yours to work on the maids. Even a Highland lass falls for such allure from time to time."

Anderley stilled, seeming uncertain how to react at first, and I couldn't blame him. One of Bree's chief complaints during the months they'd courted was about how Anderley couldn't seem to resist beguiling and flirting with other females, especially during the course of our investigations when he needed to gain information from them. To hear her jest about it now was surprising. We could be excused for searching her words and tone for hidden barbs and meanings. When she flashed him a brilliant smile, however, I joined in her amusement, realizing she was poking fun at herself as much as him.

Anderley, for his part, seemed equally as startled by her dazzling smile as her teasing. I couldn't help but wonder if this time around, he was the one being beguiled.

Gage dipped his head. "Then, Anderley, be prepared to join us, too."

The matter being settled, we scattered to our various tasks, but not before I noticed Bree observing Anderley surreptitiously beneath her lashes. I had known better than to believe that whatever had been between them was entirely over, and I could only hope that whatever happened next was less fraught than what had come before.

CHAPTER 13

Mairi MacCowan's father lived in a small cottage about a mile to the east, along the banks of the River Barbreck. Tucked into a bend of the river near a slight elevation increase, it was perfectly situated to catch the musical cascade of water over rocks. Upon first glance it appeared like many crofter cottages—a spare rectangle built from weathered stone topped by a steeply pitched thatch roof—but the closer we drew, the better able I was to pick out the finer details. Wooden trim had been fitted around the windows and carved with vines and flowers, and before the door had been built a porch of about the size, shape, and construction of a lychgate.

From these hints alone, it was clear Kennan MacCowan not only took pride in his home but also was a skilled carpenter. In fact, I began to suspect that was the position he'd held at the estate before he was pensioned off, and when we were ushered inside by a lean, stoop-shouldered man with nothing but wisps of gray hair clinging to his head, this was all but confirmed. The stone floor was crude though neatly swept, and all but bare except for the finely crafted furnishings. They were simple and unassuming, but fashioned and smoothed, and stained with such mastery that they had to be the work of a true artist.

So much so that my husband was momentarily distracted from the reason for our visit. Being an amateur carpenter himself, taught by his grandfather, he possessed a genuine appreciation for such craftsmanship. One that was evident in the number of questions he peppered Mr. MacCowan with if not the avid gleam of admiration in his eyes.

For a minute or two, I was content to allow their talk of planes, marquetry, and dovetail joints to wash over me, but the longer their conversation dragged on, the more uncomfortable I became. I wandered nearer to the hearth where he was scrutinizing the mantle, ostensibly to examine the single picture hanging on the whitewashed walls—an embroidered verse from the Gospel of Matthew, part of the Beatitudes—though I kept darting looks at Gage, hoping to catch his eye. When that didn't work, I cleared my throat once and then twice, finally drawing both men's notice. I widened my eyes briefly at Gage, trying to nudge his memory, but it was Mr. MacCowan who spoke first.

"Did ye wish to commission me to make something for ye? I'm afraid I dinna do much buildin' noo-a-days." He lifted his hands to show us his gnarled fingers. "Rheumatism. 'Twas why I agreed to be pensioned. Couldna do much anyways."

Gage flushed, clearly recognizing why I'd been attempting to signal him. He'd let his enthusiasm for Mr. MacCowan's skill temporarily blind him. "No, I apologize. We're actually here for a rather more serious reason."

"Oh?" he replied, gesturing for us to be seated.

I selected a chair below the high open window through which I could hear the river and the birds.

"I'm so sorry to have to tell you this," Gage continued as he perched on the edge of its twin. "But your daughter, Mairi, was found dead yesterday evening."

"Dead?" he replied in startlement.

"Yes," Gage replied, and then paused to allow the man to absorb this information.

Mr. MacCowan rocked back in his chair and swiped a hand over the bristles on his jaw as he stared unseeing at the floor. His skin was ashen and his eyes glassy with shock.

"Can I get you a glass of water?" I asked him, concerned for his health.

"Nay," he croaked. "Nay, thank you." He blinked through a sheen of tears as he looked up at us. "How?"

"We believe she was poisoned, though we're not certain if it was accidental or . . ." Gage broke off, suddenly hesitant to continue, perhaps concerned how the elderly man would react.

"Or murder," he finished for him, swallowing thickly around the word.

Gage nodded.

He inhaled a ragged breath, as if making himself face the possibility, and then he eyed us both evenly. "You mun' have questions for me."

Gage and I exchanged a glance, and I nodded for him to continue. My throat was too tight to speak. Somehow this man's quiet grief and acceptance was more difficult to face than the histrionics such news was often met with.

"We understand that Mairi visited you yesterday afternoon? That she often came to see you on her days off and then stopped at the manor."

"To see Liam, aye," Mr. MacCowan said. "And aye, Mairi was here yesterday. She cooked dinner, and we ate together before she left." At this, he blinked rapidly and turned his head to the side, perhaps confronting the fact that that was the last time he would ever see his daughter. I lifted my eyes to the embroidered verse. At least, here on earth.

"What did you eat?"

"Mince and tatties."

"No mushrooms? No berries?" I interjected.

"Nay mushrooms. But we did eat a few o' the blaeberries she picked on her walk here. They were from a patch we ken weel. They're no' poisonous."

I nodded. Bilberries were a common enough fruit, though stains caused by their juices were the very devil to get out. Or so I'd been told.

"Did your daughter eat anything that you didn't?" Gage pressed, just to be clear, but Mr. MacCowan shook his head.

"How was she?" I asked, switching topics, for it seemed that whatever poison she'd ingested, it had not happened here. "Did she appear healthy? Was anything preying on her mind?"

"She seemed tired," he replied. "But she often did." His brow furrowed. "And she had a bit o' a cough."

"A wet one? Or was it dry?"

"Wet. I asked if she wished to pass the night here, but she had to be back to Poltalloch by midnight in case Miss Margaret had need o' her."

"That's who she served?" I asked, having wondered what her exact position was. On our visit to Poltalloch, she had acted as more of a downstairs maid, carrying the tea tray, but I suspected that wasn't her normal duty.

"She did a little o' this and a little o' that," he replied, a reminder that, due to their nephew's profligate ways, the Campbell sisters had to do with less staff. He sighed. "And she said she needed to see Liam."

I resisted the urge to look at Gage, thinking that might be too telling.

"Did she say why she was anxious to speak with him?" Gage inquired.

Mr. MacCowan shook his head listlessly. "Nay, but surely he can tell ye that."

When neither of us responded, he looked up at us warily.

"Liam Gillies is missing," Gage explained. "And it's believed he was the last person to see your daughter."

I expected to encounter some sort of doubt or recriminations from Mairi's father about the first footman, but I was swiftly proven wrong.

"Then he mun' have been frightened," he declared. "Liam Gillies wouldna harm a flea, let alone my daughter. That lad has more honor in his little finger than most gentlemen possess in their whole body."

I found this to be a curious statement, and rather a scathing indictment of the gentlemen he'd had contact with. But before I could ponder more than Lord Barbreck and his broken engagement to Miss Campbell, Mr. MacCowan continued with a derisive snort.

"Why else do ye think I allowed him to go on escortin' Mairi home? I'd no' have done that for just anyone."

"We presumed as much," Gage told him calmly. "But all the same, we need to speak with him. To find out what he knows and whether he might have some idea how she ingested the poison. Do you have any idea where he might be? Does he have family nearby?"

Mr. MacCowan's stooped shoulders seemed to bow even further under the weight of all we'd told him. "Nay. His brother works at the shipyards doon in Clydebank, and his mam passed away a few years back."

Gage silently studied the man, perhaps uncertain how hard to press him. "Is there anything else we should know? Anything that might help us piece together what happened, and find the perpetrator if she was, indeed, poisoned deliberately."

His gaze lifted toward the door in the far corner, which I suspected led to a bedchamber. Perhaps he was thinking of his failure to convince Mairi to pass the night with him. What he didn't know, but I suspected, was that his daughter had already been poisoned before she arrived here. It was only a matter of time, then, before the toxic substance worked its way through her system.

He shook his head before allowing it to hang low.

"Well, if you should think of something, send for us at Barbreck Manor," Gage told him as we rose from our chairs. We had already taken several steps toward the door before he finally answered.

"Can ye tell me . . ."

I turned to look at his haggard face.

"Where was she found? Where is she noo?"

"The long gallery," Gage replied.

His head reared back in shock, clearly as surprised as we had been to find her there.

"And we placed her in the icehouse. It was the coolest location to put her until the authorities release her for burial." Since we had yet to speak to Barbreck about the matter, we didn't know who that figure would be. Whether the procurator fiscal would need to be called in or a local magistrate or other official could handle the matter. Few things were uniform throughout the Highlands, including their method of policing.

"You'll no' be cutting her, will ye?" His eyes suddenly blazed. "Because I willna give ye permission for that. I willna allow it."

I wasn't surprised to hear he was so adamant against it, or that he'd directed these comments toward me. Apparently, even in the depths of the Highlands, people were aware of my past. Many still viewed dissections and autopsies with fear and revulsion, convinced that if their bodies weren't interred whole and complete in a Christian burial, they wouldn't be able to rise again on Judgment Day. A fear that the present laws, which made the bodies of executed murderers the only legal supply of corpses for medical schools and anatomists, did nothing to help assuage.

Even now, however, Parliament was debating the merits of a second attempt to pass an Anatomy Act changing all that. I anticipated word from Philip, the Earl of Cromarty—my brother-in-law and a strong proponent for reform in the House of Lords—any day now on whether those efforts had succeeded.

An autopsy of Miss MacCowan might tell us more about what the poison had done to her internally—whether it had damaged her heart or lungs, her liver or kidneys—but I hadn't the heart or stomach to try to convince Mr. MacCowan otherwise if he was so set against it. And I certainly didn't have the authority.

"No autopsy is intended, at least by me. And we'll inform the authorities of your wishes," I said, refusing to flinch from his fiery gaze.

He held my gaze for a moment longer, as if gauging my trustworthiness, and then the fight seemed to drain from him. He subsided back into his chair with a weary nod, slumping forward in defeat.

I couldn't help but grieve for the old man, forced to bury his daughter when by all rights she should have long outlived him. I wondered who would look after him now.

And was surprised when I received an answer of sorts.

We had mounted our horses and steered them back down the path toward Barbreck Manor when Miss Ferguson suddenly emerged from the trees. The governess's head was bowed as if she was in deep thought, and it wasn't until we were nearly upon her that she looked up in surprise, side-stepping away from the ponies.

I studied her curiously as she hurried toward the cottage, questioning why she was there. She'd told us in the long gallery that she didn't recognize Mairi, leading me to believe they hadn't known each other. And yet here she was visiting Mairi's father. Was she merely here to pay her respects? Did she feel a responsibility to do so given the fact she'd practically tripped over his daughter's body? Or was there something more?

I cast one last glance over my shoulder before the cottage disappeared from sight to find Mr. MacCowan standing on the porch waiting for her. He lifted his arms as if to embrace her, but the foliage blocked my view before I actually saw him do so. Regardless, it seemed certain the two were not strangers, which made it difficult for me to believe she hadn't also known Mairi. I frowned, suspicious that Miss Ferguson had lied to us.

Upon our return to the manor, Gage ventured off to speak with Barbreck while I attended to Emma. My baby girl was all smiles, and I soon discovered my morose mood and gloomy ponderings were no match for her toothless grins and giggles. Part of me dreaded leaving her to travel to Poltalloch, so I dawdled, holding her on my lap as I made silly sounds and faces, making her laugh all the harder.

It was while I was blowing wet kisses on her palms, making her kick and chortle, that Charlotte found me.

"If society could see you now, they would never believe you're the same woman the scandal sheets wrote all those nasty insinuations about just three years ago." She leaned over my shoulder, making several ridiculous faces of her own as she cooed to Emma.

"Or that you were once dubbed 'The Ice Queen,'" I teased her in turn.

She sighed happily. "Babies make fools of us all."

"True." I smiled. "Or rather our love for them." I picked up one of Emma's ragdolls, wiggling it under her chin to tickle her.

"I hope it wasn't Mairi MacCowan's love for Liam that got her killed."

I looked up at Charlotte, allowing Emma to grab hold of the

doll and stuff one of its appendages in her mouth. "You heard about us finding her dead in the long gallery then."

Her expression was pensive. It was a look I'd seen before. Just six months prior, in fact, after we'd stumbled over a corpse at Sunlaws Castle just hours after she and Rye had announced their engagement. She'd worried it was an ill omen, and it had taken no small effort at first to convince her otherwise.

"Charlotte, you're not having second thoughts . . ." I began in concern, but she shook her head, cutting off my words.

"No. I know it's nonsense to believe in omens, or that Mairi MacCowan's death has anything to do with the happiness of my and Rye's marriage." She bit her lower lip, and I waited, knowing she had more to say. "But I'm not so sure my father will see it that way."

I offered her a commiserating look. She had already been nervous about her father's approval of her marriage, and murder— even of a maid and not a family member—only complicated matters.

"Then Gage and I shall just have to get to the bottom of it. Preferably *before* he arrives," I said, trying to reassure her.

"Do you think you can?" She sounded afraid to hope.

"We can certainly try."

She nodded and then flinched. "Oh, but how horribly insensitive I am." She pressed her hands to her cheeks. "Worrying about how this murder will affect me rather than the poor girl who was killed and her father. You and Gage went to inform him?"

"Yes."

"How devastated he must be. There *must* be something we can do for him."

"If I know my Aunt Cait, she's already planning something."

"Oh, but you're right. I should go see if I can help." She turned as if she intended to do just that and then stopped to look back at me. "Unless you need me to do something." She shook her head sadly. "Here you are, meant to be enjoying yourself in the country." She glanced at Emma. "Infant in tow. And yet again you're being asked to solve another murder."

Technically, we hadn't been asked to solve it. We'd simply taken the matter upon ourselves. But I suspected Barbreck was asking that very thing of Gage as we spoke.

"Does it ever grow tiresome?"

"Sometimes," I admitted.

After all, there was a reason it had been three and a half months since our last inquiry. But it seemed solving mysteries— even gruesome ones—was in our blood, for I felt my thoughts sharpening, my heart quickening, and my muscles tensing in anticipation of unraveling the puzzle presented to us.

"But as has been pointed out to me many times, I am an unusual . . . or rather, unnatural, if you prefer, person," I added with a wry grimace. "I seem unable to resist the challenge."

"Kiera, you are not unnatural," Charlotte stated with gentle firmness. "No matter how peculiar your penchants may seem to others. All I can say is *thank goodness* for them. For otherwise I would not be here." She arched her eyebrows in chastisement as much as reassurance as she reminded me of all that had been at stake during my first inquiry. Then, with a pat to my arm, she swept out of the room.

The weather at dawn had seemed fair enough, but as the morning progressed toward midday and we set off for Poltalloch Castle, a thick blanket of clouds rolled in, all but smothering what sunshine could penetrate through the cover. Much as on our journey two days prior, we could not do much talking until the horses had picked their way around the crag at the edge of the loch and we'd passed through the thickest part of the forest. However, Gage's expression upon mounting into our saddles had conveyed with no difficulty what Lord Barbreck's reaction had been to the news that a Campbell maid had been found dead in his long gallery.

As the trail widened near the lochan, Gage turned to speak to me, holding up his chestnut gelding so that I could ride alongside him. "Barbreck reacted about how we expected him to," he muttered wryly. "Raging against the Campbells. Insisting it was proof of their tampering with his artwork. Demanding we investigate."

"And in his crapulent state, I imagine he was even less pleasant than he's been the past few days," I replied.

He dipped his head in acknowledgment. "He was nursing a ferocious headache. Fairly blistered my and Henry's ears with his tongue." His thighs tightened around Titus, his chestnut gelding, easing his gait even slower so that Anderley and Bree could draw nearer. "I asked Henry to stay behind to keep an eye on him, and everyone else," he added as an afterthought. "The last thing we need is Barbreck interfering and making everything worse." He turned to his valet and my maid. "What of you? Did you learn anything from the staff?"

Anderley turned to Bree, indicating she should go first.

"I spoke wi' the cook. She was fair broken up. Apparently she's kent Mairi all her life. Told me she offered Mairi somethin' to eat when she arrived at Barbreck, but she declined. Said she thought she looked a bit peaked."

This simply confirmed what we already knew—that Mairi had ingested the poison before she arrived at Barbreck, and more than likely before she reached her father's cottage—but it was always good to gather more evidence.

"As for Liam's family," she continued. "The housekeeper said his mam was dead and his brother lived near Glasgow. She didna ken where else he might go. His friends were all at Barbreck."

"Wheaton said the same," Anderley informed us, corroborating the information given to us by all our sources—not that we'd suspected any of them were lying about such a fact. "But he did have a thought. He suggested we might check the cottage where Lord Alisdair lived."

"Wait." I turned abruptly in my saddle to look at him. "Lord Alisdair—Barbreck's brother who *acquired* the paintings I've uncovered were forged—didn't live at the manor?"

"Not according to Wheaton." The tone of Anderley's voice told me he understood exactly why I was irritated by this revelation. And the fact that no one had seen fit to inform us of it.

I exchanged a speaking glance with Gage as Anderley continued.

"He told me Lord Alisdair had lived in a cottage south of Barbreck, a few miles north of the village of Kilmartin, for as long as he or anyone on the staff could remember. That he'd liked his privacy too much and butted heads with his older brother too often to remain at the manor."

"We need to take a look at that cottage," I stated firmly. Whether it was still owned by Barbreck or not. And if I knew Barbreck, it was. Not only might Liam be hiding there, but it might also offer up some clues as to Lord Alisdair's life and his relationship with the forgeries.

"What did you think of what Mr. MacCowan had to say about Liam?" Gage asked me.

"You mean his vehement defense of the man?"

The look in Gage's eye told me he didn't view it as being so straightforward either.

"I couldn't help but wonder if he might be masking something. Though it might simply be his own guilt over not having been able to protect his daughter." I thought of the odd expression that had passed over his features near the end. "I'm not sure he told us everything he knows."

Gage nodded. "I had the same thought." He darted a glance over his shoulder toward Bree. "What of the footman Callum? What did he have to say?"

"Nothing useful," she grumbled under her breath.

"What do you mean?" I pressed when she didn't say more, risking her aggravation. It was clear she didn't wish to elaborate, but Callum's less-than-helpful comments could also prove to be illuminating.

"All he wanted to talk aboot was how much extra work Liam's absence caused him, but that he'd do it wi'oot complaint to show Wheaton hoo *he* can be relied upon."

My gaze lifted to the trees along the path where a squirrel leapt from branch to branch before scurrying down a trunk off into the forest. It was clear Callum had missed the irony of such a statement. Just as it was clear how unimpressed Bree was. It sounded as if the bloom was off the rose in regard to any admiration she'd felt for the lad.

I turned to look at Gage, trying to catch a glimpse out of the corner of my eye of Anderley riding behind him, curious how he'd taken this news. But he kept his face turned resolutely away, gazing down at the thick patch of brambles which bordered the path on that side and keeping his thoughts to himself. A wise decision.

Bree mumbled something under her breath before adding, "The only thing *remotely* o' interest that he had to say was that everyone ken Liam was waitin' for the Campbells' butler to be pensioned so he could take his position."

This wasn't entirely surprising. The thought that Liam hoped to eventually become butler at Poltalloch had briefly crossed my mind. After all, Calder had appeared older than most butlers, though some men in such a position remained there until they were forced out by either infirmity or death. Perhaps Liam had believed that his promotion to butler, and the greater income that came with it, would allow him to wed Mairi. Their closer proximity would certainly have made it more feasible.

Not that any of that mattered now.

My chest tightened with a pang of empathy for Liam. If, as we suspected, he'd had nothing to do with Mairi's death, then he must be grieving greatly. I only hoped he was somewhere safe and that his good sense would convince him to return to Barbreck.

"What of Miss Ferguson?" I asked Bree and Anderley. "The governess," I clarified. "What do you know about her?" Her presence at Mr. MacCowan's cottage this morning continued to nag at me, and I wondered what, if anything, the other servants made of her.

"No' much," Bree replied. "She seems to keep to herself. One o' the maids threw a nasty look at her back when she walked away after orderin' her to bring up the children's dinners, but I've seen worse."

Once again, this answer was as one would expect. After all, governesses were one of those positions that hovered between the upstairs and downstairs. They were a member of the staff and paid a wage, but being better educated and more gently bred, not of the same class. As such, they found themselves in a sort of limbo between both worlds, and not accepted by either. And yet, I still felt there was much more to be learned about Miss Ferguson. Much of her behavior raised too many questions. It wasn't merely her treatment of Charlotte—though that undoubtedly upset me—but also her presence in places it seemed odd for her to be.

"See what you can learn about her," I told them. "And whether she knew Mairi. But don't let her know you're asking." The less she believed we knew about her, the more easily she might slip up.

CHAPTER 14

We were surprised to discover that news of Mairi Mac-
Cowan's death had already reached Poltalloch before our
arrival. When asked, Calder the butler told us one of the trades-
men who had called at Barbreck earlier in the morning had
shared the sad report. While possible, I couldn't halt the suspicion it might have been Liam who'd shared the distressing tale.
A suspicion which was only heightened when Calder told us that
Miss Campbell had ridden out to speak to one of her foremen
but that he'd been instructed to allow us to speak to the staff
about Mairi if we wished.

As that was exactly one of the things we'd hoped to do, we
seized the opportunity before it could be rescinded. Bree and
Anderley went to the servants' hall to speak with the lower servants, while Gage and I were invited into the housekeeper's spar-
tan sitting room. A ladder-back chair from somewhere belowstairs
was added to the two stiff armchairs, the cushions on their seats
worn so thin they might have been nonexistent. The rug was

serviceable, but neither plush nor attractive, and the small book-shelf looked rather forlorn with just half a dozen books perched on it. The sole ornamentation was a rather crude watercolor of a nondescript landscape and a delightfully incongruent porcelain pig with a garland of roses around its neck. I found myself want-ing to ask questions about the porcine figure and had to force my thoughts away from it, as the housekeeper began prattling on about Mairi the moment we settled into our respective chairs.

Mrs. Kennedy was a spare woman with a neat bun of white hair perched on her head, and evidently an aversion to clutter. In regard to objects, that is. In the case of words, it seemed there could never be an overabundance.

"Puir lamb. To die so young and so *terribly*." She dabbed at the corners of her eyes with a handkerchief before leaning for-ward to vehemently add, "The lass didna deserve it, I can tell ye that. Mairi was a good girl. A hard worker. Best maid I had." She scoffed, shaking her head. "The others are helpless. A lot o' scapegraces who couldna find work elsewhere. But Mairi was different. I was groomin' her to take my place." She sighed. "Noo, it'll have to be Kady." Her mouth puckered. "Or an outlander." I remembered that Kady was the name of the maid who had dropped the tea tray during our last visit, but apparently the pros-pect of someone foreign to this area was far more horrifying.

"Your porcelain might be safer, but who knows what else might be at risk," I quipped dryly.

"Exactly!" she declared, but then her brow furrowed, plainly trying to decide if I was speaking in earnest or mocking her.

"What of Liam Gillies?" Gage asked, distracting her. "Was he known to the staff here?"

"Aye. And when I heard he was suspected o' the crime, I couldna believe it. No' Liam. He doted on Mairi. Wouldna harm a hair on her head," she declared with finality, and the gimlet glare she cast on us dared us to tell her otherwise.

"We don't actually think Liam is the culprit," Gage replied, and was awarded with a nod of approval. "We've been able to deduce that Miss MacCowan was dosed with the poison that killed her before she reached Barbreck. Most likely before she even reached her father's cottage. Which means she probably ingested it here or between Poltalloch and Barbreck."

Mrs. Kennedy's eyes widened with surprise. "Poison? I thought the lass met wi' violence."

"No. The effects of the poison were not pretty, but it was definitely poison that killed her," Gage stated. "Do you know when Miss MacCowan departed from Poltalloch? What did she eat that day? Did she take any food with her?"

Mrs. Kennedy continued to stare at us in shock. "I . . . I dinna ken. I'll have to ask."

I nodded. Those were things it was more likely the cook or maids would know. "Has anyone else been ill?"

She blinked rapidly, understanding the implication. "Nay, no' that I ken." Stiffening, she sat upright. "Should we be worried?"

"We can't say for sure," I answered honestly. "But at this point we have no reason to believe anyone else is in danger." Her face was pale with uncertainty, but I could offer her no further reassurance.

"And yer certain it wasna somethin' she ate or drank at Barbreck?"

"It wasn't."

"Because that would at least make some kind o' sense."

Gage and I shared a look.

"Why do you say that?" he asked.

Her mouth clamped shut, and her eyes darted back and forth between us. "You mun' ken. Aboot the broken engagement between Miss Campbell and Lord Barbreck?"

I nodded in encouragement, hoping to overcome her evident resistance to speak of the matter, likely born out of habit.

"Weel, Barbreck came here no' three nights past, raising a right stramash aboot some paintin' and reopenin' old wounds. We *all* heard him," she emphasized. "Everyone. We couldna keep it from the lower servants, and their mouths run like deer when there's somethin' that shockin' to share. If Barbreck's staff didna already ken, they woulda kent wi'in a day. Maybe two."

My voice rang with doubt. "And you think one of them might have taken revenge on Mairi?"

"Maybe." She exhaled as she sat back, clasping her hands in her lap. "It does sound a bit far-fetched noo that I say it aloud." She pressed a hand to her brow. "My apologies. The whole castle has been at sixes and sevens, and then to learn that Mairi's dead." Her face tightened with emotion. "Weel, it's easier for me to think o' it happenin' because o' somethin' there than because o' somethin' here."

"That's understandable."

She sniffed and dabbed at her nose with a handkerchief. "Could it o' been an accident?"

"We haven't discarded any possibilities," Gage assured her. "But the fact that no one else has fallen ill makes it seem less likely that it was an accident."

She tucked her handkerchief away and lifted her chin as if determined to face the rest. "Right then. So, it happened here. Or somewhere between here and Barbreck."

"Is there anyone here who didn't wish her well? Anyone with ill feelings toward her?"

"Weel . . . the other maids thought her a might too high in the instep, but that's only to be expected. As first maid, 'twas often her job to order them aboot or check their work. 'Twas natural they'd feel disgruntled toward her for makin' them redo their work when she believed it shoddy."

Gage tipped his head in acknowledgment. "Beyond that, then."

She began to shake her head when I spoke up, having had a thought.

"Were any of them jealous of Mairi's relationship with Liam?"

"Nay," she replied with a derisive laugh. "Dinna get me wrong. Liam is a good and sturdy lad. A good catch for any lass. But he wasna' the type to inspire jealousy. Perhaps there was some envy among the Barbreck maids, but no' among this mutton-headed lot."

Somehow I doubted the Barbreck maids were any more sensible about the men they dangled after than those at Poltalloch. From the comments I'd gleaned thus far, they were more taken with Callum than Liam. Not that Liam was unattractive, but when compared with Callum's rugged charm, there was little doubt who turned more heads. Though Anderley's presence must have thrown some sort of wrench in the household's normal operations. His smoldering, almost exotic allure must have caused Callum no small amount of competition, at least for the maids' titters.

I wondered what effect he was having on the Poltalloch maids now.

Deciding it was useless to pursue the subject further, when Bree and Anderley would undoubtedly be able to uncover more from the maids themselves, I brushed a miniscule piece of lint from my blue skirts as I attempted to casually turn the subject. "We understand Mairi often assisted Miss Margaret as part of her duties."

"Aye. Miss Margaret prefers . . . *preferred* her," she corrected herself. "And I canna say I blamed her. The other maids are too clumsy and feckless." She heaved a sigh, staring forlornly in the direction of the small window. "I suppose Kady will have to do noo. Or myself."

I wanted to ask her whether she might have heard or seen something during her time abovestairs that might have put her life at risk, but something told me to withhold the question. Not only was Mrs. Kennedy unlikely to know the answer, but she'd already proven herself hesitant to gossip about her employers. Had she not believed we already knew about the broken engagement, I doubt she would have shared it with us. So instead, I elected to enlist her aid, hoping to draw on her age and experience to help us with another matter.

"Mrs. Kennedy, I'm hoping you might be able to assist us with something," I confided, leaning toward her. "While we know Mairi was killed by poison, we are having some difficulty identifying what kind. The . . . *symptoms* are somewhat unusual."

She inhaled deeply, correctly sensing I was asking her to brace herself. "I'll help if I can."

"Do you know of a substance that causes the sufferer to bleed from their facial orifices—their eyes, nose, and mouth?"

She flinched. "That *is* unusual."

"It also causes ulcers in the mouth."

She lifted her hand to her chin as she considered my question. My gaze shifted to Gage, relieved to see that he didn't seem to disagree with my sharing such details with the housekeeper. After all, the information wasn't exactly sensitive. Several members of the Barbreck staff had seen the bleeding. If Mrs. Kennedy could identify the substance, then that would help us figure out how Mairi had ingested it and who had access to such a poison. If not, we'd risked little.

"I've *heard* rhubarb can cause bleedin' from the nose and eyes." Mrs. Kennedy raised her finger. "Just the leaves, ye mind, no' the stalks. The leaves are verra poisonous. But I've only ever witnessed them causin' severe stomach complaints, and ye said nothin' aboot that."

I shook my head, though it was possible those didn't come on until just before her death. But then where was the evidence of it?

"Then, I dinna think that can be it. No' to mention, Mairi woulda had to eat several pounds o' it for it to kill her."

Something that was highly improbable.

Gage and I thanked her for speaking with us, and then he returned to the entry hall in search of the butler while I allowed Mrs. Kennedy to escort me to the kitchen to speak with the cook. However, the cook did not take so kindly to being questioned. In fact, she wouldn't even stop bustling around the kitchen for five minutes to answer my queries, declaring herself to be too busy. The look Mrs. Kennedy gave me as she turned to leave told me she'd expected such a reception.

I might have viewed this behavior with some suspicion except for the fact that the round, rosy-cheeked woman was plainly in distress. One stiff breeze, one wrong word, and I suspected she would crumble to pieces. As a person who also felt the compulsion to *do* something when faced with a crisis, I understood what her bustling was all about.

So I did not rebuke her for her fractious behavior. I didn't counter her when she said Mairi had eaten from the same bowls of food at breakfast as the rest of the staff, and that any food she'd taken with her on her hike to Barbreck she'd fetched for herself from the pantry, and so the cook had no way of knowing. I didn't refute her when she claimed everyone adored Mairi and would never wish her harm. I didn't question her assertion that no rhubarb was grown on the estate. And when I was dismissed, I left without a fight. There would be no victory in breaking the woman, and any further questioning would only accomplish that. It was better—and far kinder—to step away and, if necessary, return to speak with her later.

Knowing the rest of the staff were in Bree and Anderley's capable hands and Gage was still closeted with Calder, I climbed the stairs to the ground floor and wandered out to the courtyard. Curious if Miss Campbell had returned, I circled the castle, peering into the stables, and then continued around to the side facing the loch. There, the courtyard ended in a small terrace before giving way to the solid stone wall of the castle and a precipitous drop down to the tiny inlet where a handful of boats were moored at a jetty.

I noticed that a narrow staircase was built into the side of the cliff face, leading to a door cut into the rock several feet below where I stood. It must have led into the cellars and servants' quarters belowground. It would be a dizzying climb but undoubtedly served both a useful purpose—offering a direct route for supplies and fresh fish from the sea to the castle—and a strategic one in centuries past. Should the castle be surrounded, escape by sea would still be possible.

I lifted my gaze to the steely waters of the loch, the boats bobbing on its surface and the green shores of the long island perched at its center. The water today was troubled, stirred up by the wind even now riffling in my ears and pulling strands of my hair loose from their pins and whipping them around my face. Its briny scent and the overcast skies roused in me memories better left buried. Memories of a time spent on the parapets of another crumbling castle looking out over a troubled sea on the opposite shore of Scotland.

It had been almost two years since Will had been killed, and yet my memories of him, of his death, still threatened to steal the breath from my lungs. There wasn't a day that went by when I didn't think of my dear friend and wish that I'd had the knowledge and foresight to prevent what his father had done to him and to keep our inquiry from ending in such a tragic way. I lifted my fingers to grip the amethyst pendant dangling from my neck. It had been a gift from my mother just before she died and was supposed to protect me. Whether it actually possessed magical qualities, I doubted, but I always felt better when I wore it. Just touching it made me feel calmer. Safer.

I blamed my distraction on those distressing memories battering at me, for I failed to note Miss Campbell's approach until she spoke.

"'Tis called *Eilean Righ*," Miss Campbell declared, coming to stand beside me. "In Gaelic it means 'King's Island,' though no one kens precisely what king it refers to." She stood tall and erect, her slim body encased in another simple but expertly tailored garment—this one the shade of new leaves. "Myself, I think it must be connected to the ancient kings at Dunadd." She turned to me. "You've Scottish blood? You've heard o' it, no?"

"An Iron Age hillfort believed to be the capital of the Dalriada." Lying just a few miles to the south at the edge of Kilmartin Glen, it had once been an important citadel of the Scots.

Miss Campbell swept her hand out as if to encompass all the land and sea before us and behind us. "There are prehistoric places dotted all over this glen—cairns, hillforts, cists, and standing stones. Some say it is the richest concentration in all o' Scotland."

I watched her face as she surveyed her domain. I heard pride brimming in her voice, but there was a tenderness also. It lit her face and softened her features.

"You love it here, don't you?" I asked softly. So softly, in fact, that I wondered at first if she'd heard me. But when she turned to look at me, I could see the reticence in her remarkable green eyes. Perhaps she feared she'd been too unguarded, or that I would misjudge her. There was no danger of that, but perhaps she didn't realize it.

Her eyes dipped to my neck where my fingers still gripped my amethyst pendant. Something shifted in her gaze, and she lifted her hand as if to touch the pendant, but then, remembering herself, she halted. "Your mother gave you that." The words didn't sound like she was guessing.

"Yes. How did you know?"

She nodded at the pendant. "She used to roll it between her fingers in much the same way whenever she was troubled."

I blinked at her in shock, and a strange tingling sensation began in my chest and spread outward as I waited for her to continue, somehow knowing whatever she said next would be significant.

"You dinna ken, do you?"

"Know what?" I whispered, feeling almost as if I was standing outside myself watching this conversation unfold.

Tilting her head, she studied the pendant as if sifting through her words before she answered. "I ken that was your mother's because . . . I gave it to her."

I stared dumbly at her as she continued.

"'Twas a wedding present. After she married my nephew Edmund."

CHAPTER 15

I stumbled back a step, almost losing my footing, and Miss Campbell reached out a hand to steady me, but I pulled away. "She . . . ? Your . . . ?" I stammered, unable to form a coherent thought let alone a question. Closing my eyes, I shook my head, trying to jar some sense into me. "No, she married James St. Mawr."

"Aye. Later." She eyed me with something akin to pity. "A few years after Edmund died."

I turned away to stare out across the loch, reaching out to grasp the low wall while I forced myself to take great gulps of the chill wind in an attempt to steady my swirling thoughts.

My father hadn't been my mother's first husband? If that was true—and I couldn't think of a reason why Miss Campbell should lie about something so easily disproved—then *why* had no one told me? My mother had died when I was eight, but surely this was information *someone* should have shared with me. When I came of age. When *my* first husband died. When I remarried.

How could I have reached the age of a score and seven years and not been informed of this?

Did Alana know? Did Trevor? I wanted to demand answers, but my sister was in London, and my brother at Blakelaw House in the Borders region—both of which were hundreds of miles away. My father had long since joined my mother in heaven. However, my mother's younger sister was close at hand, and Aunt Cait was going to answer some very pointed questions, or I would know the reason why.

But in the meantime, it was too much to grapple with. I could barely face the eddy of disquieting feelings myself, let alone dissect them before a virtual stranger.

"I'm sorry," I told Miss Campbell, gripping the wall so tightly that the gritty stone bit into my skin, but I welcomed the pain. "I'm not ready to discuss this."

"O' course," she replied kindly, though she must have had as many questions as I did.

"I . . . I need to speak with you about Mairi MacCowan," I said, floundering for something solid to latch on to. Something not related to my mother, or her pendant, or this man named Edmund. "You've been informed she is dead?"

"Aye. This mornin'. So it's true?"

"I'm afraid so." I studied her eyes, scrutinizing every shift of light, every subtle tightening. "My husband and I were there when she was found. In the long gallery. On the floor beneath the forged Van Dyck painting."

She stiffened.

"Do you have any idea why she was there?"

"I . . . no," she stammered, seeming truly disconcerted for the first time in our acquaintance. "Perhaps oot o' curiosity."

"We were told that Miss Margaret preferred Mairi. That she was more often in the family rooms of the castle than other servants."

She stared at me in bewilderment. "Aye, I s'pose so."

"Perhaps she overheard something sensitive. Something she shouldn't have." I arched my eyebrows. "Something that others didn't want her sharing." I knew I was being sharper than I needed to be, that I was in many respects lashing out because Miss Campbell had upset me with her revelation about my mother. In that regard, I was no better than the cook who had been so brusque with me such a short time ago. But I was restraining myself so rigidly, I feared if I softened my tone, I might begin to come apart at the seams.

As such, I expected her to take offense, but instead she blinked rapidly. "I dinna understand. If she was killed at Barbreck, then wouldna the culprit be—"

"She was poisoned," I interrupted. "By a substance that was slow in acting. And we've determined she must have ingested it prior to arriving at her father's cottage."

"Then . . . she ingested it here," she deduced.

"Or somewhere between Poltalloch and Barbreck," I added for the sake of clarity.

She pressed a hand to her stomach. "I honestly dinna ken what to say. Why would someone here poison Mairi?"

I searched her face for any sign of prevarication, but she seemed genuinely perplexed.

"I don't know, but it's becoming increasingly difficult to believe she poisoned herself by accident, which means *someone* wished her ill." I glanced back toward the stables, recalling my earlier suspicions about Miss Campbell's location upon our arrival. "Liam Gillies is missing. He was with her when she died, and we think he panicked, believing he would be blamed. It's imperative we talk to him to find out how she was acting just before she died."

Her green eyes met mine steadily. "And you wonder if he came here?"

"Did he?"

She scrutinized me in turn, seeming to come to some decision. "I have no' seen him. But I will ask my staff if they have and, if so, urge them to send Liam to you."

I realized there was a great deal of leeway in those statements, but under the circumstances, I suspected it was the best I would get.

Gage joined us soon after, and the next few minutes were spent relaying to him the information I'd already gleaned. Though I should have been watching Miss Campbell more closely and listening for discrepancies, I found my attention wandering—to my mother, to the things Miss Campbell had said. Her confession had knocked me off my axis, and I barely had the wherewithal to wonder if it had been on purpose. It wasn't until Gage asked a question about Miss Margaret that I was able to drag my attention back to the matter at hand.

"May we speak with her?" I asked when Miss Campbell finished answering.

Her eyes and Gage's both dipped to my neck where, without conscious thought, I'd begun to worry my amethyst pendant again. It was clear from both their faces that they knew what that meant. My first impulse was to drop the necklace as if it were on fire, but I knew that would make my fretfulness even more obvious. So I stilled my fingers, clutching it instead.

"I'm afraid she hasna been feelin' well these past two days," Miss Campbell replied. A furrow formed between her brows. "Truth be told, I almost asked Mairi to stay yesterday because, as you already ken, Margaret prefers her. I even asked my sister aboot it, but she told me she'd be fine. That it wasna fair to keep Mairi from her day off. That she looked forward to seein' her da and Liam. And I decided she was right."

"If I may be so bold," I began apologetically. "What infirmity does your sister suffer from?"

Her eyes clouded with worry. "She has weak lungs and a weak heart. Has all her life." She turned to gaze out over the loch where darker clouds appeared to be gathering in the west. "Ye shoulda seen her as a child. She was so verra fragile. Spent most o' her time indoors because my father worried aboot her so. Ye see, our brother William, who was born between us, died as an infant."

I stiffened at the name. Had I not been thinking of William Dalmay just a short time earlier, hearing it would likely have only caused me a flicker of discomfort. But in this setting, with my nerves already so raw, I struggled to stifle my reaction. Even so, Gage and Miss Campbell both noticed, though they had the grace not to make an issue of it.

"And our mother died soon after givin' birth to Margaret," Miss Campbell continued. "Father feared she would be next." Her gaze drifted again toward the horizon. "To be honest, it's somewhat of a miracle that she's lived this long."

I suspected that fact was a testament to Miss Campbell's care for her and the fresh, clean air of the Highlands. If Margaret had a weak heart and lungs, had the women lived near one of the cities—Glasgow or Edinburgh, "Auld Reekie" herself—I doubted she would have survived long.

I allowed my gaze to drift over Miss Campbell's noble profile. Between her love for Poltalloch and her affection for her sister, I supposed there was little wonder why she'd never left here and never married after her engagement to Lord Barbreck ended. She was tied here as much by her heartstrings as her duties and obligations.

She and Margaret were the youngest Campbell children to survive to adulthood, then. Which meant that Edmund's father must have been an older brother, perhaps even the eldest—yet another Sir James. If so, that would mean the current Sir James would be Edmund's older brother. I wondered if Edmund had taken after his brother in his profligate ways, if that was how he'd died. But before I could become tempted to ask, Gage recalled us to the haste of our current situation.

"Those look like storm clouds." Concern marred his brow, and I could tell the emotion was directed more at me than the weather. "I suggest we collect Anderley and Miss McEvoy and return to Barbreck before we're either detained here or caught in the deluge." He was thinking of Emma, of course. Mrs. Mackay had told us that our daughter could be fed goat's milk in an emergency, but I would prefer not to have to resort to that. In any case, I suddenly felt very anxious to return to her.

"Yes, we should go."

We took our leave as politely as could be managed. For my part, I felt wooden and awkward, but Miss Campbell seemed to understand. Better than I might have in her shoes.

We urged the horses to travel faster than they had on the journey to Poltalloch, racing the dark clouds that now seemed to be multiplying in number. As such, we mostly rode single file, and there was little opportunity for discussion. Something I was not altogether disappointed by. It gave me more time to contemplate what I'd learned before having to put it into words for Gage.

He continued to cast me worried glances and, when the trail widened enough for my pony to trot by his gelding's side, opened his mouth to speak.

"Not now," I cut him off.

He continued to stare at me until I turned to him with as level a look as I could manage while posting to the bay's trot so as to avoid being jolted. He dipped his head in acknowledgment before turning away, urging Titus to pull ahead as the trail narrowed again. What I had to say could wait, as could whatever Bree and Anderley had learned from the rest of the Poltalloch staff.

We reached the drive leading up to Barbreck Manor just as

the first fat drops of cold rain began to fall. At first, they were sporadic, but as we rounded the drive toward the portico, it began to rain in earnest. We slowed the horses to a walk beneath the shelter of the roof, allowing them to pace up and down the length of the portico while we waited for the stable hands to hurry across the yard to collect them. Normally, Barbreck's staff was much more prompt, but I attributed their delay to the rainstorm. It took a hearty soul to willingly run out in a Highland downpour, no matter one's station.

"Give him a good rubdown and an extra bucket of oats," Gage directed the man who took hold of Titus's reins as he gave his steed an affectionate pat on his shoulder. Then he turned to collect me, guiding me through the door, where Wheaton took my damp summer cloak. It had been a fortuitous decision to drape the garment over my riding habit, and I was glad Bree had suggested it.

Gage had not been so lucky. A footman passed him a towel, which he used to wipe the dampness from his bronzed face and neck and blot the worst from his hair and frock coat. Even as he rubbed one side, a single drip of water trailed across his temple, over his jaw, and down the side of his neck, disappearing under his cravat.

The sound of loud voices coming from the drawing room captured our attention, and I turned to Wheaton in question.

"The Earl of Ledbury has arrived," he said.

My gaze flew back toward the drawing room door. Charlotte's father. Of all the rotten timing. Of course, he would arrive when things were at their worst.

It was Gage's turn to appear quizzical, looking to me for an explanation. Wheaton took the towel from him and discreetly withdrew as I pulled Gage toward the edge of the entry hall.

"Charlotte told me her father is somewhat . . . critical," I murmured, reaching up to straighten his hair. "She's afraid he doesn't precisely approve of Rye. And that when he discovered a maid here has been murdered, it would only make matters worse." I glanced over my shoulder as the sound of a raised male voice penetrated through the wood of the drawing room door.

"Just a moment." Gage propped his hands on his hips as his eyes narrowed in baffled anger. "Lord Ledbury is concerned about your cousin—who is one of the steadiest and noblest gentlemen I've ever met—and yet he allowed his daughter to marry *Stratford*?"

The late Earl of Stratford had been a notorious rogue and scoundrel long before the events at Gairloch Castle when he nearly murdered Charlotte and her maid, as well as me.

"Ah, but he was an earl," I retorted wryly.

Gage's fury did not abate.

"He's a hypocrite," I clarified.

"Lovely," he muttered, resting my arm on his and leading me toward what was beginning to sound like a pitched battle.

Gage didn't bother to conceal our entrance, instead throwing the door open wide as we strode into the drawing room side by side. Everyone turned to look at us, and I surmised that my fears were correct. Charlotte perched on a sofa between Rye and Aunt Cait, with Uncle Dunstan standing behind them, stroking his beard, while Barbreck and Ledbury stood some half a dozen feet apart. Our entrance brought a temporary cessation to their volley of snarled insults, but I knew better than to believe it would last long.

"Oh, of course you're here," Lord Ledbury scoffed, being the first to react to the sight of us.

"Father," Charlotte gasped.

"How *curious* that mischief and murder should follow wherever you go." The earl's lean face twisted in a sneer which emphasized the sharpness of his nose and chin. The dainty features that were so lovely on his daughter seemed spritelike on him.

Even his tiny ears peeking out from his salt-and-pepper hair and beard.

"Father, how can you say that?" Charlotte protested. "If not for Mr. and Mrs. Gage, I would be lying dead at the bottom of a loch."

He rolled his eyes. "Charlotte, do not resort to hyperbole. I still believe you overstate the matter."

"I assure you, she does not," Gage asserted in a voice that had made larger men tremble. "My wife bears a scar from the bullet Lord Stratford fired to prove it."

I felt a twinge on my side, recalling the old wound. The bullet had only clipped me, but I still bore a two-inch-long gash where the skin had knit back together.

Lord Ledbury's eyes narrowed at my husband, as if he still might not believe him—or perhaps he simply didn't wish to—but he allowed the matter to drop. "I take it you're investigating this maid's death, then, seeing as it happened in the public rooms of the house?"

I scowled. Meaning we shouldn't have needed to investigate if it had happened elsewhere, like belowstairs, where apparently the staff was free to live and die as they would, as long as it didn't disrupt those who lived above?

"Yes, we're looking into the matter," Gage replied smoothly, though I could feel the muscles of his arm tensing beneath my own, perhaps desiring to plant the pompous man a facer.

His gaze flicked up and down my husband's form before turning away. "I still cannot understand how it was allowed to happen. My staff would never dare enter a room where they didn't belong unless it was part of their duties. And they certainly wouldn't dare to show someone from outside the staff into those rooms, let alone allow them to *die* there."

Aunt Cait's brow lowered furiously at his disparagement of her ability to manage the household staff, but it was Barbreck whose outrage was most evident. His face had reddened, and his eyes seemed to be trying to bore holes in the earl's head. I had been confronted by that enraged expression just a few short days ago, but Ledbury seemed to be little impressed by it.

"I would like to retire to my room now," Ledbury declared. "It has been a *long* journey. Charlotte, perhaps you will accompany me." It wasn't a request but an order.

"Of course, Father," she replied resignedly, pushing to her feet. Rye rose to his feet beside her, touching her arm in a show of support before she crossed the room toward her parent. Accepting the arm he crooked for her, she allowed herself to be led from the room, but not before sending me a pleading look.

What exactly she expected me to do, I didn't know. I could hardly issue a counterorder. In any case, Charlotte would need to wage at least part of this battle with her father on her own. The rest of us could only do so much. I glanced about me. Though I did wonder where Lady Bearsden was. I would have thought Ledbury's aunt would have some sort of mitigating influence on him. Perhaps she was resting, as she was wont to do in the early afternoon, and didn't yet know her nephew had arrived.

In any case, I hadn't the time or mental wherewithal to apply myself to Charlotte's problem at the moment. Emma needed attention, and then I had some questions for my aunt.

Receiving Aunt Cait's calm nod of acceptance as I excused myself twisted my stomach in knots. She *must* know about mother's first marriage, about her connection with the Campbells. After all, she had wed the nephew of their neighbor. Perhaps Mother had even been the one to introduce Aunt Cait to Uncle Dunstan. And yet, my aunt had said nothing to me about the matter, not even to remark that the Miss Campbell whom Lord Barbreck had stormed off to confront was my mother's former aunt by marriage. That fact alone made it difficult for me *not* to suspect she had intentionally been keeping the association from me.

But why? Why would she seek to conceal such a truth? Why risk allowing me to learn of it from Miss Campbell—a virtual stranger—making me feel like a fool and a child who must be cosseted from such information. And after all that I'd endured?! Whatever my mother had suffered in her first marriage, I should say I was the *most* likely to understand it.

I paused inside the door to our bedchamber, realizing I'd worked myself into a temper. Taking several deep breaths, I resolutely pushed the matter from the forefront of my thoughts to be confronted later.

There was a time in my life when that was all I had ever done—shoved disturbing things inside the closets of my mind, sometimes to be contemplated and sometimes to be locked away forever. It was how I'd survived. Providently, I no longer needed to live such an existence, though sometimes the tactic still proved useful.

I closed my eyes, exhaling one last long breath, and heard Mrs. Mackay chattering away to Emma next door. A smile tugged at the corners of my lips at the sound of her cheery voice.

I was discovering there was nothing like having a child to shift one's priorities and make things that had seemed so dire suddenly appear less all-consuming. As inconvenient and tiring as it was sometimes to have to pause every three to four hours to feed my daughter, it also forced me to slow down, to reshuffle my concerns, and it afforded me the opportunity to regularly reconnect with my daughter even in the midst of the most hectic moments. It also gave me more time for calm reflection.

Cradling Emma's downy head in one arm while the other plucked lint from between the toes of her silky soft feet—her grabby little toes collected it like a magpie—my thoughts began to drift to my memories of my mother. Because she'd died when I was young, I realized there were many things I didn't know about her. Had she hired a wet-nurse or tended us herself? Had she struggled to adapt to motherhood or taken to it easily? What had her life been like before we were born? Had she loved Edmund Campbell?

I knew she had loved my father. It had been evident in their care for each other, both when they thought we were watching and when they believed we were not. I had been one of those children who had often liked to squirrel themselves away under furniture and in tight places, making the tiny space my own. Our nurserymaids used to become cross with me, thinking I was intent on mischief, but our nanny had known this was simply my natural inclination. As a consequence of this, I often saw things I might not have otherwise, and sometimes that included my parents' private interactions.

But that didn't mean Mother couldn't have loved Edmund Campbell, too.

The specter of him was still haunting the edges of my thoughts a short time later when Gage joined us. I had spread a blanket across the floor over the rug and stretched out on my side, encouraging Emma as she kicked and squirmed on her belly. Mrs. Mackay had informed us she'd rolled over twice now from stomach to back, but I had yet to witness it.

He smiled at the sight of us and the sound of my ridiculous cajoling. "What is this?" he declared, planting his hands on his hips. "Are we having a floor party, and no one invited *me*?"

At the sound of her father's voice, Emma rounded her back, lifting her head and shoulders to try to see behind her.

"Your invitation must have gotten lost in the post," I jested.

"Lost in the post. Is that honestly your excuse, madam?"

At this comment, Emma flopped over onto her back, grinning broadly up at him.

I laughed out loud. "Of course, the prospect of seeing your father would do the trick. Not even babies can resist him," I teased, smothering her with kisses and praise for her accomplishment. He soon joined us on the blanket, and we spent several happy minutes playing with her and coaxing her to roll over for us again.

When Emma settled contentedly on her back with a silver rattle, Gage looked up at me, the concern that had been reflected in his eyes on our journey back from Poltalloch now blunted but still present. "What happened this morning?" He shifted to a sitting position, folding his long legs still encased in their riding boots before him. "You seemed . . . unsettled after speaking with Miss Campbell," he said, choosing his words with care.

I pushed upright, curling my legs to the side as I sifted through my impressions now that I was more removed from the initial shock. "Miss Campbell informed me that my mother had been a widow when she wed my father. That her first husband was her nephew."

A flash of lightning through the window over my shoulder reflected in his pale blue eyes, but otherwise there was no discernible reaction. "And you hadn't known that before she told you?" he clarified to the bass accompaniment of a thunderclap.

I shook my head.

He turned aside, swiping a hand down his face. "That's quite a revelation."

"Yes." My fingers lifted almost of their own accord to grip the smoothed surface of my mother's amethyst pendant, seeking solace from it. Perhaps that's why she'd really given it to me. Perhaps the real protection it provided had always been in my being able to touch it and know that she was still with me—even in that small way—offering me what comfort she could.

Was that how *she'd* felt about the pendant? Was that why Miss Campbell had given it to *her*?

Gage's eyes dipped to the amethyst and then returned to my face. "That must have been difficult to hear, particularly when the knowledge should have come from your family. I presume you're going to write to Alana and Trevor."

I nodded. "And I need to speak to my Aunt Cait. Though I'm not sure exactly what I'm going to say." I pushed the rattle Emma had dropped closer to her as she rolled toward me, reaching for it. She gazed up at me in contemplation and then smiled. Unable to resist, I grinned in return.

"Just tell her you want to confirm whether it's true," my husband suggested. "I suspect she'll carry the rest of the conversation."

My eyes scoured his face for reassurance. "Do you think so?"

He held out his hand for mine, and I gave it to him. His calloused fingers brushed over my own in a caress before gently squeezing. "I do."

My vision clouded with tears as I offered him a watery smile.

Seeing the hands linked over her, Emma decided this was her cue to drop the rattle and reach for them, loudly protesting the fact that they were too far away. We lowered them to her and then proceeded to tickle her.

CHAPTER 16

Is it true?" my Aunt Cait repeated a short time later when we were closeted alone in her bedchamber. Her eyes widened. "Why, yes. But . . . Kiera, are you telling me you never knew about Edmund?"

The look on my face must have spoken for itself, for she clasped a hand to her chest in what seemed to be genuine distress.

"Oh, my dear! I'm so sorry." She pressed her hand over the top of mine where it rested against the settee. "I thought for certain your father must have told you. Or Alana. Or . . . well, *someone*. But to learn of it in such a way. I'm so terribly sorry, my dear."

I sat stiffly, gazing across the room toward where rain lashed the windows. A fire burned in her hearth, the logs crackling and popping as juniper branches lent their aroma to the air. The larger part of the chamber was cast in shadow, but inside the circle of the fire's light, a warmth pervaded, slowly thawing my reticence.

"Then you weren't keeping it from me on purpose?" I asked.

"Keeping it from you? Oh, no. Of course not, my dear. It's just . . . well, it was not the happiest time of your mother's life."

My chest tightened with dread. "What do you mean?"

She turned her head to the side, seeming to gather her thoughts. From this angle I could better see the silver threading her soft brown hair, and I felt a pang at the evidence of her age. Though the largest part of my sorrow was not at the fact that my aunt was getting older, but rather that her sister—my mother—had not had the opportunity to do so. For that matter, neither had my father or Gage's mother. Emma had one grandparent left, and matters were so strained between Lord Gage and his son that I wasn't certain when, if ever, he would meet her.

Aunt Cait turned back to me with a look of resignation. "Edmund Campbell was somewhat of a scoundrel." She lifted a hand to her brow, sinking deeper into the embroidered silk cushions. "Oh, I don't know *why* I'm mincing words. He *was* a scoundrel, plain and simple. He raked hell from Oban to Edinburgh and back again. The man was as faithless as they come."

I listened quietly while inside my heart broke a little bit for my mother. It had been one thing to speculate that Edmund Campbell might have been a rogue and quite another to hear it was true. And my mother had reaped the anguish of it.

"But the real trouble was that he was a *charming* scoundrel. And your mother loved him." She lowered her gaze from where she'd been staring at the ornate stuccowork decorating the ceiling. "Each time he was caught, each time he was less than discreet, he would make the prettiest apology and she would forgive him. He would dance attendance on her for a month or two, and all would be well. And *then* he would grow bored, and . . . well, you can surmise the rest." She shook her head, her brow creasing in pain. "Greer had her heart broken so many times by that cad. If only she hadn't loved him. There was nothing she could do about the rest. But at least if she hadn't loved him, then her heart could have remained intact."

I stared dumbfounded at the Jacob Marrel watercolors gracing the wall immediately across from me, the tulips seeming to wilt before my eyes.

"I know it is not easy to hear," my aunt commiserated.

"Does Alana know all this?" I asked, wondering if this excused her at least partially for not telling me. She'd wished to shield me from the pain.

"Yes, I . . . shared it with her when she was pursuing Philip so ardently."

I looked up in surprise.

Her lips creased in subtle humor. "You're aware he was a bit of a rake in his younger days, before he wed your sister? She teases him about it often enough."

I nodded.

"Well, I feared that, even if Alana convinced him to come up to scratch, marriage would not reform him. It rarely does, you know. But in Philip's case, I was happy to be proven wrong."

I tilted my head, wondering if she would have issued the same warning to me about Gage had she not been hundreds of miles away at the time of our brief engagement. Of course, in Gage's instance, his rakish demeanor had been more of a role he employed in order to disarm others and gain information. Something that, in hindsight, Philip and Alana must have realized, or else they would not have allowed us to spend so much time alone together during those early weeks of our acquaintance.

Eager to shift the subject, I turned my thoughts to Poltalloch. "What was Mother's relationship like with the other Campbells?"

"Amicable, I would say. She gave Edmund's father and brother no reason for complaint. But I gather her feelings toward Miss Campbell and her sister were much warmer. She told me once that if she could have remained at Poltalloch with them, she would have been quite content."

I must have appeared as bewildered as I felt, for Aunt Cait's expression softened.

She reached out to gently touch my chin. "Oh, my dear, you're more like your mother than you realize." Her fingers smoothed back a strand of hair that had fallen against my temple, removing a hairpin and then refastening it to hold it in place. "Did you never wonder why your mother was content to live out most of her life in a sleepy little village in the Borders? She was quite happy there with your father. James was steady and honorable. Practical. Just what she craved."

She sat back, clasping her hands in her lap. "But we were speaking of the Campbells and Poltalloch."

We *had* strayed from the topic, yes, but part of me wanted to urge her to continue talking about my parents for as long as she could. Having her share just that little bit and then cut herself off made me feel yet again the keen sense of their loss. My memories of them had begun to fade, but Aunt Cait's words had brought them back to life, if only for a moment. It was like a faint whisper in my ear, an image formed in smoke, but when I reached out to grasp it, there was nothing to latch on to.

"They visited Poltalloch often. Usually when Edmund had stirred up some sort of trouble and needed to vanish for a time. He *did* leave your mother there a time or two when he went off on one of his escapades, but of course, he wouldn't allow her to remain there indefinitely." Her voice dipped scornfully. "Then, she wouldn't be by his side to appeal to his vanity and cater to his every whim when he tired of prowling."

"Did Mother introduce you to Uncle Dunstan?" I asked.

"That seems a logical assumption, doesn't it? But no. I met him in Edinburgh." A secretive smile played across her lips. "Though, I did contrive to pay my sister a visit at Poltalloch some weeks later when I knew Dunstan would be in residence at Barbreck."

My lips curled in amusement. It wasn't as difficult as one would think, given the proper lady my aunt presented herself to be, to imagine her contriving such a plot. All I needed to do was think of her daughter Morven. She and my sister had given Aunt Cait the devil of a time when she chaperoned them for their debuts into society.

She laughed aloud. "Yes, I can see the exact comparison you're drawing in your mind. I was, indeed, as headstrong as my daughter. But fortunately, I had my older sister attempting to restrain me and talk some sense into me. Otherwise, my already brief engagement to your uncle might have had cause to be *scandalously* short." The glint in her eyes was waggish. "I knew precisely what tricks my daughter and your sister were up to because I had been up to them myself at their age."

Her merriment faded, and she reached out again to touch my chin. "I wish you would have let me chaperone you for a season," she confided almost wistfully, allowing me to see for the first time some of what she felt in knowing what I had endured in my first marriage. And now knowing what my mother had endured in her *first* marriage, I realized perhaps she was also carrying around a measure of guilt that she had not saved me from a similar fate. "Things might have turned out differently."

"It was my decision," I reminded her. *I* was the one who'd asked Father to arrange a marriage so that I wouldn't be paraded before all of society on the marriage market and inevitably found lacking. My awkwardness had improved with maturity and the self-confidence that came from my marriage to Gage and success in solving inquiries. I no longer worried quite so much that I would say or do the wrong thing, nor cared as much what others thought of me when I did. But at seventeen and eighteen, I had felt everything acutely, even when I didn't understand it. Society would have sharpened its claws on me and tore me to shreds.

"I know, dear. It's useless to speculate." She took hold of my hand. "The fact of the matter is, in spite of all you've been through, you've emerged stronger and wiser. *You* triumphed in the end. And had you not been through it all, who's to say whether you would have ever captured Gage's heart or given birth to darling Emma. Who, as you'll recall, I predicted would be a girl," she reminded me with a wag of her eyebrows.

I shook my head. "I've been waiting for you to remind me of that." I still wasn't convinced my aunt had the ability to know the sex of the baby an expectant mother was carrying simply by looking at her, but I had to admit she had astonishing luck. Though, to be fair, the odds were in her favor, given she had a fifty-percent chance of being correct.

"And who's to say whether these murder investigations you've undertaken would ever have been solved." She tapped my knee. "I know Charlotte is glad you put your experiences to good use. And so is Rye."

I couldn't argue with that, but it did remind me about what had happened in the drawing room a short time ago. "If only we can convince Lord Ledbury of that, as well as the suitability of their match."

Aunt Cait's mouth pursed with displeasure as she adjusted the neckline of her gown striped in alternating patterns. As always, she was dressed in the first stare of fashion. At least that was something Ledbury couldn't disapprove of. When she looked up after gathering herself, her blue eyes snapped with repressed ire. "I know Lord Ledbury is a bit of a stickler for propriety, and frankly a pretentious bore, but I would have thought he'd learned from the tragedy of his daughter's first marriage that greater rank does not necessarily equate to greater quality in terms of the character of men. Apparently, I gave him more credit for good sense than he deserves."

She tugged at the lace trimming of her gigot sleeve. "In any case, Rye's lineage is nothing to sniff at. He is already the grandson of a baron, and someday he will be the son of a marquess. Not his heir, no, but there is plenty of wealth to go around. He's already been given use of, and the income from, one of Barbreck's estates in Midlothian for the perpetuity of his lifetime and that of his son's."

It was clear my aunt had been insulted, and I couldn't fault her for her outrage. Lord Ledbury had been unaccountably rude. I only hoped that if he could not be brought around, Charlotte would not bow to his pressure. But I also knew how much Charlotte disliked conflict. It tied her stomach in knots and gave her megrims. I wished her father could be more considerate of her. Surely, he must realize how happy she was with Rye and how flustered his disapproval made her.

But then, like Aunt Cait, perhaps I gave him too much credit. All I had witnessed thus far showed me he was a selfish man focused solely on his own vanity and consequence. That did not bode well for his support of Charlotte or her enjoyment of the days to follow.

"Did you learn anything helpful about Mairi MacCowan from the Campbells and their staff?" my aunt asked, breaking into my ruminations.

"Yes and no," I replied, forcing my thoughts along a different track. "Do you know if any rhubarb is grown at Barbreck?"

"Rhubarb? Probably." She gasped. "The leaves! Is that what poisoned her?"

"Maybe. Though it seems doubtful. As I understand it, she would have needed to ingest pounds of them before they would have killed her."

"True. I've only heard of people suffering severe stomach upset."

And yet, we still had no evidence Mairi had exhibited that symptom.

I turned to watch the rain running in rivulets down the glass of the nearest window. "Did you know Lord Alisdair resided in a cottage south of here rather than at the estate?"

"Yes," she replied, clearly cognizant that I was aware she *must* have known. Barbreck's youngest brother had not died until five years earlier. "But let me guess, no one told you that either." She heaved a long-suffering sigh in answer to the shake of my head. "My apologies, Kiera. Considering the fact he asked you to solve the riddle of these forgeries and figure out what happened to Mairi, I had *hoped* Barbreck was being far more forthcoming with you, but it appears I was wrong." She rolled her eyes before turning to me. "I'll be certain you're given the key and granted access."

"Thank you."

Her head tilted to the side, and her eyes narrowed in scrutiny. "Did he tell you about Lord Alisdair's Italian friend? The painter who came to stay with him from time to time."

I sat forward in my seat. "No!"

Aunt Cait closed her eyes and shook her head in disappointment. I suspected Barbreck was going to be shown the sharp side of her tongue in short order, and well he deserved it.

"Signor Pellegrini." It rolled off her tongue with a trill. "That was his name. He dined with us from time to time, and he was very charming. But I know you must be wondering now why Barbreck did not mention his existence before. I assume, like you, it's because Signor Pellegrini would be an obvious suspect for who created those forgeries."

"Did you ever see any of Signor Pellegrini's artwork?"

She crossed one leg behind the other. "As I understood it, he mainly painted murals. There are a few inside Uncle Alisdair's cottage." Her expression turned wry. "But that is not to say he did not, or *could* not, paint on canvas."

I turned to scowl into the hearth, wondering what to make of this revelation. My aunt was right. Barbreck had clearly kept it from me because he knew Signor Pellegrini would be a suspect. But that did not mean the Italian was the forger. Although, thus far, the only artists whom I had been made aware of who may have had the necessary skills to be our potential forger and the proximity to Barbreck Manor were Lord Alisdair—despite Barbreck's assertions to the contrary—and his Italian friend. The way I saw it, the forgeries were either created before they reached Scotland, or Lord Alisdair and Signor Pellegrini were our culprits. The likelihood of yet another gifted artist suddenly popping up nearby—close enough to gain access to the paintings in the long gallery—was incredibly slim.

But why would Lord Alisdair do such a thing? To sell them? I supposed it was possible he needed the money. I had always derived the impression that Barbreck was generous with his family, but maybe Lord Alisdair had acquired gambling debts or wished to make a large purchase he knew his brother would not approve of.

Whatever the truth, apparently the matter would require a great deal more thought. It was also high time we availed ourselves of the steward's help to search Barbreck's records, as he'd given us permission for. However, I didn't want to just review the art purchases but all of Lord Alisdair's expenditures. Perhaps something would stand out.

"Is there anything else I can tell you?" Aunt Cait said when I was quiet too long. "Any other way I can help?"

"Not at the moment," I told her. I needed to confer with Gage. "But I may come to you again."

"Of course. Whatever you need."

"And . . . thank you," I murmured, feeling somewhat awkward. "For explaining about my mother."

The corners of her lips curled in a sad smile. "I'm just sorry I didn't realize you were unaware of her first marriage sooner. I could have at least saved you the pain and shock of learning of it the way you did." She pulled me toward her, enveloping me in her enormous puffed sleeves and the scent of rose and sandalwood. It was the same scent my mother had worn, and a lump formed in my throat as it tickled at places in my brain that had long lay dormant. "I'm here for you any time, Kiera. Please know that."

I sniffed, blinking back tears as she pulled away. "Thank you," I choked out, seeing the same brightness in her eyes.

I somehow managed to extract myself from her chamber without dissolving into a sobbing mess, hastening toward the grand staircase, but I paused at the top.

When the day came, I wondered how I would tell Emma, tell all my eventual children, about Sir Anthony Darby. How would I explain the pain and fear and disenchantment? How would I ever be able to put it into words? For someday I would have to do so, before they learned of it in some casually cruel way from a fellow debutante, or a schoolmate, or a member of society. I couldn't hope to keep it from them, no matter how I strove to protect them from it.

Contemplating that gave me a better appreciation for what my father, sister, and brother had faced in telling me about Edmund. And I realized that my initial conviction that my experiences with Sir Anthony should have made it easier for them to do so was false. That the opposite was true. Because being able to intimately relate to some of the hurt my mother had faced only made it all that more terrible to accept. My empathy for her pain, merged with my own remembered suffering, made it doubly more difficult, for where did one end and the other begin?

It was why even now my stomach cramped and my chest felt tight. And the very thought of Emma ever having to endure something similar nearly drove me to my knees.

I vowed then and there I would do everything in my earthly power to prevent it. I would move heaven and earth to keep her safe. To keep a dishonorable person from having such control over her life.

Dragging a trembling hand across my lips, I glanced about

me, seeking distraction from my spiraling thoughts. That's when my gaze fell on the entrance to the long gallery. I hadn't returned to the room since the evening before when Mairi's body had been found, but perhaps the light of day would illuminate something we'd missed.

Redirecting my unsteady steps, I entered the gallery, the hairs prickling along my arms as I stopped to stare down its length. I'm not sure what I expected to find. Any mess from Mairi's sad demise had long been cleared away by the staff. But even so, a melancholy atmosphere seemed to linger over the space. Though perhaps that was courtesy of my mood and the stormy light filtering through the high windows.

Slowly, I paced my way down the marble floor, allowing the click of my boot heels to echo through the chamber. It somehow made it feel less forlorn to fill the space up with sound. I hesitated before the forged paintings that were allegedly created by Titian and Van Dyck, but once again, besides the fact that the paintings were frauds, I saw nothing out of place.

Logic insisted that Mairi *must* have been there for a reason. But had it been straightforward curiosity or something more? Could she have been sent here? But by whom? One of the Campbell sisters? Perhaps they'd wanted to know more about the forged Van Dyck but hadn't dared attempt to see it for themselves. But why? What had they hoped to learn?

Feeling a headache stirring behind my eyes, I rubbed my fingers over my temples, temporarily abandoning the puzzle of Mairi's presence to continue going around the room. I'd yet to examine the rest of the art hanging here or propped on pedestals, and while I didn't have the time to make an intense study of it, I wanted to take a precursory inventory. There were a number of paintings which were undoubtedly the work of a master, paintings I wanted the chance to study at leisure. Including the painting of the god of war the other ladies had been tittering about, which, indeed, appeared to be by Caravaggio. But there were also a few more pieces that just seemed *wrong* somehow. They simply didn't fit with what I knew of the attributed artist.

One of the Gainsborough portraits, for instance. It was too stiff and contrived, and it lacked the glazed effect he was so expert at, where the underpaint—usually an orange or pink-beige— was allowed to partially shine through. Or the seventeenth-century Dutch landscape whose frame proclaimed it to be the work of Saloman van Ruisdael, an artist who had been in vogue among the English. However, the composition was careless and the execution uneven.

There were also a number of Zoffany paintings I found suspect. Barbreck was plainly an admirer, but I had never particularly cared for that artist. He'd had great aptitude and had undoubtedly been capable of excellence, but his body of work was also riddled with clumsy efforts, skewed perspectives, and other symptoms of an undisciplined or indifferent creator. Such things made it difficult to tell whether the paintings hanging in the long gallery were forgeries or simply mediocre efforts by Zoffany himself.

The only thing that *was* clear was that the Titian and Van Dyck were not the sole forgeries in Barbreck's collection. How many potential forgeries there were and how endemic the problem was could not possibly be known until a full inventory was made. A task that would have to fall to me.

I closed my eyes for a moment as the dull ache behind them intensified. A pang of hunger reminded me that I hadn't eaten since breakfast, and now it was nearly three o'clock. No wonder I felt out of sorts. I decided to return to my chamber and ring for Bree. She could bring me a tray and track down Gage and the others. It was high time we compared notes and formed a plan of attack.

CHAPTER 17

Upon returning to my bedchamber, I discovered there was no need to ring for Bree. I could hear her raised voice clearly through the connecting door to the dressing room, and it was far from pleased.

"*You* dinna get to have a say in who I spend my time wi'," she declared shrilly.

The answering voice was more muffled through the wood, but I had no trouble making out the words or who the speaker was. "Maybe not. But the man is an ass," Anderley stated starkly. "Didn't you once say that men and women can be blinded to the faults of the opposite sex? That we often hold greater insights into our own gender?"

My eyebrows arched at this reiteration of a debate they must have previously had.

"Well, I thought you should know that Callum might be pretty to look at, but he's a selfish, unprincipled oaf," he finished scathingly.

"Look at you. Canna take the advice, but ye can dish it back,"

Bree retorted. "Do ye honestly think me so shallow as to only care aboot a person's looks? If that was the case, then *you* and *I* would still be courtin'."

I turned away from the wall shared with the dressing room, suddenly feeling my cheeks heat with guilt over listening to their conversation. But it wasn't as if I had a choice. I didn't even have to strain to hear their voices.

"Dinna get all puffed up, noo. 'Twasn't a compliment."

Frustration strangled Anderley's voice. "All I'm trying to say, as a . . . a friend, is that you should be wary of him."

"And all I'm tryin' to say, for the *third* time, is I'm no' a gudgeon, nor a green girl. I can look after myself."

At this, I could hear her footsteps crossing the floor, but there wasn't time to react before she threw open the door and came sailing into the bedchamber. I stood arrested by my own embarrassment, but also by the high color in her cheeks and the fiery flash in her eyes. Coupled with her strawberry blond hair, several wisps of which had tumbled loose about her face, she looked magnificent. All I could think was that it was no wonder Anderley had picked a fight. My fingers twitched at my side, anxious to capture her image in charcoal or, better yet, paint. *Portrait of a Woman in a Righteous Fury.*

When Bree caught sight of me standing near the outer door—for I'd taken no more than three steps into the room before the argument had distracted me—she flushed crimson from her neckline to her hairline. There was nothing I could say to ease either of our mortifications, so instead I decided to pretend nothing had happened.

"Bree, I've just realized I haven't eaten since this morning. Would you bring a tray up?"

"O' course, m'lady," she said, sounding relieved, even as her brow crumpled in concern. "You need to keep your strength up, 'specially while nursin' the bairn."

"I know. With everything going on, I simply lost track of the time." I crossed toward the writing desk, opening the drawer to look for paper. "Bring the tray to Mr. Gage's chamber and send for him, Lord Henry, and Anderley to meet us there." I looked up to meet her gaze. "I've learned a few things in the last hour, and I imagine others will also have news to share."

"Aye." She dipped a curtsy and then left.

I sat at the desk and jotted off a list of questions and points to consider, as well as a number of tasks to be completed, partly to organize my mind and partly to allow plenty of time for Anderley to retreat from the dressing chamber before I crossed it to reach the bedchamber that had been assigned to Gage on the other side. When I judged it to be sufficient, I picked up the list and strode toward the connecting door. I had to force myself to take a bracing breath for courage before rapping on the door. When no one answered, I opened it and, to my relief, found it empty. Gage's bedchamber was also unoccupied, and I made myself comfortable at the twin to my writing desk, angled near one of the tall windows, to continue reviewing my list.

I allowed my gaze to play over the contents of the room as I pondered. As Gage only used this room to change, sleeping in my bedchamber, I had not yet entered it, but I found its aspect to be pleasing. Deep blue drapes framed the windows and highlighted the intricate scrolling design etched in nearly the same shade of blue on the silvery gray wallpaper. In fact, the same blue chased itself around the room, in the toile bedspread, the coil-patterned rug, and the handsome Louis Quatorze chairs positioned before the hearth. Rather than a painting, a large mirror in a carved wooden frame had been hung above the fireplace, reflecting the light.

I'd barely had time to take it all in before there was a rap at the door followed by Bree's entrance, carrying a tray with a pot of tea and a plate of tiny sandwiches, which I attacked with relish. Gage and Henry followed swiftly on her heels.

"An excellent idea, darling," my husband declared as he crossed the room toward me. His voice was light, but his gaze was watchful, scrutinizing me for some indication of how my conversation with Aunt Cait about my mother had gone. I offered him a tiny smile of reassurance. "I was just going to suggest something similar." He dropped a kiss on my brow before snagging one of my sandwiches. There were plenty of them—more than I could eat—but I rolled my eyes nonetheless, for he and my brother were both notorious for filching food from my plate.

He flashed me a grin around his bite of food before turning back toward the door as Anderley slipped inside. If the valet felt any concern about my having overheard part of his and Bree's conversation earlier—as he must have heard Bree talking to me after she left the dressing room—he didn't show it. However, I did note he cast a glance in Bree's direction before focusing on Gage.

"I'm sure you can all guess why we're here," Gage began after polishing off his sandwich in two bites. "So, while Mrs. Gage finishes her meal, I'd like to hear from Miss McEvoy and Anderley. Did you learn anything of interest from the Poltalloch staff?"

Anderley looked to Bree again where she stood with her hands clasped before her. I wanted to urge them all to sit, but there weren't enough chairs. "I'm not sure there's much to tell," he said. "It seems Mairi was well-liked."

Bree snorted, cutting him off before he could say more.

His brow furrowed irritably, at either her rude interruption or her contradicting him. Perhaps both.

"No' by the other maids," Bree insisted, crossing her arms over her chest. "O' course they *said* they liked her. Most people aren't so rude as to speak ill o' the dead. But they were a slovenly bunch. Stains on their aprons, tears in their sleeves, missin' caps. At any other house they woulda received a scoldin' or worse for presentin' such a careless appearance."

I lifted my gaze to catch Gage's eye. "Mrs. Kennedy, the housekeeper, did indicate they have difficulty keeping staff. That she relied on Mairi a great deal."

Bree nodded. "I figured as much. 'Twas her job to train the others and keep 'em in line, and they resented her for it." She paused. "But I dinna think they killed her for it. No' even by accident." She turned to Anderley, her mouth curling derisively. "No' wi' the way they were carryin' on, terrified they would be poisoned next."

Anderley joined her in her disdain. "Two of them even claimed they felt ill but seemed to feel well enough after I'd escorted them to the servants' yard."

What precisely he meant by that, I didn't know. And for Bree's sake, I decided not to ask.

"It could all be a clever ruse," Henry pointed out from where he leaned against one of the bedposts.

"Maybe," Bree admitted, sharing another look with Anderley. "But I doubt it."

"Did the maids say anything about Mairi's regular duties? Or whether they'd seen her eat anything that morning before she left?" I asked, before taking a sip of tea to wash down the cucumber-and-watercress sandwich.

"They said she ate the same food as the rest of them," Anderley said. "And as to her duties, she seemed to do a bit of everything."

"Had her hand in everythin'," Bree contributed with a nod. "That's the way they put it."

"Did they mention Miss Margaret preferring her?" I pressed.

"Oh, aye," she replied with a humorless laugh. "We heard plenty aboot what a jammy assignment that was. How Miss Margaret would make ye putter aroond her room, doin' nonsensical things or fixin' her hair three different ways, just so she could talk to ye. Sometimes she'd even ask ye to sit and share her tea tray." Something that was not often done, except perhaps with the housekeeper, depending on how close of a relationship she had with the lady of the manor. "Or so they claimed," she added, seeing my arched eyebrows.

It sounded to me like Miss Margaret was lonely. What must it be like to be generally limited to the same building all of one's life, with mainly your sister and the staff for company? Her sister Anne at least got to ride out across the estate and to the neighboring village, but Miss Margaret was largely confined to the walls of Poltalloch. I felt my heart stir with empathy for her, and I wondered how hard she would take the news of Mairi's death. Perhaps we *should* have insisted on speaking with her.

Gage perched on the edge of the writing table, propping one leg over the corner. "What of you, Henry?" he turned to ask his half brother. "Anything to report?"

Between Henry leaning against the bedpost with one leg crossed over the other and Gage half-on and half-off the desk, I could only surmise that the fine art of perfecting the elegant slouch must be a family trait. In my husband's case, I knew he employed it whenever he was giving something or someone a great deal of deep consideration but didn't want to *seem* as if he was doing so. I studied Henry's countenance, wondering if his motivation was similar.

"Nothing other than Lord Ledbury's arrival." He dipped his auburn head toward his shoulder. "Unless you want to hear about Lord Barbreck's periodic bursts of temper."

None of us wanted that. And given everything I now knew he'd been keeping from us, I no longer had patience for his petulant outbursts.

I set my cup down on its saucer with a decisive click. "Well, unless Gage has something to say, I have a number of things to share." The others turned to me with interest, and when my husband didn't speak, I took that as my cue to begin. "First of all, I confirmed with Mrs. Mallery that Lord Alisdair did, in fact, live in a cottage at the edge of the estate. But I also learned that he often had an Italian friend who visited him."

Had Gage not been perched on the desk next to me, I might not have noted his subtle shift in posture. My gaze lifted to his, letting him know he was correct to assume this was important evidence.

"A friend named Signor Pellegrini, who also happened to be an artist." I turned to the others, focusing on Anderley in particular, whose country of origin was Italy, but he made no discernible reaction. "A muralist, apparently, by trade. But I presume he also worked on canvases."

Gage scowled. "And yet Lord Barbreck failed to think this was pertinent. Even when you specifically asked about artists visiting the area."

"Yes, that makes three lies of omission. Three key pieces of information he certainly knew and should have told us about."

"Three?" Henry questioned innocently, and I realized only Gage knew about my mother's connection to the Campbells of Poltalloch.

"Yes," I began hesitantly, trying to decide how much I wanted to tell them. But then I realized the matter needn't . . . *shouldn't* be a secret. The most distressing thing about it had been that it had been kept from me for so long, whether intentional or not. "I recently learned that my mother was wed to Miss Campbell's nephew before she married my father."

They all reacted with varying degrees of surprise. Bree's eyes flared wide, while Anderley barely flickered an eyelash. But Henry's was the most evident. His fair skin flushed to the roots of his hair, likely from embarrassment at his having asked the question

that required me to make such an admission. I offered him a reassuring smile, not wanting him to blame himself.

"But now knowing those three omissions," I continued, re-
verting to the original topic. "Omissions Barbreck should have
known we would find out about sooner or later, I have to wonder
whether there's more."

Gage's fingers drummed against the desk. "It sounds like it's
time we had yet another discussion with our host."

I nodded. "And we also need to take up his offer to have his
steward assist us in searching the records. But not just for the
forgeries but all the paintings Barbreck acquired, particularly
through his brother, Lord Alisdair."

My husband recognized the grim tone of my voice. "You
found another forgery?"

"Three, actually. Possibly four."

This time their reactions were not stifled by politeness.

Bree shook her head as if astonished at the absurdity. Gage
mumbled a curse beneath his breath, while Henry found slightly
more polite words.

"I thought Barbreck was supposed to be some sort of art
expert."

"Clearly not," Anderley muttered wryly.

"Then exactly *how many* forgeries are in this lauded collection
of his?" Gage demanded to know.

"We won't know until a complete inventory is taken," I replied.

He scraped a hand back through his hair in frustration.
"Which comprises what? Several hundred pieces of art?"

"At least."

The task of assessing it would have to fall to me, so if anyone should be feeling irritated, it should be me. Though, truth be
told, examining art was never truly a hardship. Even the poorly
executed ones afforded opportunities to learn something.

Henry straightened from his slouch. "I presume you believe

the likeliest explanation is that Lord Alisdair—and consequently Lord Barbreck—was duped at the beginning, when he purchased the art. That's why you think the documentation of each sale will reveal something."

"I admit that would be the easiest and most logical conclusion." I frowned. "But there are several things that trouble me about that solution."

"Such as Signor Pellegrini?"

"*And* Lord Alisdair insisting on living in his own cottage. *And* Barbreck's insistence they were authentic when they arrived. Clearly, at some point, the marquess was deceived, but I have a difficult time believing he was deceived multiple times."

"Yes, but sometimes the eye *sees* what it *wants* to," Anderley argued, gesturing with his hands. "That's how people are tricked all the time. And Barbreck's brother, and his brother's dealer before that, *knew* that they wanted to see a painting by a master."

"Perhaps, but after the debacle with the Titian, and his broken engagement with Miss Campbell, I have to believe Barbreck would have been more critical than before of the pieces his brother brought him, whether he wished to be or not."

"Actually, I believe the debacle with the Titian would have had the exact opposite effect," Anderley countered. "After all, he'd sided with his brother over his intended and her family. He'd willingly broken his engagement in defense of his brother's and their family's honor. If anything, he had even *more* invested in believing anything his brother brought to him was legitimate. For if he began to question his brother's honor, then what did that mean for his own?"

I had to admit he had a point, and I tipped my head, conceding this to him. "Whatever the case, what is certain is that Barbreck has not spent much time in the long gallery in recent years. Not with it being on the topmost floor and his trouble with his knees." I lowered my gaze to where my hand rested against the writing desk's oak surface. "Age is also not kind to the eyes, and part of me wonders whether his lordship is too proud to admit he cannot see as well as he once did."

So, if the paintings had been switched later, that could perhaps explain why he'd not noticed the uneven quality of the paintings in the last ten years or so. However, if they had been changed out much before then, I had to think Anderley was right. Barbreck had allowed himself to be blinded by pride and emotion. If only we could pinpoint when the forgeries had taken their place in the long gallery, then we might have some answers.

"You think Mairi MacCowan's death has something to do with those forgeries."

It took me a moment to realize my husband was speaking to me, and that he'd correctly interpreted my ruminations. "I know we don't have any evidence *proving* such a thing, but everything inside me is telling me it *has* to. From everything we've learned, Mairi was not a creature of whim. If she was in that long gallery, then she was there for a reason. I just don't know what. Not yet."

Gage reached out to still my gesticulating hands, offering me a gentle smile. "You don't have to sell *me* on the idea. I learned my lesson long ago never to doubt your intuition."

My insides warmed at this simple demonstration of his confidence and faith in me.

"Then if we can figure out how and where the forgeries came from, we might better understand who killed Mairi. Or vice versa," Henry summarized.

"Yes," I agreed, grateful to him for putting it so succinctly.

Gage straightened his relaxed posture. "Then, Kiera, why don't you continue to focus on the forgeries, since you obviously have the most expertise in that area."

I made a note on the list before me. "I'll finish examining Barbreck's collection so we know how many forgeries we're being confronted with and begin trying to figure out how they're related, and how they connect to Mairi." I peered up at Gage. "One of *your* priorities needs to be finding Liam Gillies. We need to know exactly what symptoms Mairi was exhibiting before she died. Maybe then we can better identify the poison she ingested."

"As to that," Bree interjected from her position standing behind the back of one of the chairs. "I wondered whether it might be some sort o' pigment. Somethin' ye would use in your paints."

I tilted my head, much struck by this idea.

"I ken how poisonous some o' those substances are. 'Tis why ye trained me to mix 'em for ye while ye were expectin' the bairn."

"And that would tie in with the art forgeries," I added, letting her know I was following her reasoning. "It's an interesting possibility. Some pigments contain arsenic, antimony, or lead, among others." I frowned. "But most of those cause severe gastric distress. And I've never heard of them causing someone to bleed from their facial orifices." I narrowed my eyes. "I shall have to think on it."

Gage's face had tightened during this litany, perhaps unhappy to be reminded of the potential dangers I faced while pursuing my passion for painting. But he knew how much my art meant to me and how careful I was with my pigments, so he kept his apprehensions to himself.

"I also find myself returnin' to Mairi's position at Poltalloch," Bree confessed, her brow scored with deep furrows beneath her strawberry blond curls.

"What do you mean?" I asked her.

"Weel . . ." She paused, seeming to sift through her impressions. "I ken ye were told that Mairi took her position at Poltalloch because there were no positions open here at Barbreck, but I've visited enough big houses like this one to ken that there are always positions open for hard workers like Mairi. Especially if they've family already on the staff."

"Then you think Mairi went to work at Poltalloch of her own volition?" I replied, having also pondered the oddness of the maid's employment choice, though I hadn't been able to see it as clearly as Bree.

Her gaze was solemn. "I think it highly likely."

"If that's true, then it raises a number of new questions," Gage remarked. "For why would she *choose* to work for a different household than her father?"

"And a different household than her beau," I reminded them. "Though I suppose we don't know exactly when Mairi and Liam began courting."

"Particularly when that different household is rumored to pay less and shows a markedly greater rate of changes in its staff," Anderley drawled, his expression conveying his opinion of that fact.

"Perhaps she was enticed there for some reason," Henry suggested, speaking into the brief silence that had fallen after all these statements.

We all turned to look at him more fully, and he shifted his feet as if uncomfortable with the scrutiny. Of the five of us, he was the newest addition to our investigative unit, and also still growing accustomed to his relationship with his half brother. It had been evident to me from the beginning how much he wished to make a favorable impression on Gage, but perhaps that also extended to our inquisitive quartet.

He squared his strong jaw with the cleft in the chin. "It stands to reason that if she chose to work at Poltalloch, and she wasn't escaping something negative about Barbreck, then there must have been something that attracted her there instead."

"You may be right," Gage said, rubbing his equally strong jaw between his fingers in thought. "I wonder if her father or Liam would know, or if it's something she deliberately kept from them." His gaze strayed toward Bree. "Miss McEvoy, see what you can uncover about the matter. But do so circumspectly," he cautioned.

She nodded. "O' course." Her whisky brown eyes seemed to reflect as much as they concealed as they met mine. "I'll also find oot what I can aboot Miss Ferguson."

I continued to meet her gaze steadily, even though I was now curious whether she already knew something, and if so, why she'd not wanted to reveal it in front of the others.

"Lord Henry and I can ask Mr. MacCowan about Miss Ferguson's visit to him when we pay him another call to ask about Mairi's employment at Poltalloch," Gage remarked, rising to his feet from his partial perch on the edge of the desk. "We'll also explore the area around Liam's former home and make a preliminary search of Lord Alisdair's cottage." He cast me a knowing smile. "Though I'm certain you wish to be there when we take a look inside."

My lips curled upward in agreement, but my attention was more consumed by the look I'd seen flutter across Anderley's features. It was evident he'd expected to be the one to help Gage question Mr. MacCowan and search for Liam, as his position in the past had always been as Gage's right-hand man. When I had begun joining Gage in his inquiries, Anderley had been forced to grow accustomed to me often inserting myself in that position, but there had still been many instances when, due to my gender and lack of experience, Anderley's presence had been preferred and needed over mine. But Henry was a man; one who was strong and fit, and trained as a gentleman in shooting, fencing, and fisticuffs. If Henry was to now ride at his half-brother's side, then where did that leave Anderley?

His and Gage's relationship as valet and employer had never been a normal one. After all, Anderley had originally been an Italian Boy—one of the countless number of children indentured by their families back in Italy to padrones, believing they would be taken to a more prosperous country and taught a trade, only to find themselves in a strange land being exploited, mistreated, and essentially enslaved. Anderley—or Andrea Landi, as he'd been named at birth—had managed to escape from his master in London and make his way to Cambridge, where he'd saved Gage from a gang of thieves who had set upon him. Since then he had worked for Gage in capacities that far surpassed the simple description of a valet and had shown himself to be as much a confidant and friend as an employee.

Watching Gage's newly discovered half brother encroach on the place he'd always held in Gage's life clearly bothered him. Though I knew he would be horrified by the idea that I had been able to glean such a thing from a simple look. Anderley was normally able to blunt his emotions, to stifle and pack them away, and refuse to give them sway. It was a technique he'd learned for his own survival. One that we recognized in each other, for I'd adopted the same strategy during my marriage to Sir Anthony, though I no longer strove to employ it. For Anderley to have allowed even a quiver of his feelings to slip through told me just how keenly he felt the cut of Gage enlisting Henry's help over his own.

"Then does that leave Anderley to search through Lord Barbreck's files with the assistance of his steward?" I prompted, careful to keep my voice strictly neutral.

"If there's time," Gage replied, leveling his gaze at his valet. "But first and foremost, I need you to assist Mrs. Gage. She may be the expert, but I know you are better informed about art than you would lead others to believe."

I turned to Anderley in surprise, not having guessed this about him.

He responded with subtle mockery. "Because I'm Italian?"

Gage arched his eyebrows in response. "You're the one who mentioned how Napoleon appropriated countless pieces of art from all the Italian states, particularly Venice, when he conquered them thirty-odd years ago, sending the best to museums and auctioning the rest for profit."

I'd not thought of that, but it presented an interesting possibility. Could some of Barbreck's collection have been acquired by his brother during those sales? If so, the discovery would be scandalous, for a British noble would have then poured money into the coffers of the enemy. However, Barbreck would not have been the first British collector to do so. At times, the acquisition of art and antiquities could be as much a madness as anything else, trumping all other loyalties, even to country.

Anderley did not respond but stalwartly stared back at him as Gage continued. "I need you to help Kiera sort through the collection and *all* the implications of it. And I need you to be available to assist Mrs. Gage or Miss McEvoy in any capacity should they require it."

Though this was phrased in as understated a manner as possible, I knew what my husband was actually saying. He wanted Anderley nearby for our protection. I couldn't fault his instincts. Not when I'd found myself in dangerous situations before. Though the same could also be said for Gage. But rather I chose to focus on Anderley, hoping he recognized the confidence Gage had in him to trust him with our well-being in his absence.

For a moment, Anderley seemed reticent to agree to Gage's request, but then he nodded once in acceptance, their eyes communicating more than their body language. Whether Anderley had agreed simply because he felt he was required to do whatever was asked of him or because he acknowledged the responsibility of his assignment, I didn't know, but I could tell he was far from satisfied.

"Then we have our tasks," Gage declared. "Henry, why don't you see that our horses are saddled while Kiera and I have a word with Barbreck."

I grimaced, preparing myself for the snarls and snaps to come.

CHAPTER 18

Contrary to what I'd expected, Lord Barbreck met our questions and accusations with sullen silence rather than loud rebuttals. Each new complaint and demand for answers was only met by more stubborn brooding. At first, I found his display as maddening as Gage, whose temper seemed to build with every unanswered query, but then I recognized our anger would get us nowhere. Not when the marquess was clearly even *more* infuriated with himself than we were.

I rested a hand against Gage's chest to quiet him before he could utter another vehement challenge. He turned his scowl on me but obeyed my unspoken request.

At first, Barbreck didn't seem to notice that we'd stopped speaking, but continued to glare out the windows of his study overlooking the formal garden. Out of the corner of my eye, I could see that Gage was tempted to break the silent stalemate, so I kept my arm linked with his, determined that we wait out the older man. I knew Barbreck well enough to realize that he wouldn't be able to keep his mouth closed for long. Not when someone else wasn't rattling on and driving his impetus to remain taciturn.

He huffed one aggrieved breath and then another, wriggling his shoulders as if finally acknowledging the uncomfortable sensation of having been trapped in his lies of omission. "Aye, I neglected to tell ye aboot Alisdair's cottage and his Italian friend," he begrudgingly admitted. "But that's only because neither is of any consequence." He glanced at me before returning his gaze to the water-speckled windows and the gentle rain that was still falling. "And I thought ye kent aboot yer mother. How was I to ken ye didna?"

"Come now, my lord," I replied in milder reproach than he deserved. "If your brother's cottage and Signor Pellegrini were truly of no consequence, then you would never have felt the need to conceal them from us in the first place."

He turned his ferocious glare on me. "Dinna try to flim-flam me, lass. 'Twas to keep ye from leapin' to the wrong conclusion, just as you're doin' noo."

"If we're inclined to leap to any conclusions, it's because you tried to keep it from us when you must have realized we would find out eventually." My voice tightened as I struggled to stifle my frustration. "You're lucky I don't view it as an insult to my intelligence."

I would like to think one of the emotions that flashed in Barbreck's eyes before he turned away was shame, but I couldn't be certain. The old curmudgeon had always been difficult to read, and that was before I'd ever been confronted with this vindictive side of him. Prior to my discovery of the first forgery, he had always been a crusty old uncle figure, prone to impertinent remarks and a dry sense of humor. But since then his cackling laugh and gentle teasing had been replaced by surly scowls and spiteful quips.

It was Gage's turn to place a quelling hand over my own

where it rested against his arm, and I made myself take a deep breath before I spoke. "We *will* be visiting Lord Alisdair's cottage. Will you provide us the key, or will we have to break down the door?" Aunt Cait had said she'd make sure I was given the key, so I knew no door-breaking would be necessary, but Barbreck didn't know that.

His gaze met mine askance, and for a moment I thought I detected a slight curl to his lip. If I'd amused him, that had not been my intent. Then he reached into a drawer in his desk to extract a thick key, plunking it down on the desk. Gage stepped forward to pocket it before the marquess changed his mind.

"Now, what can you tell us about Signor Pellegrini?" I demanded.

He arched his chin and leaned farther back in his chair, which creaked in protest. "No' much. He hailed from Rome, or there-aboots, if I recall rightly. Preferred no' to talk aboot himself. Though he was always happy to share stories aboot the great and good he'd met in his travels and painted murals for." Perhaps realizing this wasn't much of an endorsement, he then amended his statement. "He gave me no reason no' to believe him to be the upright and honorable gentleman he presented himself to be. My brother was certainly fond o' him."

That might be true, but if Alisdair had convinced Pellegrini to paint forgeries for him, then his endorsement was meaningless.

"Do you know if this Signor Pellegrini is still alive?" Gage asked, remaining focused on the facts.

"Nay, he died a few years before Alisdair in a shipwreck in the Mediterranean."

I turned to meet Gage's gaze. Then at least we knew he wasn't still lurking about creating forgeries either for himself or on the Campbells' behalf.

"You should know, I've identified at least three more forgeries," I informed him coolly, anticipating an outburst much like the other two had provoked. However, while his face and balding head flushed red, his mouth remained firmly closed. "I'm about to embark on a full inventory, and I shall notify you of the results. Are there any paintings in storage?"

At first it seemed he wouldn't answer, having returned to his sulk, but then he grumbled as he turned away, "I'll have Wheaton show you."

I studied his profile, wondering what other secrets he might be keeping from us, what other lies of omission he might have made. But I knew any further pressing on our part would only be met with stony silence.

Gage pulled me toward the door, but as we reached the entrance, I couldn't resist one last glance over my shoulder. Barbreck still sat in the same posture, but the anger that had seemed to radiate from him seconds before had dampened to something weaker. His eyes were trained on the portrait I had painted—the one of the woman who looked much like Miss Campbell. Whatever he continued to protest about his brother's innocence and honorability, I could tell that, privately, doubts had begun to creep in.

An unwanted pulse of sympathy clenched my heart before I pushed it away in irritation. While Alisdair might very well have deceived him, Barbreck still could have chosen to handle things differently. *He* was the one who had allowed his own pride to blind him for so long and cost himself and others so much. I could only hope he didn't allow that same hubris to cost those around him even more.

I met Anderley in the long gallery three-quarters of an hour later after I'd tended to Emma. I was determined to make the most of our time, and the gallery seemed like the logical place to start. As I'd requested, he'd brought paper and pencil so that we might begin a list of the paintings.

"I think our best course of action is to begin by making a note of all the pieces of art we find suspect and their location," I told him. "Then we can compare the list to Barbreck's records before returning to the paintings for further examination and testing, as needed." This would both save us time and spare the paintings any of the damage those tests might cause no matter the care I took.

A swift look over Anderley's arm showed me he'd already anticipated just such an undertaking, marking the Titian and Van Dyck down on the paper. We circled the room clockwise from those paintings, adding the alleged Gainsborough, Saloman van Ruisdael, and two Zoffany pieces I re-examined that I'd taken notice of earlier that day. Anderley also suggested we add a Filippo Lippi painting to the list, and when he pulled the small piece away from the wall, we both agreed the back of the panel on which the image was painted appeared too fresh and new.

Having finished in the long gallery, we progressed through the corridors and into other chambers, working through the house from top to bottom. Despite the fraught nature of our task, I discovered I was enjoying myself. It wasn't often that I was able to debate the merits of a painting with someone who had more than a rudimentary knowledge of art. It also allowed me to witness a side of my husband's valet I normally wouldn't be permitted to see. Anderley possessed a love for argument and debate. One that sparked in his eyes whenever we deliberated a piece's techniques and merit. At times, I even suspected he was playing devil's advocate, simply to rile me and spur on further discourse.

I began to feel empathy for Bree if this was a game he often played, but I knew my lady's maid could more than hold her own. Truth be told, I wondered if she might have derived as much enjoyment out of it as he did. Anderley's dark good looks were certainly heightened rather than diminished while making an impassioned argument, his entire body—arms, face, and feet—entering into the appeal.

And then there were times when we both found ourselves arrested by the splendor of a painting, falling silent as we stood side by side to appreciate its beauty and mastery. It was during one of these moments when my attention shifted to the man beside me, pondering the mystery he continued to present. "I wish I'd known how much you appreciate art," I remarked lightly.

He turned to look at me and then shrugged. "I enjoy it, but it is not a passion. Not like it is for you."

"But you're so well-informed." I gestured to the Velázquez hanging before us. "This is not the first time you've studied such works."

"I'm Italian," he replied, as if this justified it all, and I felt a pulse of amusement. But then he paused, perhaps recognizing that did not fully explain it. "And . . . I have a love of art, of beauty running through my veins."

I nodded, recognizing what he was trying to convey. Gage had told me his mother had been a soprano—and a successful one—before her marriage to Anderley's father. Had Napoleon not come trampling through the country, and the war had not ravaged the fragile economies of the Italian states, then it was unlikely there ever would have been a need for his family to apprentice him to the padrone, believing he was joining a traveling theater troupe. I had heard his rich tenor singing voice and wondered if he would have followed his mother onto the stage.

"What is your great passion, then?" I asked as we moved on to the next painting. "Music?"

He shook his head. "No. Not like . . . Mamma." There was a slight hesitation in his voice, as if he wasn't accustomed to allowing himself to speak her name or invoke her memory. "I'm not sure I have a great passion. I'm not sure there is room in my life for one."

I wasn't certain how to respond to this. Sometimes I forgot how the life of a servant, of anyone who was reliant on the sweat of their brow for their daily bread, could not be beholden to the whims of their desires and passions. The number of people who were able and allowed to follow such pursuits were few and far between. Even as a woman doing so, I was in the minority, for Gage, as my husband, could forbid it at any moment. *Not* that he would ever do such a thing. But the fact remained that he could.

"*'Deposizione di Cristo' di Tintoretto*," he declared as we came to the next painting, the language of his birth rolling off his tongue in easy cadence.

I turned to gaze up at the emotional scene of Christ being removed from the cross. This was the fourth or fifth Venetian artist whose work we had encountered. Perhaps there was something to Anderley's theory that some of the paintings had been acquired from the auctions that followed Napoleon's conquering of the Italian states and his confiscation of their art. I could only hope the records reflected that, though I strongly suspected they'd been modified to display a more palatable origin, and so we would have to read between the lines.

Neither of us raising objections about the Tintoretto attribution, we strolled on, entering the music room, which featured a beautifully carved harpsichord with a mermaid statue poised between the two pedestal feet supporting the wider end with the keys. The inside of the lid was painted with a pastoral scene of a forest and glade with blue mountains rising in the background. A pair of lovers stood hand in hand next to a river winding lazily toward the viewer in the far-right foreground. It appeared to me to be Italian in origin, but I was no expert in musical instruments.

"Make a note of this," I told Anderley. "I'd like to know if paintings and sculptures are the only acquisitions Lord Alisdair made."

While he bent to the task, I lifted my gaze to look around the chamber, intrigued by the mural which covered two of the walls. It was a depiction of Apollo tended by the nymphs as he plucked

on his lyre, while satyrs skipped about in the background playing pipes and flutes. From a distance, the colors and movement
were captivating, but the nearer I drew, the more flaws began to
emerge. A clumsily executed profile here and an awkward posi-
tioning of an arm there. The vibrant pigment had cracked in the
shading of the sky in the background, and yet appeared coagulated in the marbled dirt at the figures' feet.

"I wonder . . ." Anderley ruminated, as he came to stand beside me.

"Could this be the work of Signor Pellegrini?" I finished for
him, for it was obvious we had the same thought. "Lord Barbreck didn't mention anything about his having painted a mural
within the manor." I sighed. "But then, he hasn't been precisely
forthcoming."

I heard the scratch of his pencil across the paper, telling me
he was already making a notation to ask the marquess. Or better
yet, my aunt. She had been by far the most informative about
such things.

Narrowing my eyes, I scrutinized the brushstrokes in the folds
of the nymphs' gowns. A prickling sensation began along the back
of my neck, for I recognized this handiwork. I had just seen it in
the long gallery and in a painting in one of the corridors.

An artist's brushstrokes were as distinctive as fingerprints, as
unique as the swirls of color and specks of light within a person's
eyes. A student or follower could seek to emulate a master's style,
but they were never entirely successful. There were always subtle
and telling differences which could be deciphered by the trained
eye. The same could be said for forgers.

I must have made some sort of noise or sign of recognition,
for when I looked up, it was to find Anderley studying me with
almost as much intensity as I'd been studying the painting.

"You've found something important," he prompted.

"Yes." I nodded to the wall. "Whoever painted this also

painted that Van Dyck and one or more of the Zoffanys. And he may have painted the other forgeries we've found."

Anderley grasped the implication as rapidly as I had. "Then Lord Alisdair wasn't fooled into purchasing forgeries. They were created later."

I tilted my head. "Unless he purchased them in Italy from the same man who later visited him here and painted this mural. But I think it's more likely your interpretation is correct." I frowned. "That Lord Alisdair and Signor Pellegrini deliberately forged the copies, either while abroad or after they'd returned to Scotland with the originals in their possession."

"Then they either forged the copies before giving them to Barbreck or switched them for the originals at a later date."

I pivoted to gaze out the window at the broad sweep of lawn leading down toward the loch. "Perhaps they tried to fob the forged copies off first, but when they were almost caught by the Titian they sold to the Campbells, they altered their method. They gave the original to Barbreck so that the painting would initially stand up to his and others' scrutiny, and then later, when interest in it had waned, they replaced it with the copy while the marquess was away."

"That would explain why his lordship did not recognize that so many of his paintings were forgeries," Anderley agreed. "Particularly as his eyesight deteriorated."

"Yes, but . . ." I turned to look up at a pastoral landscape by an artist I didn't recognize hanging on the adjacent wall. "How were they able to make the switches without anyone noticing? Some of the forgeries are quite large." Though none of them were as massive as the one mounted before us. "Even if Lord Barbreck was away, taking part of the staff with him, there would still have been several dozen servants at work in the house and on the grounds. *Someone* must have seen *something*."

Anderley propped the book he'd used as something sturdy to

write on against his hip and tilted his head, seeming to give the matter his full consideration. "The staff of grand homes aren't precisely known for their discretion. If one of them had seen something, then the rest of the staff would know about it within hours. And if the upper servants were loyal to his lordship, then you can be certain they would have informed him of it."

"But what if the upper servants weren't loyal to his lordship?" I asked, following the direction of his speculating.

His mouth flattened into a grim line. "Then they might as easily have squashed the story among the lower staff with threats or explained it away." A furrow formed between his dark brows. "Wheaton has only been butler for about three years."

I presumed he'd learned this from one of the members of the staff, or perhaps Wheaton himself. "Which means the former butler was pensioned off just a few years after Lord Alisdair's death."

"Apparently, he had been in service here at Barbreck Manor for most of his life, and butler for forty-some-odd years. Most of Lord Barbreck's tenure as marquess."

The same span of years when the forgeries would have been swapped for the originals.

"We need to speak with him," I stated.

He nodded. "I'll ask for his direction as soon as we've finished here and then look in on Bree." Though I didn't think my expression had betrayed by even a flutter of an eyelash what I was thinking, Anderley's already correct posture straightened even further. "If one of the servants who are still here does know something, they might not appreciate her poking around."

"That's true," I readily agreed. "And Gage did ask you to see to our safety while he was away."

A pale flush tinged the crest of his cheekbones—a sight I had never thought to see, for Anderley was not easily embarrassed or discomforted, and his olive-toned skin masked much of such a reaction. Though I wasn't certain precisely which of my words had brought it about.

Wishing to spare him, I turned away, moving on to the next painting. "Just a few more rooms," I declared. "I've already examined many of the paintings in the more public areas on the ground floor, and it's doubtful the forgers would have been audacious enough to swap any of the works of art hanging there for fear of Barbreck or others noticing the change."

That didn't mean they hadn't considered it, but there was a reason the forgers had gotten away with their ruse for fifty years, and that was because they were clever enough not to take such foolhardy risks. I could only hope they'd been foolhardy in other ways.

CHAPTER 19

The list being finished, Anderley left it in my care and hurried belowstairs to check on Bree and speak with Wheaton about the former butler. This left me standing in the small parlor on the uppermost floor of the manor. As we'd descended methodically through the floors of the manor, we'd realized we'd forgotten the narrow tower that housed but two chambers, and so we'd retraced our steps up the stairs to inspect it last. But we'd soon discovered there were few pieces of art in the parlor, and even fewer in the billiards room. None were of note.

I watched as Anderley disappeared down the circular stone staircase and moved to follow, but then the staircase winding upward caught my eye. From the exterior, I'd noticed the parapet at the top of the tower and suspected there were fine views of the surrounding countryside from its height. Folding the paper carefully and tucking it into the pocket of my morning dress, I changed course.

As suspected, the door at the top opened onto a flat roof. The rain which had first poured down earlier and then drizzled had moved on to the east, leaving the evening sky painted in shades of fiery oranges and yellows. I breathed deep of the brisk air, its crispness settling with almost a bite at the back of my tongue. The vista over the trees toward the blue undulating loch to the west and the green and brown marbled crags to the north, east, and south was certainly spectacular. It possessed a light and clarity I'd yet to see an artist truly capture on a canvas, and one I readily accepted was beyond my ability, no matter how I might have strived to ensnare it with pigment.

It was that clarity which called to me now as I lifted my arms to rest them on a merlon. I'd observed long ago how often the higher I was, the clearer my thoughts became. Whether it was the loft of the library at Gairloch Castle, the tors of Dartmoor, or my art studio at the top of our Edinburgh town house, the loftier my position, the more lucidity it brought. And I definitely craved lucidity now.

It seemed that Anderley and I had uncovered the origins of the forgeries, if not the forgers' precise motive or methods, but I still didn't see how they connected to Mairi MacCowan and her death. Perhaps I was clutching at straws, seeing a connection where there was none. But even as such an excuse occurred to me, I'd already discarded it. They were linked somehow. Every instinct within me told me they were. But how?

If Gage and Henry could find Liam, perhaps some of our questions would be answered, but I was logical enough to realize it would be mutton-headed to expect he could answer them all. I turned toward the south, hoping to catch sight of the brothers returning to Barbreck, perhaps with another man in tow. Which is when I spotted her.

She was standing on the opposite side of the river at the edge of the line of trees which skirted the base of the ridge of crags which separated Barbreck from the rest of Argyll to the south and east. She was too far away for me to distinguish anything about her other than the fact that she was wearing a brilliant blue cloak, but the sight brought a lump to my throat. My mother had owned a cloak the exact same shade of azurite. Whenever she wore it, her lapis-lazuli eyes—the same color as my own—sparkled like jewels.

I hadn't thought of the cloak in years, but now I wondered what had happened to it. Perhaps Alana knew. Perhaps she'd kept it.

The woman didn't move for a long time but simply stood there, half in the shadow of the trees and half out. I couldn't see her face, but I somehow felt that she was watching me. When I shifted across the roof to be nearer to her, she whirled about in a graceful movement. Then with one last look over her shoulder, which raised gooseflesh across my skin, she vanished into the trees.

My heart pounding in my ears, I raised my hand to stop her, though what I intended to do then I couldn't fathom. All I knew was that look, that twirling movement was so familiar, and for a moment I thought for certain the woman was my mother.

Which was impossible! My mother had been dead for eighteen years. At eight years old, I'd not been allowed to view her body, but my father and dozens of other family members had. There was no doubt that her remains lay in a grave beneath the branches of an old oak tree in the graveyard next to St. Cuthbert's Church in Elwick, Northumberland. So the very idea that she was here now, watching me from the trees, was not only absurd, it also bordered on mad.

I forced a deep breath past the tightness in my chest, feeling it flutter in my lungs as I tried to dismiss the unsettling feelings that had crept over me. The woman had to be someone else. Why she had been standing at the edge of the trees, I didn't know, but she must have been there for a reason. Perhaps she had information for us. Information she was hesitant to share. Or else why hadn't she simply rapped on the door to the manor and asked to speak with us?

I scanned the trees one last time and then allowed my gaze to trail up over the boulder-strewn Corlach crag which rose above them, but there was no further sign of the woman or her azurite cloak. Forcibly turning my back on the sight, I retreated to the stairs, regaining some of my equilibrium as I entered the castle and began to descend.

A tight laugh escaped from my lungs at my silliness. Of course, it made sense that the distinctive shade of the cloak would have invoked my mother's memory, especially after learning just that morning that my mother had once been wed to a man who hailed from the castle a short distance away. But to let my imagination run rampant, to actually consider the woman might be my mother, or her ghost even, was daft.

I shook my head, hastening down the next flight of steps, and nearly collided with Miss Ferguson as I emerged in the corridor outside the long gallery. She stumbled back, pressing a hand to her chest.

"My apologies," I told the governess, reaching out a hand to steady her, but she shrugged it away. "I misjudged how fast I was moving."

She nodded, smoothing back a strand of blond hair that had come loose from its pins, and eyed me warily.

It was clear I'd given her a great fright, and no wonder. She had stumbled across Mairi's body in the adjacent room nearly twenty-four hours before, and it was evident that it still troubled her.

"Would you like to sit with me for a moment?" I asked, hoping to soothe the woman and also take advantage of the opportunity to question her.

But she shook her head and began to back away. "The children. I must return."

"Of course," I replied. I would have to ask Rye what—if anything—they had been told of the incident, and how they were handling the news. When a murder had taken place at the seat of my brother-in-law's carldom, he and my sister had agreed to keep the disturbing occurrence from their children, but with Rye's children's governess being the one who had found the body, less than a hundred feet from the nursery, that changed matters.

Before I could say more, she disappeared into the long gallery. I supposed this answered my question about whether she often used the chamber as a shortcut to the rooms and stairs on the opposite side of the castle. Not that I begrudged her its use. There was no reason she shouldn't do so. But it helped explain her presence there the previous night.

With that discovery filed away in my brain, as well as my observations about Miss Ferguson's demeanor, I continued to my own chamber and Emma.

By the time Gage returned with Henry from their errands, there wasn't time for a lengthy chat before dinner about what they'd uncovered. Moreover, the taut line of his lips as he hurried into our bedchamber from the dressing room gave me some indication that such a chat wasn't even necessary.

I reached up to adjust his cravat and affix his garnet stickpin deep within its snowy depths while he straightened his cuffs. "No luck?" I asked sympathetically.

"Liam Gillies still eludes us," he muttered in response. "There was no sign of him at his mother's croft or Lord Alisdair's cottage. We didn't enter, but the dirt hadn't been disturbed before the entrances, nor the grass from under the windows."

His jaw still glistened from his shave, and the hair at his temples was damp. I reached up to give the artful toss of curls that fell over his brow a further twist. "Well, have patience," I reminded him as well as myself. "It's only been a day, and this land isn't exactly the most hospitable or easy to search. There are any number of places he could have concealed himself, at least for a short time."

He exhaled a long breath, and some of the tension eased from his shoulders. "The stable master warned us the inland terrain is some of the roughest in Britain. Boggy valleys between rocky ridges. And that being unfamiliar with the landscape, we should be careful."

I stepped back, allowing my gaze to sweep over his appearance from head to toe.

His lips quirked at the corner. "Will I do?"

Returning to his side, I smiled softly up at him. "Always."

I arched up onto my toes, meeting him halfway as he bent to press a tender kiss to my lips.

"But we should hurry," I declared, pulling away. "Lest they begin dinner without us."

"Hungry?" Amusement lightened his voice.

"Ravenous!"

"Then let's not dawdle."

"What of Mr. MacCowan?" I asked as we made our way down the corridor, arm in arm.

"Not at home."

"So no progress made there either." I glanced sideways at him. "Did Anderley tell you about our afternoon?"

"Briefly. Oh! He did ask me to mention that he'd learned the direction of Barbreck's former butler."

I met his gaze eagerly.

"Elgin."

"In Moray?" Two hundred miles away.

He nodded.

"Well, that hampers our ability to question him." I'd assumed the man had retired to a cottage nearby, but apparently, I was wrong. Maybe he'd gone to live with family.

"Is it important?"

I opened my mouth to explain, only to snap it shut as Lord Ledbury exited the chamber immediately to the right. We checked our steps as he closed his door with a decisive click. He nodded over his shoulder to us once curtly and then strode down the corridor.

"It appears the earl hasn't softened toward Mallery or his family," Gage murmured under his breath.

I agreed, my voice hardening. "And if he continues in this vein, he's going to throw a wet blanket over the entire wedding and extinguish all of Charlotte's joy."

"An apt description."

"I wish I knew how to help." I paused. "Other than solving this murder." I sighed. "But I'm not sure even *that* will be enough."

His arm tightened around mine. "Well, don't let him extinguish *your* joy for your friend and cousin. They'll both need it to tend their own fires over the next few days." His gaze sharpened as it focused down the corridor toward where the earl had turned to disappear down the stairs. "As for Lord Ledbury, let me have a crack at him. After all, I am supposedly known for my charm and diplomacy," he added with a self-deprecating grin.

"That you are," I replied in gratitude.

Unfortunately, Lord Ledbury showed every indication that he refused to be influenced by that legendary charm. He scowled through dinner, and his scowl was still in place when the men joined us in the drawing room following their after-dinner port. When he retired soon after, I had to bite my tongue to stop myself from uttering "Good riddance" aloud.

As a consequence, everyone's spirits were dampened to some

degree, especially Charlotte's and Lord Barbreck's. Though I suspected Barbreck's mood was due more to the forgeries and ongoing murder investigation than Lord Ledbury. I was pleased to see how attentive Rye was to Charlotte, clearly sensing her distress every bit as much as I did, and the worry in her eyes seemed to soften by degrees whenever he took her hand in his.

When they wandered off together shortly after Ledbury retired, hopefully enjoying a stroll in the gloaming and a moonlit kiss, I decided it was safe for me to withdraw as well. It had been a long day, and weariness made me push to my feet slower than I wished. Gage materialized at my side, as attentive as my cousin had been, and we made our way to the door only to be brought up short by the appearance of Wheaton.

"Mr. and Mrs. Gage." He bowed. "You are just the people I was lookin' for."

I arched my brows in query.

"Your manservant, Mr. Anderley, asked me to inform you that he has somethin' urgent to relay." His eyes sparkled with a curiosity he was struggling to mask. "He asked that ye meet him and Miss McEvoy in the chapel."

Gage and I shared a look of surprise before he thanked the butler, and we hurried to answer Anderley's summons. The small chapel was located on the opposite side of the manor from the drawing room in an extension off the main block. Rising two stories, it boasted six stained glass windows, each depicting events from Christ's life, from His birth to His resurrection. The stonework was of the finest quality, with intricate tracery around the Gothic arched windows and vaulted columns supporting the roof, and the wooden pews and rood screen were topped with fleurs-de-lis and representations of the twelve apostles.

Anderley was waiting for us outside the doors. He didn't wait for us to address him before answering our most obvious question. "It's Liam. He wishes to talk."

I inhaled sharply, more relieved than I'd anticipated to discover that the first footman was uninjured and willing to speak. I supposed part of me had harbored some fear that he might have come to harm himself, though I'd refused to allow myself to contemplate it.

One of the doors was swept open by Anderley, allowing the scent of candles and old stone to sweep out and engulf us as we entered the hushed interior. I had only entered the chapel once, on my initial tour of the manor, and without the benefit of sunlight streaming through the tall windows and casting patterns from the tracery across the floor, the chamber was dim and shadowy. Several braces of candles had been lit near an alcove on the left, their flames flickering as we disturbed the air with our passing.

Bree glanced over her shoulder from where she sat in the pew nearest that alcove, her strawberry blond curls a bright halo in the gloom. Next to her slumped another figure with ash blond hair—Liam Gillies.

We crossed the room toward them, and Liam jerked his head up to meet our gazes as we rounded the pews to stand before him. It was clear that wherever he'd been hiding, it had been crude and susceptible to the elements, for the smell of dirt and damp wool assailed my nostrils. A towel was draped around his shoulders, and dirt streaked the side of his forehead near his hairline. His face was pale, and dark circles ringed the eyes that stared up at us guardedly.

"Liam Gillies?" Gage asked evenly.

When he didn't answer, Bree nudged him with her shoulder. "Go on."

"I heard you were lookin' for me," he murmured hoarsely, his eyes darting from Gage to me and back again, as if searching for confirmation. When neither of us leapt on him, he craned his neck forward, the veins on either side standing out as he made his plea. "I didna kill Mairi."

"We know," I replied softly.

His eyes flew wide, searching my face as if to be certain this wasn't some kind of trick.

"It was poison."

At this pronouncement, his shoulders sagged, and his head bowed, the heavy burden of his pain and grief evident in every line of his body.

I sank down on the pew in front of him, turning to the side to look over the back of it.

"Please, can you tell us what happened, what you observed?" Gage said as he joined me. "It could help us figure out how this happened to her."

Liam nodded, still staring at his feet. "What do ye want to ken?"

"Had you and Mairi planned to meet yesterday evening?"

He swallowed before lifting his head. It seemed like he had to force himself to speak, and I wondered if he'd gotten any rest today or the night before. "Nay. 'Twasn't her usual day off. But I was happy to see her nonetheless."

Of course he was. They were in love. Though I found it interesting that no one else had mentioned that yesterday was not Mairi's usual day off. Not Mrs. Kennedy or the rest of the staff at Poltalloch, and not her father.

"How did she seem to you when you saw her?" I inquired. "Was she her normal self?"

"She . . . she seemed tired, and she had a cough. But I just assumed she'd caught a bit o' a cold or the beginning of an ague."

"Did she complain of a stomach upset at any point?"

He shook his head. "Nay, but she felt cold. And clammy. I asked if she wanted to lie doon for a bit, but she kept insistin' she was fine." His mouth turned down at the corners. "Then she begged me to show her the paintin'. The one you'd discovered was a fake."

"Did she say why?" Though I'd tried to keep my tone even,

my eagerness must have been evident, for he hesitated a moment before answering.

"She said Miss Campbell had sent her to look at it."

Gage and I shared a speaking look.

"Miss Campbell sent her?" I repeated.

"Aye. Wanted her to report back on what she saw."

And yet when I'd asked Miss Campbell earlier that morning if she knew why Mairi had been in the long gallery, she'd denied knowing anything.

"Did she say *why* she wanted her to report back?" I asked, struggling to suppress the flash of anger I felt at Mairi's employer.

"Nay."

Gage draped his elbow over the back of the pew, his watchful expression telling me he was aware of my irritation. "What happened when you reached the gallery?"

Liam swallowed again, his arms clutching the towel tightly around him and his gaze far away. "Mairi's coughin'. It grew worse. It got so she couldna catch her breath. And then . . . and then she dropped to her knees and started twitchin', like she'd fallen in an icy loch." His tone was rough with emotion. "I tried to help, but there was nothin' I could do. And then she started to bleed—from her eyes and nose and . . . I didna ken *what* to do!" His voice dropped to a whisper. "Before I could even cry for help, she was dead."

We all sat silently for a moment, contemplating the horror of what he'd just told us.

"Puir Mairi," Bree murmured, voicing all of our thoughts, before crossing herself. Her lips moved in a short prayer. I bowed my head to silently join her.

I tried to place myself in Mairi's shoes. She must have been terrified and in great pain. But how had she come to be in such a state? What poison had she been given? And who had given it to her, and why?

I amended what we now knew about the poison. It caused not only bleeding from the facial orifices, ulcers in the mouth, and coughing, but also convulsions. Toward the end, the symptoms seemed to have progressed at a rapid rate. Liam said that she'd struggled to catch her breath, which made me wonder if her lungs had also been hemorrhaging and filling up with fluid. Whether that hemorrhaging ultimately caused her death or her heart gave out from the strain on her system, I couldn't say, but the results were the same.

Either way, this was not a natural death, nor was it caused by physical violence. Mairi had undeniably been killed by some type of as-yet-unknown-to-me poison.

What also seemed certain was that Miss Campbell had been the reason she went to the long gallery, despite her protestations to the contrary. It was possible Liam had lied, seizing on the excuse that Mairi's employer had sent her in order to explain away his infraction in sneaking her up to that chamber, but I didn't think so. I could detect no artifice in his statements, only pain and grief and confusion. Miss Campbell, on the other hand, had multiple reasons to deny her involvement, chief of them being her feud with Lord Barbreck.

I wondered how she would respond when we confronted her with Liam's assertion. Our past interactions had suggested she was a sensible and pragmatic person, but I had witnessed more times than I could count how the act of murder could drive the sense right out of a person.

CHAPTER 20

My feet dragged as I climbed the stairs to our bedchamber while Gage settled the matter of Liam's absence with Wheaton, at least temporarily. Though we didn't anticipate the footman being released from his employment when his behavior had been motivated by grief and shock, Gage wanted to be certain no actions were taken against him for the time being. I spared a moment of curiosity for how Callum, the second footman, would react to Liam's return, but it slipped from my thoughts as I sank down on the edge of the bed to unfasten the ankle ties of my slippers. I dropped each satin shoe and reached under my skirts to roll down my stockings before sinking my toes into the plush rug with a sigh.

I listened for the sound of Emma's cries or Mrs. Mackay's voice from the nursery next door, but all was quiet. Leaning forward, I reached for the watch I'd set on the bedside table, only to be brought up short at the sight of the object on my pillow.

It was a portrait. A miniature watercolor affixed in a round golden frame. Lifting it carefully, I cradled the image in my hands, recognizing the figure immediately. After all, I saw many of the same features in the mirror every morning, including the bright dots indicating her lapis-lazuli eyes.

But what was this miniature of my mother doing on my pillow? And who had put it there? I looked about me, as if the answer might be found in one shadowed corner of the room or another, but the chamber was empty except for me. I couldn't halt the flutter of uncertainty in my stomach or the way my skin pebbled as if a chill wind had blown across the back of my neck. Just as I couldn't stop my thoughts from straying to the woman I'd seen this afternoon from the rooftop.

Was this a coincidence, or was someone deliberately trying to conjure the image and memory of my mother? Flipping the portrait over, I discovered that someone had written her name on the back. Or her name as it had been when this watercolor was painted—Greer Rutherford Campbell. She had not yet wed my father and was perhaps still wed to Edmund. Alana, Trevor, and I were not even specks in her eyes.

How long I sat staring down at the lovely young woman, I didn't know, but I heard the door open and then close, and still I didn't look up. I heard the soft swish of Bree's skirts as she bustled about my dressing table and then approached.

"Is that you, m'lady?" she asked, having paused beside me.

I inhaled a ragged breath before replying. "My mother."

"You look like her."

"A bit." I reached over to prop it on the bedside table before turning to face her. "I found it on my pillow. Did you put it there?"

Her brow furrowed slightly. "Nay, m'lady." She paused, considering the matter. "But maybe Mrs. Mallery placed it there?"

I glanced back toward the painting. She was right. That would be like my aunt. Perhaps it had been in her possession, and after our conversation that afternoon about my mother's first marriage, she'd decided I should have it.

I forced a breath deeper into my lungs. Yes, that was the likeliest explanation. There was no reason for this uneasy feeling. And I would ask her about it in the morning to prove it.

Unfortunately, my aunt had not yet risen the following morning when Gage, Anderley, Brec, and I set off once again for Poltalloch Castle. Today it was Henry who was left behind, but with the important task of searching Barbreck's files with the aid of the steward. I had given him the list of potential forgeries whose purchase agreements he should locate, while also gleaning as much information as he could about Lord Alisdair's financials and his usual methods for acquiring art and from whom. Given the duties he sometimes undertook on behalf of his family, traveling far and wide to put matters in order for the Duke and Duchess of Bowmont and his various half brothers and sisters, he was likely the best person to accomplish the task anyway. He would be able to spot discrepancies or odd business and financial practices far quicker than I could, in any case.

We arrived just as Miss Campbell was striding from her door in another sensible riding habit, but at the sight of us, her footsteps checked. Our eyes met, and the subject of our private discussion during our last visit came rushing back to me. My cheeks flushed, recalling how I'd told her I wasn't ready to discuss her revelation about my mother, and I *still* didn't know if I was. Whether she sensed this turmoil or merely recognized the seriousness of our intent, she said nothing of the matter and turned to usher us inside.

Bree and Anderley were taken belowstairs, while Miss Campbell led me and Gage into the drawing room before swiveling to face us with her hands clasped before her. She didn't waste time with trite cordialities. "You've uncovered somethin'?"

"Liam Gillies has been found unharmed," Gage informed her.

Miss Campbell's hand lifted briefly to her chest as she inhaled swiftly. Though her relief appeared genuine, I couldn't help but scrutinize each movement, each flutter of her eyelashes, searching for any hint that her reactions were feigned.

"He returned to Barbreck Manor, and his recollection of the minutes prior to Mairi MacCowan's death further confirms the evidence of its cause being poison."

"Do we ken yet what kind?" Her gaze shifted back and forth between us almost in anticipation.

"Not yet." I tilted my head, trying to decipher whether this pleased her or not. "You told us yesterday that you didn't know why Miss MacCowan would have gone to the long gallery."

"I did," she confirmed after a brief pause. "And I do not."

"That's interesting, because we've learned that Mairi claimed that *you* had sent her. That you'd asked her to examine the forged Van Dyck."

The corners of Miss Campbell's mouth tightened, and her posture turned rigid. "Weel, I dinna ken why the lass claimed that, but I can assure ye I did *not*." She huffed in affront, and the sound was so much like the one I often heard Lord Barbreck make that I nearly missed what she said next. "To be sure, *why* would I send an upstairs maid wi' no knowledge o' art whatsoever to inspect a paintin' owned by my former fiancé?"

When she phrased it that way, it did seem strange.

"Then you're saying Mairi *lied*?" I pressed, wanting her to be clear.

"I suppose." Turning to stare across the room toward the hearth, her gaze clouded with bewilderment. "Though I dinna ken why she would have done so. 'Twasn't like her." She frowned. "Just as it isna like Liam to deny her anythin'. So why would such a ruse be necessary?"

Gage and I stood waiting as she sorted through the implications, much as we had already done, curious if she could come up with an explanation we had yet to consider. Gage had also taught me that sometimes silence was more effective than words. That people—both the guilty and unguilty—often felt driven to fill it, revealing far more than they ever would otherwise.

When she emerged from her musings to realize neither of us had spoken but were simply staring at her, her eyebrows dipped into an angry vee. "I dinna send Mairi to examine any o' Barbreck's accursed paintings," she snapped.

"Nay, dear," a voice behind us proclaimed. "But I did."

Gage and I turned to see Miss Margaret Campbell enter the room on the butler's arm. She paused just inside the doorway and turned to offer the man a gentle smile of gratitude as she patted his arm to send him on his way. Her sister hastened to help her, but Miss Margaret waved her off, making her way slowly toward the chair before the hearth she'd claimed during our first visit.

"I coulda told you that durin' your last visit, had I been allowed to see you." She arched her eyebrows in gentle scolding as she glanced back over her shoulder at her sister.

Miss Campbell scowled.

"You sent Mairi to examine the Van Dyck?" I repeated, crossing the room to join Miss Margaret as she lowered herself into the chair with great care.

She exhaled a small grunt as her bottom settled onto the cushion. "Aye. And before ye ask . . ." She shook her head. "I had no idea dear Mairi would come to harm. I simply wanted to gather what facts I could, to spare Anne any further pain." Her soft brown eyes hardened. "That man has caused her more than enough."

The anger faded from Miss Campbell's face, leaving only fond exasperation. "Oh, Meg."

"Woulda gone myself, if these old knees woulda held me up."

"Your lungs," her sister protested, moving to take the seat next to her.

Miss Margaret waved this objection away. "Bah!"

I looked at Gage, interested in what he thought of this exchange. It certainly seemed sincere, but a vague stirring in my gut made me wonder whether Miss Margaret was lying for her sister. Or was it merely residual confusion and anger from yesterday's revelation about my mother? Was I unfairly determined to blame the messenger in some way, shape, or form—even with a different crime?

My insides squirmed at the thought, and I had difficulty finding a comfortable position on the settee across from the two ladies. "We understand that you preferred Mairi to the other maids."

Miss Margaret looked to me and nodded, sadness transforming her lively face.

"I'm sorry for your loss," I began, offering her my sympathy. "You must have trusted her greatly."

A rattling sigh escaped her chest as she turned forlornly toward the fire, her arms hugging the shawl tightly draped over her shoulders. "Mairi was a kind lass. Didna make me feel awkward like the other maids do. And she wasna forever droppin' trays or touchin' my things wi'oot bein' invited, as if my eyes didna work right instead o' my lungs and my heart."

I couldn't help but feel empathy for Miss Margaret. It was never easy to be thought of or treated differently, to be eyed with pity or suspicion or disfavor. According to Miss Campbell, her sister had been sick all her life, forced to endure the slights and stares and complaints of the staff—both petty and great, silent and verbal. To lose the maid she could both trust and feel comfortable with must be a crippling blow, for I could only imagine she held Mairi in some degree of affection.

"Did you see Mairi the morning before she left for Barbreck?" Gage asked, adjusting the tails of his charcoal coat as he sat beside me. The gleam of his riding boots caught the morning sun spilling through the windows.

Straightening in her seat from the slumped posture she'd settled into seemed to require a great deal of effort, but she managed it, turning toward us with a grimace. "Aye. Brought me my breakfast tray before she departed."

"And that's the last time you saw her?"

She nodded.

Gage's fingers tapped against the side of his leg before he realized what he was doing and stilled them. "I don't know precisely how to ask this, so bear with me, but . . . could Mairi have overheard or discovered something in another manner?" His jaw hardened in aggravation at himself for his clumsy wording. "Could she have known something that might have gotten her killed?"

The icy expression returned to Miss Campbell's face. "I presume you're asking if she *discovered* . . ." she pronounced the word witheringly ". . . that something while she was here at Poltalloch. Something from us?"

"Or from her father. Or during one of her trips to and from Barbreck," Gage added, though we all knew Miss Campbell's interpretation was what he truly meant.

"No, Mr. Gage," she bit out. "We have no secrets here." Her gaze darted to me and then back. "None that we ever intended to keep, in any case."

"Why are you spendin' so much o' your time here?" Miss Margaret interjected. "Didna Mairi die at Barbreck? Isna that where she was poisoned?"

"Except the poison was ingested," I explained, realizing she had not been privy to our previous conversations. "And she ate nothing at Barbreck. She shared dinner with her father at his cottage, but she appeared to have already been showing signs of illness before that. Which makes us think the poison was slow to take effect. That she must have consumed it earlier in the day with something she ate."

"Then you believe whoever dosed her wi' it intended for it to take effect while she was at Barbreck?" Miss Campbell's face registered her doubt.

"Perhaps," I conceded. "If they were familiar enough with the effects of the poison to predict its course and the moment of its lethality." Such a thought caused a slight trembling inside me.

"Then if that's the case, maybe whoever they are, they *intended* to throw suspicion on us. For why would we send her to die in a place that was certain to raise questions aboot our involvement?"

Except Miss Margaret had sent Mairi to the long gallery, apparently without her sister's knowledge. So if Miss Campbell had poisoned her, she would not have anticipated her dying in such a place, only that she would be far from Poltalloch when the poison took effect.

But I didn't say this aloud, instead conceding her point with a dip of my head. At the least, it was something to consider. Had someone wished to point the blame at the Campbell sisters? And if so, who and why?

"May I take a look at your library?" I asked, knowing the question was somewhat abrupt, but I hoped that might work in my favor.

However, Miss Campbell was much too sharp. "So ye can search it for books on poisons?" she countered with arched eyebrows.

I sat still, willing the flush that was crawling its way up my neck into my face to stop. I refused to feel guilty for pursuing the information I must for the sake of our investigation, for justice for Mairi.

"I can already tell ye we do, for household purposes." She pushed to her feet. "Come wi' me. I'll show you."

With a glance at Gage, I rose to follow her from the room. After all, this was what we'd hoped for—the chance for one of us to speak to Miss Margaret without Miss Campbell's hovering presence. I left it to him to proceed with that and applied myself to keeping Miss Campbell distracted as long as possible. Even if it meant discussing my mother.

She guided me down the hall to a chamber near the stairwell. Though smaller than many noblemen's libraries, it was plainly well-used. The bookcases standing against every available piece of wall space were packed cheek by jowl with books—upright, on their sides, and even slanted sideways when that was the only available slot. One panel of smaller tomes was shelved two deep. The books were also well-loved—the leather dented and worn smooth with handling, and some of the spines were even cracked. A short stack of recently read books sat on the table between two worn chairs which had been positioned to best capture the light filtering through the windows above and behind and the hearth before. I could just picture the two Campbell sisters seated here side by side.

Miss Campbell pivoted to gesture toward a shelf in the middle of the wall near the door, her stature combative. "These three books are all we have."

I stepped closer to peruse the titles indicated. "Well, that's one more than Barbreck's library can claim," I told her with a sigh, having sent Bree to locate them the evening before. One of these was a duplicate, but the other two were different. "Would you mind if I borrowed them for a time?"

Miss Campbell glared at me as if she couldn't decide precisely how to react—outraged or bemused. It was a look I was accustomed to seeing.

"Until we know what killed Mairi, I'm afraid our inquiry into her death is rather at a standstill. And while there are a number of ways the murderer might have learned of the poison—after all, recipes and knowledge are often passed down by word of mouth from mother to daughter or cook to maid—unless someone comes forward who recognizes the symptoms, I'm afraid the only way I know of to uncover it is by studying these books."

Her posture had softened during this speech, perhaps recognizing I was simply after the truth. If the poison was found in one of the books shelved here, then yes, that would mean it was possible the Campbell sisters were aware of it, but others might be as well. Just as it was possible, even if the poison was not contained in these botanical and household management volumes, that they might have learned about it from another source.

"You are verra persistent, aren't you?" she finally remarked.

I shrugged one shoulder. "I have to be."

She studied me for a moment, a transformation coming over her face. "Aye, I suppose you do." Dust swirled upward as she slid the books from the shelf and passed them to me. "Your mother was much the same."

She looked up to meet my gaze, as if challenging me to turn away.

I swallowed, forcing my feet to remain planted where they were rather than flee. Gage needed more time with Miss Margaret.

"I wouldn't know," I replied softly. "I was just eight when she passed."

She nodded. "And children dinna often see their parents as full people—wi' flaws and triumphs, hopes and dreams—until they're older."

I supposed this was true, and I'd barely had that chance, as my father had died when I was just two and twenty.

"My aunt . . . I asked her about what you told me," I explained. "She . . . she said that Mother was happy here at Poltalloch. With you. But . . ." I broke off, uncertain how or if I should continue.

"But she wasna happy wi' Edmund," she finished for me.

I nodded.

She turned away for a moment, and when she looked back, her expression was troubled. "It's true. I held no illusions where my nephew was concerned. Edmund was a scoundrel and a rotten husband. But her husband he was."

I took this to mean, *and so he held all the power over her*, for it was true.

"And she loved him. Despite it all, she loved him." She shook her head, as if at the futility of it all. "If he'd allowed her to remain wi' us at Poltalloch, it might have made matters bearable. For a time, we even thought he might do it." Her mouth flattened. "But no one would have ever described Edmund as considerate. So off he took her." Her gaze slid toward the door. "I think Meg took it hardest."

"Your sister was close to my mother?" I replied, not entirely surprised to hear this.

"Greer was kind." Her eyes glistened with a sad wistfulness, one that brought a lump to my throat. "That's what I remember most aboot her. Her kindness. Even in spite o' the fact that life was no' always so kind to her."

All I could manage was a nod, remembering her kindness, too. Even as a child, I had seen it in the way she treated others—whether a maid or a countess. I'd recognized its extraordinariness because so many others were not.

"When Edmund died, we invited her to live wi' us here at Poltalloch, but neither o' us was surprised when she decided to return to her family." Her mouth curled in an attempt at a smile. "Years later, when she met your father, we were relieved to hear what a steady, honorable gentleman he was. Reports were they were verra happy together." She seemed anxious for reassurance that this was true, and I was relieved to be able to give it to her.

"They were," I said with a gentle smile as I conjured up an image of my parents together—the glint in their eyes, the way they leaned into each other.

"I often hear that your sister, Lady Cromarty, is thought to be verra like your mother. But I must say, *you* remind me o' her. Rather startlingly, in fact. At least, the way *I* remember her."

She was right. Alana was often compared to our mother. Once upon a time, my sister might have been annoyed by this, but now she viewed it as a high compliment and badge of honor. While I, on the other hand, had never been favorably linked to her. Yes, I had her lapis-lazuli eyes, but on me the color and shape had become too garish, too big, too witch bright. I knew I possessed some of her other features, for I saw them in Alana's lovely face, but in me these were ignored.

To hear Miss Campbell say that I reminded her of my mother made me want to weep, even as I wanted to ply her for more details. Except I suspected I already knew what she meant. When she had known my mother, Greer's life had been in turmoil—filled with sorrow and pain. She had likely been more subdued, more contained—something that had marked me all my life. Even now, when I was happier than I'd ever been, could ever imagine being, my past marked me. The trials I had been through and the anguish I had experienced had transformed me, perhaps permanently. It was those scars Miss Campbell saw in me as much as the physical traits my mother had passed along to me.

My voice quavered when next I spoke. "Did you ever see my mother again?"

She smiled sadly. "Once. When she came to visit her sister at Barbreck. Oh, we were invited time and again, even to her wedding to your father, but travel is hard for Meg. She had a bad spell and was even almost too sickly to see Greer when she visited, but your mother insisted on seein' her in her room anyway." Her eyes crinkled with amusement. "Even in spite o' your father's mild protests. She was expectin' your sister, so he was verra protective o' her in her condition."

This brought a smile to my own face, able to empathize with my mother, for Gage had been much the same way.

However, I could not dwell on that thought long. Not seeing how Miss Campbell's gaze strayed toward the door again, perhaps realizing how long she'd been away from her sister. I had no way of knowing how much time Gage needed, and I had one more question, so I launched into it before my hostess could begin inching her way toward the door.

"It's come to our attention that Lord Alisdair Mallery often received visits from a Signor Pellegrini, an Italian muralist," I told her, hoping she would view the clumsy change of topic as my having been persuaded to confide in her. "Did you ever suspect he might be the forger of the Titian?"

"I admit, the thought did cross my mind."

And yet she'd not raised the possibility herself when we visited to speak with her about the discovery of the Van Dyck as a fake. I tilted my head, wondering whether her reticence was long born of habit or something else.

"Did you ever wonder if it could be Lord Alisdair himself?" I pressed.

She'd felt no qualms about speaking ill of Barbreck's brother before. That is, until her sister reminded her it wasn't fair to tar the man with the same brush as his brother. But I was curious to hear what she would say now that Miss Margaret wasn't here to chide her.

"Aye. But then, it seemed more likely the forgeries were created elsewhere and Alisdair was duped into purchasin' them." Her eyes narrowed. "Are ye tellin' me ye believe differently?"

"I don't know exactly what to believe yet," I hedged. "But the fact that both of those men were painters, even if they weren't exactly masters, intrigues me."

She seemed to understand what I was trying to say. "All I can add to your evidence is more suspicions, I'm afraid." Her gaze dipped to the back of one of the chairs as she trailed her hand over the chintz fabric. "But I can tell ye, I've always struggled wi' the idea that Alisdair is behind it all. No' from any sense o' loyalty or affection, but rather because I'm no' certain he woulda been clever enough to come up wi' such a ploy." She glanced up with a wry frown before dropping her eyes again. "He was always easily led, usually by one o' his brothers. But perhaps this Signor Pellegrini was the one leadin' him, no' the other way aroond."

That was an interesting point to consider. I'd assumed Lord Alisdair had dragged his Italian friend into the scheme, but perhaps Miss Campbell was right. Perhaps Signor Pellegrini was the instigator.

There was a creaking sound outside the doorway and then the shuffle of footsteps slowly climbing the stairs.

"That must be my sister," Miss Campbell exclaimed, hurrying out.

When I followed her a moment later, Miss Margaret was already halfway up the steps. I paused to watch as Miss Campbell solicitously offered her arm, but while her sister took it, it seemed to me she didn't need the assistance quite as greatly as Miss Campbell assumed. I'd witnessed such a thing many times before, when loved ones smothered those who were ill, infirm, or simply old. The recipient usually either accepted the help so as not to cause an argument or was forever fighting against it. Miss Margaret seemed to have settled on the former.

I felt another vague stirring in my gut and frowned, turning back toward the library doorway. The creak and shuffle on the steps seemed to have indicated someone had passed by the library a much shorter time ago than Miss Margaret's position on the stairs would seem to suggest. Had someone followed her and stopped to listen? The butler or a maid, perhaps? I glanced about the hall. But then where had they gone? Down the servants' stair, undoubtedly.

I shook my head. If someone had been listening, all they'd heard was a lot of speculations about the motivation of the forgeries. Dismissing the suspicion from my mind, I carried the books Miss Campbell had loaned me into the drawing room.

"Any luck?" I murmured as I joined Gage where he stood gazing out the window at the countryside beyond.

"None." His eyes cut toward me before returning to the expanse of land, sea, and sky. "She knew what I was about and proved to be far more interested in talking about me."

My shoulders slumped.

"She's a canny one. Isn't that how the Scots would say it?"

I offered him a weak smile in answer to his jest and leaned my head against his shoulder as he shifted his arm to wrap it around me.

"She did reveal *one* thing to me, whether consciously or not."

I turned to study his profile questioningly.

"Miss Campbell is more distressed by all of this than she cares to reveal. Having her past—and the pain it's caused her—dredged up over and over again is eroding her composure."

I could relate to that. To feel that the grief and turmoil of one's past has been buried and laid to rest, only to be forced to confront it and all of its anguish, not once but multiple times in succession. Such a thing would prey on anyone.

That realization wedged a sharp fissure in my suspicions about Miss Campbell. For why would she do such a thing to herself, even in the pursuit of revenge? I simply couldn't see the pragmatical mistress of Poltalloch choosing such a course of action.

CHAPTER 21

The fine mist which had hung over the loch and clung to the winding glens early that morning had dissipated by the time we departed Poltalloch, leaving behind calm winds and clear blue skies. Even so, I found myself distracted as we picked our way down the trail, my eyes scanning the trees on either side of us for anything out of the ordinary. Such as a woman in a blue cloak.

I knew it was only my discussion with Miss Campbell about my mother that had conjured such a fanciful notion, but try as I might, I couldn't seem to dismiss it. I had learned more about my mother in the past two days than I had in all the years since her death. She felt more real to me now than she had in eighteen long years, and I couldn't halt the sensation that I was chasing some-thing. Something I'd longed for as long as I could remember—perhaps all my life—and it somehow involved my mother.

So wrapped up was I in my own thoughts that I almost

missed Bree's remark about what they'd learned from the staff at Poltalloch.

"Mairi kent her *before* she went to work at Poltalloch. She kent the Campbells, particularly Miss Margaret."

"Well, of course she did," I turned in my saddle to reply, confused by such a remark. "In this isolated an area, everyone would have known everyone, even those of a higher class."

"Nay," Bree retorted. "I mean she *kent* her. As in, they'd interacted before. Mrs. Kennedy said *that's* why she was hired despite her father workin' for Lord Barbreck's brother."

"But how can that be?" Gage's mount moved closer to mine as the path narrowed. "Miss Margaret is an invalid. She rarely leaves the castle. So where could they have met?"

I watched as a pair of dragonflies whirled and darted to and fro above our heads. "Perhaps it hasn't always been that way. Perhaps her illness hasn't always kept her so confined." I turned to look into my husband's eyes, shaded by the brim of his hat pulled low. "Maybe she used to be able to venture beyond the walls of the castle. They could have met then."

"True." He glanced over his shoulder. "Was Mrs. Kennedy the only one to confirm this?"

"Confirm it? Yes," Anderley answered leadingly. "But the other maids seemed to have no trouble believing it. They seemed to think this was the reason for her *preferred* treatment."

I rolled my eyes at the maids' obvious resentment. It would be easier for them to blame it on such a thing than examine their own behavior for fault.

I turned my head to peer through the trees as they crowded closer, their shade deepening. The sweat that had gathered at the back of my neck began to cool as I allowed my thoughts to turn over everything Bree had just revealed. Something she'd said was tickling my brain, trying to get my attention.

"Wait," I exclaimed in realization. "Did you say Mr. Mac-Cowan worked for Lord Barbreck's brother?" I turned in my saddle to see Bree's eyes widen warily, perhaps not knowing this was news to us.

"Aye. 'Least, that's what Mrs. Kennedy said."

My gaze darted to Gage, who seemed to find this piece of information as interesting as I did. "Now, why do you think Barbreck never told us that?"

Technically, even working for Lord Alisdair, Mr. MacCowan had been under the employ of the Barbreck estate, so it wasn't a lie. But it was definitely another sin of omission.

"For that matter, why did no one else?" Gage groused. "We're investigating the forgeries purchased or created by Lord Alisdair, and Mairi's death. Given Mr. MacCowan's connection to both, it seems a curious thing not to mention."

I had to agree. "Even Mr. MacCowan failed to speak up about it. He reacted when we mentioned Mairi having died in the long gallery, but he said nothing."

"And if the forgeries were created in Alisdair's cottage, he likely knows *something*." Gage leaned over to rub a soothing hand against Titus's neck as he suddenly flicked his mane. "We need to speak with him again."

I scowled, contemplating what sort of information Mairi's father might hold about his former employer. As yet, we had gathered only bits and pieces of information about Alisdair, about the man he'd been and what he might have been capable of. He was a mere sketch. We didn't even know how he'd died.

I took a swift breath, feeling the sensation in my gut that always alerted me when I'd stumbled upon something potentially important. It mingled with the knowledge that had been weighing on my mind since we'd discussed the poison with the Campbell sisters. "Has anyone mentioned whether there have been any other suspicious deaths, either at Poltalloch or Barbreck, or in the surrounding area?" I broached hesitantly.

My question was met with astonished silence.

"No?" I queried again when no one spoke.

"What are you thinking, Kiera?" Gage asked, knowing me well enough to realize that I would never posit such a suggestion without cause.

I took a deep breath rife with the scents of the forest, trying to find the right words to voice my unsettling suspicions. "It's only that, if whoever poisoned Mairi intended for it to take full effect when she was at Barbreck, perhaps even inside the long gallery, then they must have known exactly how long it would take to work its way through her system. And the only way they would have been able to make such an accurate calculation is if they were familiar with the substance." My voice deepened. *"Very familiar."*

Gage's expression was aghast. "You think they've used it before?"

"It's either that or simply luck or coincidence that Mairi died where she did."

No one seemed to have an answer for this, but I could tell they held as little faith in luck and coincidence as an explanation as I did.

"We need to expand our search," Gage asserted.

"I think so," I agreed. "We need to be sure."

The trail began to widen again, and the trees thinned, giving us glimpses of Loch Craignish in the distance, its water sparkling in the sunlight.

"We can speak to the staff," Anderley offered with a glance toward Bree.

"And I'll talk to my aunt," I said.

Gage's body swayed easily with the gait of his horse. "I assume this revelation was at least partially inspired by Mr. MacCowan's connection to both Mairi and Lord Alisdair, so I suppose that means we should find out how Lord Alisdair died. Barbreck said that Signor Pellegrini was killed in a boating accident, but I don't recall him mentioning the reason for his brother's passing."

"I'll ask Aunt Cait. I need to speak with her about another matter anyway," I told him, thinking of the miniature I'd found on my pillow the previous night. My eyes narrowed on the path before us. "Then I think it's high time we examined the interior of Alisdair's cabin."

After seeing to Emma, I went in search of my aunt and found her in the rose parlor with most of the other ladies. I felt a pulse of guilt at not being able to join them but then firmly squashed it. What Charlotte and Rye needed most right now was a resolution to Mairi's murder and the worries plaguing the household associated with that. Allowing myself to feel a guilt that neither of them wished me to would merely hinder the investigation.

Even so, I concealed myself at the edge of the doorway and beckoned to Aunt Cait the moment I caught her eye. Lady Bearsden was the only other person to see me, and she simply smiled in what seemed to be commiseration.

Having discreetly excused herself, Aunt Cait spoke in a low voice as she met me in the corridor, ushering me toward the morning room. "We can talk in here." The chamber's wide windows overlooked the azalea terrace of the manicured gardens. Bright blossoms in a kaleidoscope of shades bordered the path which slanted toward the massive fountain at the heart of the garden. Bees buzzed between the flowers, and a yellow butterfly fluttered around the stone urn at the border of the walk.

I paused to stare out at the lovely vista, suddenly wishing I had nothing more pressing on my mind than which color of azalea I preferred.

"You have questions?" my aunt prompted.

"Yes," I replied, forcing my gaze back to her face. "First . . ." I held out my hand. "Have you ever seen this miniature?"

She blinked, taking it from my fingers. "Why, yes. It's your mother." Her gaze darted between my face and the portrait. "She gave it to me many years ago. Before she married your father. I looked for it yesterday after you came to speak with me, but it wasn't in the place I usually kept it." She searched my face. "Where did you find it?"

"It was left on my pillow sometime yesterday evening."

She straightened in surprise.

"I found it there last night when I retired."

Furrows formed in her brow. "Perhaps one of the maids found it and assumed it belonged to you," she suggested, though her tone of voice said she was no more convinced of this than I was. If a maid had found it outside Aunt Cait's chambers, she would have shown it to the housekeeper, who in turn would have asked the mistress of the house—my aunt—who the object belonged to. It was possible that the housekeeper might have realized I was the daughter of the woman whose name was inscribed on the back, but then she would have also known Aunt Cait was that woman's sister and would still have enlisted her assistance in ascertaining the correct owner.

"I'll ask our housekeeper about it," she said, offering to do exactly as I'd hoped. "Was that all?"

"No, two more things actually. The mural in the music room. Can you tell me, was that painted by Lord Alisdair's friend—Signor Pellegrini?"

"Oh, I'd forgotten about that. Why, yes. Yes, it was."

"I suspected as much. It gives us a sampling of his work, his technique and brushstrokes," I elaborated.

"And you can then compare that to the forgeries."

"Precisely."

Her eyes brightened with interest. "And have you?"

I knew what she was truly asking and decided there was no harm in informing her of what we'd found. Everyone would know soon enough anyway. "I haven't yet had time to study them in depth, but there are indicators of his handiwork in at least some of the forgeries."

Her mouth turned down at the corners, and she shook her head. "I feel like I shouldn't be surprised, but I am." She turned to gaze out the window, her hand lifting to the locket dangling around her neck, much like I clutched my amethyst pendant when I was anxious. "Does this mean his lordship's brother is also involved?"

"More than likely."

She heaved a sigh of grave disappointment. "Oh, Alisdair."

"You knew him." It was a statement rather than a question, for the answer was obvious, but I hoped it would convince her to elaborate.

"I did. He was urbane and amusing, if a bit vain and supercilious. Truth be told, he was always a bit of a mystery—forever traveling and preferring his cottage to the manor. He liked to keep to himself."

"How did he die?"

"A sudden illness. Though he was seventy-four years old. He'd lived a good, long life."

My face must have registered my uncertainty.

"I'm afraid I was never privy to all the details, but if you want to know more about it, I can write to the local physician. Or you can speak to Mr. MacCowan. He was with him until the end."

Mairi's father. Yet again he was a figure at the periphery of our investigation.

"It's true, then? That he worked for Alisdair," I clarified, grateful she'd broached the subject for me.

Her brow lowered. "Is that something else Barbreck neglected to inform you?"

"We thought he was the estate carpenter."

She heaved a sigh of aggravation. "He's undoubtedly talented with wood, and he's been employed in a number of such projects around the estate. But his chief position was as a manservant to Alisdair when he was home, and caretaker of his cottage when he wasn't."

I thanked her and then set off to meet Gage and Anderley in the library, where I found Anderley perusing the titles on one of the bookshelves while Gage was seated in a chair near the windows reading some sort of document with creases. At my appearance, my husband glanced up and nodded before returning to his letter. Anderley took this as his cue to have our horses saddled and brought around, murmuring his intentions to do so as he departed.

My gaze strayed toward the door on the opposite side of the room, wondering if Henry was still closeted inside Barbreck's study with his records, before crossing toward Gage. He refolded the paper and pushed to his feet, meeting me halfway. There were no brackets at the corners of his mouth, so I assumed the missive had not been from his father.

"Cromarty," he replied in answer to my unspoken question, lifting the letter.

"How do they fare?" I asked, knowing my brother-in-law Philip always began each letter with a report on his family. A fact I had become tremendously grateful for this past spring during the turmoil that had flared up in London.

In the tumult of all the political maneuverings between the Whigs' labors to pass the popular and long-awaited Reform Bill and the Tories' efforts to squash it, rioting had erupted in the capital. Fears of armed insurrection had even led many wealthy citizens to make gold withdrawals, threatening the economic security of the Bank of England and further destabilizing the nation. Philip's and Alana's letters had been filled with frightening details, and I had been in genuine terror for them for a number of days. That is, until the Tories capitulated and the king had given in to the demands of the Whigs and the populace at large, leading to the passage of the Reform Act.

"They are well. Though, from the tone of his letter, I believe they are tiring of London. Especially in the heat of summer."

There was a reason most of society fled the city at the end of the social season for the cooler breezes and less fetid smells of the countryside. But there had been several pressing matters before Parliament this session, and so Philip and many of the other lords and members had remained. It was those pressing matters which turned out to be the main subject of his missive.

"They've passed it."

I looked up into Gage's expectant face, knowing only one such act of Parliament could have brought such an astounded expression to his beloved features. It caused an answering flutter in my chest.

"The Anatomy Act," he confirmed.

I pressed a hand to my neck, feeling a rising sense of relief.

Among other things, the Anatomy Act would now make the unclaimed bodies at workhouses, hospitals, and prisons available to physicians, surgeons, and medical students for the purposes of teaching and research. This would end the macabre necessity of hiring body snatchers to supply the corpses for their lecture halls and laboratories. Of a certainty, the act was not perfect. The very fact that the law it replaced had solely made provisions for the bodies of convicted murderers to be anatomized—making the act of dissection a form of punishment—by extension seemed to now criminalize the act of being poor. But at least it was a step in the right direction and should serve to eventually end the trade of the resurrectionists and their robbing the recently deceased from their graves.

Given my history with the subject, and the false accusations that had repeatedly been leveled against me—that I'd known about and assisted Sir Anthony in his procurement of bodies from body snatchers—it was no wonder such news should impact me so greatly. I suspected it would not be the end of the issue. Not while cholera still raged throughout parts of Britain and Europe, spurring violence and protests where people believed the physicians treating the ill were allowing the poor to die so that they could put their bodies to use on the dissecting table. There had been an article in the newspaper about an incident in Caithness-shire only a week before. But that didn't lessen the impact the bill's passage had on me. The sensation that I'd almost been granted a reprieve from some terrible punishment. It actually made my knees weak and tears prick at the back of my eyes.

Noticing this, Gage wrapped his arms around me and pulled me close. "Relieved?"

I nodded, still too stunned to speak. Maybe now some of the horror that had attached itself to the act of dissection would lessen. Maybe people would begin to view it in a different light. And maybe they would stop looking at me with such fear and disgust when they contemplated such things.

"Did he write anything else?" I asked a few moments later when I was able to gather the words.

"Just that he and Alana and the children will be returning to Edinburgh within the week. Now that the Reform Act and the Anatomy Act have passed, he's eager for a respite."

None of this news was particularly surprising or concerning, but a furrow formed in Gage's brow nonetheless.

I lifted my hand to his chin, urging his gaze to meet mine. "Then what's troubling you?"

"It's nothing," he insisted with a shake of his head.

But it clearly was, and I arched my eyebrows to tell him I knew it.

"It's only that . . . Philip thanked me again for my willingness to assist the Whigs in pressuring the king and the Tories, and apologized for raising any hopes of my receiving a title."

Earlier that spring, when it had appeared the Tories were going to prevent a third attempt at the Reform Bill from passing, even though the failure of the second bill had caused widespread unrest and rioting throughout London and other parts of Britain, the prime minister—Earl Grey—and his cabinet had decided they needed to find a way around them. So they had pressured the king to create a large enough number of new peers, all of whom would be Whigs, to push the act through the House of Lords. However, when King William IV had balked at the suggestion, Earl Grey and his cabinet had all resigned, forcing the king to turn to the Duke of Wellington to form a Tory government. When that had led to the tumultuous week of revolt and unrest that had me so frightened about Philip and Alana's safety, Wellington and the Tories had been forced to concede to the Whigs. Facing the prospect of seeing the House of Lords flooded with new Whig peers after Earl Grey's government was reinstated by the king, the Tories capitulated by refraining from voting on the measure, allowing the Reform Act to finally be passed.

Gage was to have been one of those new peers, but when he'd agreed to assist the scheme, he'd already known the matter was unlikely to progress that far. Everyone had expected the king to balk. So Philip's repeated apologies were unnecessary, though I didn't think that was what had brought such an unhappy look to Gage's eye.

"And?" I prompted gently.

He sighed, but I could tell his vexation wasn't directed at me. "And it reminded me of my father's last letter. How he crowed over the failure of the plot and how ridiculous it had been for the

Whigs to think it would succeed. As if most of the Whigs, myself included, hadn't anticipated just such a thing."

"He *is* friends with His Majesty," I ruminated. "Perhaps he felt affronted on his behalf."

"Yes, but why does he never feel affronted on *my* behalf."

The words were spoken evenly, almost blandly, in fact, but I sensed the pain and disappointment roiling behind them. It was my turn to embrace him, offering him what comfort I could while standing in the middle of the library when anyone could walk in on us at any moment. "Then you haven't heard from him since the Reform Act passed?" I asked, wondering how he'd broached the subject or if he'd simply pretended it hadn't happened.

"No, I imagine he's still licking his wounds."

Then he'd not addressed Gage's questions about his affair with the Duchess of Bowmont and the existence of his half brother, Lord Henry Kerr either. Their correspondence since Gage had learned of Henry had been strained and not altogether encouraging, and I knew Gage was still struggling to accept what his father had done, was *still* doing in practically denying wrongdoing and threatening to reveal certain secrets about the duchess in retaliation. Gage and his father had not been close to begin with, and this had damaged their relationship nearly beyond redemption. Whether Lord Gage realized this, I couldn't say, but he certainly wasn't making any effort to fix it.

Anderley appeared in the doorway to tell us the horses were ready, preventing me from saying more, but I arched up onto my toes to press a kiss to Gage's cheek, smelling the bay rum of his shaving soap. Then I draped the train of my plum riding habit over my arm and followed the valet out to the portico.

Lord Alisdair's cottage stood in a glen between two ridges to the east. The road which wound its way south from Barbreck to the village of Kilmartin and beyond passed not far from the cottage, but Gage and Henry had learned of a shortcut which snaked over the nearest ridge at its lowest point. It was toward this trail that Gage led me and Anderley.

As we crossed the bridge over the River Barbreck, I found myself searching the line of trees at the base of the ridge for any sign of the woman in the blue cloak but then dismissed her from my mind as we turned north. Passing through a sheep pasture, we came to a burn which boasted two cascades as it weaved down toward the river. Had we continued to the north, we would have soon reached the riverbank opposite Mr. MacCowan's cottage, but we veered south to follow the path paralleling the burn instead. It was narrow and steep at points, forcing me to concentrate on keeping my seat and not causing my mare to lose her footing, but the countryside surrounding us was lovely.

I was impressed again by its wild beauty. As we followed the course of the winding burn, the ridge to the west entirely blocked our view of the sea loch and its scent that was normally borne upon the breeze. This allowed the crisp smells of the stones and earth, as well as the scrubby vegetation that clung to its slopes, to tease at our nostrils. The ripple of the water over the rocks formed a low accompaniment to the strikes of our horses' hooves and the occasional grating call of a stormy petrel.

The trail took a sharp turn, making a rapid descent, and then emerged in a wooded glen. A short distance ahead, I could see the roof of a building emerge through the downy birch and pines as we rode toward it. This was Lord Alisdair's cottage. Though cottage was always a bit of a misnomer, for this home was nothing like the small crofts dotted here and there which boasted rough stone walls and two or three rooms. This building was also built from stone, though the surface had been smoothed and whitewashed, and was large enough to contain at least eight rooms, if not double that.

We dismounted before the main door, and I noted its intricately carved wooden panels, as well as the window boxes decorated with ornamental carvings. It reminded me of Mr. MacCowan's home and my speculation that he had been the estate's carpenter. Clearly, he'd still put his skills and craftsmanship to good use here on the exterior of the home. I wondered if he'd put his mark on the interior as well.

When Gage unlocked the door and pushed it open, I immediately discovered I was correct. From the entry hall, through the rooms, and up the brilliantly rendered staircase, the wooden details of the furnishings and ornamentations were stunning. I found myself distracted by the artistry and entranced by its whimsy, more so than the murals which covered several of the walls. I had to remind myself to focus on the reasons we were there rather than the richly textured pattern of flora and fauna carved and burned into the panels of one wall in the drawing room.

The mural of woodland nymphs and sprites—many scantily clothed—which was plastered across the wall of the dining room next door seemed almost garish in comparison. And this wasn't the only eyebrow-raising sight. Signor Pellegrini had evidently exercised restraint while painting the mural in the music room up at the manor, for he'd not done so here in these bachelor quarters. I could spot the similarities in the technique of the artist, but these murals clearly catered to a certain salacious taste. One of them even caused Gage to blush at my being exposed to it.

But the murals and exquisite woodwork aside, there were no other pieces of art gracing the walls. Whatever had hung there before had been stripped away to be displayed at the manor or placed into storage. Only one room yielded any interesting discoveries, and that was the back parlor. By the appearance of the paint-splattered floor, I surmised it had served as an art studio. In one corner stood a massive wardrobe, and I opened it expecting to find old paint supplies. Instead I located a stash of old frames and paintings jumbled together.

"Take a look at this," I told them, and waited for them to hasten over to peer inside.

By the look Anderley darted at me, I could tell he'd grasped the implications, but Gage needed an explanation.

"Forgers often use old paintings from the era and location of the artist they're attempting to replicate to get the look and feel of the canvas or wooden panel. After all, materials and techniques change over the years. These wooden stretchers, for instance." I turned over one of the paintings to show him. "Which keep the canvas stretched taut, as their name implies. The ones we use now are slightly different from those used, say, two hundred years ago. Forgers will seek out these old paintings of lesser quality and paint over them because they further the illusion of age and authenticity."

Gage nodded in understanding. "Then there's no legitimate reason Lord Alisdair would have kept a wardrobe full of paintings like this?"

I turned to Anderley as I answered, curious if he would contradict me. "None that I can think of. And given everything else we've discovered, I can only assume these are here for exactly the reason we think they are."

But otherwise, any evidence or indicators that Lord Alisdair and his friend had been creating forgeries had been cleared away. The cottage had been tidied and straightened years before, following its owner's death. Dust covers had been laid over much of the furniture and the home stripped of its valuables. If any other evidence, or even any original paintings, had still been here, they had long ago been taken away or sold.

"Unfortunately, I don't think there's anything more to see here," I said with a forlorn shake of my head as I surveyed the rest of the chamber.

"I agree," Anderley seconded.

I turned to Gage with a look of resignation. "I suppose it's time we updated Barbreck."

He didn't appear any more enthused by the prospect than I did. After all, the marquess was not going to like what we'd uncovered. "If you'd rather I do it, I can spare you the confrontation."

I moved forward to loop my arm through his. "That's very noble of you, but unpleasant tasks are always less so when they're shared, don't you find?"

His lips twitched upward at the corners. "Just don't tell Barbreck he's the unpleasant task."

I arched my chin as he led me from the room. "If he doesn't behave himself, I can make no guarantees."

"That's a spot of unpleasantness I wouldn't mind seeing," Anderley quipped from behind us.

I glanced over my shoulder to find him grinning.

"It's not often Mrs. Gage gets unpleasant, but when she does, it's always worth relating in the servants' hall."

I knew he was jesting, but I was still horrified at the thought.

"That it is," Gage agreed. When I smacked his arm, he merely laughed.

CHAPTER 22

In the end there was no opportunity for me to become unpleasant with Lord Barbreck, for Wheaton was waiting for us upon our return to the manor. Mrs. Mackay, our nurse, had requested that I come to the nursery, and I immediately dashed up the stairs with all sorts of dire situations playing out in my head. Had Emma fallen? Choked? Developed a fever?

When I burst through the door to the small nursery adjoining our bedchamber, I had half convinced myself that I would find my daughter was near death. However, the sound of her fussing quickly allayed that fear, though it didn't entirely squash my anxieties.

"What is it? What's wrong?" I said with a gasp. "Is she injured? Is she ill?"

Mrs. Mackay turned so that I could see Emma with my own eyes, lightly jostling her as she rubbed circles on her back. Her cheeks were red, and snot crusted the edges of her little nose, but her lungs sounded good and clear. That is, until she broke off from wailing to cough.

"'Tis just a spot o' catarrh. As bairns catch all the time," she assured me. "'Tisn't cause for concern, but I thought ye should ken." She observed the way my breath still sawed in and out of my lungs from my mad dash up the stairs. "Good heavens! What did Wheaton tell ye?"

"Just . . . that you'd requested I come to the nursery," I replied somewhat sheepishly.

Her smile was kind. "And ye assumed the worst."

"Well, I . . ." I had no explanation, but she seemed to understand regardless.

"The first illness is always one o' the hardest. 'Specially when it's yer first bairn."

I reached for Emma, and Mrs. Mackay passed her to me, though it didn't make my daughter stop fussing. "There's truly no cause for concern?"

"None. See, her wee nose is already drainin', and her snot's clear." Her gaze flicked up and down over my riding habit. "She's like to get it all over yer gown if ye dinna take this." She draped a small blanket over my shoulder and chest.

"But why is she so upset?"

"Weel, she doesna like havin' a stuffy nose any more than the rest o' us do. And she canna blow it oot for herself yet." She brushed Emma's hair back from her forehead. "Woke her from her nap, so she's fashed, too."

I sank down in the rocking chair, trying to take in everything she'd said while cradling Emma close. My daughter was not at death's door, but I felt just as strong a compulsion to hold her as if she was, even if she was screaming.

"Could she want to nurse?" I asked.

"Couldna hurt to try. Though she might have trouble breathin', so be prepared for her to get frustrated."

I nodded, and she turned toward the door.

"I'll just pop doon to the kitchens for some tea and tell Miss McEvoy you'll require her in aboot half an hour o' time."

I thanked her and then set about soothing my unhappy child.

I wasn't certain how much time had passed, but when I opened my eyes, it was to find Gage standing over me, gazing down at our daughter as she slumbered in my arms. It had taken numerous attempts and failures—and moving to the chair where I normally fed Emma—but eventually she had nursed and then fallen into a fitful slumber against my shoulder. Then apparently, I had also fallen asleep.

Gage's gaze shifted to meet mine, soft with tenderness, and he lifted his hand to brush it gently over my brow.

"She has a touch of catarrh," I whispered, perhaps unnecessarily, as Emma's breathing whistled and rattled from the congestion in her nose.

"Mrs. Mackay told me. Shall I take her?" he offered, reaching for her.

I reluctantly allowed him to lift her from my shoulder. "I suppose. But it took hours to calm her the first time."

She made a sound of protest before settling against Gage's broad shoulder with a tiny mewl. I felt a pulse of resentment as she easily slipped back into slumber, and then told myself I was being ridiculous. I could hardly begrudge my daughter for finding her father's strong arms to be comforting. After all, I found them to be comforting as well. And Gage was only trying to help.

I heaved a deep sigh and rubbed my eyes. "What time is it?"

"Half-past five."

I sat upright in astonishment, not realizing several hours had passed.

"I hope you don't mind, but I already spoke with Barbreck."

The deep, soothing tone of his voice did more than keep Emma asleep. It also calmed me.

"How could I mind?" I replied, for we'd only just jested about dreading doing so hours earlier. "Did he take the news well?"

"Better than I expected." There was a glint of speculation in his eyes as he sank into the couch next to where I sat. "He's mellowed in the past few days."

I pushed to my feet to draw the curtains, lest the rays of the sun shining through the window over Gage's shoulder wake Emma. The sky to the west looked like it promised rain. "Do you think he now regrets breaking his engagement with Miss Campbell?" I asked as I returned to the chair.

"I think he's regretted that for some time, whether he would admit to it or not," Gage surprised me by saying. "But the past few days have definitely given him more reasons to contemplate his fault in the matter, and the things that might have been."

Empathy stirred in my breast. Despite the fact that Barbreck had been the author of his own unhappiness—placing his brother's word, family honor, and his own pride above all else—I still couldn't help but feel sorry for the man. After all, we all make mistakes. We're all little fools in one way or another, especially when we're young.

If only he'd not allowed the incident to wedge such a permanent obstacle between him and Miss Campbell. If only he'd not placed so much trust in his brother. Discovering and reliving those failures and mistakes over the past few days must have been hard for him. But if he'd emerged on the other side more mellow, as Gage had said, then perhaps he would be better off for it. Perhaps Miss Campbell would receive the apology that was long overdue.

"He said all the artwork from Lord Alisdair's cottage was brought here, so chances are you and Anderley already saw them when you reviewed the manor's inventory."

"And the old paintings in the wardrobe?"

"He has no justification."

I expected as much. Just as I'd expected their discovery would be a blow to Barbreck. One I thought I might have been glad not to witness.

"Anderley and I also rode out to pay another visit to Mr. Mac-Cowan." Gage broke off when Emma shifted against his shoulder, softly fussing before she settled again.

"And?" I whispered.

"He wasn't there."

"Again?" This was the second time we'd been unable to locate him. "Did you ask the staff?"

"I told Wheaton to send for me if anyone sees the man."

"I suppose that's all you can do."

I frowned at the rug. His absence wasn't truly cause for concern. Not yet. Not when he might merely have gone out for a stroll or to run an errand. After all, we could hardly expect him to remain confined to his cabin. But I felt a stirring of unease nonetheless. I could think of too many unsettling scenarios which cast Mr. MacCowan as either the killer or another victim.

I pushed a strand of hair that had fallen from its pins back from my forehead and cringed at the smell that assaulted my nostrils—a mixture of horse, baby spit, and sweat. "Are you content there with Emma?" I asked Gage, who had slumped lower in his seat, his eyes drifting closed.

He nodded.

"I ordered Mrs. Mackay to take a nap, for I suspect she will be up and down much of the night with Emma. I'm going to ring Bree and ask her to draw me a bath."

I marched across the room to do just that, and when I turned back, I found Gage had already shifted so that he could recline across the couch with his head propped on the raised end. And if I was not very much mistaken, he was already asleep, or nearly so. I smiled at the sight of his and our daughter's blond heads so close, their bodies pliant with slumber.

Then I set about preparing myself for my much-needed bath, beginning with removing my amethyst pendant.

An hour and a half later I emerged from my bedchamber feeling much refreshed. I had bathed and washed my hair, Emma had been fed and passed back into Mrs. Mackay's care, and I was now dressed in one of my favorite gowns for dinner. The elaborate pleats of the deep neckline accentuated my shapelier form, and the pattern of blue and indigo birds complemented my eyes, as did the deep blue sapphire necklace Gage had gifted me for my twenty-seventh birthday two months past.

I closed the door with care and set off down the corridor toward the grand staircase, only to nearly collide with Miss Ferguson as she hastened down the second set of stairs. It was almost a repeat of our encounter the previous afternoon.

"Oh," she exclaimed, her eyes seeming caught by something on my chest—either my necklace or the low décolletage of my gown. She blinked. "I beg your pardon."

"No harm done," I replied with a disarming smile. "Is anything wrong?"

But rather than calm her, my words seemed to fluster her instead. "Nay. O' course not," she stammered before dipping a hasty curtsy. "Excuse me."

Before I could utter another word, she'd hurtled herself down the next flight of stairs. I couldn't help but wonder at and worry about the governess's behavior. Before, she'd been defiant and almost domineering, especially toward Charlotte, but now she was fidgety and nervous. I supposed finding Mairi's body like that could have caused such a drastic change in her. Maybe she feared the poisoner would strike again, at another servant, but I felt there might be something more. I was still curious about her visit to Mr. MacCowan.

I'd been waiting to question her again until Bree had reported back with what she'd learned about the governess, but perhaps it was time to speak with her regardless. Whatever Bree had uncovered thus far would simply have to be good enough.

With that decision made, I resumed my stride down the corridor, only to be almost assaulted again. I flinched to the side as Henry's door flew open, and he came hurrying out still tugging on his coat sleeves.

"Mrs. Gage," he gasped at the sight of me. "My apologies! I should have been looking where I was going. I haven't injured you, have I?"

"Just my composure," I assured him. "And please, isn't it past time you began calling me Kiera?"

He nodded and corrected himself. "Kiera."

I offered him a gentle smile and then reached up to adjust the folds of his cravat that he appeared to have mangled. "You seem to be in a hurry."

"I lost track of the time," he explained as he submitted himself to my ministrations.

"Still searching Barbreck's records?"

"Yes. I'd hoped to be finished before dinner, but I've still another few hours of work, at the least."

My gaze lifted to his face before returning to the cravat. "I take it the records are not as organized or straightforward as they should be."

"That is putting it mildly," he muttered.

"Then I am doubly grateful to you for taking on the task. There." I patted his chest as I finished.

"Thank you." He grinned bashfully. "Now I shall at least look presentable."

Looking up at him from this vantage, he looked so much like his brother that I felt my affections stir for him, warming my chest. Despite all the distress it had caused Gage to discover his father's infidelity to his mother, I was glad he now had Henry. And that Henry was just as eager to have Gage in his life as Gage was to get to know him. Though relations between Gage and his maternal relatives had improved, there was still a void in Gage's life where his family should have been.

When Henry offered me his arm, I accepted it.

"Have I missed anything interesting, then?" he asked, as we began descending the stairs. "What discoveries have you made today?"

I filled him in on our visit to Poltalloch and Alisdair's cottage while he listened attentively. I paused as my recitation ended, allowing my thoughts to return to the records he'd been searching. "What of you? Have you been able to ascertain anything of pertinence?"

"I can tell you that I've located several of the paintings you asked about specifically in the records, and they seem to be legitimate sales, for what that's worth." Meaning that the documents could have been falsified.

"Did Lord Alisdair purchase them?"

"Yes. At least, it appears so. The records aren't always clear." His jaw was tight with frustration. "I'll be better able to explain tomorrow."

Though I wanted to press him for details, I knew when it was best to leave matters in more capable hands. When he'd had time to sort through all the records and their implications, he would explain. In any case, we were fast approaching the drawing room where the others had gathered before dinner.

However, we needn't have hurried, for we were far from the last to arrive. Brady and Poppy, as well as Lord Barbreck, had yet to make their appearances. For all the tension in the room, you would have thought those present were suffering from some great agitation, and I swiftly deduced I wasn't entirely wrong. Lord Ledbury had plunked himself down in the middle of the room and appeared to be resisting all attempts to be charmed or cheered, or even to conduct a peaceable conversation. I scowled at the man, angry at his petty, selfish behavior. He seemed determined to ruin his daughter's happiness, and I'd had just about enough of him.

Releasing Henry's arm, I marched across the room toward where Morven stood gazing at a marble bust of a young man with a chipped nose and looking spectacularly bored. "We have to do something," I declared without preamble.

Fortunately, she didn't require one. Her eyes sparkled with mischief. "What did you have in mind?"

We pivoted to stand side by side, gazing out at those congregated around the room. "I no longer care whether Lord Ledbury enjoys himself. He's resolved not to. So, I suggest we stop factoring him into the equation. If he doesn't like what we're doing, he's always welcome to retire to his room."

"Like a naughty boy," Morven teased.

"I suggest we proceed as if he wasn't here," I posited. "And if that was so, what would we be doing?"

"Playing parlor games and such," she suggested eagerly.

I agreed. "Charlotte loves them." I sighed. "Now, whether she'll be able to enjoy them with her father staring broodingly on or sulking in his room remains to be seen. But at least we have to try."

We stood silently, contemplating this. Or at least I thought that was the path both our thoughts had taken, but Morven proved me wrong.

"May I stop minding my tongue at dinner as well?"

I turned to find her lips pursed as if suppressing an impish grin and laughed, drawing some of the others' gazes. "Yes. I know your mother meant well by counseling everyone to be on their best behavior, but honestly! If Lord Ledbury cannot even make an effort to be pleasant, then why should we curb our speech? You Mallerys are far from the most outrageous members of the ton. In fact, I doubt you would even make the list."

"I feel I should be insulted," Morven replied. "But I take your meaning. We're all shockingly tedious in our observance of morals and fidelity."

I shook my head, knowing she was being facetious. "Come! Let's rescue Charlotte, who I fear is about to turn to stone."

It took effort on our parts, but with some skillful manipulation of the conversation over dinner and the assistance of several allies—chief among them Lady Bearsden— we managed to salvage the evening and hopefully the entire wedding party. Once most of the others caught on to what Morven and I were doing, they joined along easily enough. Only Lord Ledbury and Lord Barbreck seemed determined to resist our good cheer, but when they retired early, the last vestiges of reticence fell away from everyone, including Charlotte.

I couldn't recall an evening when I had laughed so hard or so often, and at the silliest things. It was as if our normally cheerful demeanors had been bottled inside the stifling atmosphere of the house, and now that the cork had been released, we were bubbling over with mirth.

It was an evening I would remember fondly in the days to come. One I would wonder if we would ever return to.

CHAPTER 23

The calamities began small.

Poor Emma could not be calmed, and her cries could be heard through the nursery door, if not echoing through half the manor. She nursed fitfully, and any time she was laid in her cradle, she howled, struggling to breathe through her congested nose. So she slept in short snatches against Mrs. Mackay's or my shoulder. Near dawn she finally fell into an exhausted slumber in her cradle, but Gage and I didn't have time to enjoy it. There was too much to accomplish that day.

I must have looked a fright when Bree answered my summons an hour after dawn, for she offered me a sympathetic smile. "The bairn wouldna rest?"

I blinked back at her blearily and then yawned. "Not until about four o'clock. Couldn't you hear her?" I shook my head as if to dislodge the sound of her cries.

Bree urged me to sit at the bench before the vanity, wrapping my fingers around a cup of coffee rather than my usual morning cup of chocolate. "I thought this might be more useful this mornin'."

I simply nodded and lifted the dark brew to my lips, savoring its bitterness. While the coffee slowly took effect, Bree bustled about the room, laying out my clothes and readying the items I would need for my toilette. Once I'd washed my face in the basin she'd filled with warm water and returned to the bench, she began unbraiding my hair and pulling the brush through my long tangles.

While she worked, my thoughts filtered back through the events of the previous evening, recalling a particular altercation. "Bree, have you been able to learn anything about Miss Ferguson?"

She glanced up at me in the mirror. "No' much, I'm afraid. Other than the fact the other maids are no' so fond o' her. They think she acts a might too high in the instep, bossin' them aroond like she's one o' their betters."

"Well, she is the governess." And so entitled to give orders to the lower servants to a certain degree.

"Aye, but I take it she's done nothin' to foster kind feelings toward her, only resentment."

I wasn't surprised to hear this after witnessing the way she'd spoken to Charlotte. If she could treat a countess like that, how much more belittling and condescending would she be to a chamber maid?

"Where did she come from?"

"Somewhere o'er near Glasgow. That's as much detail as I could glean given Mr. Mallery was the one to hire her."

And so the housekeeper or butler would only know the details she'd provided them herself.

Perhaps I needed to have a chat with Rye then.

That being decided, I slid open the drawer in the vanity to remove my jewelry box. The house being filled with only family and close friends, I'd not taken the precaution of having it stored in the safe but simply locked it between uses. Bree handed me her copy of the key from her pocket so I wouldn't have to retrieve my own, and I opened the box. When I didn't find the object I was looking for on the top tray, I frowned. Lifting out the three levels of trays below it, I grew increasingly more agitated as my quarry remained elusive.

"Have you seen my amethyst pendant?" I asked Bree as I scrutinized each tray spread out across the vanity again. My more expensive pieces of jewelry were all there, including the sapphire necklace I'd worn the night before, but not my mother's amulet.

"Nay, m'lady. Did ye put it in the box last night?"

"Yes, before I bathed." I looked about me, searching the table and then the drawer the box had been set in. "Did you see it last night when you put my sapphire necklace away?"

"I . . . I'm no' sure, m'lady," she admitted. "I wasna lookin' for it, and Miss Emma was wailin' so. I was in a hurry to finish my tasks and get oot o' the way."

I scowled, leaning over to search the floor. "It must have fallen out. It has to be here somewhere."

We both dropped to our knees, searching under the furniture before opening every drawer, but the pendant was nowhere to be found. I dropped back down on the bench, my stomach twisting in knots at the idea that my mother's final gift to me was lost. Or stolen. Almost four months earlier, it had been ripped from my neck by an Edinburgh criminal, and I'd feared it was lost for good, but a friend had retrieved it for me. To think that it had been taken again left me feeling shaken and vulnerable.

"I'm sorry, m'lady," Bree gasped, and I suddenly realized she was near tears.

I seized hold of her hand. "It's not your fault," I assured her. "I was distracted, too."

"But I ken how much that pendant means to ye."

"Yes, and I suspect someone else did, too," I stated grimly.

She followed my gaze to the jewelry box, where I was trailing my fingers over the keyhole. "Ye think someone picked it?"

"I do. Look at these knicks." I could feel the indentations from whatever tool they'd fumbled with or used to force the lock. I frowned deeper. "And now that I think about it, I'm not sure the box was even locked. The key turned too easily, and there was no click of the lock tumbling."

"But who would do such a thing?"

"I don't know." My voice hardened. "But I'm going to find out."

After Emma was sorted and I was dressed, I made my way to my aunt's bedchamber. My neck felt bare without the familiar weight of the pendant my mother had given to me, and I found myself pressing my hand to my chest, as if convinced my senses were playing tricks on me. Aunt Cait was preparing for the day, but she welcomed me into her chamber, and we chatted about Emma's catarrh and the evening before while waiting for her maid to finish her hair.

Her tasks completed, the maid slipped from the room, and my aunt reached for my hand. "Thank you for what you did last night," she told me, her gaze earnest. "Morven told me it was your idea, and I'm glad of it." Her mouth tightened at the corners, and she shook her head. "I never should have instructed the others to tame themselves and defer to Ledbury. But well, I wanted to make matters easier for dear Charlotte. Sadly, that's not how it turned out." She sank back for a moment, subdued by her own thoughts, and then straightened, flinging her hand in the air as if to physically brush them away. "But no more of that. We shall simply be ourselves, and Ledbury can go hang if he doesn't like it."

A smile cracked my lips at hearing my aunt voice such a thought.

"However, you didn't come to speak to me about that." Her eyes softened in concern. "Something has happened."

Faced with her empathy, I suddenly found it difficult to speak. "My amethyst pendant. It's missing."

Her eyes widened with alarm. "The one your mother gave you?"

I nodded and then proceeded to explain about the locked jewelry box and my suspicions that it had been picked.

"This is serious, Kiera," she replied, pressing a hand to her heart. "It means someone in this household is a thief."

But not for the usual reasons. After all, they'd left the more expensive pieces of my jewelry untouched.

"Were you able to uncover anything about the miniature that was placed on my pillow?"

She blinked at the shift in topics but swiftly accommodated. "None of the staff claim to have done such a thing. In fact, only my maid and the housekeeper admitted to having ever seen the portrait before."

"Then how did it end up in my room?"

"I don't know. Perhaps a guest?" she suggested.

I'd considered the same thing. "But wouldn't they have simply given it to me if they'd found it?" It would have been the more logical thing to do.

She shrugged, having no better answer than I did.

I dipped my head. "We'll have to ask."

She reached out to touch my knee. "Why don't you let me handle that, as well as asking everyone about the pendant. I'm sure you have a dozen other things to see to."

I conceded to her wishes, knowing she would be able to go about the matter in a much more diplomatic manner. The loss of the pendant was too personal to me.

I excused myself and went in search of Gage to inform him of what had happened, but discovered he and Anderley had already set out for Mr. MacCowan's cottage, hoping to catch him at an earlier time of the day. I couldn't fault him that logic, but I was still disgruntled not to be able to share my upset with him. Feeling agitated and out of sorts, I found myself wandering through the rooms, unable to settle to the tasks I needed to accomplish.

It seemed to me that whoever had placed my mother's miniature on my pillow and taken my pendant was out to make trouble. To cause me pain and doubt by conjuring thoughts of my mother. Why they would do this—toy with her memory—I couldn't answer. But as for the who . . . My thoughts immediately shifted to the woman in the blue cloak, whom I'd not seen again and had yet to identify.

Grateful Bree had chosen a walking dress for me that morning, I sent a maid for my bonnet and pelerine and set off down the drive in the direction I had seen the woman. She wasn't there, of course, but I scoured the tree line for any sign of her passing—a trail, a broken twig. When this yielded no results, I continued walking, too exasperated to return to the manor. Part of me wanted to fling my bonnet to the ground and stomp on it while the other part of me simply wanted to sit down and weep. I knew some of my distress was the fault of my restless night and my worry over Emma—needless though Mrs. Mackay had told me it was—as well as all the unanswered questions we faced about Mairi's death and the forgeries, but it was easier to seize on the loss of the necklace as my chief source of discontent.

Lengthening my stride, I set out for the shores of the loch, hoping my brisk pace would expend some of the anxious energy pulsing through my body and lull my frenzied thoughts into submission. The ground was wet from the previous night's rain, dampening the hem of my gown, but I continued undaunted. Only when I reached the rocky shore of the sea loch did I stop just shy of the lapping tide.

I stood there for some minutes, my breath rasping in and out of my lungs and my thoughts continuing to spin frantically, until finally the pounding of my heart began to slow. Tipping my head back, I closed my eyes, allowing the sound of the waves rolling up onto the rocks to calm me. The gentle rippling of the water soothed something inside me, smoothing the jagged edges of my distress, much as it had smoothed the stones along the shore for thousands of years.

When I opened my eyes, I could see the green slopes of Eilean Rìgh in the distance. I stared across at its shore, comforted by the knowledge that the waves that continued to wash the rocks before me would eventually wash over it, and then the tip of the Craignish peninsula, and then farther out to sea to the ends of the earth. Its push and pull was one long, unending rhythm.

Not wanting to break the spell, I didn't turn when I heard footsteps edging closer over the rough ground, as if their owner didn't wish to startle me. Not until he was already at my side. Henry offered me a sheepish grin, his auburn hair ruffling in the breeze.

"My apologies if I'm disturbing you. Perhaps you wished to be alone?"

I took that to mean that my expression wasn't particularly welcoming, and I strove to rectify it. "No. I was simply lost in thought. You're more than welcome."

He still eyed me doubtfully but moved a step closer.

"Did you wish to speak with me?" I asked, noting his lack of hat. Perhaps he'd seen me leave and stepped out of the manor to find me. Then I realized how early the hour still was. "Have you already finished searching Barbreck's records?" The evening before, he'd said he still had at least several more hours of work to do before he was done.

"Nearly."

My brow furrowed quizzically. "Then?"

He cleared his throat, clasping his hands behind his back. "Well, I . . . I saw you leave the manor, and when you disappeared from sight, and well . . ." He shifted his feet. "I know Gage worries for your safety, so . . ."

I arched a single eyebrow. "So, you followed me?"

"Yes."

I wanted to feel disgruntled at his presumption, but I knew he was merely concerned with my well-being and his brother's favor. It wouldn't be fair to snap at him given those considerations.

"I didn't intend to walk so far," I told him. "I simply needed to clear my head, and this is where my feet led me."

He nodded and then, after a pause, ventured to say more. "I like to walk, too. It's easier to think when I'm alone. Easier to breathe."

Whether he intended to or not, his last statement and the manner in which he'd wistfully murmured it had been rather revealing. For no one would classify the massive castle in which he'd grown up with the rest of the Duchess of Bowmont's children, or their palatial London mansion in Grosvenor Square, as stifling. That he still needed to escape its confines from time to time said much about his state of mind. I knew he loved the family to whom he'd been born, including the duke, who had claimed him. But evidently, he was still searching for something. The duchess had told me as much when I first confronted her with my knowledge of Henry's true parentage.

I wished I knew how to help him find it, but I recognized it was something he had to discover on his own. Unfortunately, I was afraid that part of his hope of finding it involved initiating a relationship with his natural father. Every bit of my experience of Lord Gage told me that Henry's hopes of that would be utterly dashed. All Gage and I could do was try to help him find resolution another way and bolster him when Lord Gage ultimately failed him.

As if reading the bent of my thoughts, Henry broached the subject of many of our anxieties. "Sebastian hasn't heard from his father, has he?"

I was surprised but also pleased to hear him use Gage's given name in private conversation. Only his father and I ever said it with any regularity, and the tone in which Lord Gage uttered it left much to be desired. "Not for at least two months," I admitted, deciding I wasn't breaking a confidence by telling his half brother this. After all, the topic of their father must be a fraught one between his sons at the moment, and I suspected they were both eager to spare the other that pain in bringing it up.

"Then he doesn't know whether Lord Gage has followed through on his threat." His threat to reveal certain secrets about the duchess if Sebastian was told about Henry's real parentage and his relationship to him.

It was an implied question even if he uttered it as a statement, and I shook my head in answer, unable to ease the concern reflected in his eyes. "But . . ." I hesitated a moment before concluding that if my husband had not intended for his brother to know what I was about to reveal, then he would simply have to forgive me, for it was done with the best of intentions. "I do know that Sebastian has made various counterthreats against his father."

Henry's eyes widened in surprise.

"After all, Lord Gage is not without his own secrets. Several of which he might find very . . . inconvenient to become known. So, I would not fret much over the matter."

He turned to gaze out at the loch, I suspected at least partially to conceal how stunned he felt. Clearly, he had not anticipated Gage doing such a thing—further jeopardizing his own relationship with his father to protect Henry and his mother—the woman who had helped Lord Gage break his marriage vows to Gage's mother. But then Henry was still coming to know Gage. Coming to understand his fierce loyalty and code of honor, his desire to protect the innocent, no matter who they were or how he felt about them.

I wondered if he was also thinking about his brother, Lord John Kerr, whom he'd escorted somewhere overseas to escape potential punishment for the crime he'd committed at Sunlaws Castle seven months prior, during the winter holidays. Gage and I knew the predominant reason he'd given into familial pressure to do so was out of love and loyalty, as well as the fear that his brother might do himself harm on the journey, and so we'd made peace with that. But that didn't mean Henry had.

Deciding it was time to change the subject, I returned to the most pressing matter at hand. "Then you still can't summarize for me what you've found in the records?"

His lips pressed together as if weighing his options, and then he sighed, as if resigning himself to fate. "I can tell you what I've uncovered so far."

I smiled. "You don't like being rushed into giving a pronouncement until you've gathered all the facts, do you?"

Hearing the teasing note in my voice, he huffed a laugh. "I suppose it comes from growing up with older brothers who were all too hasty to rush everything."

"I can understand that." I tilted my head. "And I promise to not presume that whatever you have to tell me is your complete and final word on the matter."

He grinned more easily. "Fair enough. I was able to match all the items you specifically requested I find records for to some sort of purchase agreement, including the harpsichord. However, there is something . . . inauthentic about some of them." His brow furrowed as he tried to explain. "The same names appear over and over. Which is not entirely surprising, as it seems he used the same dealers many times, and they often have sellers who are eager to part with multiple items. But . . . I question whether there are actual people behind some of their names."

"Why do you say that?" I asked in interest.

"Many of them appear to share the same address. And their names . . . they seem rather ubiquitous. Akin to using John Smith in English."

"Then the exact origins of some of the paintings are undoubtedly questionable," I concluded, thinking of the paintings taken from Venice and other places in Italy by Napoleon.

"Undoubtedly. However, that does not mean they weren't authentic paintings when they were purchased and transported to Barbreck Manor," he cautioned.

"But Lord Alisdair *was* the person to purchase all of them?"

"Yes."

I gripped my chin, contemplating everything he'd just told me, and whether it furthered our investigation. "Were you able to find dates for the purchases?"

"Yes, and I noted them each on the list you gave me. Starting with the Titian purchased in 1774 and ending with one of the Zoffanys in 1821."

"Wait. Did you say he purchased the Titian in 1774?" I asked with a frown.

"Yes." His eyes scoured my features. "Is that significant?"

"What's significant is that Lord Barbreck told me that Alisdair acquired the Titian specifically on Sir James Campbell of Poltalloch's behalf, and yet *he* didn't receive the painting until 1778, for that's the year Barbreck's engagement to Miss Campbell ended, and that event followed swiftly upon the heels of their acquiring it and discovering it was a forgery."

"That means Lord Alisdair had the Titian in his possession for almost four years before he delivered it to Sir James."

I nodded. "And if Lord Alisdair *had* acquired that painting specifically at the direction of Sir James, I struggle to comprehend his keeping it for four years before turning it over. I recognize that his journeys may have taken a considerable number of months or years to complete, but four? Wouldn't he have shipped some of the objects he'd acquired home before then?"

"Unquestionably. And he did. I found the shipping documents, as well as letters from Lord Alisdair detailing the number of cartons and descriptions of the items shipped, as well as the names of the vessels and ports where they would arrive."

Then Lord Barbreck had lied again. I clenched my hands into fists as my temper spiked. Four years was plenty of time for his brother or Signor Pellegrini to have created the first forgery. I wondered if they'd concocted the scheme soon after Sir James had asked him to acquire a Titian. Had they seen this as their chance to pocket some money and keep the Titian? Or had it all been about conceit? Had they been so vain that they believed themselves equal to such a masterful painter and so thought to prove it by fobbing off their own work as Titian's?

I'd opened my mouth to say something scathing about the Mallery men of that generation when I heard the sound of a horse's gallop approaching. Turning toward the road, I spied Titus's chestnut coat before I saw Gage's tall form in the saddle. My stomach pitched, for he wouldn't have urged his gelding into such a fast gait without good reason. The grave look on his face as he pulled up on Titus's reins only confirmed my fears.

"We found Mr. MacCowan," he told us. "He's dead."

CHAPTER 24

I gasped, wishing I'd given more credence to the concerns that had stirred within me the previous evening. But then, that might have already been too late.

"We think it might be the same poison that killed his daughter. Will you come to confirm it?" Gage asked me.

"Of course," I replied without a second thought, moving forward to take the hand Gage reached out to me. Before accepting it, I glanced back at Henry, wondering how he would follow.

"I'll return to the manor," he said, answering my unspoken query. "I have those records to finish up."

I nodded and then dismissed him from my mind as Gage removed his foot from the stirrup so that I could hoist myself up behind him in the saddle with his assistance. Once I was settled, with a scandalous bit of leg showing above my kid leather boots, we set off. The fact that he hadn't positioned me before him across his lap told me he intended to go quickly, and indeed, I was forced to tighten my grip around his torso as Titus's strong legs charged back in the direction they'd come.

The firm muscles along Gage's abdomen and legs posted to the gallop, partially lifting me as well, but not having access to the stirrups, it was impossible for me not to be jostled about at least slightly. As such, I was more focused on clinging to Gage and avoiding dropping my weight too forcefully onto Titus with each hoof strike than on my surroundings. So by the time I'd noticed the flash of azurite blue in the trees bordering the drive—the same trees I'd searched a short time earlier—we had already flown past. I whipped my head around to look over my shoulder, but whatever I'd seen had disappeared, whether back into the trees or because I'd imagined it.

Gage lowered his upper arms, trapping mine around his torso, perhaps worried by the fact that my grip had slackened, and I was forced to return my attention forward. The word "stop" hovered on my lips, but then I swallowed it back down, already knowing we would find nothing if we returned to the spot where I'd thought I'd seen a flash of blue.

I locked my gaze on the back of Gage's neck, disconcerted by the fact that I couldn't decide if what I was seeing was real or an illusion. Of a certainty, it was not my mother, for I didn't believe in ghosts, and even if I did, she would not be haunting me here. *No*, I thought, taking myself firmly in hand. *If* there was a woman, then she was one of flesh and blood. And bent on making mischief. My hands fisted in Gage's coat.

Gage slowed Titus as we passed through the stable yard and then pulled him up even further as we veered onto the trail which led past the gardens and into the woods that paralleled the north shore of the river. Though no longer galloping, the horse maintained a steady trot, and we soon found ourselves entering the clearing where the MacCowan Cottage stood. The glade was quiet except for the rushing of the river. Anderley stood guard outside the door, beneath the porch that had been carved to look like a lychgate. His expression was grave and his pallor rather a greenish hue.

Gage helped me to dismount and then led me toward the cottage, only to pause on the threshold. "I warn you, the smell . . ." His face was pained. "It's somewhat foul."

"Not somewhat," Anderley muttered.

I nodded. I'd faced the smell of decomposition many times, and while never pleasant, I was prepared. However, with the current temperatures, it was rather early for the body to have reached that stage. After all, we had seen Mr. MacCowan alive a little over forty-eight hours earlier. He could not be that far gone. But before I could point this out, Gage opened the door, and I discovered the scent he had been alluding to was not from decay.

I nearly gagged as the foul stench of feces and vomit filled my nostrils. Digging in the sleeve of my dress, I extracted my handkerchief and pressed it to my nose and mouth. It did not block the vapors completely, but it was better than nothing. The space immediately inside the door was as neat as before and the stone floor swept clean. But in the doorway between the main living area and what must have been the bedchamber lay Mr. MacCowan.

"We found him lying on his side with his arms outstretched like that, but we rolled him over to check for signs of life," he explained, pressing his own handkerchief to the lower half of his face. "He was cold to the touch."

I could tell immediately that rigor mortis had set in, for his body had stiffened in the position in which it had been found. The scent was stronger near the body, making me suspect it emanated from the bedroom. Forcing myself to ignore the impulse to flee, I knelt beside the body and reached for his fingers, attempting to manipulate them, but they remained unpliant. "He's been dead for some time."

Lying as he was in the doorway, I had to examine him upside down, but I had no desire to move any closer to that stench than I had to, so I leaned awkwardly over the body to better view his features. Tracks of dried blood led from his nose and eyes and had dripped on the floor where he lay. I pushed down on his chin, cringing at the sight of the ulcers and his rotting teeth. From the bluish-purple tinge of the skin on the left side of his face, I could tell that was the side on which he'd lain. I pressed my fingers there, and the skin did not turn white but remained bluish-purple. "At least twelve hours," I declared. "Probably more like eighteen."

"Then he died the evening after we visited him. Only a day after his daughter."

"That's what it looks like," I replied as Gage helped me to my feet.

"Killed by the same poison?"

"It certainly seems like it." The fact that we hadn't seen any signs of Mairi's stomach distress didn't mean it hadn't occurred. After all, she'd traveled some distance between Poltalloch and her father's cottage, and then on to Barbreck Manor. She could easily have become sick in the woods between either destination, but I suspected it had most likely occurred between the cottage and Barbreck. She'd declined any food, and Bree had said she'd looked pale and nervous, all of which could be symptoms of recent nauseas and purging.

"Have you searched the pantry for any food he might have eaten?" I asked.

"Not yet."

I turned to help him do so, eager to escape the terrible smell, only to be brought up short by the sight of the painting hanging over Mr. MacCowan's bed. I could see just a sliver of it, but it raised the fine hairs along the back of my neck.

"Kiera?" Gage murmured in confusion as I began carefully

picking my way around the body, bracing myself for the full onslaught of the noxious odor, but I had to see what this painting was. My artistic sensibilities could already tell that it was masterful, and logic told me that it almost certainly had bearing on our investigations.

As the painting came more fully into view, I nearly gasped aloud. It depicted a furious seascape of crashing white-tip waves and roiling gray and orange-tinged clouds, as if to reveal the angry sun behind. At the center was a storm-lashed boat tipping precariously to the right as it rode the foaming tip of an enormous wave, threatening to toss all of its terrified occupants from its confines. No, they weren't all frightened. One figure on the right was calm and peaceful, as if he'd just woken from slumber. This, I suspected, was supposed to be Jesus, and the other brightly attired figures in the ship were his disciples.

I had seen the same painting hanging in the home of Thomas Hope in London. Or nearly the same. Christ's robe in this painting was a lighter blue, and there were a few other minor alterations. Hope's painting had been by Rembrandt, and this painting bore all the same hallmarks—the vibrant colors, the movement of light, the emotions conveyed by the characters and how they seemed to waver from one to another flawlessly. Whether it was by Rembrandt himself or one of his pupils, it was certainly a masterpiece. And worth far more than a man of Mr. MacCowan's position could afford.

The most feasible explanation for how he'd acquired it was that Lord Alisdair had given it to him. Perhaps it had been a gift, but if so, it was an extravagant one. For this was no forgery, but the real thing.

Gage called my name again, recalling me to where I was, and the stench I'd been able to momentarily forget while so absorbed in my study of the painting. Now it slapped me in the face. I gagged and turned away, studiously avoiding looking near the corner where I suspected the chamber pots sat.

Hurrying from the room, I exited the cottage and moved a dozen steps into the clearing, gulping great gasps of fresh air as I wrestled with my breakfast as it was threatening to reemerge. When the worst had passed, I turned back to face the men. I realized we couldn't just leave Mr. MacCowan like that.

"Someone is going to have to . . ."

"Yes, but not you," Gage replied sternly, easily following the direction of my thoughts.

I nodded, grateful such a task would not be mine and slightly ashamed that meant someone else would have to endure it.

"Now, what did you see in the bedchamber that was so interesting?" Gage demanded, moving aside his coat so that he could prop one hand on his hip.

"The painting on the wall. It was by Rembrandt. Or at the very least, one of his pupils."

His and Anderley's eyebrows both arched skyward.

"How could a man of MacCowan's means afford a Rembrandt?" Anderley asked the obvious question.

"He couldn't. Lord Alisdair must have given it to him."

"Or he stole it," the valet suggested.

I considered this but then shook my head. "No. I don't think so. Everything we've learned about Mr. MacCowan thus far has told us he's a scrupulous fellow." I paused. "Though, he was undoubtedly anxious for us not to see it during our last visit. Remember how he glanced nervously toward the closed bedroom door," I said to my husband. "Regardless of how he acquired it, he must have known it would arouse questions and suspicions."

We all fell silent for a moment, our gazes sliding back toward the cottage.

"Something is not adding up here," Gage declared.

"No, it's not," I agreed.

His voice was taut with bewilderment. "Why would Lord Alisdair gift his manservant a priceless painting?"

"Maybe it was to keep him quiet. To guarantee his silence," Anderley suggested.

"About the forgeries," I concluded, and he nodded. My eyes narrowed in thought. "If Lord Alisdair and his friend, Signor Pellegrini, were creating forgeries, then Mr. MacCowan *must* have known about them. And if he'd known about them, then it's entirely feasible his daughter Mairi knew also."

Gage shifted his stance, planting *both* hands on his hips. "Is that what this is all about, then? Punishing those who were involved in or knew about the forgeries."

But who was doing the punishing? Lord Barbreck? I couldn't see it. Though there was another possibility.

"Or if not punishing them, then perhaps silencing them instead," I postulated.

Both men turned to look at me.

"But Lord Alisdair and Signor Pellegrini are both dead," Gage said. "So that would mean there's another person involved."

"Someone determined to keep their involvement secret," I elaborated.

"Yes, but who?"

I didn't have a ready answer for him.

"There is the former butler," Anderley suggested. "After all, we suspect he was the one who aided Lord Alisdair in switching out the paintings."

"Yes, but you told me Wheaton had said he'd moved to Elgin. Why would he come all the way back here to silence two fellow servants who might or might not have been about to reveal his part in the scheme? How would he have even known?"

"A letter?" He frowned. "I admit, it doesn't sound very promising."

"What of the person who purchased the originals from Lord Alisdair after he made the switches?" He dipped his head in emphasis. "Now *that's* someone with a great deal to lose if the scheme is revealed."

He was right. We hadn't yet been able to locate the legitimate paintings, which meant they'd more than likely been sold. When and to whom, we didn't know, but the works of art had to be *somewhere*.

"Perhaps Henry will have some idea who that might be after he finishes going through the records," I said, feeling even more grateful now for Gage's half brother's thoroughness.

But in the meantime, there were other things to see to. "We didn't search the pantry," I reminded them.

"We'll do it when we return," Gage assured me. "But I didn't see anything on the tables. So, however Mr. MacCowan ingested the poison, it's probably already been cleared away. Likely by Mr. MacCowan himself."

I pressed a hand to my mouth, pacing away a few steps in bewilderment before returning.

"What is it?"

"We're fairly certain Mairi was poisoned *before* she arrived here. The two of them shared a meal together, including the bilberries she'd brought with her, and then she died a few hours later. While her father seemed unaffected a full twelve or four-teen hours later. Which tells me he wasn't poisoned from the same thing Mairi was. So . . ." I flung my hands out in exasper-ation. "How was he poisoned?"

"Maybe the poisoner brought it to him later," Anderley said.

"But wouldn't he have been on guard?"

"Maybe not if he knew them well," Gage argued. "If he trusted them, he might have suspected nothing." He tilted his head. "*Or* maybe they slipped it into something while he wasn't looking."

"Then they would have needed to visit him soon after we left."

Gage's head lifted, his eyes fastening on something behind me. I whirled around, thinking of the woman in the blue cloak, but I spied someone more familiar. And potentially much more interesting.

"Someone we might have even passed while we were departing," I finished leadingly, glancing over my shoulder to catch Gage's eye before I took a step toward the woman approaching. "Miss Ferguson, what are you doing here?" I called.

"Is it true?" she gasped. Her cheeks were streaked with tears, and her eyes looked a little wild. "Is he . . . is he dead?"

Who Mr. MacCowan was to her, I didn't know, but he was clearly important. However, that didn't mean she hadn't also killed him. After all, poisoning could be done from a distance so that the poisoner need not even touch their victim or watch them suffer and the life drain from their body. She might have loved him—and Mairi—and still killed them.

But faced with her distress—even if she was the cause of it—I couldn't withhold my empathy. "I'm sorry."

She hiccupped on a sob and turned to hurry toward the door.

Gage moved to intercept her. "My condolences, Miss Ferguson, but you can't go in there. You don't want to," he amended.

"But someone should see to him, someone should . . ." She blanched, and her words broke off as if his last statement had just registered with her. "What . . . what happened?" she asked in a hushed voice. "How did he . . . ?"

"Poison. Likely the same as his daughter."

Miss Ferguson buried her face in her hands and wept, prompting my husband and his valet to look to me imploringly. Apparently, comforting sobbing females was a woman's job.

I stepped forward, wrapping an arm around her shuddering shoulders. "Come with me," I coaxed gently, steering her toward a pair of rocks positioned beneath the cool shade of an oak tree.

I perched beside her, passing her my handkerchief when I realized she had none of her own. When her tears had slowed and the worst of her trembling subsided, Gage sidled over to join us while Anderley remained respectfully at a distance, though still within earshot.

"How did you know Mr. MacCowan?" I asked as she dabbed at her eyes.

Her hands stilled. "He . . . he was my uncle."

My gaze snapped to Gage's, not having expected this. "Then Mairi was your cousin?"

She nodded.

"But when you found her in the long gallery, you told us you didn't know who she was."

Her head bowed low. "I was afraid."

But that wasn't all, and we allowed the silence to stretch, letting her know we knew this.

"And I . . . was maybe a little ashamed." She peered up at me through red-rimmed eyes, fallen strands of her honey blond hair shielding her face. "I hadna told anyone she was my cousin."

"So it was a secret."

"It wasna a secret," she retorted defensively, raising her chin so that I could see her blotchy face more clearly. She crossed her arms in front of her. "I just dinna like to share things aboot myself."

Because she didn't want the other maids to find out about her lowly connection? Or was she more worried about concealing the less-than-genteel side of her ancestry from her employer? Considering the romantic designs I'd wondered if she had on him after hearing Charlotte's concerns, and witnessing Miss Ferguson's treatment of her soon-to-be new mistress, perhaps she'd worried that would make Rye look at her differently.

"I suppose governesses aren't often related to simple parlor maids," I remarked leadingly.

"My mother married above her station. Though no one would've known it upon meetin' her. And she taught me the same."

"Then when we last saw you here, you were coming to offer your uncle your condolences?"

"Aye."

"Is that all?"

"What do you mean?" She furrowed her brow in confusion, but by the guarded nature of her stance, I suspected she knew exactly what I meant.

"You didn't bring him any other comforting measures? Any food or drink?"

She stiffened, glancing warily at Gage and then Anderley, before turning back to me. "I didna poison him, if that's what you're tryin' to imply. Why would I? I just told ye. He's my uncle."

"Yes, and yet you kept it a secret. One I suppose no one can verify but you."

"I have another aunt. In Oban. *She* can verify it."

I scrutinized her features more closely, wishing I could tell whether the panic I saw suffusing them was at the idea of being *accused* of such a crime or being caught. "You must recognize how suspicious it seems that you were the last person known to have visited Mr. MacCowan, and also the person to find Mairi, meanwhile keeping your relation to them concealed." I tilted my head. "Why *were* you in the long gallery that night?"

"I often pass through there. 'Tis a quicker route to the servants' hall and laundry, and I can avoid the bustle o' the kitchens. *And* Lady Stratford and Mr. Mallery's chambers are on that side o' the house." She was becoming almost belligerent now in the face of my questioning, and I arched my eyebrows, letting her know I was not impressed. She flushed.

Deciding to switch tactics, I tried to elicit her help instead, to see what she might unwittingly offer up. "How did your uncle seem when you left him two days past?"

"He'd just lost his daughter! How do you think . . . ?" She broke off, biting her lip as she turned her head to the side.

We waited, giving her a moment to compose herself.

"Sad. Tired," she murmured in a more subdued voice, lifting the handkerchief to dab at her cheeks as a few more tears trickled from the corners of her eyes.

"Was he showing any signs of illness?"

She looked up at me uncertainly, perhaps thinking I meant to trick her, and then shook her head. "Nay."

I nodded, my mouth flattening as I considered what she'd said. "What of the pantry? Did he take anything out of it to eat?"

She shook her head again. "Nay, and I offered to get him something. Told him he had to keep up his strength. He'd only let me fetch him a glass o' water." Her eyes hardened. "And I didna put poison in it."

"I wouldn't have thought you did," I replied evenly. "Most poisons are bitter and difficult to conceal the taste or appearance of. You wouldn't slip it into water."

The way she glared back at me told me she had something she wanted to say—something highly uncomplimentary—but she was wise enough to keep it to herself. It was while she was staring at me with such palpable loathing that I realized she had a far more cold-blooded motive than keeping her relationship to the MacCowans secret. One we had not yet addressed.

"What did you think of your uncle's painting?"

Her brow pinched. "What painting? My uncle was a carpenter."

"The one hanging in his bedroom."

Her gaze flitted toward the cottage, some of her antagonism fading. "I never went into his bedroom." Her eyes returned to me, rapidly scrutinizing my features. "Is it . . . ?" Her hands tightened around the handkerchief she clutched in her lap. "What kind of painting is it?"

I traced the dagged edge of my pelerine fabric, making her wait for my answer, curious what she might reveal. But I saw only eagerness—the type of an avaricious nature. Arching my chin, I decided on a vague tactic, not daring to look at either of the men, lest they give me away.

"It's unclear. It will have to be examined more closely to determine its value. But given the recent discovery of forgeries in Lord Barbreck's collection—all of which were acquired by his brother, whom your uncle worked for—his possession of such a painting raises a number of delicate questions."

Some of her enthusiasm faded, as if she didn't know how to respond.

I tilted my head in scrutiny. "Who stands to inherit your uncle's property? You?"

"I suppose," she replied hesitantly. "Or my aunt."

I turned to stare at the structure before us. "But the cottage belongs to the estate, does it not? As well as some of its contents? It was part of his pension."

She swallowed. "Yes, I believe so."

I lifted my gaze to meet Gage's. "Delicate questions, indeed."

Of certain, the ownership of that Rembrandt was in question. If there was no documentation stating that Lord Alisdair had signed over the painting to Mr. MacCowan, then it could be argued that it had been granted for his use solely during his lifetime or as furnishings in the cottage. In that instance, Lord Barbreck was almost certain to claim ownership—and win. Unless there was no documentation Lord Alisdair or the Barbreck estate had ever owned such a painting in the first place. Then it could be argued that Mr. MacCowan had somehow acquired it on his own. Though, in that instance, it was also likely that Barbreck—with his far greater resources, power, and influence—would still ultimately win. Miss Ferguson's and her aunt's only hope of claiming the painting was if Mr. MacCowan had held clear documentation of ownership, and from Miss Ferguson's deflated countenance, it didn't appear as if she expected such a thing.

Unless this was all an act. After all, that painting provided a credible motive for her wanting her cousin and her uncle dead. Miss Ferguson was far from stupid. If she *had* murdered them to gain possession of it, she would have already thought through and researched all of the ramifications.

Before I could ask any further questions, we were joined in the clearing by several other members of Barbreck's staff, as well as Uncle Dunstan. Miss Ferguson seemed to recognize that their presence had granted her a reprieve, for she exhaled in relief, her shoulders dropping.

Gage crossed to speak to my uncle while the two footmen and two maids stood hesitantly to the side. I cringed, aware of how unpleasant the task before them would be. Then I noted Liam's presence and his wary posture and pallid skin. I rose from the rock to go to him, pausing only long enough to tell Anderley to keep an eye on Miss Ferguson. Though where I expected her to run, I didn't know.

"Should you be here?" I asked him gently, ushering him to the side, for it was evident he felt some affection for Mr. MacCowan.

He shuffled his feet, staring at the ground. "I need to be here," he ground out. "For Mairi."

My heart squeezed at the pain written in every line of his body, even his vocal cords.

When his eyes dared to lift to mine, I nodded, letting him know I understood. "He spoke highly of you, you know." I offered him a look of commiseration. "Said you were honorable and trustworthy."

Liam blinked several times and turned his head to the side.

"I just thought you should know."

He bobbed his head, and I did the only kind thing I could for him. Leave him to grieve without my looking on.

"Nay, lad," I heard Uncle Dunstan respond to Gage's request that he escort me and Miss Ferguson back to the manor. "You go while I handle matters here." His gaze flicked toward me. "You and Kiera have visitors."

It was on the tip of my tongue to ask who when he answered for me.

"The Campbell sisters."

My surprise must have been perfectly evident, for a smile cracked my uncle's somber face.

"Aye. Ne'er thought I'd live to see the day. 'Least no' while my uncle was still alive." He waved us toward the path. "Go on."

Gage's expression was pained. "I warn you, it's not pleasant."

Uncle Dunstan was unfazed. "I imagine no'. But we'll manage just the same. We're transportin' him to the icehouse?"

To lie beside his daughter until their burials.

Gage confirmed this and then pivoted to have a quiet word with Anderley about securing the painting and bringing it to the manor. I gestured for Miss Ferguson to join us, ushering her toward the trail as Gage finished his instructions. Then I issued my own brief directive to the dark-haired valet, for I'd not missed the unpleasant scowls he'd periodically aimed toward the second footman—Bree's friend Callum.

"Behave yourself," I murmured with a warning glare.

The look he gave me in return was one of complete innocence, but I strongly suspected Callum would not finish this task with unsoiled livery.

CHAPTER 25

We were silent for much of our trek back to the manor, with Miss Ferguson marching in front of us while Gage led Titus by his reins. Once the trees thinned and the manor came into view, the governess cast a defiant glare over her shoulder before diverting her steps down a different path, presumably one that led toward the servants' entrance. I only just resisted the urge to roll my eyes at her insolent behavior. She certainly wasn't winning any points from me.

I would need to say something to Rye. After all, she was the governess to his children. The difficulty was in knowing exactly how much to reveal. If she was guilty, then I didn't want her anywhere near my cousin's children. But if she wasn't, I didn't wish my hasty judgment to jeopardize her position. However, the children's safety had to come first. Perhaps confining them all to the nursery with the other nurserymaids and Brady's children's governess would solve the problem temporarily. Then at least she wouldn't be alone with them.

"Do you think she did it?" Gage asked once Miss Ferguson's angry stride had carried her far enough away that she wouldn't overhear.

I darted a glance at the unpleasant governess out of the corner of my eye. "I think she's covetous and exceedingly unpleasant." I heaved a sigh. "But those things don't make her a murderer."

He nodded, and Titus's bit jangled as he adjusted the reins in his hand. "The discovery of that painting certainly alters things. But I've been thinking. If it *was* the motive for the murders, then why didn't Miss Ferguson, or whoever killed him, remove it from the cottage *before* the body was found? After all, you estimated he'd been dead for approximately eighteen hours. That's a large window of opportunity for them to have taken it."

"Yes, but they probably weren't aware who knew of its existence, and whether that might complicate their efforts to sell it. Not to mention, where would they store it? Miss Ferguson couldn't just waltz up to her room and hide it under her bed. She would have needed someplace dry and secure. Someplace where no one would stumble upon it by accident."

Gage gripped my elbow to help me navigate around a large puddle in the middle of the path while he and Titus strode straight through it. "Maybe they'd had a place in mind, but then your discovery of the forgeries in Barbreck's collection and our subsequent investigation complicated matters."

I looked up from examining the hem of my gown for splatters. "You're thinking of Alisdair's cottage?"

"It fits all your parameters."

I had to concede he had a point. I pressed my hand to my head, which had begun to ache. "I don't know what to think just now. It's all a bit of a muddle." I lifted my gaze hopefully toward the pale stone of the manor. "Maybe whatever has brought the Miss Campbells to Barbreck will help to make sense of it."

We found everyone gathered in the drawing room, including

Lord Ledbury with his pinched face and Lord Barbreck with his long one. The marquess sat stiffly in the chair he seemed to prefer near the hearth, watching Miss Campbell out of the corner of his eye while trying to appear as if he was not doing so. For her part, Miss Campbell also seemed determined not to glance in his direction and, by all appearances, was more successful at it.

I was most surprised to see Miss Margaret seated next to her sister, her shoulders bowed but her eyes alive with interest as she took in everyone and everything. I wondered when she had last left the confines of Poltalloch. Our prior conversations seemed to imply it had been years if not decades. As such, I couldn't blame her for her curiosity.

We greeted them before sitting on the sofa opposite where others had moved to make room.

"We apologize for the delay," Gage told them before glancing toward my Aunt Cait. "But I imagine the reason for our absence has already been explained."

Aunt Cait nodded. "It's just awful. Poor Mr. MacCowan."

"Was it poison, the same as his daughter?" Jack asked. His wife, Morven, shot him a quelling glare, as if her busybody self hadn't wished to ask the very same question.

"I'm afraid so," Gage said.

"Then that makes our reason for comin' here all the more pertinent," Miss Campbell informed us in a tight voice before reaching out to touch her sister. "But perhaps this conversation should be conducted wi' just Mr. and Mrs. Gage."

"Och, dear. We've made 'em too curious noo," Miss Margaret replied, patting her sister's hand where it rested on her arm. "Let 'em listen. 'Twill do no harm."

"If you're sure?" she asked doubtfully. Her eyes were fretful, but I thought it was more on behalf of her invalid sister's health than whatever she was about to reveal.

"I am." She cleared her throat. "I've had a thought. Aboot the poison. Ye see, I . . . I dinna eat so much as I once did. Often I dinna feel like eatin' anythin' at all. Which troubles my sister." She darted a look at her sister out of the corner of her eye, whose mouth had primmed. "So sometimes I encourage the maids who attend me to take food from my tray. Treats and sweetbreads and such. Whatever they like. So, my trays are no' so full when they return to the kitchen, and my sister willna pester me aboot my lack o' appetite."

No wonder the other maids had been jealous of her partiality to Mairi. Except, in this instance, it might have saved their lives.

"Did Mairi take food from your tray? Did she take food the morning of the day she died?" I specified.

She nodded. "Aye. And dinner the evenin' before."

"Meg!" Miss Campbell exclaimed softly in scolding.

Miss Margaret's face flushed guiltily. "'Tis only that you nag me so when I canna help it." Her eyes glistened with shame. "But if that poison was meant for me, and Mairi—and her father—ate it instead . . ." She broke off to take a deep breath. "I dinna ken if I'll ever be able to forgive myself."

Miss Campbell clutched her sister's hand firmly. "What nonsense!"

She turned to her sister in startlement. "But Anne . . ."

"*If* the poison was in your food, if it *was* meant for you, then it's no more your fault that it killed Mairi than it is the Stuarts lost the throne. No one blames ye."

"She's right," Gage assured her. "But it does alter things considerably if Miss Margaret was, in fact, the intended target and not Mairi and Mr. MacCowan."

I nodded. It also meant that, for Mr. MacCowan to have been affected, Mairi must have taken some of that food to him. But he'd told us she'd only brought him the bilberries she'd picked from a well-known patch along the way.

I frowned. No, wait. That wasn't right. We'd never specifically asked if she'd brought any food with her. He'd told us about the berries when I asked if the dinner she'd cooked them had included mushrooms or berries. So it was possible she had brought him something from Miss Margaret's tray. He *had* told us that Mairi hadn't eaten anything he hadn't also consumed.

"What did Mairi take from your tray, both at dinner and breakfast?" I asked Miss Margaret.

She sniffed, wiping her nose with her handkerchief. "A bit o' cheese and a plum, and a raspberry compote wi' some oat cakes."

"The compote, then, would be the most likely culprit," I declared, shifting to look at Gage. "Which would have been transported in a jar."

"I told both Mr. Mallery and Anderley to examine the pantry. They should be able to tell us whether such a jar is in Mr. MacCowan's cottage."

"Then we may have some sort of confirmation soon enough." I focused my attention on the sisters—Margaret with her head and eyes downcast and Anne with her back rigidly straight and a martial gleam in her eyes that did not entirely mask her fear. "Do either of you know anyone who might have wished Miss Margaret—or either of you—harm?" I asked not unkindly.

Miss Campbell's gaze flicked momentarily toward Lord Barbreck, but she did not actually speak his name. "No' Meg. Who could wish to harm her?"

Barbreck seemed chastened by this look. Enough that it prodded him into speech. "Anne, I ken I havena been kind or even very civil these last decades," he admitted in a gravelly voice. "But I would ne'er wish you . . ." He nodded to Margaret. "Or your sister to come to such an end."

She listened to this avowal with quiet dignity and then, with the same controlled grace, nodded in acceptance of this partial apology. It was easy to see why my mother had so admired her.

"Could it be a member of your staff?" Gage inquired with

some reluctance. Servants were often blamed for the sins of their employers, which had made us leery of accepting such a suggestion in the past. But maids and footmen were people, too, with their own failings and prejudices, and so they could never be entirely ruled out.

"Our staff is very loyal," Miss Campbell replied.

Except we knew that they weren't. Their upper servants, perhaps, but not the maids who came and went with distressing regularity, as their housekeeper had confided.

"Perhaps it was an accident," Aunt Cait suggested, drawing all of our gazes. "Maybe something was mistakenly added to the compote." She waved her hand in the air. "Some herb or berry or whatever the poison was. After all, accidents do happen."

The others began to murmur about this possibility, and I had to admit she was right. Accidents did sometimes happen. But it disturbed me that the poison had caused such an alarming end to its victims, and yet no one thus far had recognized it. If it was a simple herb or berry found in this region, wouldn't *someone* have identified it by now?

The door behind me opened softly, and I glanced over my shoulder to see Bree entering. "Ye rang?" she queried as she crossed the room toward where I stood, cradling Emma before me so that she could gaze out the window.

A pair of birds must have made a nest above us under the eaves or in a crevice in the edifice of the building, for periodically the two sparrows would playfully soar and dive in front of us before swooping back up to their perch. Each time they did, Emma reached out a little hand as if trying to catch them and exclaimed, "Ah-ah," in approval of their antics. Bree grinned as Emma squirmed in excitement, and I noticed how it highlighted the charming smattering of freckles across Bree's cheeks and nose.

"Well, noo. I can tell *someone*'s feelin' better," she remarked, offering the child her finger to grip.

"Yes. Mrs. Mackay gave her a warm bath this morning, and she made a liniment of camphor and lavender to spread on her chest." I'm sure it also helped that she'd been able to breathe well enough to nurse and fill her belly.

"Aye, I can smell it. My mam used to do the same. Works a treat."

Emma cooed in response to this, as if to agree, and Bree and I laughed at her adorable enthusiasm.

"Is that right?" I told my daughter, pretending I understood exactly what she was saying. "Well, you don't say."

She tilted her head up and reached for my chin. I pretended to nibble the tips of her fingers, to her grinning delight as I carried her toward the rug. "Lay that blanket on the floor," I directed Bree, nodding at the quilt draped over the back of a chair. "Emma can show you what a marvelous roller she's become while we talk."

Once we were settled on the floor, with Emma on her belly between us gnawing on her fist rather than attempting to roll, I turned my thoughts to the investigations. "You heard that the Campbell sisters visited Barbreck this morning?" I queried, straightening the fern-green skirts of my gown where I sat with my legs draped to the side.

"Aye. Miss Margaret thought the poison might o' been meant for her."

I was pleased to hear she was already informed about at least some of this morning's developments. "Yes. Did any of the maids at Poltalloch mention her coaxing them to take food from her tray?"

"Aye, one o' 'em. I suspected it was one o' the reasons they were so jealous o' her preference for Mairi."

I turned my head to the side, nibbling my lip in thought. "Then Miss Margaret wasn't lying. At least about that part."

"Do you think she's lyin' aboot somethin' else?" From Bree's tone of voice, I could tell she was doubtful, though she didn't wish that uncertainty to be evident.

"Probably not, but I do wish she'd told us everything earlier. As it is, we now have to reexamine what we know and try to make connections we weren't trying to before."

Her eyes reflected her understanding of my frustration.

I frowned at the blocks of the quilt below me. "The most baffling question we have to answer is *who* would wish to harm Miss Margaret. And why?" I gazed hopefully at Bree. "Did the staff have much to say about her?"

"No' much more than that she's an invalid who gives gifts. Or *lets* them take 'em." She tilted her head, gazing up at the ceiling in thought. "I gather most o' 'em rather pity her. They see her as some sort o' tragic figure."

And Miss Margaret had realized this. She'd alluded to as much. But none of that really seemed to offer a motive for killing her.

I reached over to smooth out the blanket where it had become rumpled beside Emma. "I suppose the person with the most obvious motive for killing Miss Margaret is her sister. After all, Miss Campbell has been charged with her care all her life, which has tied her to Poltalloch." I shook my head. "But she genuinely seems to love her sister, just as she loves Poltalloch. I don't believe her life would change much even if her sister died."

Bree nodded in agreement. "That's the impression I've gotten from the servants aboot her as well. Other than the typical sisterly squabbles, they rub along rather well."

"Then where does that leave us?"

She shrugged. "Everyone seemed to like Miss Margaret.

She'd caused none o' 'em any grief. How could she, wi' her being ill her whole life? She's harmless."

I frowned upon hearing her words, wishing I understood why they made the base of my neck tingle.

"What?" Bree asked, noticing my look. "What is it?"

"I don't know," I admitted. "Maybe it's just that . . . we know full well that no one is ever truly harmless. Our past inquiries have taught us that. So . . . maybe we're dismissing someone we shouldn't."

"Miss Margaret?"

I narrowed my eyes, wishing I could isolate the precise reason why my instinct was humming. "Maybe. Or maybe someone else." I pushed to my feet. "One thing I *do* know is that I'm not going to allow another day to slip by without identifying that poison. Perhaps that will be the key to unlocking the answers we seek."

Emma chose that moment to finally demonstrate her new trick, flopping over onto her back to grin up at me. I dropped to one knee, joining Bree in heaping her with the correct amount of praise for this achievement, and then lifted her into my arms to fetch Mrs. Mackay. Once she was safely in the nurse's care, I gathered up the books I'd borrowed from the Campbells and made my way through the house to the library with Bree in tow.

While Bree rang for tea and pulled the two books on poisons I'd already identified from Barbreck's shelves, I sat at one of the tables to begin perusing the first of the Campbells' books. Thus settled, we spent the early afternoon searching the pages for even a hint of what the poison might be, but it was to no avail.

I slammed the last book I'd been scanning and leaned forward to bury my head in my hands. "Why can't we find it?" I demanded to know of no one in particular.

Bree shook her head. "I dinna ken, m'lady. It must be rare, indeed."

I sighed, turning my head to stare at the groaning shelves. That, or someone here or at Poltalloch had removed any books which mentioned it. I allowed my gaze to trail over the section which had contained these books, but the only gaps in the spines came from the spot where Bree had pulled them. Sinking back in my chair, I tried to think of another way we might find our answer, but my brain was too tired.

"I've been thinkin' aboot what you said," Bree remarked, forcing me to drag my gaze from the table where it had landed to her face. "Aboot no one truly being harmless. And I keep comin' back to the peculiarity o' Mairi's employment."

I recalled her interest in Mairi having taken a position at Poltalloch when her father worked for the Barbreck estate, and how she'd learned Mairi had been acquainted with Miss Margaret *before* she was hired. "Go on."

"I can't help but wonder whether there's a connection between Mr. MacCowan workin' for Lord Alisdair and Mairi workin' for the Campbells. Lord Barbreck may've severed relations wi' the Campbells, but that doesna mean Lord Alisdair did, even if he *did* try to sell them a forged painting."

I considered this and had to agree with her logic. "You're right. Stranger things have happened. Though, given what we've uncovered about the forgeries, I doubt either of the Campbells will admit to the association if I ask them about it."

Bree leaned forward over the table. "I'd like to look into it. Speak to the older servants who might remember somethin'—both here and at Poltalloch."

I searched her eager face, admitting that if anyone could wheedle the answers we sought from these Highlanders, it was Bree. But still I hesitated to send her off on such a task alone, especially when we weren't aware of the exact nature of the danger we faced.

"Very well," I agreed, and her face brightened. "*But* . . . you can't go to Poltalloch alone."

She didn't argue, perhaps recognizing the wisdom of this as well. "I can ask Callum . . ."

"Not Callum," I stated, leaving no room for argument. "We already know his judgment isn't the most assailable. And not Liam either," I told her before she could make the suggestion. I locked gazes with her, already seeing in her eyes that she knew what I was going to say, and she didn't like it. "It has to be Anderley."

She heaved an aggravated sigh but did not verbally protest.

"I know your relationship is strained at the moment, but he's the only member of the staff I completely trust to see to your safety, no matter how vexing and difficult he is."

Her lips twitched at this last comment, and I seized my advantage.

"Understood?"

"Aye. No matter how vexing and difficult."

"Good." I glanced toward the window where blue skies still reigned. "He should have returned from Mr. MacCowan's cottage by now, and I presume you wish to begin immediately, so go find him."

Before she could reply, the sound of raised voices drew our attention toward the corridor.

"I've never set foot in such a *depraved* house in all my life," the man declared, and I needed only one guess as to who it was. "Poisonings, forgeries, theft, murder! Why, it's more than disgraceful. It's entirely beyond the pale. And I cannot comprehend why you would wish to ally yourself with such a family, with such a household."

I moved toward the door to find Lord Ledbury practically foaming at the mouth while Charlotte clutched Rye's arm with her hand. My cousin appeared torn between anger and concern, and concern won out when Charlotte faltered back a step and pressed a hand to her brow. She did seem rather wan. Though this appeared to have no effect on her father or his towering fury.

"Perhaps we should repair to the . . ." my aunt began in placation, only to have Lord Ledbury make a rude noise before pivoting on his heel and storming off.

I hastened closer, worried for Charlotte's well-being, but Rye was already leading her toward the stairs.

"Oh, it's nothing," she replied with a gasp to my expression of concern. "Just a megrim. I . . . I suffer from them from time to time."

I nodded, remembering she'd suffered from them at Gairloch Castle when she was married to the odious Lord Stratford. I'd suspected then that her megrims were a symptom of extreme stress and anxiety, and now I was certain of it.

But what could I do but allow her to lie down and rest? Yes, I could solve Mairi's and Mr. MacCowan's murders. That would be a start. But I was becoming more and more certain that wouldn't solve Charlotte's problems with her father.

CHAPTER 26

Charlotte did not come down to dinner that evening, and blessedly, neither did Lord Ledbury. This was not something any of us were altogether surprised by, and it allowed the conversation to flow more naturally without Morven or I having to spur it on. But while the company was more congenial, I couldn't say that it was any more cheerful, not with the murders and Charlotte's unhappiness preying on many of our minds. Rye, in particular, looked dejected. I suspected his quiet, good-natured soul had never been objected to in all his life, and Lord Ledbury's rejection, coupled with Charlotte's megrim, had brought his spirits low.

I wished I could promise that at least one of the investigations would be resolved soon, but we were hindered by a lack of evidence. In the case of the forgeries, while we had strong suspicions and indicators that Lord Alisdair and Signor Pellegrini had been the culprits, we hadn't uncovered definitive proof and were unlikely to *ever* find it now that the events were so far in the past, and everyone with any knowledge of the devious goings-on at Alisdair's cottage was dead.

Anderley had returned from Mr. MacCowan's cottage earlier that afternoon with a jar that contained the remains of raspberry compote, which seemed to confirm Miss Margaret's suspicions, but we couldn't prove that the poison had come from the jar. Not without sophisticated lab equipment and the knowledge to operate it to extract the information we sought. All we knew was that it was possibly from Miss Margaret's tray, and it was plausible both Mairi and her father had eaten from it. But they'd also eaten a number of other similar things.

The truth was, until we figured out *what* poison was used, we couldn't move forward with the investigation. Having escorted Bree to Poltalloch, Anderley was going to speak to the cook about the raspberry compote, and maybe she would have some inspiration, but I doubted it. It was more likely she would refuse to divulge anything beyond the most rudimentary details out of fear that she would somehow be blamed.

Regardless, I'd elected to keep my thoughts on Miss Ferguson to myself for the moment. For if that poison had come from Poltalloch and had been intended for Miss Margaret, I didn't see how the governess could be involved. There was no need to sully her name needlessly.

Too tired to even play a hand at whist, I excused myself from the drawing room soon after the gentlemen joined us, but before I reached the stairs, I heard Morven calling after me. I turned as she approached, wondering what had brought her hurrying from the room. When she held out her hand and opened it, my heart leapt in relief.

"I found this under the sofa." Her topaz eyes scrutinized mine as I took the amethyst pendant from her grasp, clutching it to my chest. "Mother said it was taken from your room."

"Yes. I was afraid it was lost forever," I answered in a tight voice as the back of my eyes stung with tears.

Morven pressed a hand to my shoulder, offering me a consoling smile.

"Thank you," I told her sincerely.

"Of course."

I sighed, my gaze dropping to the purple gemstone. But then I frowned, examining the chain and clasp—both of which were new since the last chain had been snapped by an Edinburgh criminal. "Though I don't understand how it ended up under the sofa. I know I put it in my jewelry box. I distinctly remember doing so."

Morven shrugged one shoulder. "Maybe someone was making mischief."

I looked up at her, pausing in consideration before confiding, "Did your mother also tell you I found her miniature of my mother on my pillow one evening?"

Her eyes widened. "No, she didn't." A vee formed between her brows. "Mischief, indeed."

I began to tell her about the woman in the blue cloak but then for some reason stopped. I wasn't sure why. Perhaps because I would have to explain the significance of the azurite color. Perhaps because it sounded ridiculous, even to me. Whatever the case, I merely nodded emphatically to her reply.

"Why would someone *do* these things?" she asked in genuine bewilderment.

"I've been asking myself the same question."

She turned to look over her shoulder in the direction of the drawing room. "Let me think on it." Her eyes sparkled with intrigue. "Maybe I can provide *you* with some answers for a change."

I smiled. "That would be nice."

She embraced me and then returned to the others. At least one mystery was solved. Though it had left another in its wake.

I climbed the stairs, but rather than exiting into the corridor that would lead to my bedchamber, I continued up the next flight to Charlotte's. I rapped softly before opening the door to peer inside. The lights were all extinguished save the fire in the hearth, which revealed her lying on her bed in the flickering glow, and the scents of lavender, yarrow, and feverfew drifted from the room.

"Kiera?" she murmured.

"May I come in?"

"Of course."

I shut the door gently before crossing the room to perch on the edge of her bed. "How are you feeling?"

A cloth was draped over her forehead, and she opened her eyes briefly before answering. "Better. A little."

She allowed me to take her hand in mine. "Is there anything I can do?"

"No. Celeste knows what to do."

I remembered her maid. She had nearly died with us at Gairloch.

Turning to gaze into the fire, I searched for the right words. "I'm sorry I've been so distracted by the inquiries . . ."

She squeezed my hand, halting me. "There's no need to apologize." Her eyes fluttered behind their lids.

"Maybe. But I still wish I could have been with you more these past few days, to stand beside you, to offer my support."

Her lips quirked into a pained smile. "You're a good friend, Kiera. But your being there wouldn't have made contending with my father any better or any easier." She sighed. "He is who he is. And I just have to accept that." Her voice strengthened. "Just as he'll have to accept that I'm marrying Rye. Or not accept it, I suppose. The choice will be his. But that's not going to stop me from doing it."

I felt the tears I'd been biting back earlier resurface. "I'm so happy to hear that, dearest. You deserve to be happy."

"I don't know that I *deserve* it," she countered. "I don't know that any of us do. But I'm *going* to be. Happy, that is. And I'm going to stop trying to make everyone else happy as well. If they want to be, they can decide they're *going* to be for themselves."

"Bravo, Charlotte," I exclaimed as tears streamed down my cheeks. I knew this was a momentous realization for her. She'd spent so much of her life trying to please others, deferring to their wishes and tying herself in knots to do so, that she'd lost sight of what made *her* content. That's one of the reasons I'd always adored her great-aunt, Lady Bearsden, for she'd never let Charlotte cater to her happiness over her own.

Her eyes opened to meet mine in a moment of solidarity before closing again.

"I shall leave you to rest then," I said, squeezing her hand once more before rising to my feet.

"Kiera?" she murmured before I could go.

"Yes, dear?"

"Don't fret about me. I know what needs to be done. You just focus on finding that murderer."

"Is that an order?" I couldn't help but quip.

"Will it help if I make it one?"

I smirked, for she knew me too well. "Maybe."

"Then, yes. It is."

"Yes, my lady," I replied with a mock curtsy she couldn't see. Or maybe she could, for she snorted.

I left the room with a smile. It was the last one I would wear for some time.

I woke with a start to the sound of banging on our bedchamber door. Sitting upright, I clasped the sheet to my pounding chest.

Meanwhile Gage had already vaulted out of bed and pulled his dressing gown on over his bare torso as he crossed the room. He yanked open the door only to be confronted by a frantic Anderley. I'd never seen him looking anything less than cool and collected, but his dark hair stood on end, and there was a stain across the collar of his white shirt.

"It's Bree," he gasped. "We think she's been poisoned."

Panic clutched my throat, making it difficult to speak. "What are her symptoms? Where is she now?" I scrabbled for my own dressing gown.

"She started vomiting . . . about an hour ago, on the trail back from Poltalloch. I . . . I lost track of the time. *Oh Dio!*" He broke off to exclaim, clutching his hair in both hands.

"It doesn't matter," I told him, thrusting my arms into the sleeves, even though he evidently realized it did. "What else?"

"She . . . she became lethargic. And cool and clammy to the touch. What does that mean?"

"It could just be a result of her vomiting," I tried to reassure him even though my heart stuttered with fear. "Which is a good thing. If she ingested the poison, then we need her to vomit it back up. *All* of it back up." I hastened forward to grip his arms, seeing the wildness in his eyes. "Where is she now?"

"The servants' hall with the cook. I didn't know . . ."

I nodded, cutting him off. "Bring her to Gage's assigned chamber and tell the cook I need a bottle of ipecac or whatever foul remedy they have for making someone vomit, as well as clean water and chamber pots."

He whipped around and ran down the hall, disappearing into the stairwell.

I stood in the doorway, pressing a hand to my heart as I tried to process what had just happened. Bree had been poisoned while she was investigating on our behalf. Gage's arms wrapped around me, pulling me into his chest, and I allowed myself one moment to absorb his comfort before pushing him away. Fear was clawing its way up inside me, and if I didn't *do* something, it might take hold entirely.

"Wake Mrs. Mackay," I told him as I moved toward the dressing room door. "Ask if she knows any other remedies that might help Bree."

Vanishing inside, I hastened across the room and pushed open the door to Gage's assigned bedchamber. It was cold and dark, and I yanked open the drapes over the windows to allow the moonlight to spill into the room. I stripped the bed of many of its pillows and lowered the linens, ready to receive Bree's body.

Gage joined me soon after, making me suspect Mrs. Mackay had already been aroused by Anderley's knocking. "She suggested ipecac, the same as you. But without knowing exactly what she was poisoned with, she couldn't say what else might counteract it."

Pressing my hand to the bed pole, I bowed my head, reeling from my failure to uncover the poison sooner. If I had been able to identify it, we might have already caught the killer, and then Bree would not have been asking more questions of both staffs. She would never have been poisoned herself.

I tightened my grip around the smooth wood, welcoming the pain it caused the fragile bones and muscles in my hand. Then I forced myself to resume my task. Mentally whipping myself was not going to do Bree a bit of good. Ridding her of the poison would.

"We need a fire," I told Gage as I knelt beside the bed, searching under it for the chamber pot.

I didn't have to ask twice. The hearth was soon crackling, and the candles throughout the chamber were lit. Enough that I could clearly see what state Bree was in when Anderley strode through the door carrying her.

Her skin was deathly pale, and her head rested listlessly against his shoulder. I could tell now that the stain on Anderley's shirt was vomit rather than blood. That she must have cast up some of her accounts as he cradled her in just such a position, for it stained her yellow bodice and skirts as well.

"Lay her in the bed," I ordered him as two maids followed in his wake. I directed them all on what to do and then shooed the men from the room. I thought for a moment that Anderley was going to argue, but Gage clapped a hand on his shoulder and escorted him through the door.

With the help of the maids, I propped up Bree and pressed the bottle of ipecac syrup to her lips, forcing her to drink. While the concoction did its work, I had one of the maids fetch one of my simplest nightdresses from the dressing room while the other maid and I stripped Bree of her soiled garments. She shivered in the cool air, but it allowed me to search her for other symptoms. Finding no marks or rashes, we swiftly dressed her and bundled her under the covers, waiting and watching for the ipecac's effects. We didn't have to wait long.

Several long, exhausting, monotonous hours followed—for Bree and for us—broken only by her heaving and my brief departures to nurse Emma. I was surprised to find Gage was absent from our chamber, but then I realized that, of course, he would be sitting up with Anderley, going over his and Bree's every movement that afternoon and evening, as well as every element of the inquiry. Good, because in my muddled, terrified state, nothing made sense to me.

Night eventually gave over to day, and Bree finally lay still and quiet, her beautiful strawberry blond curls a limp, grimy mop against the pillow. I sat beside the bed, watching her chest slowly rise and fall, praying we had done enough. Part of me itched to dose her again, just to be certain, but I knew she had nothing else left to give. Any more, and we risked killing her from dehydration.

After an hour had passed without further incident, the maids and I poured a sip of water down her throat. We bathed her as best we could without waking her and then changed her into another clean nightdress—this time one of her own fetched from her chamber. I dismissed the maids a short time later, continuing to ply Bree with short sips of water as I kept vigil over her. I knew I should seek rest myself while I could, but I was too frightened that she might slip away if I wasn't there to keep watch, to will her to keep breathing.

When it came time for Emma's next feeding, I didn't even leave the room. I must have drowsed through much of it, the calm that flooded me whenever I nursed my daughter nearly lulling me to sleep. So when Mrs. Mackay extracted a sleeping Emma from my arms, I startled slightly.

Some minutes later when the nurse returned, I looked up in confusion.

"I've asked one o' the nursemaids from upstairs to sit wi' Emma," she informed me. "And glad she was to do it, usually bein' run off her feet by the bairns upstairs. So, I can sit wi' Miss McEvoy for a spell."

"Oh, I can't . . ." I protested.

"Ye can. And ye *should*. You're no good to her, or yourself, or Emma in this state." She urged me to my feet. "Noo, go and get some sleep, m'lady."

I shook my head, feeling perilously close to tears. And I knew that if I wept, I might just fall apart completely. "No, I really can't. Even if I lie down to try, I know my mind won't let me. So, I'm better off just staying here."

But Mrs. Mackay stood her ground. "Nay, you're no', lass. Go and get some fresh air then, at least."

I sighed wearily and then nodded. With one last look toward Bree, I allowed Mrs. Mackay to usher me through the door. My footsteps managed to carry me through the dressing room and into my bedchamber almost by pure momentum, but then they stopped. I stared at my reflection in the long mirror, realizing at some point I'd changed into a morning gown, though I didn't recall exactly when. My normally bright eyes were flat, the light inside them dimmed by fear, and the skin across my cheekbones appeared taut, like frayed rope ready to snap.

I snatched up my shawl from the vanity bench and charged through the door, down the lesser-used staircase, and out the door next to the chapel. I had no destination in mind other than to keep moving.

The sky was leaden—suitable to my mood—but the clouds didn't seem to threaten rain. Even if they had, I didn't think that would have stopped me from striding northeast, past the gardens, and out onto the moor. The sun was hidden from view, but I estimated the time to be close to midday, and my stomach began to protest in hunger at my never having broken my fast. I ignored it, welcoming each pang as my due for not having protected Bree.

If she had been poisoned by the same substance as Mairi and her father—and we had no reason to believe she hadn't—would her fate be the same? Had too much of the poison already worked its way into her system before we'd induced vomiting? Had it all been in vain?

I hugged my shawl tighter around me, refusing to contemplate that possibility. Bree was my maid, yes, but she was also my friend, and if I lost her . . .

I shook my head, desperate to drive the thought from my mind. Bree was strong. She was a fighter. Her breathing had been regular when I left. Her color had been pale but growing healthier. Another few hours should tell us whether she'd escaped the worst or . . .

My footsteps arrested in the middle of the tall grasses, the damp from the dew having already soaked the hem of my skirts. I should turn back. I should be with her. Just in case. I closed my eyes against the sudden press of tears.

Who was doing this? Who could be so cold-blooded?

Bree *had* to have been getting close to the truth. That's the only thing that made sense. Why else strike at her?

So what exactly had she uncovered? I forced myself to think back over our conversation in the library the previous afternoon. She had wanted to further explore the connection of Mr. Mac-Cowan's employment with Lord Alisdair and Mairi's with the Campbells. She'd said Mairi had known the Campbell sisters before she went to work for them, but how?

The most likely scenario was that she had met them through her father, who worked for Lord Alisdair. We'd discussed the possibility of the Campbells and Lord Alisdair having been cordial. Was that the connection? Was there something about that relationship they—or someone else—had wished to remain hidden? What was I missing?!

I was on the verge of turning back when I saw a flash of blue out of the corner of my eye. My gaze jerked to the nearby tree line where the woman in the azurite blue cloak stood watching me. I couldn't see her eyes beneath the shade of her hood, but I could feel the weight of her stare nonetheless.

She stood arrested as I began to walk toward her, slowly at first, and then with more urgency. I thought perhaps she meant to help, but then she turned and began to move off into the trees.

My heart kicked in my chest. "Wait!" I called, lifting my skirts to run, the grasses whipping at my ankles. "Please, wait!"

When I reached the trees, I didn't even break stride but continued on, following the same narrow trampled path she had. She glanced over her shoulder once but kept going, gliding between the trees, seeming to hide and reveal herself with each alternating step. I was panting and gasping for air, desperate to reach her, and yet she seemed to move without effort up the trail, even as it climbed.

Through the trees up ahead, I could see a lightening, and I pushed myself to move faster, hoping to catch up with her in the clearing. But by the time I reached the glade, she was already at the other side. "Please!" I gasped one last time, bending forward over my knees as I struggled for breath. I didn't know if I could go on. Until she turned back toward me again, lifting a gloved hand to the edge of her hood in profile.

The way she clutched the trim of her hood. The manner in which she gripped it, as if she might throw it back at any moment. My heart stuttered. I had seen my mother make just such a gesture dozens, if not hundreds, of times. Even eighteen years after her death, I remembered it.

I blinked my bleary eyes, testing their focus. It couldn't be. It wasn't possible. I had to be seeing things. If she would only show me her face.

When she set off again through the woods, I couldn't just let her go. Not without knowing for sure. Not without understanding what I was seeing.

I stumbled forward, pushing through the pain and exhaustion. She was so tantalizingly close and yet too far away. I could hear the sounds of the river growing closer, a steady ripple beneath the birdsong and my own panting breaths. The trees here grew thicker, and I kept losing sight of her for multiple seconds before catching a glimpse of her again. And still she moved incessantly onward.

I should have been more mindful of my surroundings. I should have stopped to wonder at her motives. However, in my weary, sleep-deprived, guilt-lashed haze, I couldn't think straight. I was operating on pure instinct—and a false instinct at that—one born of grief and loss and the desperate wish to see my mother again. But before I realized any of this, it was too late.

When she disappeared from view, I raced onward, determined to find her. Bursting through the last line of trees, I thought she must reappear. Instead, all I saw was open sky. I realized too late that the land ended here, dropping precipitously into the river. I flailed, the earth crumbling under my feet as I began to topple over the edge.

CHAPTER 27

K iera!" a voice shouted, grabbing onto me from behind and
hauling me back from the brink.

I gasped in shock and terror and relief, my knees giving out
beneath me.

Gage wrapped his strong arms around me and pulled me
away from the cliff edge. "Kiera, what on earth were you doing?"
he demanded, his voice tight with anger but also fear, for it shook
at the edges. "Didn't you hear me calling for you?"

I hadn't, but I couldn't answer him. It was all I could do to
grip the lapels of his coat, clutching them for dear life as something split open inside me and I began to weep.

He gathered me up in his arms, carrying me through the trees
and out into the clearing we had passed. There he sank down in
the tall grasses and heather with me still cradled in his lap, allowing me to sob myself dry.

When finally my tears had slowed, he passed me his handkerchief and pressed a kiss to my brow as I mopped at my face. "Better?" he asked tenderly.

"A bit," I admitted, my tone muffled by congestion.

"Now." He pressed his fingers gently to my chin, lifting it so he could look me in the eye. "What happened?"

My cheeks warmed in shame and embarrassment.

"I saw you leave the house and followed you out of the gardens, fearing the worst about Bree." He broke off in his explanation. "Is she . . . ?"

"She was still resting quietly when I left her. Nurse Mackay offered to sit with her."

He nodded slowly, perhaps wondering why I hadn't lain down to rest, but he didn't press the issue. "When you suddenly broke into a run and darted off into the trees, I didn't know what to think."

"Then you didn't see the woman in the blue cloak?"

He appeared startled. "No." His gaze flickered over my features. "Who was she?"

"I don't know. But . . ." I lowered my eyes, twisting the handkerchief, before forcing my gaze back to his. "It's not the first time I've seen her." I explained about the previous sightings as well as their potential connection to the appearance of the miniature on my pillow and the loss and recovery of my pendant.

His expression was grave. "Kiera, why didn't you tell me about any of this before?"

I lowered my gaze again, too ashamed to look into his face. "Because we were just so caught up in our investigations, and I wasn't sure she was even real," I admitted on a broken whisper. "Part of me thought . . ." I trailed off before forcing myself to continue. "She reminded me of my mother."

Rather than scold me for my foolishness, as he should have done, he pulled me close, resting his chin on my head. At first,

I felt brittle in his arms, but I couldn't withstand his efforts to comfort me, and soon melted into his embrace, even as I still berated myself for my folly.

"Deliberately, I assume." His voice rumbled in my ear.

"Yes, I suppose so."

"Kiera, they were taking advantage of your love for your mother, and the memories her connection with the Campbells has dredged up. They were misleading you. And I suspect if you hadn't been so exhausted and distraught over Bree, you would have realized that."

He was right. Or at least, I hoped so. I should have recognized my mother never would have run away from me like that, drawing me into danger. It was only, I'd wanted so badly for it to be her. It was a raw ache I could feel clear down to my bones.

"I miss her."

"I know," he replied, brushing back the tendrils of hair clinging to my face. "It's different now, isn't it? Having a child of our own. I find myself wondering what my mother would say or do. How she comforted *me* when I was crying in the middle of the night."

I looked up into his beloved face. We had always been united in our grief over the loss of our mothers at too early an age, and even more so now.

His eyes narrowed as he gazed out into the glade. "I see so much of you and me in Emma, but I also see glimpses of my mother. Sometimes they're so fleeting, I'm not sure they were ever really there and not just my wishful thinking." He smiled sadly. "So, you see, I understand. At least, partially."

I trailed my finger over the cleft in his chin. "I just feel so close to her here. Closer than I have in years. Because people haven't been afraid to speak of her as if her name alone would cause me pain. It does, but it's a good pain. Do you know what I mean?"

"I do." His eyes glistened with sadness. "My father practically banned mentioning my mother from conversation after she died. Until I met you, until you forced me to tell you about her, I hadn't uttered her name in years." He nudged me gently. "Thank you for that, by the way." His mouth flattened. "I suppose I should have done the same for you."

"It's not that you didn't," I protested. "But . . ."

"You needed to hear it from people who knew her," he finished for me.

"Yes." I frowned, searching for the words. "And . . . I suppose I needed to more fully understand the woman she was, not just the parts grasped by my eight-year-old brain. I needed to know that resilience is in my blood."

Gage's face was soft with affection. "That it is." His mouth flattened. "But I still wish you'd told me."

"I know," I admitted. "I should have trusted you. I should have trusted myself." I wrapped my arms around his neck. "The next time I see a figure lurking in the bushes, you'll be the first to know. Even if I'm partially convinced it's my mother's ghost."

Gage's eyebrows arched. "I suppose that will have to be good enough."

I pressed a kiss to his lips, running my fingers through the hair at the nape of his neck. "Thank you for saving me."

"Kiera." His voice was naked with emotion, but rather than speak, he used his mouth in other ways to show me how much he cared.

When eventually we pulled apart and found our way to our feet, he took my hand in his, our fingers twining, and guided me back toward the manor.

I glanced behind me as we left the clearing. "Where do you think she went?"

"I don't know," he admitted, needing no clarification as to who

I was talking about. It had to be the woman in the blue cloak. "But I suspect she's long gone."

He was undoubtedly right. So I shifted my thoughts back to the troubles at Barbreck. "Where's Anderley?"

"Resting. Or at least, he should be." He frowned. "There's no telling whether he listened to me."

"What was he able to tell you about what happened last night?"

"Between his berating himself that he'd allowed her to convince him to split up so they could question more of the staff?"

My heart went out to Anderley. I remembered how he'd looked when he banged on our door in the middle of the night. He felt guilty for not protecting her. Perhaps even guiltier than I did. And I strongly suspected Bree would not appreciate either of us blaming ourselves. In fact, I could just hear her scolding us for such ridiculousness, that she could take care of herself, thank you very much. Except she hadn't.

"He said the cook confirmed she'd made about a dozen jars of raspberry compote some weeks past, but that no one else had fallen ill from eating it," Gage said.

"Then the poison was added later." I frowned. "What of Bree? Who did she talk to? What did she uncover?"

"He said he didn't know. That Bree was unusually quiet on the ride back to Barbreck. He'd thought she was merely puzzling over something, until she became ill near the spot where the trail skirts closest to Loch Craignish."

"Then I suppose he doesn't know if she ate anything that was offered to her?"

Gage shook his head, lifting aside a low-hanging branch for us to pass under.

"Well, hopefully Bree can tell us herself. Though . . ." I pressed my lips together, ruminating on the matter. "Bree is wiser than that. I find it difficult to believe she would have accepted *anything* from Poltalloch."

"But I imagine they took food from Barbreck in their saddlebags."

I looked up at him, following the bent of his thoughts. "Yes."

We quickened our steps, veering toward the stables so Gage could ask where the saddlebags had been taken.

"Anderley was just here askin' for 'em," the stable hand told us, his eyes sharp with interest.

Gage thanked him and we hurried off toward the servants' entrance, finding Anderley just inside the door, already searching through both bags. "You've had the same thought we have," Gage told his valet.

"That someone poisoned her food," he practically growled. "Yes."

Though he was more neatly groomed than he had been the previous night, there were dark circles under his eyes, and his olive skin was wan with fatigue. But I was one to talk. I must have looked much the same. Or worse, since I'd been sobbing not thirty minutes earlier. My eyes still felt raw and gritty.

I moved closer to examine the items he'd set on the table near the door. Even in the dim passage, I was swiftly able to pick out the most likely culprit. "This." I seized the jar of deep red chutney. Opening the lid, I carefully smelled. "Rhubarb with cherries." I clamped the lid back on. "They must have hoped the bitterness of the poison would be masked by the tart fruit." I thought back to what the housekeeper at Poltalloch had told us about the poisonous qualities of rhubarb leaves. "Or that we'd attribute her illness to an improper preparation of the rhubarb." I glanced at the motley collection of food. "But I would throw out the rest of it just to be safe."

"Then someone must have snuck into the stables to tamper with it while you and Bree were otherwise occupied," Gage surmised, taking the chutney from me to examine it. "Or added the poison before you left Barbreck."

Anderley's jaw hardened as he turned his face away, his fists flexing at his sides as if he wanted to hit something. He managed to contain himself, turning back to us. "How is Bree?"

"She was resting comfortably when I left her," I assured him. "And I'm going up to check on her again now."

"May I see her?"

My breath caught at the raw emotion I heard in his voice. I could relate to the desperate need stamped across his features to ensure that Bree was safe and well. "Yes, of course."

I led both men up the stairs and rapped softly on the chamber door before opening it a crack to peer inside. When I was certain everyone was decent, I opened it wider to reveal Bree still lying beneath the rumpled white sheets.

Mrs. Mackay rose to her feet. "She woke aboot an hour ago."

"She did?" My heart surged with hope in my chest.

"She did," she confirmed with a gentle smile. "Asked after all o' you, and I was able to convince her to drink more than those dribbles o' water you've been givin' her. We talked for a wee bit, and then the puir lass fell back asleep. She's puggled."

"What did she say?" I asked, knowing I wasn't the only one whose interest had been piqued by those words.

"As to that," the nurse replied, her expression growing more serious. "Perhaps we might step into the next room so we dinna wake the lass. But first I mun tell ye that she thinks the poison was in the chutney in her saddlebag. She said it tasted off somehow, and so she spat it out and stopped eatin' it."

I pressed a hand to my chest, grateful she'd detected the taste and spit it out. Otherwise, the consequences didn't bear considering. "We'd just deduced as much," I began to explain, but Anderley spoke over me.

"Why didn't she say something?"

Mrs. Mackay's steady gaze shifted to the anxious valet. "I

dinna ken. But I suspect she figured there was nothin' to be done until you'd returned here and could get help."

"Yes, but we could have ridden faster," he protested.

"Not in the dark," Gage reminded him. "You might have broken your necks."

"You did well," I told Anderley, knowing he wouldn't listen, but it needed to be said regardless.

His gaze dropped to Bree's face, which was soft in repose. Whether she would be pleased at the idea of Anderley seeing her in such a state—with her hair still lank and grimy and her lips chapped and dry—I didn't know. But given his evident anxiety and the way he was looking at her, I suspected her looks didn't matter one iota in how he felt.

"Let's step through the dressing room," I suggested. "We can leave the door cracked." Now that Bree had woken once and spoken to someone, I felt less anxious about her state. Though by no means was she out of the woods.

"May I stay with her?" Anderley asked. "Just for a few minutes."

Had they been of the upper classes, it would have been a highly improper request. Even as servants, it bordered on inappropriate. But I had always found such strict rules to be ridiculous anyway. Anderley would never harass a woman, let alone one who'd been ill and could barely lift her head. Even one he loved.

"For a few minutes," I confirmed and then turned to lead the others from the room.

Even so, Mrs. Mackay, Gage, and I stood just inside our bedchamber, with the two doors leading to and from the dressing room wide open. I nodded for Mrs. Mackay to tell us what she'd learned from Bree, but she said something even better.

"I think I may ken what the poison is."

If any lingering lethargy had remained, it was pulverized by this statement. "You do?"

She nodded. "Miss McEvoy and I were discussin' her symptoms, and those o' the MacCowans, and the fact that both were hidden in deep red dishes."

That *was* an interesting distinction. I'd overlooked the coloring in favor of the strong flavors.

"It brought to my mind the jequirity bean." Her gaze darted back and forth between me and Gage. "Do ye ken?"

I shook my head. "The jequirity bean?"

"Aye. Mayhap ye ken it as the paternoster pea. 'Tis the seed o' a flowering plant. It's not native to Scotland, or England for that matter, but the red beans are often used for jewelry—necklaces and such, and especially rosaries."

"And they're poisonous?" I clarified, surprised to discover such a bean would be used in those objects.

"No' by touch. The poison is deep inside the hard shell and has to be crushed or chewed to be released. 'Twas used in trials by ordeal long ago." She tilted her head. "Though some o' the accused were informed ahead o' time that if they swallowed the bean whole, it would pass through them, leavin' 'em unscathed." She lifted her finger. "*But* if it *was* chewed, 'twas supposed to cause a right terrible death, includin' bleedin' from the eyes, nose, and mouth."

"That's it, then," I exclaimed. "That's our poison." I turned to Gage. "Then we just need to find these paternoster peas and figure out who possesses them."

"I ken someone who does."

My eyes widened in surprise, and I could tell from her expression that the answer troubled her.

"Who?" Gage asked.

"Miss Ferguson."

Gage and I shared a look of misgiving.

"I noticed she carries a rosary, and it's made from paternoster peas."

As if joining the voices of accusation in my head, we heard a wail from the nursery next door.

"Thank you for telling us," I told the nurse.

She nodded and then hastened to the nursery to check on Emma and relieve the nursemaid. Meanwhile I stood rooted to my spot, wishing I'd spoken to Rye and insisted we lock up Miss Ferguson until the matter could be investigated further instead of letting her return to her charges and wreak more destruction on those around her. I hadn't thought to ask Mrs. Mackay whether she'd said so, but Bree must have also seen her rosary—or maybe Miss Ferguson had thought she had—and hadn't realized the significance of the beads.

"We don't know yet for certain that it was her," Gage reminded me, rubbing circles in my back. "There may be someone else with jewelry made from paternoster peas."

"That would be awfully coincidental."

"Maybe. Maybe not."

"And will that person also have motive for wanting Kennan and Mairi MacCowan dead?"

Gage had no answer to that. "We need to question her."

I agreed. "But not here. At her uncle's cottage. Let's make her walk through the rooms and see how she reacts."

"But first . . ." He turned me to face him, resting his hands on my shoulders. "You need to rest."

My eyes widened in alarm. "We can't leave her to wander free . . ."

"Oh, we're not," he replied with a humorless chuckle. "Leave it to me and Anderley to isolate her and prevent her from causing any further trouble."

"And Bree . . ."

"I'll enlist your aunt or cousin to watch over her. *And* I'll even make Miss Ferguson taste any of the food bound for Bree's room if that will make you feel better."

I looked up into his patient gaze and realized I wasn't demonstrating a great deal of that trust I'd promised to show in him. He and Anderley knew full well what was at stake, and Henry and my family could be relied upon to help them.

I exhaled wearily. "That might be taking it a tad far." After all, the poison couldn't be hidden in just anything. "But order the kitchen staff to throw out the chutney and anything red or pink that the paternoster peas might be hidden in."

"I will."

I bowed my head forward, resting it against his chest. "Very well," I conceded gracelessly, though given half a chance, I think I might have been able to fall asleep standing right there.

"Good. Now," he declared, setting me away from him. "Lie down before you *fall* down. I'll bring Emma to you, and when she's done, I'll whisk her away so you never need rise."

I offered him a weak smile. "Be careful. I might grow accustomed to such service."

"Oh, darling," he murmured, wrapping his hand around the back of my neck. "You could have had such service from the day of her birth. You're the one who wouldn't let me." He dropped a kiss to my lips and then left to do all he'd promised.

CHAPTER 28

Gage was right. Just a few hours' sleep had made all the difference in the world. And it had turned out I'd missed even less than I'd feared.

Gage had confined Miss Ferguson to her bedchamber after questioning her about her rosary and her movements the afternoon before, and she had been singularly uncooperative. In the interim, Rye's children were left in the care of the nurserymaids and their cousin's governess. I wished I could have been the one to explain to Rye our suspicions about his governess, but Gage said my cousin had taken the news fairly well, all things considered. It had helped that Charlotte was with him, so while Rye had been evidently shocked and distressed, and concerned about his potentially poor judgment in hiring her, he'd not faced those emotions alone.

Meanwhile belowstairs, with the help of several of the kitchen maids, Anderley had scoured the kitchen, pantry, scullery, and cellars for any evidence of the poison or further tampering with the food. After all, the paternoster peas had to be ground up somewhere. But their search proved unsuccessful. Though, for the sake of safety and thoroughness, they had gotten rid of all the red food already prepared.

Bree continued to recover and regain her strength, even bathing and eating a bowl of beef broth. I visited her in her room before setting out for Mr. MacCowan's cottage, relieved to see a bit of color return to her cheeks and her bright intelligence glinting in her eyes. Let it suffice to say, I did not leave her room dry-eyed or without some reluctance. However, I knew she was in excellent hands, for Anderley was staying with her, along with Lady Bearsden, who held a soft spot for the pair. I didn't hold much faith in her ladyship's abilities as a chaperone should our maid and valet need such a deterrent, but her presence was meant as more of a deterrent to gossip about them anyway, ridiculous though that might be.

The leaden skies of the morning had not abated, and by the time we reached the glade where Mr. MacCowan's cottage was located, the shadows had already lengthened. A cool wind blew in from the sea, rattling the leaves in the trees overhead and sending them scuttling across the path before us. We had elected to walk, with Miss Ferguson leading the way next to Henry, while Gage and I followed.

If Miss Ferguson's attitude could be summed up in one word, it would be *defiant*. A stance I could understand if she was afraid she was about to be caught for the crimes she'd committed. But if she was innocent, her surly, uncooperative manner merely made her seem guiltier.

However, as we entered the clearing, her angry strides shortened and then stopped before the door. We allowed her a moment to gather herself, and then Gage prodded her to move forward. "Go on, then." She jerked forward as if pulled by strings and slowly opened the door. I crumpled the handkerchief clutched in my hand, having it at the ready in case the stench that had permeated the building the day before had not been completely cleaned away.

I needn't have worried. The only scents to assail my nostrils were the harsh fumes of whatever cleaning agents the maids had used. We moved into the main room, and I noted the pantry cupboard doors gaped wide, showing they'd been emptied of all their foodstuffs. The door to the bedchamber had also been left open, though the floor where Mr. MacCowan had collapsed between the two rooms was scrubbed clean of any trace of blood, leaving a paler patch of stone than that around it.

Miss Ferguson crossed her arms in front of her as her gaze darted around the cottage, looking as if she half expected something to leap out at her. Her eyes eventually fell to that patch on the floor between the two rooms, and her face paled, obviously deducing the reason for its discoloration. Then they lifted to meet mine, their depths frantic.

"I didna kill 'em," she blurted, and then gestured toward Gage. "I didna even ken those beads on my rosary were poisonous 'til ye told me. How could I?" Her voice rose in pitch. "I mean, who strings a *rosary* wi' somethin' that can *kill* ye?"

"Perhaps your mother warned you of them, or you read about them in a book? There are any number of ways you might have learned about them," Gage pointed out with faultless logic.

"But I didna!" She stamped her foot, some of her earlier defiance returning. "I would *never* have killed my uncle and cousin. Especially no' for a *paintin'*." She motioned wildly toward the bedroom. "I assume that's what ye think. That I hoped to inherit it. Well, I didna. I didna even ken aboot it. And 'twill likely go to my aunt anyway."

She was right. There were problems with the painting being her motive, but that didn't mean there wasn't another one as yet unknown.

"The fact of the matter, Miss Ferguson, is that you are the

only person who has been discovered to be in possession of the source of the poison," Gage informed her sternly, his stance widening as he towered over the petite woman. "You were also seen visiting Mr. MacCowan at this cottage by me and Mrs. Gage, and you concealed your relationship with both victims." His eyes narrowed. "You also had access to the kitchens at Barbreck Manor and could easily have poisoned Miss McEvoy's chutney yesterday afternoon."

"But I didna!" Her eyes were wide with panic, and her chest rose and fell with each anxious breath. "I would ne'er hurt Miss McEvoy. I would ne'er hurt anyone!" She clutched her head between her hands, staring at the floor several feet away. "I didna put poison in Miss McEvoy's chutney," she stated more calmly, though her voice was still ragged with distress. "And I didna put poison in my cousin's or my uncle's food." She clasped her hands before her, as if in prayer, as her gaze bounced between the three of us. "Please! You have to believe me."

Part of me wanted to. I didn't want to believe the woman who had been charged with the care and education of Rye's children could do such a thing. But the evidence as Gage had laid it out was difficult to ignore or dismiss. She *was* the only person in possession of the poison. Or at least, the only person we'd discovered so far. There was a possibility someone else had access to paternoster peas.

There was also the question of how exactly she'd contrived to dose her cousin, Mairi, with the substance. We'd shifted our focus to the raspberry compote once Miss Margaret had come forward to suggest she might have been the intended target, and the compote might still have been the substance containing the poison, but it might also have been something else. Miss Ferguson might have met her cousin on her day off as she was journeying to her father's cottage and given her something then.

Or maybe I had been wrong about the length of the poison's

latent period—the time between consumption and effect. After all, the time between Bree's having ingested it and her beginning to vomit had been shorter, though I wondered if my maid had either consciously or unconsciously induced her own vomiting. I would have to verify that. But it was possible the poison struck more quickly than I'd believed, and Mairi had consumed it after arriving at her father's home, but he had not eaten it until later. Though that would contradict Mr. MacCowan's assertion that she'd eaten nothing he hadn't. And what of her cough and the other symptoms she'd exhibited on her arrival at this cottage?

Whatever the truth of those details, Miss Ferguson was still our most viable suspect, and unless a better one presented themselves or she could prove her innocence, our chief suspect she would remain.

I scrutinized Miss Ferguson's features, thinking back to our conversation the day before. "You say you didn't know about the painting, that you don't expect to inherit it, and yet yesterday when I asked you about it, I could sense your interest." She turned her head to the side, her shoulders inching upward. "It was perfectly apparent that you weren't as indifferent as you wished to seem. Perhaps you were intrigued by the money you could make from selling it."

She surprised me when she suddenly snarled, "I dinna want anythin' to do wi' any paintings my uncle might o' possessed."

Gage and Henry appeared just as taken aback as I was.

I narrowed my eyes, realizing she knew much more than she was saying. "Why is that?" I pressed, careful not to divulge anything that might muddy the waters of her guilt or provide her an excuse for her actions.

She clamped her mouth into a tight line, perhaps angry at herself for revealing as much as she had. How much loyalty did she feel toward her uncle and cousin? Would she still keep their secrets, even in death?

"*Obviously*, ye already ken they were involved in the forger-ies," she snapped, her gaze searching mine for confirmation. "Well, involved in keepin' it all quiet anyway."

"Go on," I coaxed when she broke off.

"Uncle worked for Lord Alisdair. 'Twas wi' him mornin', noon, and night whenever his lordship was at Barbreck, and cared for his cottage when he wasna. And when Mairi's mam died, my cousin was there, too. Helpin' oot or playin' quietly in a corner. They kent all his secrets."

"Yes, but how did you learn about them?"

A vee formed between her brow. "One summer when I was eight, my mam decided it was time I got to ken my other relatives. Or at least, that's what she claimed," she sneered. "She really wanted me oot from beneath her feet while she hosted a house party. One my father couldna afford." She exhaled irrita-bly. "But I digress. She sent me here to stay wi' Uncle Kennan and Mairi. At Lord Alisdair's cottage."

I straightened. "So, you witnessed firsthand what he was doing?"

"Aye, though I didna truly understand until much later that what he was doin' was wrong, or why my uncle was so insistent we no' talk aboot it."

Gage's gaze met mine, as shocked as I was to discover we had a firsthand witness. Albeit an unreliable one, at best, given her age at the time and her current predicament.

"Did Lord Alisdair have many guests?"

"A few." She eyed us more evenly now that she was resigned to talking. "I suppose ye already ken aboot Signor Pellegrini."

I indicated we did. "Did he assist Lord Alisdair?"

"Oh, aye. He was in the thick o' it. And there were a few others who visited Lord Alisdair from time to time. An elderly gentleman and a lady." Her expression turned guarded. "She seemed to be *verra familiar* wi' him. She always came and went in a cloak."

A lover, perhaps? One intent on hiding her identity. Miss Ferguson seemed to think so.

"Did you notice whether any of them ever left with paintings?" I asked.

She shook her head. "Nay. But . . . I'm no' sure they woulda done so while we were watchin', even if we were just bairns."

She had a good point. Not every nobleman was ignorant of the watchful eyes of the servants that surrounded them, especially if they were doing something they wished to hide.

I crossed slowly toward the door to the bedchamber. "Then when I mentioned a painting hung in your uncle's bedchamber, you assumed it must be one of Lord Alisdair's forgeries."

"Or worse, one o' the originals he'd stolen." She lofted her chin haughtily. "I spoke the truth. I dinna want anythin' to do wi' it. And I imagine it rightly belongs to Lord Barbreck anyway."

I moved into the bedchamber, relieved to find that the stench was gone, aided no doubt by the window that was left partially open. I allowed my gaze to trail over the contents. A paler rectangle than the surrounding wall was now evident above the bed where the painting had once hung. Anderley had brought the suspected Rembrandt back to the manor, where it sat in the marquess's study. The objects littering the remaining surfaces were spare—a comb, a bit of string, a razor.

By far the most surprising discovery in the room was the closet which had been hidden behind the carved paneling along one wall. When I'd peered into the room the day before, I'd had no suspicion there was a cupboard concealed behind it. I moved closer to investigate.

"Anderley said they found it yesterday when they were searching the cottage."

However, I didn't hear anything else he said, as my eyes had fastened on something inside. Reaching up, I removed the garment from the peg and turned to show the others the azurite blue cloak.

Gage's pupils dilated, immediately grasping the implication, and as one we turned to Miss Ferguson.

She still hovered in the doorway, eyeing the cloak with disinterest. Or a fair approximation of it. At the sight of our faces, she stiffened, her eyes widening in uncertainty. "What?"

Henry's expression behind her also registered confusion.

Gage swiveled to loom over her. "Did you attempt to coax my wife over a cliff this morning?" His voice cracked like a whip, making even me start.

Miss Ferguson cowered backward, only to be brought up short by Henry. "Nay! I-I would ne'er . . ." she stammered.

Gage's eyes bored into hers, and she was shrewd enough not to look away. "Where were you around eleven?"

"Wi' the bairns in the schoolroom. I've been wi' them all day. Ye can ask the nursemaids. They saw me. And heard me. The walls in the nursery are verra thin."

She was right. If she'd disappeared for long enough to lead me on such a merry chase, someone would have noticed. We would need to speak with the nursemaids, to be sure, but I didn't expect to discover she'd lied.

I pressed a hand to Gage's back, hoping to calm him. I'd rarely seen him so furious.

He slowly backed away from the governess. "We'll be verifying that."

She nodded, still watching him warily.

I draped the cloak over my arm, trying to decide whether it had been hung here to deliberately cast blame on Miss Ferguson or simply because it was a convenient hiding location. Smoothing my hand over the woolen fabric, I found a hair. Holding it up to the light, it appeared to be either pale blond or gray. But had it come from the wearer or been picked up elsewhere—like the inside of the closet?

My gaze lifted again to the cupboard. Had the cloak always been stored there, or had the culprit just decided to rid themselves of such an incriminating piece of evidence? I tilted my head, scrutinizing the panels on the outside and the manner of construction that had allowed it to remain concealed. I could have sworn I'd seen something similarly constructed, and recently. Clearly Mr. MacCowan had crafted it himself. I'd already noted what a talented carpenter he was.

And then it struck me like a thunderbolt.

I spun about to share my epiphany with Gage, only to clamp my mouth shut again at the reminder of Miss Ferguson's presence. "Let's return to the manor," I instructed instead, striding past them toward the door, anxious to confirm my suspicions.

I didn't pause to wait for the others, trusting they would catch up. In less than a dozen steps, Gage grabbed my elbow to check my pace. "What is it? What have you realized?"

I adjusted the cloak draped over my arm, and I glanced over my shoulder toward Henry and Miss Ferguson, who trailed several feet behind. "Let's just say, this cloak has given me a fair idea where the paintings are."

His eyebrows arched. "All of them?"

I cast him an enigmatic look. "We shall see."

While Gage secured Miss Ferguson once again in her chamber and enlisted Liam's assistance in standing guard, I took care of Emma and changed into my crimson riding habit with the assistance of the upstairs maid who had been summoned to sit with Bree so that Anderley could join us on our next excursion. I was relieved to see Bree making such a swift recovery but had insisted she remain in bed until at least the following morning.

Something she had strenuously argued against, but I had prevailed, with the added promise I would visit her later to tell her about everything we'd learned that day. And hopefully soon I would have even more to reveal.

Hastening down the steps to the library, where I was to meet Gage, Anderley, and Henry, I was forced to check my steps when Charlotte and Rye suddenly stepped into my path. From the intent looks on their faces, I deduced they'd been waiting there with the sole purpose of intercepting me.

"Gage spoke with us briefly," Charlotte said, perhaps uncertain I knew. "How likely is it that Miss Ferguson is the culprit?"

I grasped hold of her arms above the elbows, rumpling the enormous ice blue gigot sleeves of her gown. "First, let me say how glad I am to see you looking much recovered from last night," I told her, hoping to calm some of the anxiety that wreathed her face.

She exhaled deeply. "Thank you."

"And second, we're still uncertain." I shifted my gaze to Rye. "I don't know how much Gage told you, but Miss Ferguson was in possession of a rosary made from the poison, and she concealed the fact that Kennan and Mairi MacCowan were her relatives."

Rye and Charlotte shared a look of shock that told me they hadn't known at least one of those things.

He shook his head in bewilderment. "I'm just still so astonished by the idea that Miss Ferguson would do such a thing."

"Yes, but you do like to believe the best of people," I pointed out. "Which is admirable," I hastened to add. "Except in a case like this."

Rye turned to his fiancée with sad eyes. "I'm sorry, Charlotte. I should have taken your concerns about her more seriously sooner."

Charlotte clasped his hands between hers. "Oh, but darling, you couldn't have known it would be as bad as this. I certainly didn't."

"Now, let's not be hasty," I warned them. "The evidence against her is unsettling, but it's by no means definitive. There's still a possibility she's not the killer." I studied both of their faces. "Have either of you spoken with her in the past few days?"

"I have," Rye admitted. "As I'd alluded to, Charlotte had expressed some concerns."

I nodded, having been the one to encourage her to take those concerns to him.

"And I wanted to address them." He cleared his throat. "To be honest, she seemed to me to be quite chastened. Perhaps a bit too much."

I wondered if this had been a ploy by Miss Ferguson or simply more evidence of the general malaise and uneasiness which had plagued the governess during the days after she'd stumbled upon her cousin's dead body. I supposed it depended on whether she was guilty.

"She promised to be more respectful," Rye continued. "And in general, appeared to be quite receptive to my requests and suggestions. She seemed pleased to learn that she and the children would be moving with us to the estate near Edinburgh my great-uncle has gifted us the living from as a wedding present."

I considered this piece of information, wondering if some of Miss Ferguson's general disagreeableness had been a result of her apprehension that she and the children would be left at Barbreck when Rye and Charlotte departed after the wedding. After all, the place was clearly not one of happy memories for her.

"Thank you for telling me that," I said. "And as I cautioned, don't be too hasty. There are still questions to be answered. I can't really say more." I began to move away. "Excuse me."

"Of course . . ." Rye murmured after me even though I'd already turned away, intent on finding one of those answers.

CHAPTER 29

N ow, then. You've got us here," Gage declared with impatience. "So out with it." He spread his arms and turned in
a circle in the entry of Lord Alisdair's cottage. "Where are the
paintings?"

I merely continued to smile my enigmatic smile as I led them
into the drawing room, enjoying being the sole possessor of the
answer to this riddle for a moment longer. I only hoped I proved to
be correct; otherwise, my husband would never let me live it down.

"Open those drapes," I directed, moving toward the paneled
wall I had admired during our last visit. Then I had been distracted by the craftsmanship and artistry, but this time I was
entirely focused on the construction.

Late-afternoon sunlight flooded the room as Anderley threw
open the drapes across the massive southern-facing window. With
the stage now set, I gestured toward the panels with a theatrical
flourish. "Hidden in plain sight." I arched my eyebrows as Gage
continued to stand immobile and then turned to examine the

wood, trusting he would soon apprehend. Lightly, I ran my fingers over the grooves in the panels, searching for a mechanism like the one that had opened the closet in Mr. MacCowan's bedchamber.

"Of course," Gage exclaimed behind me and then hurried forward to assist me.

I grinned at his evident excitement.

Soon all four of us were studying the grooves and joints, kneeling and rising on our tiptoes to inspect every inch, but it was Henry who found first one mechanism and then another just above it, opening both with loud snicks. We slowly backed away as the panels swung outward like two massive doors. It was a false wall. One concealing two feet of extra space. And on the real wall behind it hung about a dozen paintings.

I gasped, pressing my hands to my mouth as goose bumps rose across my entire body. I couldn't help it, for before me hung a stunning array of masterpieces. There was the Titian, and there the Van Dyck. The Gainsborough, van Ruisdael, Zoffanys, and all the others, plus two more I had missed.

"Well done, my clever darling," Gage declared, draping his arm around me to pull me to his side and dropping a kiss to my hair. "I take it these are the originals."

Barely able to tear my gaze away from the display before me, I peered sideways at him long enough to note the amusement twinkling in his eyes. "Yes!" I gestured toward the brilliance before us. "Can't you tell?"

"Only through your eyes. And Anderley's."

I darted a glance at the valet, finding him similarly transfixed. At least I wasn't the only one.

"So, Alisdair didn't sell them," Henry summarized needlessly. "He kept them."

"Yes, his own private collection." A furrow formed in my brow. "Which means his motivation wasn't greed."

"Envy, then?" Gage suggested. "Or revenge?"

I frowned, puzzling over what I knew of the youngest brother of the marquess. "Or maybe it *was* greed. But not of money."

"Of beauty," Anderley finished for me.

I turned to meet his gaze, seeing that he understood the same thing I did. "He wanted these works of art for his own, but Barbreck held the title and the money. The only way he could possess them was through trickery."

I looked up at the wall, my eyes seeking out the Titian. And from what we knew, it had all started with this work by the renowned Venetian artist, which was supposed to go to Sir James Campbell of Poltalloch.

I ruminated on that first forgery, wondering at his audacity. When it had been discovered, what had he thought? Had he been surprised his brother had defended him so stringently, or had he expected it? Had he felt guilty Barbreck had broken his engagement because of him? Or had that been his intention? Or if not his intention, then a pleasing consequence.

As for Signor Pellegrini, I supposed we might never know what his motivations were. Perhaps Alisdair had paid him—in money or in kind. Or perhaps as a frustrated artist who had been forced to resort to painting mediocre murals to make his living, the reward had been seeing his works hung in such a grand place as Barbreck Manor's long gallery alongside other masterpieces. He may have seen this as a sort of vindication and proof of his genius, as well as the unfairness of the powers that be who may have judged his other work unworthy. Maybe it was both.

Turning my back on the paintings, I crossed to the window, peering out at the rugged Argyll scenery and ruminating further on what Anderley and I had concluded about Lord Alisdair. He had coveted beauty. In art, yes. But what about also in women?

I thought of the lady Miss Ferguson had remembered visiting Lord Alisdair. How she'd seemed anxious to hide her identity by wearing cloaks, of all things. If she'd visited him often, then she must have lived nearby, and there were a small number of ladies residing in this part of Argyll.

Could Alisdair have coveted his brother's fiancée? And what of Miss Campbell? Would she have willingly taken up with the man who had attempted to swindle her father and wrecked her engagement?

Maybe if Alisdair had admitted the truth. If he'd apologized and expressed remorse. After all, Barbreck was ultimately responsible for his decision to end the engagement. I was certain Miss Campbell would have seen it that way. But I wasn't as certain that the lady I had come to know would have accepted such a relationship, whether as his lover or business associate. Yes, love and hate could be powerful motivators, but Miss Campbell, in her own way, was just as prideful as Barbreck, and I struggled to see her in either role.

Gage joined me at the window. "You've thought of something," he stated, his eyes sharp with concern. He knew me too well. "What is it?"

The words to theorize a bitter betrayal formed on my tongue, but I swallowed them back, shaking my head. I wasn't ready to share such a nasty suspicion. Not without further contemplation, without further proof. But for the moment I focused my thoughts on the next step.

"Barbreck should be informed the paintings have been found."

That would be betrayal enough for one day.

Gage nodded, but I could tell he wasn't convinced that's all I'd been deliberating.

In the failing light of the day shining through his study windows, Lord Barbreck looked as if he'd aged a decade in the space of the past week.

As we'd finished telling him about our discovery of the paintings, his head had sunk back against his chair, and he'd closed his eyes. One might have expected him to feel some relief upon learning his paintings had not been sold, or damaged, or lost forever. But I didn't think it was relief that made his head suddenly too heavy to hold up. It was grief. And sorrow. And shame.

Gage and I waited quietly for him to speak, allowing him the dignity of deciding how he wished the rest of the conversation to go. If asked, I would have said I anticipated he would nod his head in thanks and then dismiss us so that he could continue to brood in solitude. But apparently, he'd already done enough of that.

"I ne'er suspected him, ne'er doubted him. No' in the fifty-odd years since," he told us in a weary voice, lifting his head. "Maybe that was naïve o' me, but when I asked and he swore it was a genuine Titian, I believed him. But . . ." He held up his liver-spotted hands and sighed. "It turns oot he lied." He reached inside the central desk drawer and extracted a miniature portrait that he clutched in both hands and gazed down at longingly. "And *I* was an even bigger fool than he."

I didn't need to see the image he was looking at to know whom it depicted. And the fact that he'd kept it all these years told me without a shred of doubt why he'd never married another.

"I always believed I was right. That I'd preserved our family's honor. That Anne had been the one who lost oot, but I was wrong." His brow crumpled. "It was me."

"You're not the only one who lost out," I remarked. "Even if they were *your* actions and *your* foolishness."

His stare hardened at my bluntness, but I was not about to gloss over the truth now.

"Miss Campbell lost, too."

His shoulders bowed, and his eyes fastened once again on the image in the portrait, acknowledging this fact.

"She deserves an apology," I pressed, but with less bite.

His mouth tightened in a firm line. "Aye, she does. Tomorrow." He looked up to meet my gaze evenly. "Will ye join me?"

Though it might have been a plea for help in doing so, I didn't think it was. He appeared determined to finally do the right thing whether I accompanied him or not. Rather it seemed more of a desire to have witnesses, to make his apology a public statement as well as a personal one.

I only hoped Miss Campbell proved as worthy of that apology as I wanted to believe.

I glanced at Gage before answering. "Of course."

Barbreck dipped his head in gratitude, as I'd expected him to do five minutes before, and then returned to his contemplation of the miniature.

When after some moments he didn't speak, we excused ourselves, closing the door to his study with a gentle click. I paused before the painting hanging several feet away of *Christ at Emmaus* by an unknown artist, likely a Venetian based on the color and light. Tracing the brushstrokes and falls of shadow quieted my mind.

"Well, at least that's one mystery solved," Gage remarked, standing just beyond my shoulder.

I didn't comment, still unable to voice the dark suspicions swirling in me, trying to take shape. Part of me hoped my husband would attribute my failure to reply to my absorption with the painting, but the rest of me grasped he knew me far too well and was far too attuned to my idiosyncrasies to ever let it pass without notice. And the rest of me proved right.

"Kiera?"

"Hmm?" I hummed distractedly.

When he grasped my shoulders, turning me to look at him, I knew I was not going to be allowed to escape his interrogation with such a shallow ploy. He searched my face for the answers I didn't yet know how to give. "Why aren't you more pleased? You found the real paintings, and now they can be restored to their rightful place. What more could you ask for in that regard?"

I turned my head to the side, glancing at the study door. "For Alisdair not to have meddled." Though *meddle* was much too innocuous a word. One for aunties trying to arrange marriages and sisters interfering in well-laid plans. Perhaps *transgressed* was better. Or *betrayed*.

"Yes," he replied solemnly, matching my tone. But I could tell from the intent look in his eyes that he was not going to be so easily diverted.

Which made the sudden appearance of Morven and Lady Bearsden all the more fortuitous.

"Kiera!" Morven exclaimed, raising her arm to hail me as if I was across the garden rather than twenty feet down the corridor.

Before turning to greet them, Gage gave me a look that told me our conversation was not finished, merely temporarily suspended. One I ignored, determined as I was to avoid it until I was ready.

"What is it?" I asked my cousin as she bounded forward with Lady Bearsden trundling along more slowly behind her with the aid of her cane. Noting the triumphant gleam in her eyes, I trusted we weren't about to be informed of another poisoning.

She clasped my hand between hers. "You remember you told me about the miniature showing up on your pillow, and then I found your mother's missing pendant?"

I lifted my other hand to press it to the amethyst. "Yes?"

"Well, *I've* uncovered something."

"Have you?" I replied, trying to suppress some of the amusement I felt at the victorious tilt of her head. She was clearly quite proud of herself.

"I spoke to some of the staff, and one of the maids recalled seeing an older woman entering your chamber."

My eyes widened at this pronouncement and then immediately shifted to Lady Bearsden's face.

"The maid told me she'd *thought* it was Lady Bearsden, so she didn't say anything," Morven continued.

"But it was not," Lady Bearsden proclaimed with a harrumph. "As if I would enter another guest's room without their being there or having their leave to do so."

I struggled to hide a guilty flush, for I'd done just such a thing numerous times in the past. Of course, it had been in the pursuit of one of our inquiries, but that didn't absolve me entirely. Mercifully, neither lady seemed to notice.

"Yes, but the maid couldn't have known you'd not been given leave to do so," Morven pointed out. "And she wasn't going to be so impertinent as to *ask* you."

Something whoever the culprit was had counted on.

"I suppose you're right," Lady Bearsden replied, seeming slightly mollified.

"Would you say this maid was particularly perceptive?" I asked Morven.

"I should say not," Lady Bearsden grumbled. "Naming *me* the culprit."

"What I mean is, would she have noted the details? Or would she have simply seen an older lady entering my room, and so assumed it was Lady Bearsden since she was the guest who most easily fit that description?"

"Definitely the latter," Morven proclaimed. "When I pressed her on whether she was certain it was Lady Bearsden, the only details she could recall was that she was dressed like a lady and had white or gray hair."

I frowned. "She didn't see her face?"

"No."

Then, for that matter, the intruder might have been *anyone* dressed in disguise with a wig. Though I couldn't imagine why anyone would go to such lengths just to employ a few pranks. Which told me that they weren't merely larks but the work of someone much more intent on preying on my mind. Someone like the woman in the blue cloak.

I turned to look at Gage, knowing he was thinking of Miss Ferguson, but someone else had come to my mind. The same person whose possible involvement had been troubling me since the governess mentioned a lady had regularly visited Lord Alisdair. The same person who had made sure I was aware of my mother's connection to her and her gift to her of the amethyst pendant even now hanging around my neck.

Could Miss Campbell have snuck into the manor? Could she have been the woman to don the blue cloak? That first time I'd seen her from the battlements, she couldn't have anticipated I would do so, but perhaps she had seen me standing up there and realized the effect it had on me. Perhaps that's when she'd decided to keep exploiting it.

I had to admit it was possible she *could* have done all that. Though that didn't answer whether she *had*.

Just contemplating the idea of it left me feeling cold inside, for I had liked Miss Campbell. I had felt a growing affection for her, particularly in light of her relationship with my mother. But if she had sought to exploit that connection to some nefarious effect, then I had been well and truly fooled. At least temporarily.

I turned to look up at the painting behind me, forcing my eyes to follow the sweeps of that long-ago painter's brush, to breathe through each swipe as if I was making it myself while my mind grappled with the unsettling possibility that Miss Campbell was complicit in the forgeries, and perchance a poisoner. For if she was the lady who had been such a regular visitor of Alisdair, she had almost certainly known of his dishonorable activities. Activities Mr. MacCowan and Mairi had also known about, as well as her presence at Alisdair's cottage. And if she had been the older woman sneaking into my chamber and skulking about in a blue cloak, then she had been intent on at least hindering my efforts to investigate. She had also left the cloak inside Mr. MacCowan's cottage, which made me suspect it wasn't the first time she'd been there. She might have poisoned both servants to keep them quiet about her past.

After all, it was my discovery of the forgeries which appeared to have set everything into motion. Before then, Miss Campbell must have felt relatively safe from discovery. Alisdair and Signor Pellegrini were dead. The MacCowans were unlikely to speak up about it or be believed if they did. But once I'd realized the Van Dyck was a forgery, everything had changed. We started asking questions, and she must have feared it was only a matter of time before the MacCowans talked.

It was a disconcerting feeling to suspect that my knowledge and actions—no matter how innocent or well-meaning—might have initiated the events that had led to other people's deaths. Usually the murders we investigated had little, if nothing, to do with us, for they transpired for reasons independent of us, and we either happened to be nearby or were called in later to investigate. But this time was different. And while the notion of my feeling guilty about it was absurd, I did, in at least a small way, feel culpable.

Which made Miss Campbell's involvement all the more troubling to contemplate. Though, if she was our culprit, we still required proof—something we were sadly lacking at the moment. And something we needed to remedy.

I turned to find Gage watching me, and I gave him a slight nod, letting him know I'd accepted it was time we talked. But first, there were two things I needed to do.

"I'm exhausted from the past few days," I told Morven, suddenly feeling all the hours of sleep I'd lost the past two nights to Emma's catarrh and then Bree's poisoning. "I think I'll take a tray in my room for dinner. Will you make my excuses to your mother and Charlotte?"

"Of course," she replied immediately, her face crinkling in empathy.

"You've had the devil of a time," Lady Bearsden commiserated. "But you'll rest easier tonight, dear." Her optimism was kind but, given everything that still weighed heavily on my mind, not very encouraging.

I excused myself, saying I needed to see to Emma, and trusted Gage would find a way to excuse himself from dinner as well. However, rather than go straight to my bedchamber, I deviated to the room where Bree was currently recovering. I found the door open and her sitting up in bed, her complexion still pale and dark circles under her eyes. But the signs of her recent sickness were somewhat mitigated by the fury in her eyes as she glared at Anderley with her arms crossed over her chest.

"She keeps trying to get out of bed," he explained to my arched eyebrows.

"Aye, well, I can fetch a book five feet away. I'm no' that helpless," she groused.

Anderley's mouth was set in a mulish line. One that rivaled even Bree's.

I suppressed a sigh. "Gage and I will be taking dinner in our chamber tonight," I told the valet. "Why don't you go and see if he requires anything. I'll sit with her for a time."

He nodded, striding from the room with a brief backward glance.

When his footsteps had receded down the corridor, I turned to my maid with a look of mild chastisement. "He was very worried for you. You must realize that." My lips pursed wryly. "Or are you determined to be stubborn?"

CHAPTER 30

Bree turned away, her obstinate expression lessening by only a degree.

"I don't think I've ever seen Anderley in such a state, and well, I don't think I ever wish to again," I admitted, allowing some of my own distress to creep into my voice as I sank down in the chair next to the bed.

She looked up at this, allowing me to see some of the fear she must have felt during her ordeal after she'd realized she'd been poisoned. "He was rather gallant," she admitted. "Held my hair back while I cast up my accounts."

"I've always thought that was an excellent indication of a man's heroism," I replied with sincerity, thinking of how Gage had done the same for me after merely a few hours' acquaintance when neither of us was very sure of the other.

She flushed. "I couldna seat my mount after that, so he took me up before him. Carried me up the stairs, too, didna he?"

I nodded.

She seemed embarrassed by this.

"You had just been *poisoned*," I reminded her. "No one expected you to be able to function. And all we could think to do was purge it from you as best we could." I grimaced. "I'm sorry about that."

"Dinna be. I understood why it had to be done, and under the circumstances . . ." She lifted her hands as if to indicate her being alive. "I canna complain."

We sat silently for a moment, each of us contemplating what might have been, and then I inhaled deeply, knowing if I gave way to such thoughts, I would never ask the questions I needed to.

"Has the physician been to see you yet?" I asked, knowing a rider had been dispatched early that morning.

"Nay."

I frowned but did not comment on that further, knowing Bree didn't hold the answers to what had delayed the doctor. Instead, I explained how we'd deduced that the poison had been put in her chutney, and that she'd survived because she'd not ingested more than a few drops and we'd purged the rest in quick order. She confessed to some lingering stomach cramps, but that was to be expected given the violent vomiting twelve hours prior. I also told her how Mrs. Mackay had been the person to finally recognize the poison was the paternoster pea.

"I wondered when she got that glint in her eye after we talked this mornin'," Bree confessed. Her brow furrowed, and she glanced toward the window where outside the gloaming had fallen. "Was it just this mornin'?"

I smiled in commiseration. "Yes."

"And noo that ye mention it, I do recall my mother tellin' me stories aboot the beads used to make some rosaries." Bree had been raised a Roman Catholic and still attended mass whenever possible during our travels. "But do ye truly think Miss Ferguson did it?"

"I don't know," I admitted. "But thus far she's the only one we've discovered to have access to the poison."

"Aye, but there are other Roman Catholics nearby who likely own rosaries. Even the Campbells are Catholic, if somewhat lapsed. That is, if Mrs. Kennedy is to be believed."

I perked up at these last comments. "Did you see any rosaries while you were at Poltalloch yesterday?"

"Nay, but then I didna go searchin' through their drawers and chests where they'd most likely be kept."

I tilted my head. "What *were* you able to learn?" I asked, having wondered what had triggered the poisoner to target her.

She heaved a sigh. "No' much. And believe me, I've been replayin' every conversation I had yesterday, tryin' to figure oot if I missed somethin'."

"You were trying to pry into the connection between Mr. MacCowan working for Lord Alisdair, and Mairi working for the Campbells, and how Mairi had already known the Campbells before going to work for them," I reminded us both and then informed her of the progress we'd made in the forgery investigation. How we'd located the original portraits behind a false wall Mr. MacCowan had built and all the details Miss Ferguson had remembered from her time visiting as a girl. "Does knowing that help you in any way?"

Her eyes narrowed as she gave the matter her serious consideration. "Well, I've been thinkin' that if Mairi had met the Campbells before goin' to work for 'em, then maybe she'd met them—or one o' 'em anyway, since Miss Margaret dinna leave Poltalloch much. Then maybe she met them at Lord Alisdair's. Maybe Miss Campbell visited there wi' her brother, or maybe she went by herself . . ." She broke off, and I could tell she was contemplating the same thing I had. She looked up from the toile counterpane over her legs to meet my level gaze. "The lady," she finally dared to say.

"I wondered about her, too," I admitted.

"Then you think . . . ?" Her words fell away as she sank her head back against her pillows, seemingly stunned and at least slightly unsettled, given the fact the person in question might have poisoned her.

"Did Miss Campbell know you were there asking questions? Did she know what you were asking about?"

"Aye, she kent we were there. We told her we were there to speak to the staff aboot the poison again after Miss Margaret's suggestion she might o' been the intended victim." Her eyes were apprehensive. "But she might have figured oot we were after somethin' else. She might o' overheard."

I rested my elbow on the arm of the chair and propped my chin on my fist, pondering Miss Margaret's revelation. Had the poison been in her raspberry compote? Had Miss Campbell known how her sister coaxed the maids to take her food? Had she gambled on her doing so that morning with Mairi? If so, she had taken a tremendous risk, one that would call into question the affection she seemed to hold for her sister. Or had the poison been added later or been given to Mairi in some other form? Or by some other poisoner?

I pressed my hand to my head, wondering if my exhaustion was making me muddled.

"What are ye gonna do?" she asked as if afraid of my answer.

"Speak with Mr. Gage," I reassured her, pushing to my feet. "And nothing else for tonight. So get some rest. I promise not to ride off into trouble."

She smiled tightly. "I'll try."

So will I, I thought, not having any more confidence I would get much rest than she seemed to. *So will I.*

The next day dawned too early. Emma woke just after six o'clock demanding an early breakfast, and it had taken considerable effort to crawl out from beneath the covers to answer her summons. It didn't help that the dawn was cool—one of those Highland summer days that felt more like autumn. Though I tried to console myself with the fact that at least it wasn't raining, especially since we would be venturing out in just a few short hours.

Gage played lady's maid for me, as the evening before I'd ordered Bree to stay abed until she felt well enough, or at the very least until midmorning. Though I strongly suspected her to be up on her feet the moment the clock struck that hour.

"Stop fretting," he told me as he finished lacing my day corset, dropping a kiss on my shoulder. "The answer will present itself. It always does. And fretting won't make it come any faster."

He was right, about the latter part in any case. Though I'd long feared our investigative skills would one day prove not up to the challenge. After all, not every criminal was stupid, and evidence wasn't always there or straightforward.

We had discussed the inquiry for hours the previous evening before falling asleep, sometimes going over the same points multiple times, but the answer was no clearer. Whether the poisoner was Miss Ferguson or Miss Campbell or some other player was not yet evident. But from his knowledge of and correspondence with the region's procurator fiscal, Gage strongly suspected that as the evidence currently stood, the official would charge Miss Ferguson for the crime. Given my current doubts, this did not sit well with me. I wanted to be certain of her guilt.

Especially now knowing the procurator fiscal was a Campbell himself, a relative of the Duke of Argyll. The Campbells of Poltalloch might be a minor branch of the family, but they were Campbells nonetheless, and clan loyalty ran strong in the Highlands. Had Miss Campbell counted on that? If she was the culprit, had she been relying on her family connections to smooth away any difficulties if she was seen or any evidence happened to point toward her? I couldn't dismiss the possibility.

The procurator fiscal certainly hadn't been in any rush to investigate the crime, telling Gage he would rely on him and Lord Barbreck to handle the matter fittingly until he was available. While it was true that the jurisdiction of some officials covered several thousand square miles of land, and so they could not be expected to arrive promptly at every suspected murder, I also knew the status of the victims slowed his response. Had the MacCowans been of a higher rank, the inquiry into their deaths would undoubtedly have taken higher precedence. Yet another example of the inherent injustices in our legal system. But in this case, also helpful to me and Gage in not having the man breathing down our necks, potentially hampering our own investigation.

So it was no surprise that I had these inherent injustices in mind when I was informed a short time later that the local physician had finally arrived to examine Bree.

"I'm a verra busy man, Mrs. Mallery," I heard him telling my aunt as I entered the room. "I canna be expected to come oot to see every maid or footman who falls ill. Ye should o' called the surgeon o'er at Kilmilford."

"But she was poisoned, Dr. Brown," Aunt Cait reminded him.

"Aye, and there's no' much I could do for the lass if that was the case. But as I'm here noo, I may as well take a look at her." He set his black bag down with a thump on the table next to the bed where Bree sat with her mouth clamped firmly shut, minding her place, though I could tell by the look in her eyes that she was wishing this Dr. Brown to the devil. I was doing much the same from my position standing near the door.

After a very rudimentary examination, which had not taken Bree's comfort much into consideration, he closed his bag with a snap. "She'll recover. 'Twas likely no' more than a bit o' gastric fever."

"It was not gastric fever," I retorted, having had enough of the supercilious man. "Two people have died from poisoning by jequirity beans, and Miss McEvoy only survived because she consumed very little of it and we dosed her with ipecac soon after."

Dr. Brown's head reared back, visibly taken aback by this pronouncement. However, he wasn't about to take my word for it. After all, I was merely a woman. "That's highly doubtful, Miss . . ."

"*Mrs.* Gage," I bit out. "Perhaps you know of my husband—Mr. Sebastian Gage. Or my father-in-law, Captain Lord Gage, friend and confidant of our king." I wasn't above using the connection when it had its usefulness. Like putting this cad in his place.

"I see." He stood stiffly, his gaze assessing me. "Then perhaps it's possible."

I wanted to roll my eyes, but my mother had taught me better manners than that.

Though apparently her sister had not taken those same lessons to heart. "Oh, for goodness' sakes," Aunt Cait snapped. "Do climb down from your high horse, Dr. Brown. My niece is never wrong about such things."

I'd thought the physician was shocked and appalled before, but her assertion made his back straighten as if a pike had been driven through it.

My aunt ignored his high dudgeon. "Now, did you receive my letter?"

"Your letter, ma'am?" he replied with wounded dignity.

"Yes, the one I sent you several days ago to ask about Lord Alisdair Mallery's death. You examined his body, did you not?"

"Aye, and I assure you there was nothing untoward aboot it, if that's what you're implying."

"How did he die?" I interrupted.

He turned to me with a sniff. "He had been sufferin' from a long-standing respiratory illness, which resulted in internal hemorrhaging and tachycardia, and ultimately heart failure."

If he'd thought using medical terms would deter me, he was sadly mistaken.

"Diffuse hemorrhages?" I challenged.

It took him several seconds to respond. "Aye."

"How did they present? I assume you didn't perform an autopsy, so what were the symptoms?"

His face was growing red with suppressed fury, probably at my questioning his findings. "I found dried blood inside his mouth and around his nostrils."

I turned to meet my aunt's gaze and then Bree's, for they both knew what that meant. Lord Alisdair might have been killed by the same poison. In fact, given the pattern of events, I would have gone so far as to suggest that he had. And since Miss Ferguson had not yet been employed here at that time, that almost certainly ruled her out as a suspect. Which left but one probability.

"Thank you," I told the physician as I whirled toward the door, anxious to find Gage and inform him of what I'd learned.

I breathed a sigh of relief as I noted both Campbell sisters were seated in the drawing room at Poltalloch Castle. They both had to be present for the plan Gage and I devised to work. In truth, calling it a "plan" was rather loftier than it was. It was really more of a forlorn hope, a last-gasp effort. For if someone didn't break rank or let slip the information we sought, then all we were left with were theories and suppositions.

They greeted us cordially enough, though I could see that Miss Campbell had armed herself with the typical icy reserve she donned whenever Lord Barbreck was present, for which no one could blame her, least of all Barbreck himself. However, Miss Margaret was openly hostile. Her eyes snapped angrily, tracking the marquess's every movement. Her feelings about him were quite unambiguous, and it was clear they stemmed from his past treatment of her sister.

Lord Barbreck lowered himself into the chair nearest to Miss Campbell, a move which seemed to surprise her based on the rigid tension in her frame. As we were there, at least ostensibly, in support of his lordship, Gage and I made polite small talk, waiting for Barbreck to direct the conversation. After taking a moment to catch his breath, he dived into the heart of the matter.

"Miss Campbell, I wanted to come here myself to inform you that there's been a development," he told her in a respectful voice.

All the room fell silent, the sisters waiting to hear what Barbreck would say, and Gage and I scrutinizing Miss Campbell's and her sister's every flutter of an eyelash.

"Mr. and Mrs. Gage have found the original paintings. *All* the original paintings." He paused for a moment to let that sink in. "Includin' the Titian."

Miss Campbell took a quick inhalation of air, as if for a moment she'd forgotten to breathe, and then resumed her rigid stillness, while Miss Margaret turned her head to the side, her jaw tight with anger.

Barbreck bowed his head. "Apparently, I was wrong aboot Alisdair. Verra, verra wrong. I trusted him. I placed family honor and my belief in him o'er everythin' else, and he deceived me." His voice broke on the last, and I watched Miss Campbell check the impulse to reach out to him. Her eyes told me she was not unaffected, even if the rest of her features remained stiff and unyielding.

Inhaling noisily through his nostrils, he forced his gaze up to meet hers. "I've come to apologize," he declared. "I was wrong, Anne. You were right. And I was a bloody fool to let it end our engagement."

The ache and the naked longing in his eyes brought a lump to my throat, as well as Miss Campbell's, for she hiccupped, seeming to struggle with her own emotions.

She did reach out then, resting her hand over his where it lay on his chair arm. "We were both fools, Donald," she admitted softly. "We both put our pride before all else."

Seeing them thus affected me greatly, and I reached up to swipe at the tears gathering at the corners of my eyes. They had both let hard-heartedness and stubbornness separate them for so long, but whatever love had been between them was evidently not completely extinguished. Unless Miss Campbell was acting. But seeing her now, seeing them together, I struggled to believe such a thing was possible.

Perhaps we'd been wrong. Perhaps I'd been trying too hard to make all the pieces fit, to connect both investigations when the simplest answer was the right one. Miss Ferguson had killed her uncle and cousin for the painting or to protect her past or in revenge for some slight.

But in our absorption with Barbreck and Miss Campbell's reconciliation, we had forgotten about Miss Margaret, whose voice suddenly snapped like a clap of thunder.

"You're goin' to forgive him? Just like that? After all the pain he's caused ye? Fifty-four years o' it."

"Meg . . ." Anne began, but her sister would have none of it.

"Well, I'm no'!" Her eyes flashed fire. "Because I remember every minute o' it. I remember every tear and every outburst. Every lonely year ye spent here wi' naught but me for company, wishin' for love and children, and a life ootside these four walls. He stole that from ye! He stole it all wi' his stupid pride!" She pushed to her feet, rising far quicker than I would have believed she could. "So, no, I'll no' forgive him." Her eyes narrowed spitefully on Barbreck. "I'll never forgive him."

She began to stride angrily toward the door but crumpled after two steps.

"Meg!" her sister gasped as Gage and I rushed to Miss Margaret's aid.

Her face was scrunched in pain.

"Deep breaths," I coaxed as Gage attempted to help her sit.

"My cane. I forgot my blasted cane," she bemoaned through gritted teeth.

"What hurts most?" I asked as I scoured her for injuries.

"Your hip," her sister exclaimed.

"Nay. It's no' that," Miss Margaret groused. "'Tis my leg."

"This one?" I reached down to make a precursory assessment of it through her skirts. "It doesn't appear to be broken, but it may be badly bruised or sprained." I turned to my husband. "Can you lift her? Perhaps you should carry her to her chamber?" I looked to Miss Campbell for confirmation.

"Aye." She glanced over her shoulder toward where the butler stood in the doorway. "Calder will show ye the way."

Gage hefted Miss Margaret into his arms and moved to follow him. My gaze trailed over the floor, searching for what had tripped her up in the first place. Or had her old legs simply given way?

Miss Campbell grasped my arm anxiously. "Mrs. Gage, you have some medical training."

"A very little," I replied. And almost exclusively on dead bodies.

"Will you examine her? Make certain it's no' serious. I can send for Dr. Brown, but he'll take hours to come, if he deigns to come at all."

Having firsthand experience of this Dr. Brown, I well understood what she was saying, so I reluctantly agreed. "Of course. I'll do what I can."

She thanked me, and I hurried after them.

I found Gage settling Miss Margaret in her bed on the floor above, arriving just in time to hear her make a jest.

"If I'd kent taking a tumble would result in my bein' carried aboot by such a bonny gentleman, I might o' fallen sooner."

Gage adjusted the pillow beneath her head, his eyes glinting with amusement as he looked up at me as I crossed the room.

"Miss Campbell has asked me to ensure you don't require the physician or the surgeon," I explained to Miss Margaret, whose pleasure seemed to dim at my appearance. I supposed I couldn't begrudge her that. After all, I rather enjoyed having Gage's attentions all to myself as well.

My husband nodded, and I could tell he was thinking the same thing I was. Though this wasn't how we'd hoped to achieve it, the sisters had enabled us in our plan to separate them anyway. "I wish you a swift recovery," he told Miss Margaret, offering her his most charming smile. "So I can enjoy more of your delightful company."

Her lips curled in pleasure. "That'll give me motivation enough."

Gage chuckled lightly as he closed the door.

She sighed, lapsing back into her pillows. "You're a lucky lass, Mrs. Gage."

"That I am," I agreed, surveying our surroundings as I approached the bed. By all accounts, Miss Margaret spent a great deal of time in this chamber, but at least it was a lovely one. The walls were hung with thick tapestries of knights and horses, and the floor was covered in a plush medallion carpet. I noted a clump of mud near the foot of the bed and felt a pulse of dismay that Gage must have tracked it in on his boots, marring the pristine rug. I would have to inform the butler. The four-poster bed was constructed of pale oak and draped with fine linen, creating a cozy nest from which she could still see out the window toward the rippling waters of the loch.

She turned toward the view now, looking small and frail against the massive bed, and I felt my heart swell with sympathy. How many times had she done just that, wishing she could venture farther? She had mentioned her sister longing for a life outside these four walls, but I suspected that part was just as much a confession about herself. Given that context, I couldn't fault her anger at Barbreck on her sister's behalf. Honestly, it spoke well of her that she was outraged and anxious to protect Miss Campbell in whatever small way she could. Would I not do the same for Alana? Would she not for me?

"Is your leg the only thing causing you pain?" I asked.

"Everywhere pains me, lass," she replied wearily. "But aye."

I nodded, lifting her skirt a few inches so that I could prod and manipulate the leg. "Tell me if anything hurts when I press," I told her.

She didn't respond, but I trusted she would.

Feeling awkward touching her like this, I tried to make conversation as I examined her ankle and began moving upward. "I can understand your anger at Lord Barbreck," I began, hoping to elicit her confidence. "And your surprise at your sister's easy forgiveness. I admit, as furious as she'd seemed on earlier visits, I did not expect such an easy acceptance from her."

This was not entirely true, for while affronted, Miss Campbell had never seemed as enraged as I might have been in her shoes, but I needed to nudge the conversation in a certain direction.

The muscles of Miss Margaret's leg tensed under my hands, but I swiftly realized this was in anger, not in pain. I also noticed that her lower limbs were far stronger than I'd expected. The musculature was much more developed than I had anticipated for a woman who had been ill all her life and hobbled merely crossing a small room.

A disquieting feeling began at the base of my spine. One that would not be dismissed. And for good reason.

CHAPTER 31

Aye, Barbreck hurt her terribly. He hurt us all. And continued to do so o'er the years. Spurning us." Miss Margaret heaved a sigh, her muscles relaxing again. "But Anne has always been more forgivin' than me. 'Tis somethin' I've ne'er understood."

"I suppose I can relate to that," I continued, shifting the aim of my conversation as my unease grew. "Living the life you've led, it must make you less patient of others' foibles and excuses."

She turned to look at me then, and I struggled to mask any change my discovery had wrought in me. My mind was racing as I tried to grasp all the implications of her musculature and maintain control of our conversation.

"Aye." She tilted her head as if scrutinizing me, and my heart kicked in my chest. "As it must you."

I realized then she was speaking of my past with Sir Anthony and the scandal of my involvement with sketching his dissections. "In some ways, yes," I admitted, lowering her skirts. "But in other ways, I think it's made me more patient. It's certainly made it easier for me to empathize with those who have suffered tragedy or distress." I could tell that I had her full attention now and decided to prod a bit further. "Lord Alisdair, for instance. What motivated him to do such a terrible thing? Did he ever regret it? Did he ever consider telling them the truth?"

Something flickered on her face, tightening the corners of her eyes, and I wondered if I'd shown my hand, but perhaps it was merely displeasure at my having credited Barbreck's brother with having any heart. "I didna ken Alisdair weel, but what I did glean was that he was as vain and self-absorbed as they come, and just as easily led."

I found this comment interesting. Was she testing me? "Then you don't think he was the intellect behind the forgeries? That it was his friend Signor Pellegrini's idea?"

She shrugged. "Who else?"

But there was an undertone to her voice, a sly insinuation. I knew then that she was lying, and what's more, she was enjoying it. The truth lurked in the glints of her dark eyes, waiting to be seen by those who had the desire to look and the ability to discern it. Her innocence and infirmity . . . was it all a façade?

I wanted to kick myself for not questioning it sooner. After all, I'd noted how flushed and healthy she looked—unlike someone with a lung and heart condition. I had wondered at her ease in climbing the stairs. That is, until Anne caught up with her and she'd slowed to accept her help. One of the servants hadn't been listening outside the library door—it had been Margaret. She'd hurried up the steps to make it look like she'd passed by much earlier. But in my defense, who would ever suspect such a thing? To pretend to be infirm not for a week or a month or a year, but for decades—an entire life! Perhaps her illness had started as something real as a child, but at some point she must have overcome it. Her muscles seemed to tell that tale, as did her complexion and her breathing—when she wasn't intent on playing the invalid.

Mairi had acted as her maid, so she must have known. She must have seen Margaret at Lord Alisdair's cottage, leading him about to whatever end. That's why she'd been hired, why Margaret preferred her. She'd kept her ruse a secret. Kept it until I'd recognized the first forgery. Then, either because she'd threatened to talk or because Margaret had simply feared she might, Margaret poisoned her and her father to guarantee their silence about her involvement.

Which meant she'd probably also been the woman in the blue cloak who had plagued and misled me, and the older woman seen sneaking into my chamber. It had been Margaret, not Anne.

The pieces all seemed to fit, but what proof was there? Her strong musculature didn't tie her directly to the murders. Neither did a tone of voice or a glint in the eye. This wasn't an accusation that could be made with such flimsy evidence. If my suspicions were wrong and she was innocent, such an accusation could do great harm not only to Margaret but also to my family's relationship with the Campbells. But if I was right, then Margaret was dangerous, indeed, and who knew what further havoc she might wreak? I couldn't leave this to chance. I needed to find some sort of proof, or else coax her to give herself away.

"What do you think will happen now?" I asked, sitting on the wooden stool next to her bed and allowing my gaze to drift over the contents of the room as if contemplating the future.

"Wi' Anne and Barbreck?" She grunted. "I imagine they'll be more friendly noo, but I dinna expect much more to come o' it than that. They're too old to wed."

My eyes caught again on the clump of mud I'd blamed on Gage. What if it hadn't come from him but from Margaret herself? "Are we ever really too old to wed?" I posited. "I once heard about a gentleman who was two and ninety when he married his third wife."

"Aye, maybe," she conceded as I slipped the clasp of my gold bracelet and allowed it to fall to the floor while she wasn't looking. "But Anne will ne'er leave Poltalloch noo. She loves it so."

Kneeling to pick up the bracelet, I lifted aside the bed skirt and peered underneath to find a pair of boots flecked with dirt and mud before quickly rising to the chair again, making a great show of refastening my bracelet. From the corner of my eye, I could see Margaret looking at me askance, but I did not turn to acknowledge it. It was more important I feign no knowledge of what I'd just seen. That she had, indeed, been out and about recently, and Mairi was no longer here to clean up the evidence of it.

"Miss Campbell's love for Poltalloch is unmistakable. But 'never' is also a very strong word," I replied, continuing to prod at the potential of the future, hoping to find a vulnerability.

"She would be a fool to do so," she snapped. "At least here she would be master o' her own domain, given our nephew's disinterest in the estate. There, she'd only be under Barbreck's thumb and contending wi' his cantankerous whims. They'd no' last a day wi'oot screaming at each other." She breathed deeply, calming her sudden flash of temper. "Nay. She'll realize all that."

Or Margaret would helpfully point it out to her.

"She'll stay here." She nodded as if the matter was decided.

"You know her best," I replied obliquely, allowing my gaze to travel again over the contents of the room, searching for any further evidence of Margaret's guilt. If I could just find the paternoster peas. Regrettably, there were any number of places where she might have hidden a rosary or the loose beans, and what excuse did I have to begin searching for them?

Then she offered me one herself.

She pressed a hand to her chest, her face constricting in pain. "My heart."

I leaned toward her.

"Could you . . ." She gasped before waving her hand toward

the bureau on the opposite side of the room. "There's some medicine . . . in the top drawer . . . will you . . . ?"

I hurried across the room, opening the drawer indicated. "Which one . . . ?" I broke off as my eyes caught sight of the rosary strung with bright red beads nestled inside. It took me less than a second to register that there were no medicine vials inside the drawer beside it, and less than another second to realize that Margaret had known precisely what she was doing when she directed me to this drawer. It had not been providence but machination. The bottom dropped out of my stomach as I whirled to face her.

She had risen up onto her supposedly weak knees, her eyes blazing back at me with unholy fury. But it was the tip of the knife she held out toward me that most alarmed me. It was small, about the size of a *sgian-dubh*, but wickedly sharp. Only when I recognized she was still several paces away, that surely I could reach the door before she could reach me, did the panic in my chest ease so that I could take a breath.

"'Twas my boots," she demanded. "They gave me away, didna they?"

"Your legs, actually," I replied as conversationally as I could manage, deciding my best course of action was to keep her talking. Regardless of her physical fitness, she was still seventy-odd years of age and would eventually tire of perching in that position. When she moved, so would I. "They're not those of an invalid."

"'Twas a gamble pretendin' to trip like I did," she conceded. "But I had to force Anne's thoughts away from bloody Barbreck and back to me," she snarled, using far stronger words. Words I'd rarely heard a lady utter.

"You didn't want your sister to leave you," I realized with a start.

Her eyes narrowed. "If *I* was never goin' to be allowed to leave, then neither was she."

Her vehemence was unsettling, and I found myself wishing I could recall what was on top of the bureau behind me. Was there something I could throw at her? A book? A figurine?

"Then your illness . . . ? Was it ever real?"

"Aye, it started oot real enough. I was a sickly child. But then I was never allowed to get better. My father had already decided my place, and it was at Poltalloch, as a companion to my aging relatives." Her lips curled upward at the corners. "So, I arranged matters to my liking."

I blinked, stunned by the turn in our conversation. "Then, *you* convinced Alisdair to paint a forgery of the Titian?"

"Dinna act so surprised. I've always been good at convincin' others to do what I want." Her eyes hardened. "Except my father. God rest his soul." The manner in which she said it planted in my brain the chilling suggestion that he might have been her first victim, though she didn't admit it outright. "As I said, Alisdair was led easily enough. After all, I was quite beautiful at seventeen. And I didna really lose my looks until a few years ago. Aboot the time Alisdair suddenly grew a conscience." Her sneer told me she didn't think much of those who were bound by such a thing. "Before that he was happy to do what I wished, wi' the knowledge that he was not only foolin' his pompous older brother by possessin' the genuine paintings he'd so coveted but also occasionally sleepin' wi' a Campbell woman in his bed."

"But why? Why continue the ruse for all that time?" I asked in astonished bewilderment. "Your ploy had worked. Alisdair painted the forgery, and then I presume you were the one to damage it to convince your father to contact that expert who decried it. You took quite a risk thinking that would cause a rift wide enough between Barbreck and your sister that it would end their engagement."

"Nay, I just recognized Barbreck's pride couldna withstand the accusation."

I blinked at her cool assessment of the situation. "So, you'd already ruined your sister's engagement and kept her at Poltalloch. Then why continue? Especially after your father died? Couldn't you have done what you wanted then?"

"'Twas too late," she snapped. "I'd already lost all those years, any chance at a life and a home o' my own. Gentlemen dinna marry spinsters when they can have young and nubile debutantes for their brides." She sat back on her heels, tipping the knife as if to idly examine the blade. "Besides I liked kenning that Barbreck was slowly bein' deprived o' his precious collection, and that he'd no' idea it was happenin' right under his nose, or if he did ken, he was too proud to admit it. Barbreck looks on *me* with pity," she practically spat the word. "But *he* was the one too stupid to see the truth. *He* was the one bein' duped. And by his own brother, no less." She glanced up at me as if to see what kind of effect her confessions were having on me. "And as for Alisdair, I liked watchin' his jealousy grow, no' dwindle wi' every painting he took. And 'twas no hardship to endure his attentions. At least, no' initially." Her smile was feline. "I wouldna offered myself if it was."

"All this time, you kept the scheme going. Until, as you said, Alisdair grew a conscience."

"Aye. Then his usefulness was at an end, and . . . you can imagine the rest." She shrugged one shoulder as if the matter was of little importance. "There wasna even a hint o' suspicion, except from Mairi and MacCowan. But they wouldna dared to say anythin'." Her gaze sharpened. "Until you showed up."

"And I noticed the forgery." I'd already deduced this much.

"I could feel Mairi watchin' me, and I ken 'twas only a matter o' time before she or her da talked. I couldna let that happen."

She shifted her leg as if to begin climbing down from the bed, and I sidled a step toward the door, only to stiffen in shock as the knife she'd held came flying past within inches of my head to embed itself in the wall with a thunk.

Margaret tsked. "Really, Mrs. Gage, did you honestly think I was goin' to let you simply walk oot o' here?" She now stood by the bed, brandishing two more knives. "I canna ride. I was ne'er allowed. But I can throw wi' deadly accuracy up to twenty feet. 'Twas one o' the skills I *could* practice while confined to my room." She nodded toward the walls. "Why do ye think there are so many tapestries in here? They're to cover the holes."

I realized with sickening clarity that I'd made a fatal miscalculation. Margaret might have pretended to be infirm for fifty to sixty years of her life, but she was far from helpless, and she did not allow herself to be hindered by the same scruples as other people. I had no doubt she would kill me, find a way to make it look like an accident, and feel no remorse in doing so. Only smugness at her own cleverness.

But I had a daughter who needed me. A husband and family and friends who relied on and loved me. I was not going to let her take me from them. And I was *not* going to let her outwit me. Yes, she was cunning and resourceful, but so was I. And I could be ruthless, too, when the situation called for it.

Pivoted slightly away as I was, I slowly, ever so slowly, tried to slide my hand through the slit in my mauve pelisse to where my pocket had been tied beneath without alerting her. I had taken to wearing one whenever we were in the country or someplace I didn't want the bother of carrying a reticule about my wrist. I had also long ago learned to never leave my pocket pistol behind, especially while we were in the midst of an inquiry.

But I feared I would never reach it before Margaret tired of talking. She seemed to like the sound of her own voice, as well as the opportunity to brag about her predatory, manipulative feats, but she was far from stupid. Eventually she would decide enough was enough, and I knew I had no hope of extracting the gun before she hurled her next knife.

It was then that I spied the second door just a few feet away.

It was partially concealed by one of the tapestries, and there was no telling what was behind it or if it was even unlocked, but at the moment it was my best chance of escape.

"That must have been a lonely way to grow up," I said, hoping empathy might have some effect on her, or at least keep her talking while I worked out a plan.

But my compassion seemed to have the opposite effect, making her brow lower in anger. "Dinna pretend to sympathize wi' me. That ploy willna work. And dinna try appealin' to the fact you're Greer's offspring. It willna save you either."

My heart stuttered in my chest, but I forced myself to breathe in and out as evenly as I could. "Your sister told me you were both fond of her," I charged.

"O' course we were. Greer was worthy o' fondness."

This pronouncement might have softened me toward her if she wasn't wielding a pair of knives, intent on killing me.

"And Anne has kept a watchful eye o'er all o' her offspring from afar, all these years. So we ken all aboot yer bein' an artist and yer turn as an investigator, as weel as yer more ghoulish past." Her lips curled with a cruel delight that then just as swiftly disappeared. "But I didna anticipate ye identifyin' the forgeries, though I shoulda." She scrutinized me from head to toe. "Yer mother always saw too much, too."

I stilled at this pronouncement, uncertain what she was implying. What had my mother seen?

"'Tis why she left. And why she returned. To confront me. She kent I'd poisoned Edmund. Put it in his brandy flask. And she wanted me to ken it, though she could ne'er prove it." Margaret gestured with the knives, making me flinch. "As I said, I liked Greer. I liked havin' her here. But Edmund kept takin' her away."

Aunt Cait had told me the same thing. How my mother had been happy here, but her feckless husband kept returning for her, only to betray and abandon her yet again.

Margaret's expression turned black. "I didna expect her to leave and ne'er return. At least, no' until it was too late."

With each moment that passed, I could feel the clock silently ticking down. Margaret's mood was darkening, her umbrage growing, and it was only a matter of time before she struck. Having abandoned my efforts to reach my pistol as futile, I instead reached for the handle of the drawer in the bureau behind me and slowly began to pull it out, hoping my wide skirts masked the movements. Much as I loathed the current fashion for swathes of bulky fabric and ridiculous puffed sleeves, I had never been so glad of them.

"And if she'd stayed?" I challenged. "What would you have done then? Killed her, too?"

"Only if she crossed me," she replied chillingly, as if such a response was perfectly reasonable.

Each tug of my hand ratcheted the tension within me that it would be the one she detected. Feeling I'd risked enough, I lifted my fingers to slide them into the one- or two-inch gap I'd made. The tips brushed against coarse wool, and I clamped hold. "It was you in the blue cloak, wasn't it?" I accused.

One eyebrow arched upward in satisfaction. "The same shade as your mother always wore."

"And *you* who placed her miniature on my pillow and stole my pendant, only to drop it under the sofa when you came to plant that lie about the poison being for you."

She shrugged. "I tried to save ye from this fate, but ye persisted in pursuin' yer inquiry."

"You tried to lead me off a cliff," I snapped, my temper igniting at her implication that she'd been doing me a favor. I yanked the woolen garment out a little further, crumpling it in my fist.

"That, too," she readily admitted.

"*And* you poisoned my maid!"

"Aye, she was sniffin' too close to the truth." Her gaze met mine sharply in accusation. "But *you're* the one who sent her here into danger."

I lifted my opposite hand to point at my chest. "I am not about to take responsibility for *your* malicious actions, you selfish witch. You delight in hurting others, and you care nothing for anyone but yourself."

"Guilty as charged." Her dark eyes were bright with intent, and I knew in the next moment she would raise her knife. This was my only chance to escape.

Praying the garment I'd snagged had enough heft to it, I hurled it across the room at Margaret and darted toward the second door. Thrusting aside the tapestry, I grasped the handle and yanked open the door, diving behind it just as I heard the thwack of another knife striking the wall where I'd been standing.

Pulling the door shut, my gaze frantically searched the space into which I'd run for something to prop under the knob. The chamber was a parlor of sorts, its contents dimly lit by the sunlight filtering through the thick drapes still pulled across the window. Catching sight of a second door, I dashed toward it, only to freeze just short of opening it.

This door must open onto the same corridor as Margaret's bedchamber. And if that was the case, then she might very well be standing out there right now waiting for me, having predicted my route. I spun around, searching for some alternative means of escape, but there was none. The only means out of this parlor were through that door or back through Margaret's bedchamber and out to the same corridor. I was effectively trapped.

I pressed a hand to my wildly beating heart, ordering myself to think. Dropping my hand to where my pocket lay beneath my pelisse, I felt the hard lump of my pistol. I still had that, and Margaret was as yet unaware of it. But I would rather not have to shoot her, even after all she'd done, even if she deserved it. I felt ill at the notion. I might be capable of ruthlessness when it was required, but that didn't mean I had to be merciless.

My gaze darted between the settee, the drapes, and the chair, formulating a plan. Rushing over to the sofa, I grabbed the blanket lying over its arm and stuffed it behind one of the drapes, creating a lumpy shape. I snapped up the footstool and crouched behind the wide bergère chair. With everything in place, I pulled my percussion pistol from my pocket. Cocking the hammer, I said a swift prayer. That my ploy would work, that the shot would be loud enough for Gage to hear it. Then I lifted the pistol and fired at the far wall.

The report of the gun reverberated in my ears and the recoil rocked me back on my heels. Regaining my balance, I dropped the pistol and picked up the footstool, holding it in front of me like a shield just as Margaret burst through the door. I'd trusted the gunshot would spur her into action, making her realize she had seconds to silence me before help arrived.

She didn't waste time on words or taunts, and I flinched as first one knife and then another sailed across the room to strike the mound in the drapes where, in the low light, I'd hoped she would think I'd concealed myself. But when a body didn't crumple to the floor, and she advanced to discover why, I was ready for her. Using every ounce of might I possessed, I hurled the footstool at her head, hearing the wooden base connect with a loud crack.

Rising to my feet, I cautiously inched forward to stand over her. When she didn't move, simply lay there with her eyes shut and the footstool covering half her torso, I began to shake. I crossed my arms over my chest, feeling the cold fear I'd refused to give sway swamp me.

Fortunately, Gage chose that moment to come hurtling into the room, pistol drawn, and skidded to a halt at the sight of me and then Miss Margaret unconscious on the floor.

"It . . . it was Margaret," I stammered, moving toward him. "Sh-She's not infirm. She hasn't been for a very long time. And sh-she's behind it all."

He gathered me into his arms just when I thought my knees would give way, holding me tightly as I trembled and buried my head against his chest. His lips pressed to my temple and then my ear, whispering words of comfort.

Miss Campbell tumbled into the room soon after, her eyes wide with shock. Whether or not she'd heard everything I'd said to Gage wasn't clear, but when she moved to kneel by her sister's side, I cautioned her.

"Careful. She may have more knives. And she throws them."

Miss Campbell stiffened, her gaze lifting to the drapes where one of the knives was still sunk into the fabric while the other had fallen to the floor. Now that I had time to think, I was surprised one of them hadn't shattered the window glass.

How much Miss Campbell knew about her sister, her lack of infirmity, and the events that had transpired wasn't yet clear, but her alarm was genuine. And when she rose to her feet without even shifting the footstool off her sister's insensible form, and gathered up the knives before thrusting them into a drawer in the nearby writing desk and turning the key, I took that as some measure of her anger.

CHAPTER 32

The consequences of the discovery of Margaret Campbell's treachery were swift and immediate. Her sister contacted the procurator fiscal herself and swore out testimony against her—all the various odd occurrences over the years when Margaret had seemed to disappear or behaved strangely, all the small incidences Anne had never dreamed would add up to multiple murders. Anne also encouraged her staff to testify to everything they knew, and that, combined with the evidence we'd gathered and the confessions Margaret had made to me, formed a rather compelling case against her. Within days, Margaret was taken up in irons, still sporting a sizable lump on her head, and transported to Campbelltown.

Margaret's actions in coercing Alisdair to paint forgeries could not be criminally prosecuted, but that did not stop them from wounding Anne—and Barbreck—terribly. To know that two people they had each loved so dearly had conspired to hurt them so deeply was not an easy scar to bear, but it did seem to draw them closer together. Perhaps they'd realized they'd already lost too much time, and what remained was infinitely precious. As such, I wasn't surprised when Anne was invited to Charlotte and Rye's wedding, even as small as the guest list was.

Charlotte was positively stunning in her gown of pale blue satin with her golden tresses swept high on her head. In truth, I didn't think I'd ever seen a more radiant bride, but it wasn't merely her physical beauty, but also the love that shone in her eyes when she looked at my cousin. A sentiment Rye echoed standing up with her, holding her hands steadily in his.

It brought a tear to my eye, knowing how much sadness they'd both endured to get here and seeing their joy now. I found it difficult to take my eyes off them, and I suspected everyone else's gazes were riveted on them as well. But when I looked up into the small audience populating the pews, I noticed one set of eyes staring back at me instead.

I dabbed at the wetness in the corner of my eye and smiled at Gage, feeling every ounce of his love directed at me. He looked so dashing in his deep blue frock coat, his golden hair artfully tousled. It had only been three hours since I'd last been in his arms, but I already longed to be there again.

My confrontation with Margaret had changed me. It was a situation I'd walked into with no expectation of danger, and yet Margaret had turned out to be more intent on killing me than perhaps anyone I'd ever faced. Given that fact, and its unpredictability, I'd found myself more determined to live each moment to the fullest. Whether Gage realized this or not, I wasn't sure, but I suspected my inability to keep my hands off him might have given him some clue.

My gaze drifted to the right to find Lord Ledbury observing the ceremony with at least a look of tolerance. I wanted to believe that even a man with as callous a heart as he seemed to possess couldn't sit there unmoved. I knew from Charlotte that he had tried and failed one last time to persuade her not to wed Rye, but she had stood up to him, as she'd pledged to do, and she seemed lighter for doing so. Or perhaps that was just her joy in marrying Rye overshadowing everything else.

Regardless, now there was nothing Lord Ledbury could do. The vows were spoken, and Rye tenderly kissed Charlotte to much applause, even from Rye's children and a contrite Miss Ferguson, whom Rye and Charlotte had decided to keep in their employ probationally. Ignoring all protocols, we swarmed them with well wishes. I laughed as Lady Bearsden flapped her arms, tears streaming down her face as she declared how happy she was.

Later that evening, I cradled a sleeping Emma in my arms while Gage reclined on the bed beside us. Her belly full and her nose now clear, she'd drifted off to sleep. My love for her had also somehow grown deeper from my frightening experience, though I would have sworn before that would be nigh impossible. Because of it, I treasured each smile, each babble, each trusting moment she rested in my arms just that little bit more.

The chamber being so cozy and peaceful with just the three of us populating it, I was reluctant to disturb it by returning Emma to her cradle. Especially with the view I had of Gage's muscular torso while he had his arms clasped behind his head. There was a spot on his neck just above his clavicle that I particularly wanted to press my lips to.

However, Gage's thoughts seemed to have followed a slightly different path.

"I wonder why Margaret never took any of the paintings for herself after Alisdair died, or why she didn't try to sell them?" he ruminated as he gazed across the chamber at the Van Dyck that Barbreck had insisted be temporarily hung in our chamber. Truthfully, I would have preferred that it be returned to the long gallery where it belonged, not associating many happy memories with it, but I knew Barbreck had intended it to be a grand token of gratitude, so I hadn't argued.

"It was never about the money," I told him quietly. "Or the art."

He turned to look at me. The memory of what Margaret had done, and what she'd tried to do to me, passed between us. His hand stole into mine. "It was about control."

I inhaled past the tightness that had settled in my chest. "She and Sir Anthony would have made quite the pair."

He squeezed my fingers. "But neither of them will ever trouble us again."

I breathed deep once more, offering him a small smile. "No."

Lifting up on his elbow, he trailed his fingers across my jaw, cradling it as he kissed me. He was just deepening it when there was a knock at the door.

Pulling away, he sighed. "Who could that be at this hour?" he groused as he climbed from the bed.

Emma made a soft grunting noise, smacking her lips in her sleep, and I smiled down into her sweet face. I could hear Gage's low voice conferring with someone in the corridor. When he turned back toward us, closing the door, he held a letter.

"That was rather late delivery," I remarked. "Or did the staff forget to give it to you in the midst of all the excitement earlier today?"

"Anderley said the rider told Wheaton it was urgent," he said, moving closer to the light cast by the fireplace.

I frowned, trying not to worry that something had happened to Philip, or Alana, or one of their children, or even my brother Trevor. For who else would send us such an urgent message?

When he hesitated briefly after examining the seal before breaking it, it did not alleviate my worries. I watched as he unfolded the letter and began to read. Moments later, tension furrowed his brow and corded the muscles in his arms and neck.

"What is it?" I asked, alarmed by the changes in him.

He finished reading and then appeared to scan the lines once again as if unable to believe what he was reading. "It's . . . from my father's valet." He looked up at me, shock and pain radiating from his eyes. "Father was attacked."

"When? Where?" I gasped, sliding my feet to the side of the bed to go to him, still holding Emma.

He glanced back down at the missive. "Three days ago. In Yorkshire." His eyes met mine, uncertain and afraid. "Apparently he was on his way to Edinburgh. To see me." His gaze dipped to our child. "To see Emma."

He seemed to be held immobile, stunned and unsure what to do. After all the hurt his father's actions—past and present—had caused him, and the unpromising nature of his recent correspondence, I could understand his bewilderment and indecision. So I took command of the matter for him.

"You wish to go to him, don't you?"

"I . . ." He blinked. "Yes."

I nodded, crossing to the bell-pull to summon Bree and Anderley. "Then, we'll leave at first light." My eyes dipped to our sleeping infant. "Or as close to it as we can manage." I rapped once on the nursery door before entering. Then I laid Emma in her cradle and briefly explained the situation to Mrs. Mackay, trusting she would begin packing what she could while her charge slept.

When I returned to our bedchamber, Gage was still standing where I'd left him, staring at the rug a few feet in front of him. I wrapped my arms around his torso and pressed my head against his chest, hoping some of my warmth and comfort would penetrate through his haze of astonishment and fear. His arms lifted to embrace me back almost perfunctorily and then in earnest as he lowered his chin to my head.

"I'm sorry, darling," I whispered. "I know this isn't the reunion you'd hoped for with your father. I can't imagine how worried you must feel."

He inhaled deeply. "There's nothing I can do until I reach him. Until I know . . . how bad it is."

"His valet didn't say?"

"Not in so many words, but I know Lembus. He wouldn't have written to me unless it was bad. Very bad."

I tightened my arms around him, pouring my love into him. A thought occurred to me. "Henry should be told."

I wasn't certain how he would react to this bit of interference, but all he did was nod, his chin scraping against my hair. "Yes."

We stood that way several minutes longer, knowing there were dozens of things to be accomplished before we could depart in the morning, and yet needing the comfort the other provided and the solidarity of knowing that, whatever happened next, we would face it together.

We would both need the solace of that connection in the days to come. For we would soon learn that Henry's existence as his son was not the only secret Lord Gage was keeping. And the revelation of at least one of those secrets had far deadlier consequences.

ACKNOWLEDGMENTS

Many thanks go to the following:

My husband and daughters, for all their love and support, and for providing ample inspiration for Gage and Emma.

My large family, for all their love and support, and for giving me so much material to draw on for Kiera's extended family.

Jackie Musser and Stacie Roth Miller for their always impeccable feedback and advice.

My editor, Michelle Vega, who just "gets" me.

My agent, Kevan Lyon, for her steady hand and guidance.

The entire team at Berkley—you are all amazing!

The brilliant artists and artist historians whose masterful paintings and research aided in the conception and execution of this book. Any errors are entirely my own.

And God, for his never-ending love and faithfulness.

Ready to find
your next great read?

Let us help.

Visit prh.com/nextread

Penguin
Random
House